# BORDERED

# BY

# DARKNESS

Dakotah Anne

*For my past, present and future self;*
*I did it!*
*And for my beloved cousin Abby;*
*We did it!*

# Contents

# Prologue

It all started with a war raging between two neighboring planets. One desired power and possession; the other only peace and freedom. The smaller of the two planets—holding beings that bring light and life—were at a disadvantage over the weapons their neighboring planet used against them. Knowing the planet's impending doom, parents tried to escape to ensure their own or their children's survival. One family managed to secure an escape pod for their daughter, hoping a new planet would offer her a safe haven. Instead, a malfunction with the escape pod caused the young woman to land on a gloomy, desolate planet void of any life, light, or love. Overwhelmed by her loss and having no way to fix the pod to leave the planet, she only had one solution. Only knowing how to bring light to the darkness, she used her ability to bring life. Plants sprouted from the dull soil and animals grew, overwhelming the abyss with beauty.

For two years, the woman, Sanaa, tended to the world, and she finally felt as if she was home.

One day, Sanaa was tending to a stubborn, black field. Her power flowed from her fingertips into the cold soil, urging the world to bend to her, when suddenly, it listened. Delicate flowers of white, pink, and blue bloomed from the soil, overcoming the blackened land, expanding towards the sun to take their first breath of life. She sat back, watching the flora pop up around her, the only sound the gently shifting of soil.

Something rustled in the fresh grass behind her, causing her to whip around, her long moonlit colored hair swatting her in the face as she did so. Cautiously standing, she faced an unknown man that had joined her, apparently intrigued by the glow coming from her; the result from the pureness of her power within her. The man introduced himself as an explorer from another planet, coming across the flourishing planet on his way home. Although skeptical at first, Sanaa and the man, Doran, became friends. She slowly introduced Doran to her powers—bringing plants and animals to life, healing any living creature, helping to keep someone alive, and even bringing back the dead. He offered to take Sanaa back to his home planet, so she didn't have to be alone, but she refused, not wanting to desert everything she created. The man understood, deciding to stay with her on Cosima so she wasn't alone.

As time passed, the two friends fell in love and started a family. With Doran inviting his home planet to settle with him and Sanaa, their family and the planet's population prospered over time. Troubles of payment, property, and food arose, bringing to attention that someone needed to be in charge to help keep peace between everyone. It was decided that Sanaa and Doran, who founded the planet and were the eldest, should rule as the King and Queen of Light with their posterity living by their rules. They built a beautiful kingdom, placing a silver and white palace in the center of the new town.

While Cosima shifted into its warmer months, the kingdom was once again at peace, until an ominous storm slowly circled in the distance. Every day, the brewing sky grew worse, never relenting. Concern and fear arose in the kingdom, unsure what the storm was or where it came from.

The king and queen decided to follow the storm, to find an explanation. The answer came to them as they neared the outskirts of the storm. The beautiful green field that once flourished, had returned to its original black and withered state. Dead. An uneasiness formed in the queen as they ventured to the center of the storm. A bleak town came into view dominated by a dark stone castle. The streets were lit by cobalt blue lamps. Dreary strangers glared and shielded their eyes as the king and queen slowly made their way through the town. All the life the queen had once created had vanished.

The royal couple conversed with the self-proclaimed Rulers of Darkness and Death; figures cloaked in shadows who governed these people. Seeking a new home, they discovered the green planet, deeming it suitable for building their kingdom. While attempting to welcome the newcomers, the dark rulers noticed the power the Queen of Light had. The rulers ordered their guards to do whatever means they needed to get the power from the queen. Doran and Sanaa escaped, not having a chance to try and reason with the King and Queen of Darkness.

Back in their kingdom, Doran and Sanaa urgently warned their people of the newcomers, powerful beings who wielded dark magic and could take the life of anything they wanted.

A war broke out between the two kingdoms. Light against dark. Fearful for her life and their youngest daughter that was on the way, Sanaa stayed in the palace while the king fought alongside with their children and people. The war lasted for years. The queen's heart broke at the sight of her falling kingdom, her people once again at a disadvantage not able to overpower their sinister power. Memories of when she was younger and leaving her home planet resurfaced as she looked at the never-ending storm overwhelming the once blue sky. The green that once thrived all around, now a stygian, unhealthy black. Eyes brimming with tears, she stared at the letter clutched in her hands. Everything she created was disappearing. Everyone she loved, including her husband and children, now gone. Sanaa couldn't bear the thought of losing everything again, especially her youngest daughter.

Ensuring the safety of her daughter, Sanaa sought the King and Queen of Darkness, determined to come to reason with them. She reasoned with the King, arguing her case that the war needed to stop, otherwise there would be nothing left of the planet. The king refused, stating he would not stop until he got her power. Sanaa pleaded with him, throwing him every excuse possible to try to change the king's mind. Hopeless, Sanaa kneeled before the king's throne, her tears a testament to her desperate plea for resolution as she gazed at his shadowed silhouette. She couldn't deal with more loss of her family, her people, a repeat of her home planet. The king reiterated his desire for her power, promising to end the war once he had it. Sanaa stood back on her feet, stating she would be more than willing to give her power if she could, but admitted her inability to do so. She reasoned that he could not hold her power. If he did, it would be worthless and disappear. She begged for a solution, even if it meant her own death and the loss of her power, it would all be for nothing. The king sat in the silent shadows as the queen cried, repeating her pleas over and over, offering solutions to the king. It wasn't until she offered to provide all the necessary food provisions for the dark kingdom that he finally agreed. Food in return for sparing their lives.

A pact was created. To start anew, both kingdoms were torn down, building new ones in their place next to each other to help create a balance between the darkness and light, so neither overpowered the other and resources could easily be passed to the Kingdom of Darkness. In an attempt to keep past greediness of power from resurfacing and ruining the pact, it was decided that both the King of Darkness and Queen of Light anoint their children to rule in their steed. The Prince of Darkness, who was only a few years younger than the queen's daughter, would rule the kingdom of Tenebris, while the Princess of Light ruled the kingdom of Luxregnum. They hoped it would ensure history did not repeat itself. Despite creating a pact to ensure both kingdoms live, the king and queen refused to have either of their people interact, deeming the other inferior than their own. A border wall was built to separate the kingdoms, to prevent any interaction and possibly cause another war to break out or break the new balance the King of Darkness and Queen of Light managed to create. Sanaa grew a forest border, separating the kingdoms and the rest of the world. Marking where they could not expand outside of their kingdom if they wanted the balance kept.

Rules and directions were given to both children in case something were to happen to the balance. If it were to break, they could ask for the King and Queen's help to restore it, but only if they went together. Everything was in place, allowing the king and queen to leave the newly formed kingdoms and watch their children from a fortress afar, only helping when necessary, not aware of the troubles to come.

# Chapter One

"Princess Ciana?" A voice echoes distantly. "Your Highness?" the voice asks again, closer this time. Ciana shakes her head, snapping out of her trance. As Ciana stands on a stool, she observes a small woman with short, curly, dirty blonde hair retrieve a book from the scattered mess on the floor.

"Oh, sorry, Kuma. I was lost in thought," Ciana apologizes, grabbing the books from Kuma's shaking hands. "Was there something you needed?"

"I came in to see if you needed any help." Kuma motions to the messed-up bookshelf as she picks up more of the fallen tomes. "Are you looking for something?"

"I was looking for the book on our world's history or the simplified version of it. I thought it was here in the library. Abrie from the orphanage is coming for a little field trip with the children, and I wanted to share some of our history with them."

Kuma hands the rest of the books to Ciana, straightening her black and white maid outfit as she takes a step back.

"I thought people couldn't come to look around the palace because of how unsafe it can be for you."

Ciana nods slowly. "We can't, but these are children ranging in age from three to sixteen. They cannot do anything to me. Besides, the orphanage and I have... a long history together. It will especially be good for the younger children, since they don't know much about our history compared to the older children, so learning about it here at the palace will make it more fun and memorable." Ciana tosses her long, blonde hair over her shoulder, turning her attention to Kuma, who looks unsure.

"So you're going to read the whole book to them?" Kuma's eyebrows furrow.

"No," Ciana says with a chuckle. "I'm going to show them something that no one has seen that ties back to the King and Queen of Light when they first came to this planet. I just want to make sure I have all my facts right before I give some details about our history to the children."

"That's a good idea." Kuma lights up. "The children will love whatever you have planned for them. I believe I know where the book is as well!"

Ciana perks up. "You do? If you could get it for me, I would appreciate it."

"Of course! I'll grab it right away." Kuma starts for the library door.

"Kuma!" Ciana calls before the maid disappears out the door. "I also wanted to ask if you'd help with the tour? An extra hand will be needed."

"I would love to help." She smiles before leaving the library.

Sighing, Ciana leaves the room as well, traversing the palace's marble hallway to the only balcony overlooking the town.

"All is quiet," she whispers to herself, watching a group of children play with a ball outside of their red and white brick houses, white lanterns blazing on either side of their doors. Rolling her shoulders, she slouches forward so she can lean onto the railing. The small act releases the tension in her body, easing the stiffness of her spine. Always having to hold a perfect posture in front of the kingdom and her staff, the small moments of relief allow her to breathe a little easier.

"Your Highness?" a strong, crisp voice requests from behind. Ciana stiffens, straightening and turning to see the armored guard bowing before her; his graying black hair a slight mess from the helmet that's tucked securely under his arm.

"Yes, Zomo?" Ciana acknowledges, releasing the breath and tension once more, turning back to the town. She's known Zomo for so long and is the only person around whom she can be herself. Just Ciana instead of *Princess* Ciana. He's the only one in the kingdom who knows everything she's had to go through. He joins her at the railing, easing his elbows onto the stone the best he can with his armor on.

"Is anything the matter?" he wonders.

"Why do you ask?"

His gaze lingers on the kingdom before he shifts his attention to Ciana. "You're here on the balcony when you should be preparing for the orphanage."

"Why does that make you think something is wrong?"

Zomo cocks his head, giving her a knowing smile. "You're forgetting how long I've known you, Ciana. Whenever you're on the balcony, it's to help you think and clear your mind of something. If I recall you once referred to it as your 'thinking balcony'?"

The corners of Ciana's mouth twitch as she tries not to smile. He isn't wrong. The balcony is one of the few places she goes to help come up with a solution if it's not thumbing through the plethora of books in the library. Looking over the town reminds her of who this all will benefit, helping her form the best solution to aid her people, but she isn't ready to admit something is unsettling at the back of her mind.

"I'm just enjoying the view before the children come," she insists.

"You can't lie to me, Princess Ciana." He nudges her shoulder gently, receiving a very un-princess-like wrinkle of her nose in response. "What's on your mind? Do you not want the children here? Are you scared that if you let them in something will happen?"

"No," Ciana bites, then sighs, shaking off the harshness of her tone. "I'm not scared of the children being here. They aren't the ones who think I'm in no position to rule."

"Then tell me what it is, so I can take care of it."

"I'm not sure." She drums her fingers on the stone, considering the reason she is out here. With a quick glance, she notices Zomo watching her, patiently waiting for her to continue. Zomo is as loyal as they come. He's the only person who would believe her—Ciana would trust him with her life—and so, she decides to be honest with him. "Something doesn't feel right, but I don't know what it could be."

"Do you believe another riot could be in the works?"

"I'm not sure."

He gives a single nod. "Let me check it out. Scout out the town to ensure no one is trying to cause any trouble. If they are, I'll break it up before they get a chance to do anything."

"That's fine. Take Ritesh and Eyal with you as well." Ciana shifts, watching as the guard straightens, facing her.

"Yes, Your Highness." Zomo bows with a fist over his heart before leaving the balcony. Ciana looks over the town once more, before she takes a deep breath, straightens her spine, and returns inside to head to the kitchen.

"Please make sure the apples and carrots are cut up and fresh," Ciana informs one of the cooks, examining the assortment of snacks being prepared. "The children won't eat them otherwise."

"Of course, Your Highness." The cook scribbles the note on a piece of paper.

"We're going to have a little picnic in the garden so they can eat and play. Please be sure to have everything we need set up and ready before we're there so we do not keep the children waiting."

"Yes, Your Highness."

"Is there anything else you need from me?" Ciana asks, glancing at the clock.

"No, I believe we have everything. If there is anything, we will be sure to come find you."

"Thank you."

"Princess Ciana." Kuma grins, entering the kitchen with a white-covered book. "I found the book for you."

"Thank you, Kuma. I don't know what I would do without you." Ciana carefully grabs the book, staring at the white cover for a moment. The sense of dread intensifies slightly, making Ciana frown.

"Princess Ciana, are you alright?" Kuma whispers, breaking her trance.

"Yes, I'm fine." Ciana forces a smile, holding the tome to her chest. Wanting to dive into the pages right away, she pivots and heads to her thinking balcony once more. Kuma's soft footsteps trail behind her.

Returning to the railing, Ciana rests her elbows on the cold stone, flips the book open, and scans through the worn pages.

*The Darkness,* Ciana repeats in her mind. *The queen felt uneasy from the darkness. But nothing's wrong.* Ciana looks out at her town taking in the calm tranquility of her people. Vendors call out to passersby, enticing them to buy their products. Children's laughter and squeals of delight echo in the air as they play in the streets and a park Ciana knows is hiding behind some of the buildings. She lets her gaze drift over the rooftops until they halt on the border. A shiver trails down her spine. *Nothing's changed, so why does it feel like something has?*

Ciana looks at Kuma, who's staring at her hands, fidgeting slightly. Even though her handmaid hasn't been with her long, Ciana feels she can trust the woman with her honest thoughts. Every time she sees her, Ciana is reminded of herself when she was younger. It wouldn't be the first time she's confided in the handmaid, but Ciana knows her spoken words are safe between the two of them. "Kuma?"

"Yes?" She looks up.

"Have you noticed anything different in town or perhaps even in the palace? Like something feels amiss or doesn't quite belong?"

Kuma stares at the border, then quickly glances over the town. She shrugs. "I haven't noticed anything, nor do I see anything amiss at the current moment. Might I ask why?"

"Something doesn't feel right." Ciana sighs, dropping her focus to the book. "It's as if we are on the brink of something. I'm not sure what, but it feels... ominous."

"There was an attempt on your life a few weeks ago. Do you think you're a bit anxious from that encounter?"

Ciana's body tenses, remembering the fear that overtook her when she heard metal hitting metal behind her while at the farms, preparing the next cart to send over the border. Zomo had intercepted a man who was hiding in the cornstalks, ready to strike her with a long silver dagger as she examined the wheat across from the corn. How the man knew Ciana would look at the crops in the area he was hiding is still a mystery, but Ciana thought it best to leave the crops to her guards in case it were to happen again. She's tried to stay sheltered in the palace ever since. Only leaving when she needs to, being sure to have protection when she does.

"While I'm still furious about what happened, I don't believe that's what's bothering me now."

Kuma frowns, biting her cheek. "Did you get word of something else that may be targeted towards you?"

"No, but Zomo is out checking the town, just in case."

"Do you think you're nervous because of the children? They are going to be the first visitors we've had in the palace."

"I don't have any reason to be nervous with them." Ciana exhales sharply, running a finger over the page she has open. The ink feels as if it's been embossed against the thin paper, the dense letters still sharp despite the pages fading in color.

"If there's anything I know about you, Princess Ciana, it's that you want this visit to be perfect. I think you might be worrying about something going wrong with them, even if you don't realise it," Kuma suggests.

Ciana nods, closing the book. "You're probably right. I do want things to go smoothly. I'm sure I'm just overly worried about everything being just right." Ciana takes a few deep breaths, giving Kuma a smile. "Thank you."

Kuma bows her head slightly. "I was hired to help you, so I'm trying my best to do so."

"You're doing a great job at it," Ciana praises, reaching to squeeze Kuma's hand gently. The handmaid beams.

"Is there anything you need in preparation for the children?" Kuma asks, shifting the conversation.

"Everything should be set, we just need the children themselves."

"When will they be arriving?"

"Within the next hour."

"Okay. May I be excused until they arrive then? I have some things I need to finish up before I forget," Kuma shyly asks, avoiding eye contact with Ciana.

"Of course, Kuma. I'll have someone get you when they arrive."

"Oh, thank you!" Kuma sighs in relief, scampering off. Once the balcony doors close, Ciana relaxes her smile. Resting her chin on her palm, Ciana stares at the town once more. She'll need to portray a soft joyfulness around the children, but for now, the untroubled appearance can fall and she can try to clear her mind.

*I don't think I'm worried about the children. That can't be it. But what else could it be?*

"Your Highness?" Zomo's voice echoes in the back of her mind.

*I can't be worried. I've never had a feeling like this before. It's almost as if I can actually feel something wrong. But what could cause it?*

"Your Highness?" Zomo's voice whispers through her thoughts again and she doesn't feel the tap on her shoulder.

*The queen felt uneasy with the darkness,* Ciana recalls. *But they're on the other side of the border. Nothing's changed, at least from what I can see.*

"Your Highness!" Zomo shouts, startling Ciana from her inner-dialogue.

"Zomo! Don't do that!" she breathes, placing a hand over her racing heart.

"I'm sorry, Princess Ciana, but you weren't responding. I came to give you a report."

Ciana blows out a long breath, calming herself. "Right. Of course." She clears her throat, adjusting her posture, and tapping the book against her hand. "Did you find anything wrong?"

Zomo shakes his head. "I did not. Everything in town appears as it should; nothing is wrong. There's no word of anyone planning anything against you either."

"That's good, but it doesn't help me." Ciana bites her bottom lip. Even with his assurance, the impending sensation still sits heavily in her stomach. "Are you sure there was nothing weird or out of place?"

"No, Your Highness. Everything is just as it should be."

"On this side at least," Ciana mutters, looking back toward the direction of the border. "You don't think it's something in the other parts of the kingdom?"

"Eyal scouted that area, which is why it took me longer to return. Everything in the kingdom is fine."

Ciana hums a reply, shifting to face the border. "Then it's got to be something on the other side."

"The other side of what?"

"The border," she replies softly, eyes glued to the red and white brick wall.

"Your Highness?" Zomo cocks an eyebrow.

She follows the shadows from the houses; the tips reaching and stretching to climb over the wall to the other side. Ciana stares at the shadows as if waiting for it to show her the answer. Shaking her head, she faces Zomo. "Something isn't right, Zomo. I haven't had a feeling like this before, something is *wrong*. If it's nothing in my kingdom, then it must be something on the other side of the border. It's the only thing that makes sense."

"And how would we know? We can't cross the border. We don't interact."

"I'm aware of that," she grouses with a huff. "There is one thing we can do, though. Fetch Kuma for me, please, then meet me in my study."

"Of course, Your Highness." Zomo bows, leading them through the balcony doors and down the marble hall, breaking away from Ciana as she heads to her study.

*We've never had a problem. Why would something change now, after all these years?* Ciana sets the book on her desk, flipping it open once more as if hoping it would tell her the answer. The word darkness keeps standing out as Ciana skims through the pages.

"Your Highness, I found Kuma as you requested." Zomo's voice speaks from afar.

*It has to be something on the other side of the border. It's the only explanation.*

"Your Highness!"

Ciana looks up, startled. Zomo and Kuma exchange glances. "Sorry, Zomo. Thank you." Ciana takes a few deep breaths. "Kuma, I would like you to send a letter to Tenebris."

Kuma's eyes widen, taking a step back. "To the *Kingdom of Darkness*?" she blurts.

Ciana nods. "To the prince, specifically."

"The *p-prince*?" Kuma stammers, blinking wildly at the princess. "We can't interact with the kingdom, let alone *him*. Why do you want to send a letter? How would we even do that?"

"I have a feeling that something's wrong and it's not just my nerves or worry about today's visit. I need to make sure there isn't something happening in his kingdom."

"Princess Ciana, you can't send a letter to the prince for an update on any trouble in his kingdom," Zomo includes. "So what if there is? Why would it be any concern of ours?"

"It wouldn't, unless it puts our kingdom in danger."

"You believe the kingdom is in danger?" Zomo arches a brow, slightly taken aback from Ciana's statement.

"Not yet, which is why I need to ensure all is well in Tenebris."

"If you don't think we're in danger, then why bother with a letter?" Zomo remarks.

"I'm following my instincts, Zomo. I can feel that something's off and it's better if we prevent danger before it starts," Ciana tells him, rubbing her temples. Zomo nods in response.

"Princess Ciana, we still aren't allowed to interact with the people of Tenebris." Kuma steps forward.

"It's not an interaction; it's a letter. We do have a little communication with their kingdom, as you know. When we send over food, they return with a detailed list of what else they may need on the next shipment. It's how we know how much and what exactly to send."

Kuma laughs. "I would hardly call that communication."

"Regardless, according to the statutes, the prince and I may communicate with each other in an emergency. Even if there isn't a problem on their side, it's better I check than to have something happen in their kingdom that may find its way to ours."

"How would the letter reach the prince? We still can't cross over."

"No, but we do have animals. We will send the letter via horse." Ciana stands from her chair.

"Will the horse know where to go?"

"Yes. We'll send one of the horses that takes the food over. It'll know the path to the kingdom. From there, we'll hope that the prince receives it. It shouldn't take longer than a couple hours before we hear back."

"What would you like me to write to him?"

"Address it to the Prince of Darkness, let him know we have reason to believe something has shifted the balance."

"Are you sure?" Kuma asks. "There isn't any proof—"

Ciana lifts a single hand, hushing her maid. "Tell him the Princess of Light believes something is amiss; whether that be the balance or something else does not matter. We need to ensure everything is well."

Kuma nods. "Anything else?"

"No, that is all. Please send it right away, Kuma."

"Of course, Your Highness." Kuma dips into a curtsy then departs.

Ciana looks at Zomo. "I want you nearby the remainder of the day, just in case we missed something in town."

"Your wish is my command." Zomo bows his head. Ciana glances at the clock on the wall.

"The children will be here any moment." Ciana huffs, rubbing her temples as she paces around the room. The last thing she wants is to let the children know anything is wrong. Stopping next to her desk, she leans against it, rolling her shoulders forwards to release the tension from her upper body and spine. Hanging her head, she closes her eyes. Ciana takes a long inhale, using the second of quiet to push the dreaded feeling from her mind. Exhaling through pursed lips, she straightens her posture, holding her head high as she flutters her eyes open. She turns and smiles at Zomo. "Let's go greet them."

Excited whispers filter through the grand entrance doors as she approaches. Ciana straightens her baby blue dress, nodding at the waiting guards who slowly swing open the large wooden doors, revealing the orphaned children and their housemother. Smiles spread across the children's faces as they see Ciana.

"Princess! Princess!" they greet, running up to try and hug her.

"Children, this is not how we act towards the princess." The tall woman with curly red hair sighs, gathering the children away from Ciana.

"It's alright, Abrie," Ciana reassures her, turning her attention back to the children, hugging a few of them. "Are you ready to see parts of the palace?"

"Yes!" The children grin, bouncing from foot to foot, a few of the younger children grab hold of Ciana's outstretched hands.

"I have some rooms I'd like to show you I think you'll all enjoy." Ciana smiles, leading them down the white marble hall, their footsteps echo off the polished floor, trailing up the marble columns towering over them to the ceiling above. "Then I have a surprise if you all behave."

"Oooo." The children giggle, clapping their hands.

Kuma runs down from the opposite end, slowing her pace as she nears the group.

"Sorry I'm late, Your Highness, but I got the letter sent," Kuma breathes, her face a light shade of pink.

"It is all right, Kuma. We haven't started the tour quite yet. Children, I would like you to meet my handmaiden Kuma. She will be joining us today."

One of the girls raises her hand. "What's a handmaiden?"

"A handmaiden is someone who helps me with whatever I may need."

"Like what?" one of the younger boys asks.

Ciana smiles at him. "Like ensuring I know what paperwork to sign. Knowing what documents need to be sent out right away. Informing me when meal times are. And more."

"You don't know when to eat?" Giggles escape from the children.

"As the Princess, I have many responsibilities. Sometimes I get so busy I don't realize how much time has passed. Kuma keeps track of the time for me. She's been working for me just over two weeks and has already done an excellent job." Ciana gives Kuma a warm smile.

"Why don't your parents help? The king and queen?" a boy blurts.

"Ah, that is an inquisitive question. One that I'll happily answer later. But right now, I want to show you the ballroom."

Ciana guides the children to the white and gold ballroom, the lush green garden, the silver-crested tiara in her study, and peeked in the cold, deserted dungeon before bringing them to the most important room in the palace.

"This way." She leads them back up the metal stairs towards another flight of stairs to a landing with one set of double doors. "I think you will like this room. This is the most important room."

Ciana opens the door, letting the children into an observatory-type room brightly lit from the skylight ceiling. The air around them lifts, almost as if the room is floating in the clouds. The spacious room holds nothing but a single stand displaying a white blob of light, surrounded by glass in the middle.

Drawn to it, the children's faces are illuminated by the white light. Their excited whispers fill the room.

"Do you all know what this is?" Ciana walks up behind some of the children.

"Yes!" The children's eyes light up.

"The heart of our kingdom. This helps keep our kingdom healthy and strong. Without it, darkness would overrun us. The Queen of Light herself gave it to us."

"It's smaller than I imagined," Abrie comments, peering at the heart.

"It is the same size as a regular heart, but it is very powerful."

Ciana stares at the heart for a second, wringing her hands together slightly, the dread from earlier returning as she feels the heart's pulse beat irregularly.

*No,* Ciana holds back her gasp. *No wonder I could feel something off.*

Ciana glances up at Kuma, who's watching her closely. Her heart pounding.

*Something is wrong, and whatever it is, it's affecting the kingdom. It needs to be stopped before it gets worse.*

"Your Highness?" Kuma whispers, pulling Ciana away from her thoughts.

Ciana puts on a smile, clasping her shaking hands together, forcing a calm voice as she turns her attention back to the children. "Let's move on, shall we? You were all well behaved, so I'll take you to your surprise." Zomo holds the door open as they file out of the room. Ciana falls back so she can whisper to Kuma.

"I'll catch up with you, but could you please lead the children down to the antique room?" she requests, stopping next to Zomo.

"Yes." Kuma nods, hastening her walk so she can lead the group. Ciana turns her attention to Zomo.

"Please tell me we've heard back from the prince."

"No one has reported that we've received anything," Zomo informs her.

"He better respond soon. The heart is beating irregularly. *Something* is affecting the kingdom. You didn't see anything here, so it has to be something on his side." Ciana wrings her hands in front of her. "Why did this have to happen today?"

"As soon as we hear from the prince, you will be the first to know. When did you first start feeling like something was off?"

"Just this morning."

"I'm sure whatever it is, will pass. The prince still has time to get back to you and fix whatever it may be."

"*If* he gets back to me."

"I'm sure he will, just give him time."

"I'll wait, but not if things don't improve any time soon."

"I'm sure they will, Your Highness. Now I suggest we rejoin the children. I'm curious as to this surprise you have planned for them."

"It'll be a first for everyone." Ciana takes deep breaths, walking down the stairs to catch up with the children.

# Chapter Two

The children whisper excitedly outside the light oak doors, shut tight and locked, to keep everything inside. Ciana weaves her way through the children to stand with her back to the door.

Abri shushes the children. Ciana smiles at the excitement, patiently waiting for the children to quiet before she explains what lies behind the doors. "Your surprise is in the antique room. There are a lot of valuable items in there, so you aren't allowed to touch anything. If you don't behave, we will leave immediately. Do you understand?" Ciana looks at the children's eager faces, watching them nod, keeping each other quiet. Lights flicker on as Ciana unlocks and swings the doors open. The children gasp filing in as noiselessly as possible.

Display cases line the room, showcasing anything from the first currency created to the first weapon. Ciana leads the children down the rows towards the back of the room.

"You have clothes in here?" One of the older children laughs, pointing to a well preserved suit. "What's so important about that?"

Ciana smiles. "Everything here goes back to the beginning, when the queen and king first started living in this world. The clothes you see belonged to the king and some of their children."

"Why?"

"As a memorial. As you know, the Queen of Light landed on this planet when it was dead. She gave it life with her powers, creating what we have today." Ciana walks the children to a few preserved plants, before leading them to a dirty, brown bag and notebook, propped open to a drawing. "The king then found the planet and discovered the queen. This is the bag he used during his time traveling to different planets along with a drawing he did."

"He was very good!" a young girl comments, looking at the detailed drawing of some plants.

"He was." Ciana nods, leading them to the next case holding a diagram for a gun and sword. "When the people of Tenebris came, they wanted to take our power. As our power can't be used as a weapon, the king and queen had to find some way to give them a chance of defending themselves. As a result, they figured out how to make guns and swords, based on what the king had on his home planet."

"Why?" A boy looks at the gun prototype.

"The people of Tenebris can kill anything with a simple touch. So, being able to defend from a far was the best option; hence the gun. But they didn't always work due to technicalities from being made so fast without proper testing, so they had to fight with swords as well. But even then, they only did so much against their power."

"What does this have to do with keeping clothes?"

Ciana chuckles. "The king and immediate children of the queen lost their lives in the war. She kept some of their clothes to help remember them. When Luxregnum was created after the pact was solidified, she moved them here to keep them safe."

"Are any of your clothes down here?"

"No." Ciana laughs, leading them to the end of the room, where two metal doors wait. "Now, what I'm about to show you is very old, but sturdy. You can play in what I'm about to show you, but you must be respectful to it."

Ciana opens the metal doors, revealing a large stone room. The air grows slightly colder as they enter. The children gasp, running up to one of two old, worn-down pods.

"These are the pods that the queen and king traveled in before coming to Cosima. The larger pod was the king's; built for the long travel he did. The smaller pod was the queen's; small and sleek to easily take off in an emergency and travel for a shorter amount of time," Ciana explains motioning to the pods accordingly.

"Your Highness." Zomo approaches Ciana. "No one has ever been in here."

"I'm aware."

"Then why are you allowing the children to be here?"

"It's part of our history. Parts from the queen and king's home planets. If we're ever in need of leaving the planet, we have the pods as guidance."

"But—"

"We only kept them locked away in case Tenebris got ideas about overruling us and wanted to ensure we had no means of escape. Having the children down here won't hurt anything," Ciana remarks, watching as the children, Miss Abrie, and Kuma look around the pods. "These pods are the oldest items we have. The majority of our structures are based on either the pods or from the king and queen's home planets, such as the motion censored lights, the brick buildings, the farms, and any sort of technological items."

One of the older girls walks out of the larger of the two pods, looking between the two. "I don't understand." She sighs, scratching her head. Ciana joins her. "The king was from a different planet than the queen, right?"

"That is correct."

"And the queen was the last from her planet... the king didn't have her powers, right?"

"Yes."

"With our powers, we age gracefully, don't look a day over twenty but can live for a long time, so how did the king live so long? Wouldn't he have died before the queen?"

"You have a very inquisitive mind. That is true. The queen actually gave some of her power to the king, so he became like her. That's how he was able to live for so long. It's the same for the rest of the king's people who came to Cosima. When they arrived, the queen gave them some of her power as well."

"We can do that?" a boy gasps, overhearing the conversation.

"Only the royal family has the ability to transfer power to someone in that way. You guys can just heal with your powers."

"What else can you do with your power?"

"So why didn't the queen just give her power to the King of Darkness?" A girl waves her hand.

"It wouldn't have worked. The power would disappear. Think of it this way; imagine if our bodies were a cup, the king when he first arrived didn't have any powers, his body was like an empty cup. Because of that, the queen was able to fill the cup with her power. The King of Darkness on the other hand already has power. His cup is already full and there's no room for the queen's even if she were to try to give him some of her power. His cup would overflow and not gain anything from it. But if I were to give one of our own people some of my power, it would work because you already hold the same power, I would just be enhancing it in a way. Does that make sense?"

The children nod, before the girl raises her hand once again. "How old are you then, Princess Ciana? You were born during the war, which happened so long ago."

"Let's see, the queen is roughly five hundred and twenty years old, so that would make me"—Ciana counts on her fingers—"four hundred and four years old."

"Wow, that old? Is it the same for the other side of the border?"

"I'm not entirely sure, we don't know much about the other side, but I would assume it is. Otherwise, the queen probably would have come back if the King of Darkness died, since she wouldn't have much of a need to stay away anymore."

"Why did they leave?"

"The king wanted to ensure that his greed for power didn't interfere with what he and the queen had built so both of their people could live. The queen went with him to make it fair and keep an eye on him in case he went back on his word."

"Does your mom never help you? Even if you need it?" More children gather around to listen.

"No, I'm on my own unless it's something I absolutely cannot do myself."

"But weren't you only ten when you started ruling? Wouldn't she have helped you then?"

"Yes, she did help then. Just as the King of Darkness helped his son, who was only six at the time."

"As ruler, why don't you have the title of queen?" Abrie asks, folding her arms across her chest.

"In the royal line, we keep our title until the higher up has passed. So even though I am the ruler, I will keep the title of Princess until the queen has passed. Or if I were to marry, that would also give me the title of queen as my husband would automatically get the title of king." Ciana glances at Zomo who nods.

"I see." Abrie slowly nods, Kuma also nods in understanding.

"Why did the king only agree to the pact after the mention of us providing their food?" one of the older boys questions, sitting in front of Ciana.

"I'm not entirely sure, but based on the little information we know about them, he probably agreed knowing that their supply of food would shortly run out once our people die."

"Not if he had our power!"

"You mean *her* power," a kid corrects his friend. "So why is your power different from ours?"

"Like I said, the power would have disappeared, which the queen was aware of. So in return to supplying all their food they let us live."

"Which is why we're so close to each other and have the border wall to help hold the balance, right?"

"That is correct." Ciana chuckles to herself, pleased that the children are wanting to understand everything.

"It doesn't seem fair, us providing them with food when they give nothing in return."

"It may not, but it is. It was either they let us live over food or we lost our lives. It was the only thing the king agreed to, so the queen took it to help us."

A quietness settles over the children as they nod, taking in everything she has to tell them. Ciana lets her gaze dance over them until a girl at the center of the group raises her hand. Ciana gestures for her to speak. "We always hear about the balance between us and the people of Tenebris and how it can't be broken. I don't understand what that means."

"Everything has a balance. We have a pure power, while the people of Tenebris hold an impure power. Alone, these powers don't have any problem, but when the Kingdom of Darkness started to build on the planet, their power began to overrun ours. This was shown by a storm that appeared and wouldn't go away. When the kingdoms were rebuilt, the king and queen managed to find a balance so their darkness would not overrun us, especially since we're so close to each other. If that balance between our powers broke, it would mean something physically happened to cause a shift. The result would be the darkness coming into our kingdom."

"There's no storm now."

"You're right. There isn't. It disappeared once the balance was created."

"If it's so dangerous, why are we so close to the other kingdom?" another girl inquires.

"It's to help even out the balance."

"What?" The children's faces scrunch up, trying to understand.

"Here, maybe this will help you understand." Ciana chuckles. "Kuma, do you have any paper on you?"

"Oh, yes I do." Kuma reaches into her pocket, handing Ciana a blank piece of paper.

"Perfect, thank you." Ciana rips the paper into five pieces, folding them just enough so they stand, forming a box, with one separating the middle. "This paper box represents the land Tenebris and us have. Half is theirs, the other half is ours. As you can see, everything is split equally, both sides are balanced with the same amount of space. It's the same for the powers; both kingdoms' abilities are able to thrive within their side, never intersecting or crossing over to the other. The outside edges represent the forest border we have from the rest of the world. Everything is fine, right?" The children nod. "If the balance broke, the darkness would start coming over here." Ciana touches the corner of the middle paper, causing the entire thing to collapse. "Even the tiniest bit can cause the downfall of our kingdom, because their power is so impure compared to ours." Ciana sets the box back up again. "The same even if we were to expand past the forest." Ciana once again touches the corner of one of the outer papers, causing it to collapse once more. She grabs a piece, tearing it in half again, trying to add it to one side of the box. "As you can see, if we were to expand, it still wouldn't work, but if both kingdoms expanded..." Ciana tears another piece, making the papers stand again. "It balances everything back out."

"Ooooh!" The children sigh.

"So if we stay in our box, our powers are evened out enough, we don't have any problems. Which is what the heart helps... with." Ciana's smile falters as she thinks back to the heart.

*At least that's how it's been until now.*

One of the boys raises his hands. "So what else could break the balance?"

"I'm not entirely sure. It has never happened before..." Ciana's heart begins to race.

*Could it be happening now? No, it couldn't.*

"A good example would be if someone harmed the heart. That would definitely..." Ciana trails off.

*That would definitely set things off. The palace is heavily guarded, so I would know if someone harmed it. There's got to be something else happening.*

"Your Highness?" Abrie questions, watching Ciana drift in thought. Ciana shakes her head, smiling again.

"Sorry about that," Ciana apologizes.

An older girl wearing worn-out pants and a favored shirt raises her hand. "If the balance is broken, how is it fixed?"

"Only the queen and king's power can fix whatever caused it in the first place and restore everything. There was a map created and given to both rulers, so we know where to find them. Without their power, the balance cannot be fixed."

A boy, who appears to be around fifteen, shoots his hand up. Ciana nods in his direction, waiting for his question. "What's the difference between your power as princess and the queen's power? Couldn't you just restore everything?"

Ciana hesitates, watching as the children exchange curious whispers. "I think that is enough questions for today," she finally replies, standing.

"Wait!" the boy calls out. "I want to know more about your power."

"That is something you are all too young to fully understand." Ciana stares at the paper box on the ground.

*I need to know if there's something wrong in Tenebris. If something is happening with the balance, then it needs to be fixed, but wouldn't there be more signs?*

"Princess Ciana?" Abrie tries to get her attention.

*I could just be overthinking things. It's probably not anything major, like I think it is.*

"Princess Ciana?" Ciana looks up at Zomo, who's coughing, before turning her attention to Abrie.

"I'm sorry, yes Abrie?" Ciana smiles.

"I was just going to relay that some of the children are getting hungry."

"Oh, yes!" Ciana glances at the nearby clock. "Lunch should be ready. I was thinking of having it out in the garden. Give the children some fresh air again."

"Thank you, but I think we'd better head back to the orphanage. I'm sure you have a lot to attend to."

"No. No, I'm merely lost in thought," she lies, trying to play off her distractions as nothing more than daydreaming. "Please stay for lunch."

"Thank you, but no. I think it best we end our visit here."

"Are you sure? The cooks have prepared a lovely meal for the children."

Abrie nods. "I'm sure. I don't want to keep you from your duties."

"Will you at least take the food with you?" Ciana urges. "That way you don't have to worry about making a meal when you get back."

"That's not necessary, Your Highness."

"I insist." Her tone hardens, but Ciana can't stand the idea of them leaving hungry. "It'll go to waste if I keep it all here. I can't possibly eat it all by myself." She stares at Abrie almost pleadingly. "Please," she adds more softly.

Abrie glances at the children, letting out a sigh before answering, "I wouldn't want it to go to waste."

Ciana releases a sharp breath, grinning. "Thank you. Kuma, could you go tell the cooks to pack the lunch for the children?"

"I will let them know." Kuma curtsies, leaving the room.

Ciana helps Abrie gather up the children, leading them back to the grand entrance. Kuma joins them a few minutes later, carrying a large, woven basket.

"The cooks said there should be plenty of food for the children to have dinner as well," Kuma tells Abrie as she hands over the basket.

"This is too much, Your Highness." Abrie smiles, securing the basket.

"I want to help as much as I can. Even if it means providing two meals. Feel free to keep the basket; you'll have much better use of it than me." Ciana returns her smile.

"Thank you for letting us tour the palace."

"Anytime Abrie. If you want to do it again, please let me know."

"I will. Thank you." Abie bows her head, before ushering the children out the doors. Ciana follows them to the first step, watching as they make their way down the stone street.

"Zomo?"

"Yes?" Zomo joins her side.

"Still no word from him?"

"That is correct. I'd give him until the end of the day to reply. Who knows what he has going on."

Ciana sighs, crossing her arms. She looks toward the border. "There hasn't been anyone strange in the palace, correct?"

"No one but the staff has been in the palace, until the children, of course."

"No problems at the border gate?"

"The guards stationed there have never seen anyone from Tenebris come through that forest."

"Hmmm." Ciana lets out some air. "I don't think I can wait to hear from the prince. I want you to scout out the kingdom for anything that might be out of place. Anything that may be wrong. Go from border to border, look at everything you can. I just want to make sure we didn't miss anything. Take Ritesh and Eyal with you again. If you see anything, let me know immediately."

"It will be done." Zomo bows, walking back into the palace. Ciana lingers outside a second longer, her heart dropping as she sees two townsmen talking and pointing at her from the street. The whispers and pointing used to be a good thing, the awe and respect given from her people, but now it meant nothing but speculation and potential plotting, watching her every move for one mistake to try and use it against her. Taking a deep breath, Ciana turns and goes back inside the palace.

# Chapter Three

Ciana circles the heart, examining it closely. She rubs her temples, feeling a small headache beginning to form.

"Your Highness?" Ciana pivots to face Zomo as he enters the room. Crossing her fingers behind her back, she hopes he's bringing her good news. "The kingdom has been thoroughly scouted. We looked everywhere, and there is still no sign of anything."

"That's good..." She nods absently. "And have we heard back from the prince?" With bated breath, Ciana awaits the answer she's been longing to hear.

"I'm sorry, Princess Ciana. There's been no reply. The horse hasn't even returned, so who knows if he even received the letter?"

Ciana lets out a frustrated sigh. "It's been almost a day since we sent it. It shouldn't take him this long to respond with a simple yes or no."

"Do you still feel as if something is off?"

"Yes," she replies tartly, then flutters a hand toward the center of the room. "The heart is still beating irregularly, and this stress is causing a headache."

"Is there anything else you propose we do?"

"I don't know. There's not much we can do until we know for sure if Tenebris has a problem. Until then, post a few guards to patrol the border wall and watch for anything unusual."

"Right away, Your Highness." Zomo bows, leaving the room. Ciana looks back at the heart.

*Nothing's gotten worse. That's a good sign. Whatever could be happening over the border isn't a major problem. But why would I feel like something is wrong if it is in Tenebris?*

Ciana resumes her pacing, round and round the heart, only stopping when Kuma pokes her head through the door.

"Princess Ciana?" she questions.

"Yes, Kuma?"

"We received something from the Prince." Her voice falters at the mention of him. Ciana perks up, her anxiety lessening.

Ciana crosses the room in hurried strides. "What did he say?"

"You're not going to like it." Kuma hands Ciana a wrinkled note. Turning the paper over, she's met with... nothing.

"That's it?"

"That's all we got."

"There's nothing written." Ciana crumples the paper, walking back to the heart. "Thank you, Kuma."

"Would you like me to dispose of the paper for you?"

Ciana frowns at the paper clutched in her fist. "Yes, please. I'd appreciate it."

"Of course, Your Highness." Kuma takes the blank reply and exits. Ciana returns her focus to the heart, feeling its irregular pulse.

*What am I going to do? Something is wrong, but I can't fix it if I don't know what it is. The queen didn't go over what I was supposed to do if the prince didn't get back to me.* Ciana wipes away a stray tear, taking a staggering breath as she leaves for her room.

Ciana flips through the worn pages of the history book, tapping her fingers against the white cover underneath as she reads. She glances up from her desk to a knock on her door.

"Come in!"

Kuma enters with a glass of water. "Here's the water you requested."

"Oh, thank you, Kuma." Ciana takes the glass, drinking half of it immediately.

"Are you feeling alright?"

"Yes. Just a small headache from stress."

"Have you eaten anything lately?"

"Not since breakfast. I've been trying to figure all this out."

"Your Highness, you need to eat. I'll have the kitchen make you a meal. That might help your headache as well," Kuma offers, departing for the kitchen before Ciana can refuse.

Ciana gently turns the pages, scanning for anything useful. One page catches her eye. She stares at the passage, eyes dancing over each word carefully.

*The Queen of Darkness,* she muses, taking in the small inscription. With a huff, she lets her mind trill over what she's read. *What happened to the Queen of Darkness? The king left, but we don't know what happened to her. Could that be the reason behind all this uneasiness? I wonder if we have any other history books with more information about her.*

In search of any other historical accounts on the unaccounted Queen, Ciana heads to the library. Turning a corner, she sees Zomo running toward her, sweat coating his red face.

"Your Highness," he breathes. "The border... on the far end of the kingdom... I came back as quickly as I could."

"What is it?" Ciana urges, her nerves rising once more. Zomo doesn't answer as he struggles to catch his breath, gulping in air. "Fetch my horse!" With a curt nod, Zomo rushes down the hall as Ciana hurries to her room to grab a shawl, then makes her way to the main entrance. As Ciana approaches, the guards open the door to reveal Zomo atop his spotted brown horse, holding the reins of her black and silver mare, and another guard waiting on a black horse.

"Let's go!" She clicks her tongue, urging her horse to follow Zomo down the stone roads. The brightly lit brick and wooden houses blur as they fly past. The horses' hooves clap against the stone road beneath them, entangling with the sound of the townspeople making purchases with one another, murmurs from some as they watch Ciana ride past and children playing in fresh grass yards or around marble lamp posts. Ciana looks up ahead where thick, green trees melt into the blue sky; marking where the kingdom ends.

"Over here," Zomo calls over his shoulder as they ride away from the town, near the area where the forest trees meet the tall red and white brick wall separating the two kingdoms. She takes in the shadows looming around the trees, how the deep green canopy sways, providing tiny glimpses to their trunks, before the sun shining off the armour of a few more guards waiting beside the wall distracts her.

"Oh, no," Ciana gasps, hopping off her horse. Her wide eyes follow a black edge creeping over the top of the wall, confirming what she feared would happen. The guards bow as she passes by. "No, no, no. I'm not seeing this."

"Your Highness, is it what I think it is?" Zomo asks, worry filling his voice.

"Yes," Ciana utters softly. "The balance has broken. The darkness is spreading to our side."

"How could this have happened?"

She shakes her head. "I'm not sure."

"Did the prince ever send back a reply?"

"Yes, but there was nothing on it."

"Your Highness, look!" One of the other guards points at the darkness. Ciana's heart races as she watches it branch down the wall like a deadly shadow ready to envelop them all. She takes a few steps back.

*No, no, no. It can't be spreading. Not now. Not this fast. I need to get a hold of the prince, but can't let my people see this in the meantime.*

"Create a perimeter. Make sure no one sees the darkness. It's still at the top of the wall, but if it continues to spread, it'll be more noticeable, and I don't need a panic," she tells her guards.

"Yes, Your Highness. For how long would you like us to keep up the perimeter?"

"Until I say otherwise."

"Right away." They bow as Ciana walks back to her mare with Zomo.

"What needs to be done about the balance?" Zomo asks, mounting his horse.

"I need to get in touch with the Prince of Darkness. He has no choice but to respond since the broken balance will affect both our kingdoms. If something happened on his side, then hopefully it can easily be fixed." Ciana clicks her tongue, starting their way back to the palace.

"Princess Ciana!" a man in town yells, causing Ciana and Zomo to slow their pace, allowing the man to approach. Zomo positions his hand to rest on the hilt of his sword, secured in its holster.

"What can I do for you?" Ciana addresses the man.

"You've been ignoring our requests," he affronts her. Ciana's eyebrows furrow, not sure what he's referring to.

"I'm afraid I don't understand. Requests for what?"

He scoffs. "Don't be inane, *princess*." Ciana frowns, not surprised that her people would dare speak to her in such a way, but still hurt by his comment. Zomo eases his horse between her and the man, creating a protective wall."

"Watch your tone or lose your tongue," Zomo warns.

"She's the one who's been ignoring *us*." The man's eyes blink in her direction. "She clearly doesn't care about her own people."

"I do care," Ciana counters harshly. Everything she's ever done has been for the kingdom; for her people. Why can't they see that? "There is a lot that happens behind the palace walls, and I get many requests from the town. I apologize, but I cannot recall one inquiry for—"

"I was referring to *all* of them," the man interjects.

Ciana glances towards the wall, her anxiety building as they sit there instead of riding to the palace to form a plan. "I have reviewed and replied to the most important requests and concerns. Now if you can please excuse me—"

"But not the rest? All our requests should be important to you, Ciana." The man's tone holds a sharp edge

"You will address the lady as Princess Ciana or Your Highness," Zomo corrects through his teeth.

"Every request is important, and I do take the time to look through each one. However, it would be impossible to reply or make promises on the hundreds of inquiries that cross my desk, *sir*." Ciana's hands tighten on the reins. This conversation needed to end. "Now, if you'll excuse me, there is something of the utmost importance I must address—" Ciana reiterates as calmly as possible.

"Apparently not. You don't even come to town meetings to discuss items with us," he persists.

"Do *not* interrupt Her Highness again." Zomo scowls.

"Zomo." Ciana shakes her head slightly when he turns his attention to her. With a frustrated puff of air through his nose, Zomo eases his horse back a single step. "I am more than willing to come to town meetings," Ciana begins, straightening in her saddle. "However, I am never informed when they are."

"You never ask," the man counters.

"I have." Ciana closes her eyes for a moment, taking a few subtle deeper breaths to try to steady her racing heart. Her eyes drift behind the man, noticing other townspeople slowing or stopping to listen. A town proclamation in the middle of a potential disaster is the last thing she needs right now. "With every complaint I receive regarding my attendance at your meetings, there is always a response asking for the time and the location of the next meeting. And yet, I still have not gotten a reply from *any* of you, nor an invitation." A few of the patrons behind the man scurry away, while others ease even closer. "Now, excuse me. I must be going." Ciana gently kicks her horse, starting to move away from the man.

"Of course. Running away from what you don't want to deal with. Just like you always do!" the man yells after her. Ciana bites her tongue, using all her strength to restrain from jumping off her mare and tackling the man. She meets Zomo's eyes, giving him a knowing look. He nods in understanding, turning to the other guard in a whisper. The guard nods, dismounting his horse while Zomo takes its reins.

The man stares the guard down as he approaches, before the guard forcefully twists one of the man's arms behind his back, pushing him in the direction of the palace, slowing their walk as they walk past Ciana.

"This conversation will continue after I've finished dealing with an urgent need that requires my attention. Until then, you will have plenty of time to think about your lack of respect towards me."

The man glares at Ciana and Zomo before the guard continues to move him forward. Ciana looks at the rest of her people, who also give her glares as they walk back to their lives.

"I think we're done here, Your Highness," Zomo states as he gently kicks his horse, starting his way back to the palace. Ciana follows.

At the palace, Ciana writes a letter to the prince, informing him of the broken balance. On the outside of the note she writes 'Urgent' in big letters, hoping that he will give it more attention than the last one.

"Here, Kuma, please send this off to Tenebris right away." Ciana hands over the letter as she makes her way to the library.

"Yes, Your Highness." Kuma nods, running off down the hall.

Ciana grabs as many potentially helpful books as possible to combat the darkness.

*There's got to be something that I can do to prevent the darkness from spreading.* Ciana rubs her temples before flipping through the books. *Nothing, nothing, nothing.* She sighs, pushing away a few of the books.

Kuma enters the library, finding Ciana at one of the tables. "I got the letter sent, Ciana."

"Thank you, Kuma."

"The cooks also have your meal prepared."

"Thanks, but I don't have the time to eat."

"Princess Ciana, you need to eat."

"I have a lot more important things on my mind, Kuma." Ciana sighs, her stomach grumbling in protest.

"Princess Ciana," Kuma warns. "Your health should always be important. Don't make me drag you to the dining room."

Ciana smiles, standing from the table. "And I know you would," she replies. "You're right. I need to eat something."

"Regardless of what's going on, it's important to keep your strength." Kuma opens the door, curtsying as Ciana walks by.

"Are you going to make sure I eat all my food?" she teases.

Kuma chuckles. "If I must." Ciana flashes her handmaid a smile.

A butler brings out a plate of roast chicken, setting it in front of Ciana along with a glass of water. "Here you are, Princess Ciana."

"Thank you." Ciana smiles, drinking her water. The butler bows, leaving her alone. She stares down at the bleak beans against the white rice on her plate, bringing her mind back to the darkness.

*I hope I get a response soon. I can't risk it spreading further into the kingdom. There's nothing I can do to fix it.*

Ciana takes a bite of her meal, struggling to come up with a solution. Finishing her water, Zomo enters the dining room in search of her.

"Your Highness," he greets.

"Please tell me you're here to tell me we got a response," Ciana pleads.

Zomo shakes his head, averting his gaze for a brief second. "I'm sorry, Ciana. It would be too soon. I came to inform you that a perimeter has been set up, two guards are watching the wall where the darkness has continued to spread."

Ciana slumps in her chair, raking her hands through her blonde hair. "Of course it is. Zomo, I don't know what to do."

"Can't you go to the queen and king, since we know the balance is broken?"

"I can't, or else I would have left already."

"Why not? Isn't that what they told you to do?"

"Yes, but I can't go without the prince. I just have to wait for him to respond to me." She shakes her head in frustration. *Why is he refusing to reply?!*

"Why must you go with him? Why can't just one of you go?" Zomo adjusts his helmet under his arm.

"It's to help prevent any possible wrongdoings."

"What do you mean?"

"It's for accountability." Cianna sighs, fiddling with the fork on the table; anything to keep her hands busy. "Going together ensures that one of us isn't going to try and sabotage the other kingdom. If we don't, then the king and queen won't help in case we are going to them with ill intentions. The balance was created by both kingdoms, so both need to go to get it fixed."

"I see, but didn't you say you were hoping the problem could be easily fixed?"

Ciana nods. "Whatever caused this to happen, hopefully it is small enough so we don't have to go to the fortress. But if not... we'll have no choice."

"Hopefully it won't come to that," Zomo says, his voice a bit uncertain. "In the meantime, have you figured out what we can do to prevent the darkness from spreading?"

"That's what I was trying to figure out before Kuma urged me to eat. It's what I'm going to do right now." Ciana scoots her chair back, standing.

Zomo dips his head in a bow. "I will let you be, but please let me know if you come up with anything."

"I will." Ciana makes her way back to the library for the rest of the day.

# Chapter Four

"Your Highness!" Zomo runs into the dining room the next morning. Sweat caressing his red face. He bends over, trying to catch his breath.

Ciana turns in her chair to face him, fear crossing her eyes. "Please tell me you're running in here to tell me we got word from the prince."

Zomo shakes his head, straightening his posture. "I wish," he breathes. "The darkness... it has spread."

"Show me." Ciana pushes her breakfast away, following Zomo to the grand entrance. Without bothering to wait for someone to bring her a horse, she climbs behind her guard on his. Zomo whips the reins, taking them down the street.

Ciana's jaw drops as they near the wall. Darkness fully engulfs the entire section and some plants at the bottom. Zomo extends his hand, helping her off the horse so she can get a better look. The guards stationed bow as she nears.

Examining the ominous area, Ciana's pulse quickens. Before, the darkness merely sat along the top, but now... she had hoped nothing would happen overnight.

"If it spread this quickly overnight, then who's to say how much it'll continue throughout the day and another night." Ciana exhales sharply, rubbing her temples; her headache lingering from the previous evening.

"Princess Ciana, if I may?" One of the guards steps forward.

"Yes?"

"You can bring life. Can't you just revive what the darkness has touched?"

Ciana presses her lips together, shaking her head. "If I only could. Watch." She crouches next to the blackened plants. Ciana gently places her hands on the leaves. The void of life sends a chill up her body, pulling at her as if it would take away the life within her. Pushing the feeling aside, she focuses on the plant, imagining it alive, thriving and pulsing with the sunlight. A warm sensation flows from her fingertips to the plants, reviving it to a fresh green. As soon as her hands are off the plants, the darkness overcomes it, killing it instantly. Ciana takes a step back as the darkness spreads a little more. "I can't revive what the darkness has destroyed. Only the queen has that power."

"I wasn't aware, Your Highness," the guard apologizes.

"It's alright."

"Princess Ciana," another guard speaks up. "If your powers cannot stop it, what are we to do to prevent it from spreading? The town will start asking questions since it's becoming more obvious."

Ciana feels the eyes of her guards on her, but Zomo's presence keeps her from erupting in rage at the question. With a forceful swallow, she straightens, looking each of the armored men in their eyes. "I will go to the king and queen," she says, deciding right at this moment that there is no other way.

"But, the prince," Zomo presses.

"Yes, I know, Zomo," Ciana snaps, giving him a small glare. Closing her eyes, she forces her mind to settle. It's not their fault the prince hasn't responded. "I know," she repeats, more gently. With a final glance at the guards, Ciana turns, walking back to Zomo's horse. Staring at the darkness will not help anyone; she must do *something*.

Zomo helps Ciana back onto the horse before getting on himself. "Continue guarding this area. Let no one approach. Expand the perimeter if needed. If anyone begins to question—"

"Tell them," Ciana interrupts, "that by order of the *princess*, to..." she hesitates, wanting to say nothing more than to have them kindly butt out, but, as their princess—their protector—she needs to not only ensure they feel safe, but be honest with them too. "Tell them it is being handled with the utmost urgency."

"Yes, Your Highness." They salute. Zomo glances at Ciana, then whips the horse's reins.

"Kuma, I need you to write an urgent letter for me, please," Ciana requests, pacing her study.

"What would you like me to write?" Kuma readies her paper.

"It's to the Prince of Darkness. Tell him the balance has broken, and the darkness has continued to spread on our side. We must go to the fortress before it destroys our kingdom. Also tell him I am not pleased with his lack of answering when we have a life-threatening situation in our hands. Tell him if he fails to respond, I will have no other choice but to make him, since both our kingdoms will be affected," Ciana lists. Kuma frantically writes every word, making sure she doesn't miss anything.

"Anything else?"

"No…" Ciana taps her chin. "No, I think that's all. Please get it written and sent over the border right away."

"I will, Your Highness. Don't worry." Kuma stands from her seat, swiftly leaving the study. Ciana continues to pace.

*Things will only get worse if we don't go to the fortress. It's the only way to fix the balance now. The prince better reply this time. I don't know what else I could do to reach him except for crossing the border, but I don't want to do that if I don't have to,* Ciana thinks, making her way to her room.

*There's nothing else I could do. If he doesn't respond, I'll have no choice but to cross over to convince him.* She sighs, running a hand over her face as she walks out onto her balcony to look at her glowing town. The warm sun beats down on her, embracing her in its rays. Tears trickle down her cheeks. *Why did this have to happen now? Why couldn't it have happened years ago or years from now? This couldn't have come at a worse time.*

Ciana stirs her soup, occasionally taking a bite. Her hope slowly fades as the hours pass with no word from the prince. Zomo strolls in, taking a seat next to her.

"Hi Zomo," she acknowledges, resting her head on her hand.

"I came to give you an update." He gives her a small smile.

"Go ahead."

"The darkness is still spreading. So much so that the town has noticed."

Ciana grimaces. "Have you been telling them it's being handled?"

"Yes, but they're still questioning as to what it is and how it happened. We will have to tell them the truth, eventually."

"We will, but now is not the time for a panic. Not until I get word from the prince." Ciana frowns, taking a drink of water.

"Still no word from him?"

"No. Kuma is looking to see if anything has come back from him right now, but he took his time on his last letter."

"Did you mark it as urgent?"

Ciana's head bobs. "As was the last one, despite that, we didn't receive a reply."

"I'm sure he'll respond to this one."

"He'll have to if he wants his kingdom to survive. We just can't afford to waste any time."

"I understand, Your Highness. Would you like me to check on Kuma to see if she's gotten anything?"

"Yes, please, or if you can find any good news for me to take my mind off of things, I would appreciate that as well."

"I'll go take a look." Zomo stands, giving Ciana a quick bow before heading to the door. Kuma runs through the door as Zomo opens it, a piece of paper in hand.

"Ciana!" she breathes, setting the paper next to Ciana's bowl. "He replied."

"An actual reply or another blank piece of paper?" Ciana asks, picking up the paper.

"I'm not sure. I didn't read this one." Kuma pulls out the chair beside Ciana and plops down, eager for the princess to open it. Zomo stalks back, peering over Ciana's shoulder. The princess unfolds the paper.

"I'd like to see you try," Ciana reads aloud. She crumples the note, shoving her chair back. "You would think he'd have a little heart," she seethes. Although she's never met the prince, Ciana could tell she wouldn't like him. A royal who refuses to acknowledge a very real, very *fixable* threat is no right ruler. With fists clenched, Ciana stares at her feet, mind trilling through every other option. This was ridiculous. Nothing would work without the prince—she *needs* him, and that thought alone fueled the wrath that's been burning softly inside her since she first saw the darkness.

With a resolute sigh, she straightens. "This isn't going anywhere. I must speak with him in person."

"But, Your Highness—" Zomo begins.

"I have made up my mind, Zomo. Either you accompany me or I shall find someone else more suited to the task." Without hesitation, the guard nods. "Bring Ritesh and Eyal as well, and meet me at the entrance."

"Yes, Your Highness." Zomo leaves.

"What are you going to do, Ciana?" Kuma questions, eyes wide with curiosity.

"If he will not respond respectfully to my letters or take action, then I have no choice but to visit him myself. Maybe then I can talk some sense into him."

"You can't honestly mean to cro—"

Ciana looks at her handmaid, jaw tight. "Yes, Kuma. I'm going to cross the border. I must." Kuma deflates, shaking her head in wonder. The princess leans in, lowering her voice, but keeping it clipped and sure. "I wouldn't go around telling everyone that I am going to cross, but it's the only other way to try to make him come with me. The balance needs to be fixed."

"I won't say a word." Kuma air zips her lips, throwing away an invisible key.

"I'll be back as soon as I can," Ciana goes on.

"Do you need anything for when you cross?"

"No. It shouldn't take long, and I'll have some guards, so I'll be safe. I'll grab a shawl, but nothing else. The less I come off as a threat, the better it will be."

"Alright. Be safe."

"I will." Ciana gives her maid a reassuring smile, then leaves the dining room, heading to her room. Throwing a shawl over her shoulders, she rushes to the grand entrance where Zomo and two other guards are waiting.

"We are ready, Your Highness," Zomo announces as she approaches them.

"Good." Ciana looks each guard in the eyes. "We're going to Tenebris. The Prince of Darkness needs to come to reason so we can get things back to how they were before," she explains, brushing past them.

The guards exchange a look. "We can't cross the border," one of them says, but Ciana doesn't turn to see who. "It's against the rules. We aren't to interact with those scums."

Ciana whirls, holding her ground. "I'm quite aware of that, but he isn't responding to our requests. The only other option is for me to talk to him personally." Shaking off the stiffness in her shoulders, she turns and continues toward the border gate. "I'll try to convince him of the urgency myself," she calls back.

"Won't crossing upset the balance more?" Zomo asks, catching up to walk—quickly—beside her.

"The queen said once it's broken, nothing will make it worse, except for not taking care of it."

"Princess Ciana, let me and a few guards go then, not you," Zomo implores. "You should stay here to ensure your safety. We will bring weapons; make sure the people of Tenebris know we are serious about our inquiry."

"No," Ciana counters firmly. "No guns; your swords are enough. We don't need any more trouble. I need to convince him myself. This way, he can see how serious this is. If it were just you and some guards they might think you were up to something nefarious."

"And they won't because you're there?"

"I'm hoping not," she utters. "This is the only chance we have of making him see that we have to go to the fortress, and soon. I must be the one to go."

The guards stationed outside the border gate bow as Ciana approaches. Ciana eyes the foreboding path on the other side of the large brass gate. The gloomy, black trees and lack of sunlight give Ciana a big unwelcoming. The thought alone of going to where life is hardly existent makes her heart race.

*It's the only way,* she reminds herself.

Turning her attention to one of the guards, she lifts her chin. "Open the gate, please."

"Your Highness?" The guard looks at his partner, clearly unsure of what to do. Ciana, nor anyone, has demanded the gates be opened for anything other than the food runs. "It's early for a food delivery, and we haven't gotten a request for one from Tenebris either..." he offers.

"We're not sending over any food. Open the gate. I need passage."

The guards exchange glances with each other before they look at Zomo for answers.

"Her Highness has good reason to cross," he informs them. "I will accompany her, along with Ritesh and Eyal. As for right now, obey Her Highness's order and tell no one where we have gone. Open the gate."

"Of course." The large brass gate swings open, her trio of guards on her heels. The singing of birds and sounds of critters decreases almost in an instant as if Ciana had entered a soundproofed room. Ciana takes a deep breath, staring into the path ahead of her, the midnight void almost whispering how if she were to move forward, she'd never come back.

*There's no other option,* she reminds herself as the gate swings shut behind them. There was no going back.

# Chapter Five

Large withered trees tower over them. Branches reaching, entwining with their perished neighbors across the shadowed path. A chill trickles down Ciana's spine as the air grows cold and eerie as she steps under the thick canopy. Her gaze traces up one of the blackened trees, noticing how even though they are barren, the branches are still thick enough to block out the sun and clear blue sky. The only visible light comes from the glow Ciana and her guards illuminate, allowing them to see just enough to stay on the path.

Another step. Ciana pauses, listening for sounds of the forest, a simple scuffle of a creature running to a tree, but there's not even a wind whistling through the branches, no birds chirping, no movement whatsoever other than the steps of Ciana and her guards. The silence is almost foreboding and palpable, so tense it presses against her eardrums.

A branch snaps, echoing like a gunshot through the trees. The guards tense, hands instinctively moving to rest on the hilt of their swords, ready for whatever could be waiting for them. Ciana places a hand over her racing heart, forcing her breath to steady.

"Be on guard for anything. Don't cause any trouble, just protect," Zomo instructs the other two as he tries to peer ahead. "Princess Ciana, permission to let Ritesh scout ahead?"

Ciana meets Zomo's gaze. *Scout ahead? What would there be to scout for? There's nothing but us in this desolate forest!* She nods, looking back around the forest.

Zomo gives Ritesh a curt nod, who unsheathes his sword in response, jogging up ahead.

*It's just precaution,* Ciana tells herself. *There's nothing here, and if he does come across anything it might just be the kingdom. There can't be any creatures of darkness, right? That wouldn't be possible...* Ciana's breath quickens at the thought. Taking a few deep breaths, she calms herself. *They can't bring life to anything, that I'm aware of at least. There isn't anything to worry about. I have my guards, the forest is silent, nothing bad can happen.*

Ciana walks over to one of the trees, frowning as she gently touches the brittle trunk. "It breaks my heart how there's no life," she whispers.

"What was that, Your Highness?" Zomo questions.

"Nothing." Ciana shakes her head. *Everything the queen brought to life. Dead. All because of their powers, whether intentional or not. It makes no difference.*

The sound of footsteps jumps Ciana out of her thoughts. Zomo readies himself, relaxing when Ritesh comes into view.

"There's an opening up ahead, sir," Ristesh informs Zomo. His blonde hair sticking out from under his helmet.

"What kind of opening?"

"It's hard to tell, even with our light, it's so dark. I didn't go any further when I came across it because I saw a dim, blue hue in the distance."

Zomo releases a heavy sigh. "You sure about this, Princess Ciana? What if he doesn't listen?"

"He has to if he wants his own people not to starve to death. Keep going," Ciana answers.

The group continues along the shadowed path, Ciana's guards cautiously looking around as they venture further into the trees. Nearly tripping over a dead twig, Ciana picks it up, examining it the best she can. The coarse black skeleton of what should be wood crumbles as she rubs it between her fingers.

*How could such a dark power exist? Why would anyone want to live without having any... life around them?* Ciana releases the remains of the stick through her fingers, sprinkling them to the ground as she looks once again at the trees around them. *If the entire forest is dead, why don't they just tear them down?*

"This is the opening I came across," Ritesh acknowledges as a small clearing comes into view, a faint blue hue glowing in the distance just as he had reported. Zomo nods, turning to Ciana, raising an eyebrow as if inquiring if they should continue.

"Keep going," Ciana orders, fixing her eyes on the glow, a pit forming in the bottom of her stomach.

"How do we know we're going in the right direction? What if the blue light isn't the town?" Zomo inquires, continuing down the path.

"We've stayed on the path the entire time. The light has got to be the town." Ciana takes a breath. "I don't know what else it could be. We keep going."

The blue intensifies until they can see the dim town lit by blue. Zomo halts, grabbing Ciana's arm and gently drawing her back.

"This is our last chance to go back," he says, eyes dancing over her face, looking for the slightest hint of fear or uncertainty.

Ciana bites her tongue, forcing her face to remain stoic. Turning away from Zomo, she takes in what she can see of this part of Tenebris. Houses made from sable wood and black stone silhouette against the dark blue lamps. The blue flames flicker on top of the thin posts, appearing like wisps of spirits overlooking the graveyard-like yard. Her eyes drift to the people walking the dim streets, faces downturned and expressionless, almost like they're mourning a loss; so opposite of her own kingdom.

Her town is truly a beacon of light and joy, and this... this was more than just the Kingdom of Darkness—this was a town giving off warning of death and despair.

*How can one live like this? Without any glimpse of happiness within them?* she wonders, taking in the murky colors and lack of even the slightest hint of joy. *Would they even appreciate being saved? Would they even let me? Would my people even appreciate what I'm doing for them?*

Ciana shakes off her negative thoughts. She knows this is the right choice. Saving others is always the right choice, regardless of who it is.

"We continue, no matter what," she tells Zomo, peering at him over her shoulder. With a resolute nod, they continue, stepping out of the treeline into view. The townspeople stop to stare, their expressions of ominous disgust illuminated by the cobalt blue light. They turn to shield their eyes as Ciana and her guards walk by. Ciana holds her head high, wringing her hands together in front of her, pushing all negative thoughts from her mind. Glancing down at her hands, she forces them to gently clasp together instead, trying to hide any nerves rushing through her body.

Ciana notices a group of children playing around a lamp post. One of the girls swinging around the pole slips off, landing onto the hard ground. Ciana looks around as everyone ignores the cries of the girl tenderly holding her arm. Her friends run off snickering.

*Poor girl, why isn't anyone helping her?* Ciana runs over, kneeling beside the girl, giving her a warm smile as the girl shrinks back, eyes wide with fear.

"Princess Ciana!" Zomo counters, rejoining her.

"Shhh, it's okay," Ciana soothes the girl. "I'm not going to hurt you. I want to help you." Ciana speaks softly, slowly reaching for the girl's arm.

The girl's breath quickens, warily watching Ciana's hands hovering above her arm, before meeting her eyes again.

"Please?" Ciana pleads. The girl holds her breath, tears swelling in her eyes, nodding ever so slightly. Relieved the girl is allowing her to help, Ciana gently places her hands on the arm. Focusing on the injured limb, she closes her eyes to imagine it healed. A warm tingling sensation runs down Ciana's arm to her fingertips as the rest of her body feels light, as if a burden was just released. The cold ground and air warm around her. A soft collection of gasps and whispers ripple behind Ciana from the townspeople watching. The girl stops crying, trying to pull her arm away from Ciana's grip.

"I'm almost done," she reassures the girl, knowing she's feeling a warm sensation from her healing power. The girl pulls her arm away the second Ciana lifts her hands, scrambling to run away without a word.

"How dare she touch one of our children!" a woman yells. Ciana presses to her feet as her guards surround her, ensuring no one can sneak up unnoticed.

"Disgusting." A man spits.

"I helped her!" Ciana defends herself, clenching her fists. "She was in pain, and none of you were doing anything!"

"What are you doing on this side of the border? It's against the rules." A man staggers up to them, his clothes dirty and torn in places, black bags under his eyes. Ciana nearly takes a step back, caught off by the statement, remembering where she was. Feeling her nails dig into her palms, she takes a deep breath, clasping her hands together.

"Where is your prince?" Ciana demands.

"I don't have a prince, but I would love a princess." He laughs, sending shivers up her spine.

"You have no right to be here," another man speaks up, walking up to Zomo.

"I do at the moment. Where is the Prince of Darkness?" Ciana requests again.

"That is no concern of yours. You and your guard friends should leave before our patience runs out."

"We will not leave until we speak to the prince."

"Then I guess we'll do this the hard way." The man cracks his knuckles, signaling more men to join him, circling around Ciana's guards.

*Why are they threatened by my presence?* Ciana panics slightly. *They know they have the upper hand. I just want to help. I knew it wouldn't be easy coming over here, but I figured they'd ignore us and throw insults from afar or just keep a close eye on us.*

"Watch it, buddy, we mean no harm," Zomo reasons.

"Why else would you be here besides to hurt our children?"

"I did not *hurt* her!" Ciana reiterates, frustration building inside her. "If you give me a moment to expl—"

"What is going on?" a strong voice demands, making the men back away. Ciana peers over Zomo's shoulder to see a young man with messy brown hair and dark eyes, his tan skin complementing his casual onyx clothing. He looks at the men in turn before shifting his attention to Zomo. "Well, if it isn't the Princess of Light's personal walking torches." He smirks. "Why are you here?"

"She touched one of our children. Assaulted her," a man answers.

"I *healed* the girl. None of you were paying attention to her when she was crying," Ciana huffs, turning her attention to the young man. "I am here to talk to the prince." The young man cranes his neck, locating her behind her guards. Even from a distance, she can tell he's at least three inches taller than her, making him slightly more intimidating. Ciana keeps her eyes locked on him as looks her over, emotionless.

"And the Princess herself." He acknowledges. "I can take you to him."

"Thank you." Ciana nods to Zomo to follow the young man as he starts to lead them up one of the cobblestone streets.

*At least someone over here has a little decency.*

They walk through the dreary cobblestone streets of the town, before a large stone castle appears from behind a hill. Opening the big wooden doors, he leads them into a somber throne room, lit by more blue lamps.

Ciana and her guards stop as the young man walks up to the empty throne. "Tell me, Princess, what brings you to my Kingdom of Darkness? Wanting to cause trouble?" He leans back on the lone throne. "You've got some nerve wandering over here."

Ciana pushes past her guards so she can see him better. "Trouble has already begun, Prince..."

"Prince Kieran."

"Kieran. If you read any of my letters, you would know that the balance has been broken. Your darkness has started branching over to my side of the border," she explains calmly.

"And?" He scoffs, lazily draping his arms over the side of the throne. "If you got my replies, you should know that I couldn't care less about that. Doesn't sound like my problem."

"We have got to fix it."

"Ha! There is no *we*," he sneers. "Why should I care?"

"If we do not go to the fortress to fix it, we will all die."

"Again, why should I care? Your people mean nothing to me."

"I didn't just mean *my* people. Everyone over here will also die if we do not fix the balance. We supply your food. Once we die, there will be no one to grow food for you. That was the main reason the pact between kingdoms was made; we all live and you wouldn't have to worry about finding a new home."

Kieran sits forward on his throne, absorbing what she was saying. "Hmmm, that does sound serious. In that case... you'll have to find another prince to go with you." He shrugs, relaxing back into his throne.

"You know very well that it has to be the both of us."

"And I know very well that I don't want to go on a long trip, especially with *you*. So tough luck."

"Have some heart, Kieran, please. The darkness is spreading fairly quickly and is jeopardizing my—*our*—kingdoms."

"Still don't care. There's no way the darkness could be spreading as fast as you say. It doesn't work like that."

"How would you know unless you caused it?"

"I know how our darkness works, Princess. It doesn't just consume unless we want it to. If it's the balance, then it would still take a while to spread. It can't be more than a few specks of black on your side."

"I'm afraid it's much more than a few specks," Ciana mocks. "Its engulfed an entire section of the wall in just over a night."

"Sure. Whatever you want to say." Kieran scoffs again. "If that's really the case, then I suggest you figure out another way to fix whatever set off the balance in the first place. If that's really what it is."

"I do not know what set it off. Whatever you or your people did on this side messed it up."

"Hang on now, Princess." He straightens in the chair. "I replied to the accusation you sent. I told you there were no problems over here, especially anything that would set off the balance. If anything, it was your side, so look there first instead of blaming my people."

"You sent no such thing to me. All I received was a blank piece of paper. My side did nothing. I checked that first. Regardless, we still have to go to the fortress."

Kieran waves his fingers in the air. Ciana doesn't notice at first, but realizes he's playing with a black flame between his fingers. "Are you saying I'm lying?" He gives her a side eye.

"I'm just relaying what I received on my end. However, as the Prince of Darkness, I wouldn't be surprised if you *were* lying."

"I'd watch what you say to me, Princess. I can easily harm you quicker than your guards will have time to react. I wouldn't accuse me of lying. As dark as I can be, lying sure isn't something I do," Kieran warns. Ciana's guards adjust their posture. "Something obviously had to happen, but it wasn't from over here. I'm aware of everything that happens in my kingdom. In my last letter I said I'd think about going if you found the source."

"I told you, I don't know what happened to set things off."

"Then you have your work cut out for you. You all can leave now." Kieran casually gets off his throne, walking towards the door.

"Kieran, please," Ciana pleads, taking a few steps after him. "I would not be over here if it wasn't serious. Our kingdoms will both die if we do not do anything. I can't go alone, you know that."

"It's *Prince* Kieran," he corrects, stopping at the doorway, turning his head just enough to emphasize his title without completely looking at Ciana. His head drops the slightest bit when he looks back ahead. "You have the power of life, just revive what the darkness is killing."

"I can't," Ciana replies, half-way defeated. "I've tried. It immediately withers once I stop using my power on it."

Kieran lets out a soft sigh. "You're positive it's the balance?"

Ciana rolls her lips in, biting them. Thoughts of wanting to reiterate that's why she came over in the first place fill her mind. Of course it was broken. She's already told him this. Instead she manages a soft "yes" before silence occupies the space between them. Perhaps he was considering going with her after all.

She waits with bated breath, watching the prince's back. His posture straightens as he shakes his head. Hope blooms in Ciana's chest as he turns around, but it quickly fades when she sees his eyes narrowed and menacing.

"It's impossible. Unless you broke it by coming over here. I don't want to see you over here again, otherwise it will be the last thing you do," he growls before pivoting on his heels.

"I always thought there was some good in everyone, even over here. I guess I was wrong." Prince Kieran disappears through the door. "Let's go." Ciana returns to her guards, heading toward the main entrance. Walking back through the town, two of the townsmen trail them, ensuring they cross the border back to the Kingdom of Light.

*It's hopeless. Without him agreeing to go with me to the fortress, the darkness will just have to spread. Maybe once there's no more food he'll realize how he was wrong in not going.* Ciana nearly stops as her thoughts spark an idea. *That's it! That's what I'll do. I'll stop the food provisions, just until he agrees to come with me. The next cart full is supposed to cross over in a couple of days so the timing is perfect. We provide their food, so unless he wants his people to starve he'll have no other choice.*

# Chapter Six

A week later, and no letter from Prince Kieran has arrived. Ciana hoped that by ceasing all supply runs, she'd prove to him that her kingdom and the people within are just as important as his. She had hoped he would give in and be forced to go with her by now, knowing their food supply from the last cart should have been out a few days ago, and yet... silence. She even had Kuma check the letters she received after writing the prince to confirm he wasn't lying, but only found the two.

The darkness has inched its way further along the wall and towards the town, making it harder to block off from the townsmen. The sight has started a panic among her people, concerned for their safety. Two days ago, no longer able to play it off as an experiment, Ciana addressed her kingdom, informing them of the darkness and how she is doing everything in her power to resolve the issue, by even reaching out to the Prince of Darkness to help aid her. She promised her people that she will protect them and no harm will come to them or the kingdom. Ciana hadn't been sure how much hope she'd inspired in them, but she knew it couldn't have been much based on the public disapproval towards her and the worry that was still stirring in the town.

"Princess Ciana!" Zomo runs into her study that late afternoon, a gun slung over his shoulder.

"Yes?"

"The prince is at the gate. Requesting to speak with you."

"What?" Ciana jumps from her chair, knocking it to the ground, following Zomo out the front door. Hopping behind him on his horse, they ride over to the border gate.

"My orders are to wait until the princess is here," a guard shouts through the gate.

"Look, she's here. Can you open the gate now?" Kieran's voice argues from the other side, fiercely pointing at Ciana.

"What are you doing here?" Ciana hops off the horse, striding up to the gate.

"What do you think?" he sneers. Ciana examines the prince; his tan skin now a slight shade paler, dark bags under his eyes and his cheekbones slightly more shallow than before. "You took away our food. My people and I are furious; you are breaking your part of the pact," he continues, speaking through his teeth. "So I want to see this engulfed wall to see if it really is from the balance breaking and not just you overreacting to a mere shadow." Kieran crosses his arms, eyeing them all. Ciana stares at him through the gate. "What? Don't trust me now?"

"You finally see the importance of keeping *my* people alive then?" Ciana smiles, proud that her plan did in fact work. Kieran grimaces. "You seemed pretty set on not wanting anything to do with this."

"You gave me no other choice. Although I did consider relocating..."

Ciana blanches. "What?"

"*But* it seemed easier to come see this darkness for myself than to uproot an entire kingdom." The prince holds her stare, a half-cocked grin on his lips.

Biting back the unladylike response she wanted to spit at him, Ciana takes a breath and forces a tight smile. Regardless of her plan almost failing, he was here nonetheless. "I see." She holds back a glare, turning her attention to the waiting guard, hesitating.

*He almost moved his kingdom, didn't he think coming to look at the darkness and going to the fortress would be easier? He's the Prince of Darkness, could he have a trick up his sleeve?*

Kieran heaves a sigh. "You're seriously hesitating now? After everything you did to get me over here?" Ciana keeps her eyes on the guard. "Fine. If you don't want me here anymore, then I'll just let your kingdom die, and it'll be on you. We don't have to go to the fortress. I'll prepare my people to leave." He turns to go back to his kingdom.

"Wait!" Ciana stops him.

*It doesn't matter. If he's willing to go, then I better take him on his offer while he's still willing. I just have to trust him. We can't waste any more time.*

"Open the gate," she orders her guards.

"Princess Ciana, we can't let him on our side," Zomo whispers, Kieran faces them again, his features darkening slightly indicating he can hear.

"We have to, Zomo. We have to fix the balance before it gets worse. Open the gate, please." Her guards follow her order, allowing Kieran to step over. Zomo cocks his gun.

"Try anything over here, and it will be the last thing you do."

"Do not start anything, Zomo. This way, Kieran." Ciana leads the way to the end of town, keeping to the wall to help make sure none of her people see him.

Ciana frowns when she sees the expanding darkness. Zomo stands with the two stationed guards, explaining the situation as Ciana and Kieran approach the darkness.

"It's continued to spread, and at this rate, it will overcome the kingdom in maybe a week," she informs Kieran who traces his fingers against the black wall.

"And you don't know what caused it?" His eyebrows furrow as he draws his hand away, rubbing his fingers together as if the darkness left a residue.

"No, but we can figure that out after we talk to the queen and king."

Kieran turns to Ciana, shaking his head with a frown. "I was hoping you were overexaggerating and were worried about nothing serious, but—"

"But," Ciana interrupts, hope blooming in her chest.

"It seems I was mistaken."

Ciana studies his features, looking for any sign of deceit or mistrust. Finding nothing but almost a hint of annoyance and confusion, she lets her gaze wander back to the darkness. "And this is not you?"

"No, it is my darkness." Kieran rubs the back of his neck. "I just don't know what could have caused it." Ciana opens her mouth to retort about how he couldn't know what caused it when it *is* his darkness, but he quickly continues. "And I'm telling you the truth. Nothing's changed in my kingdom other than lack of food, and if it's nothing over here then something else must have caused the balance to shift."

"Does this mean you'll come with me to the fortress?" Ciana smiles.

"Yes. Let's go so this can be over with." Kieran turns to walk to the forest.

"Hang on, Kieran. It's going to be a long trip, we need to bring provisions. It's obvious you didn't bring anything with you, so I suggest we pack what we will need and meet back at the gate, then we can leave." Ciana begins to walk away.

Kieran lets out a single chuckle. "I'm already ahead of you, Princess."

Ciana whips back around. "What do you mean?"

"I already brought a bag of provisions. I left it on my side of the gate." Kieran walks towards the gate.

"But you didn't think I was telling the truth about the darkness." Ciana follows, arms crossed. "How could you be prepared to leave?"

"No, I didn't believe you and still hoped you were wrong, but I'm not as stupid as you might think I am. I know to listen to my gut instinct."

"And it told you to come over prepared to leave?" Ciana raises an eyebrow.

"Yes."

At the gate, Kieran crosses over, grabbing a black bag that was obscured by the wall. Slinging it onto his back, he rejoins Ciana and Zomo.

"Are you prepared to leave, Princess?" Kieran smirks. Ciana holds back a glare as she starts towards the palace. Kieran follows with Zomo on his heels.

At the palace entrance, Ciana quickly explains to her guards what's happening as they cock their guns. Upon entering the palace, Kuma hurries towards Ciana.

"Your Highness, I was looking everywhere for you. I—" Kuma stops short, stumbling backwards at a loss for words when Kieran enters behind Ciana. Her face drains to a pale color, and she appears on the verge of collapsing.

"It is alright, Kuma. He's not staying long," Ciana quickly reassures her.

"But–but—"

"I know, I know. Go to my room. I'll be up shortly."

"Ok," Kuma squeaks, running into the nearest room.

"Huh, what a wimp," Kieran snorts. "She almost reminds me of someone."

"Watch it, *Prince Kieran*. Don't refer to her Highness in that manner." Zomo digs the barrel of the gun into Kieran's back. Kieran whips around, slamming Zomo into the wall, gun forced against his neck. A slow shade of purple colors Zomo's face.

"Watch it, you moron. I wasn't referring to the Princess of Goodness here. Don't threaten me with anything again unless you want me to kill and destroy everything over here. So don't push it."

"Let him go, Kieran, do *not* kill him," Ciana orders. Kieran glances over his shoulder at her, before he releases the gun, stepping back. Zomo collapses to the floor, gasping for breath. "Zomo, please do not threaten him. I know you are doing your job, but we do not need any battles to start," she adds towards Zomo, sweetly.

"Hmp, goodness in everyone, huh?" Kieran scoffs.

"Yes." She smiles. "Now I will be right back, and both of you better still be alive. I won't take long." Ciana leaves down the hall, up one of the marble staircases to her room. Kuma immediately bursts into questions once the room door closes.

"Your Highness, why is he over here? Why are you *allowing* him to be here? What if he does something to us? Or does something to the heart?" Kuma rants, nervously moving around the room. Ciana gently grabs her shoulders, looking into her eyes.

"I know we're not supposed to interact, but we have no choice right now." Ciana releases her grip, fear filling her eyes. "The balance is broken. Our kingdoms are both in danger if the prince and I don't take care of it."

"But why is he here?"

"The balance can't be fixed without going to the queen and king. He's here to go with me so we can fix everything. It's the only way."

"There's got to be something—"

"There isn't, Kuma." Ciana shakes her head, grabbing a large bag. "I've tried to think of another way, but there's nothing else we can do. I will do *anything* to save my people, even if that means we have to work together. I really don't want to, but our hands are tied." Kuma nods, grabbing some clothes from Ciana's dresser, handing them to her.

"Do you think you have enough for the trip?" Kuma chuckles when Ciana comes out of her closet in a pair of pants and a shirt suitable for traveling. Ciana looks at the largely stuffed bag, the sides bulging, ready to explode at any moment.

"I think so." She smiles, grabbing a slip of paper off her bookshelf and some coins she stuffs into her pocket. "Thank you for your help, Kuma. I'll be back before you know it." Ciana pulls her hair back in a ponytail.

"Be safe, Your Highness. We need you to come back." Kuma curtsies, holding the door open.

"I will." Ciana throws the bag over her shoulders, the weight nearly causing her to topple backwards as she goes back to the entrance.

"Are you ready to go?" Zomo asks, glaring at Kieran.

"Yes,"

"Okay, let's get this done and over with." Zomo heads for the door.

"No, Zomo. I'm sorry, but you cannot come with us."

"Your Highness, you can't expect me to let you go on a dangerous journey alone with *him*."

"There will be no dangers along the way."

"You'd just slow us down, making us stop every second at every sound," Kieran mumbles.

"How can you be so sure?" Zomo eyes Kieran, holding back a remark to his comment.

"When the map was given to us, the queen was explicit that there were no dangers. If we were ever to go to them, she wanted to make sure we wouldn't be harmed along the way. No harm will come to us. You still can't come with us. The king and queen will not help if there are more than us two. It can only be us."

"But I—"

"Please Zomo. I am sorry. I wish you could come, but we need to get the balance fixed, so it *has* to be me and Kieran. There's no one else I can trust to keep the kingdom in order until I return. I know the people will listen to you. Keep an eye on the heart, make sure it is safe, and make sure things do not get out of hand, especially if the darkness reaches town and the crops. Both sides should still get their fair share."

"Do you even know where to go?"

"I do." She waves the piece of paper.

Do you have any food? Or any form of protection? You've never been without a guard."

"I can provide us with food and I already told you there will be no dangers. If we do come across anything, Kieran can easily take care of it."

"Pfft," Keiran huffs.

"I can at least escort you to the forest border," Zomo decides.

Ciana nods. "That I will allow."

"Oh, can we just go already?" Kieran rolls his eyes. "We're losing daylight."

"We are going." Ciana walks past him to the front doors, heading towards the side of town closest to the border wall once again.

"Why not just go through the town?"

"I don't need my people to panic if they were to see you."

"Right." Kieran kicks a small rock.

"Your Highness, are you sure I—" Zomo starts when they reach the forest border.

"I am positive, Zomo. You have to let me do this if you want things to go back the way they were."

"Of course, Your Highness."

"I will be safe; nothing will happen. Just take care of things here."

"Yes, Your Highness."

"Let's go, Kieran." Ciana walks into the forest; Kieran follows closely. "So it begins."

# Chapter Seven

Ciana occasionally glances over her shoulder to make sure Kieran is still following as they make their way through the forest in silence. Every glance back is the same as Kieran seems lost in thought, his gaze fixed on the ground in front of him, a hand running against the trees. The ground vibrates as a tree crashes to the ground, making Ciana whip around.

"What in the world?" She gasps as she notices the black trail of trees behind Kieran. "Kieran, why are you killing the trees?" she accuses. Kieran furrows his brows at her before turning around to witness the scene behind him.

"What? It's not hurting you. The balance is already broken any-way."

"Still, there is no need for you to kill them."

"I can do what I want. I'm bored."

"Good, it's supposed to be an uneventful trip. Now I think we take a right here." Ciana points at the fork in the forest, reading the map.

"That's not right. We're supposed to take a left at the twin trees."

"The what?"

"The twin trees. The two trees growing from the same trunk?" Kieran points to a pair of trees a few feet away from them.

"We still take a right," Ciana dismisses, glancing at the twin trees marked on the map.

"Let me see that." Kieran rips the map from her hand as she walks past.

"Careful! That's our only map to the fortress, unless you brought yours."

"I am being careful, and no, I didn't bring mine because I have it memorized. Now we take a left."

"I doubt that."

"I just told you about the tree marked on the map that is right here in front of us!" Kieran exasperates.

"There's no way you have it memorized," Ciana dismisses, starting down the path on the right.

"You're going the wrong way, Princess. We're supposed to take a left here!" Ciana walks back to Kieran.

"No, we aren't, look." Ciana points to the marked line on the map leading to the left. "Oh."

"Told you. You should have taken map lessons." Kieran shoves the map back into her hands, walking ahead down the path on the left.

"I did."

"Well, you obviously failed." Ciana watches from behind as Kieran rummages through his bag, pulling out a silver bottle, twisting the cap off and taking a drink of what Ciana assumes is water. Replacing the cap, he shoves the bottle back in his bag. "Now what was this heart you mentioned to that one guard, the moron?"

"Zomo? He's not a moron."

"Eh, don't care." Kieran shrugs, killing another tree.

"The heart is not any of your concern, so I wouldn't worry about it."

"Well, I am. It must be important for you to tell what's-his-name to keep it safe."

"It still does not concern you, Kieran." Ciana sighs, rubbing her temples. She peers at the dancing shadows on the ground from the setting sun, a light breeze rustling the trees. "You took us down the wrong path. This isn't right."

"Did not. The map says it is this way."

"There's supposed to be a landmark of some sort." Ciana holds up the map, looking at a circle marked with the words 'Two In One Landmark'.

"You mean something like rocks shaped like a bear?"

"I'm not sure. The map doesn't specify what it looks like. But I think it would be trees, not rocks."

"It's rocks. Why in the world would it be trees?"

"Kieran, we're in a forest! Why would it be rocks?"

"There are rocks in the forest, duh."

"Not big enough for a landmark."

Kieran whips around. "Princess, have you ever been in a forest?"

"Not until recently, have you?"

"Half my kingdom is a forest, of course I have, and we have rocks that are big enough to be landmarks. I'm telling you, it's rocks."

"There hasn't been one big rock since we've been in here!" Ciana snaps.

"Ugh, look!" Kieran roughly pulls Ciana next to him, forcefully pointing in the distance to a shadowed figure shaped like a bear. "See? Rocks." He pushes her away from him.

"Don't push me like that." She glares. "Those aren't rocks."

"Of course they are."

"Then why are they getting bigger when we aren't moving?"

Kieran looks back at the bear figure, which has gotten bigger in the minute they were standing there and was still growing. A low growl sounds from behind them. Ciana watches Kieran slowly turn his head around.

"Okay, miss know-it-all, how do we get out of this?" he whispers as a bear walks up from behind, the dark figure of the bear joins the second one as they begin to circle around them.

"Why are you asking me? You're the one that brings death." She slowly folds the map, pocketing it.

"And you bring life, so you must know how to deal with the things you create."

"That's not how it works," Ciana stiffens as one of the bears comes and sniffs her. "As the Prince of Darkness, I figured you knew how to deal with everything," she mumbles under her breath.

"I do. It's a nice perk." He gives her a smug smile.

"Then why don't you get us out of this?"

Kieran's gaze darts between the bears, a hint of a smile forming on his lips before it quickly falters as he looks back at Ciana. "You can't just go around changing your mind about what's okay for me to kill. You were so upset about me killing the trees, but you *want* me to kill innocent bears? Never thought I'd hear that from you."

"I never said that. Just do something so they go away."

"Like what, Princess? I only know how to kill things."

"Fine, let's just hope they go away." Ciana holds her breath as the bear stands on its hind legs, sniffing her head. Ciana closes her eyes, trying her hardest to keep her legs and hands steady, her heart trying to escape her chest. She shrinks as the bear licks her face.

*Bleh. Of course they have to make sure I taste good.*

Hearing the bear land back on four legs, Ciana opens her eyes, one at a time. The two bears back away, gently bobbing their heads and grunting as if having a conversation. Ciana glances at Kieran, who looks relaxed with his arms folded across his chest as he watches the bears.

*Why does he look so calm?*

The bears turn back around, both advancing to Ciana, who starts to back up.

*What's happening?* Her heart races. Kieran curiously watches as the bears focusing their attention to her.

"Kieran?" Ciana whispers as she continues to back away. He doesn't respond.

*They're going to devour me.*

"Kieran?" she pleads louder, glancing up at him.

"What?" He sighs.

"What do you mean, what? Can you give me a little help?" Ciana backs into a tree, her heart beating in her throat as the bears continue to advance on her.

"Why are they only focusing on you? You're nothing special, you don't have nearly enough fat on you to make a satisfying meal." He taps his chin.

Ciana's mouth drops. "That was not what I asked. If you think you'll make a better meal, could you at least get them focused on you instead? Or do something to get them away from me?" Ciana holds her breath, her limbs clinging to the tree behind her, waiting for the teeth to sink in.

"Fine." Kieran casually walks in between Ciana and the bear, creating black flames that engulf his hands. Slowly approaching the bear, he holds his hands in front, only for the bear to grunt and move around him back to Ciana. "No, you don't. You can't have her, she's mine."

Kieran throws one of the flames to the ground in front of the bear. The black flames shoot up, creating a barrier.

"Oh, so I'm yours to burn?" Ciana questions, eyeing the heatless flames.

"The flames aren't going to hurt you, but I got the bear away from you, didn't I?"

"Yeah, one bear. The other one isn't blocked by your flames." Ciana points out as the second bear comes around the tree to her, nuzzling itself between Ciana and the tree, breaking her hold on it. "You're some hero." Ciana staggers forward, hardly able to stay standing with her shaking body.

"Hey, I tried!" Kieran counters, folding his arms across his chest, the black flames on his hand and the ground disappearing. The bear walks behind Ciana, nudging her forward with a grunt. Another shove and she stumbles, nearly falling on her face.

*What is it doing?*

"Kieran, will you please try harder and do something?" Ciana fights back tears.

"What else do you want me to do? You don't want me to kill them. They're not eating you, so I don't see why you're so worried."

"I don't get how you're so calm." Ciana stumbles again as the bear pushes into her.

"I'm never scared. I can kill these beasts before they have a chance to do anything to me. I'm more curious as to why they like you so much."

"Who cares? Just get them away from me!"

"Princess," he huffs, pinching the bridge of his nose. "If you were in any real danger, I'd help you and just kill them regardless of what you say, but clearly they're trying to take you somewhere."

"What makes you say that?" Ciana stumbles forward once more, trying to calm her trembling insides.

"They keep pushing you forward. Kinda a big clue if you ask me."

"How do you know they aren't taking me away to eat me?"

"They're bears, they don't care where they eat. I say let them lead you, maybe they won't eat you if you do." He smirks. "Or maybe they will."

Ciana looks at the bears. *Maybe he's right. It can't hurt to try, right?* With less resistance, she eases forward, following the other bear, who is already making its way down the path.

Glancing over her shoulder to see if Kieran is coming, she watches the second bear move from behind her in front of the prince, blocking his path with a low growl.

"Well, excuse me," he huffs back at the bear, folding his arms across his chest. The bear growls again before trotting after Ciana and the other bear.

The bear in front guides her through the towering trees to a hidden cave, where two bear cubs run out to greet them. Ciana comes to a halt, not wanting to intrude their home. The bear from behind runs past into the cave, coming back with another small cub in its jaw, gently laying the baby bear at Ciana's feet. She looks down at it, not sure what's happening or what they want until she sees the bear is not moving.

"Oh," she breathes, forcing herself to kneel. "You want me to bring back your cub?" The bear grunts. "I can, but just this once. You can't eat me afterwards either." She gently places her shaking hands on the little body, focusing on the bear cub. Imagining its alive, a tingling sensation of energy runs through her arms down to her fingertips. Barely visible in the brown fur, a small black tally mark appears on the stomach of the bear cub as its chest begins to move up and down.

Eyes opening, the cub yawns and stretches as if it had taken a nap. The bear gently nudges the small cub until it stands more alert, running around the bear before joining its siblings. A smile spreads across Ciana's face, standing up and watching the other bears greet and lick the newly revived cub.

*They wanted to be reunited.*

The bear stares at Ciana with its obsidian eyes, carefully approaching her; the bear gently nudges her trembling hand up, rubbing its head against it. Ciana cautiously scratches the bear's head.

*Please don't change your mind,* Ciana pleads. *Please let me leave in peace and in one piece.*

The bear licks her hand, making her flinch before it joins the rest of the family, running up to the cave.

Relief washes over Ciana as she stumbles away from the cave in the direction they had come from her heart beating even faster. Finding a sturdy tree, her legs turn into water, finally giving out, her mind blanks as she stares absentmindedly to the darkening sky above.

"There you are!" Kieran heaves, appearing between two trees. "Told you they weren't going to eat you. I mean I did have my doubt and they would anyway since they're wild animals, but they didn't. What happened?" He looks at her laying in the dirt.

"Glad you were concerned," she says, voice shaking.

Kieran tilts his head, watching her hands against the dirt. "You're shaking."

"Really? I didn't notice." Ciana takes in some deep breaths.

"Wanna go back?" Kieran challenges.

"No. I just need a moment. Thank you very much."

"Well, hurry up then. I want to get this over with as soon as possible."

Ciana takes a few more deep breaths. Her legs wobble as she stands up, dusting the dirt off her clothes. "Then let's continue." She walks ahead.

"I still want to know why the bears didn't eat you."

"Like you care."

"I don't." Kieran runs up next to her, smirking. "I want to know so I can prevent it next time."

"They wanted me to revive one of their bear cubs."

"How'd they know you could do that?"

"I think they sensed it? Smelled it? Tasted it? I don't know. Either way, they must have known I could help bring it back while you would only kill them."

"Or they understood what we were saying and went based on that."

"I don't know, but your black flames of death sure are a big give-away."

"Like they would know. Oh look! It's the landmark!" Kieran points to a crescent moon shaped rock up ahead.

"How do you know that's the one we're looking for?"

"Didn't you listen to anything when our kingdoms were created? Our parents told us that the landmark would represent both light and dark. Which is why it's marked 'Two In One' on the map. Both kingdoms are represented in one thing."

"And that's a crescent moon because?"

He rolls his eyes, frustrated with her lack of understanding. "The moon comes out when it's dark, but gives off enough light so it's not pitch black. Goodness, princess, what *did* they teach you in that happy little kingdom of yours? Clearly, nothing of importance." He scoffs, then gestures toward the formation. "And it's made of rocks, so who was right?"

"Don't get cocky with me. You were the one who thought a bear was a rock formation, remember? If you knew it was a crescent moon this whole time, why did you think it was the bear?"

"Okay, and? I wasn't saying it was *the* landmark. I was just pointing it out to show you that they exist. It was just an outline, so how was I supposed to know it was a real bear?"

"You live in darkness, you should have known since you should be used to it!" Ciana's fists clench. She takes a few deep breaths to calm herself down. "It is getting late, so let's agree on a safe place to spend the night," she continues in a more delicate manner.

"Why not just continue through the night? We'll get there faster."

It takes everything in Ciana not to turn and shake him. What is wrong with him?

"Are you afraid of the dark, princess?" he drawls.

She'd had enough of his retort for one day. Spinning on him, she clenches her fists into her hips and glares. "I'm sorry, but nighttime means it's time to *sleep* in my kingdom. What do you do when it gets dark? Engulf things in your dark flames and make a sacrifice to the shadows?" She rolls her eyes, sarcastically.

"Why do you keep doing that?" Kieran examines her carefully, his voice softening the slightest bit.

"Keep doing what?" She exhales sharply, stepping over a root. Rolling her shoulders, she releases some of the tightly wound tension.

"You keep switching between personalities."

"I do not know what you are talking about."

"Yes, you do. Back in your kingdom, you were so nice, goody-goody and proper, but now you keep switching between that and talking back to me. I don't know much about you, but since you're the Princess of Goodness and Light, I'm pretty sure you aren't supposed to act how you have been. It's... odd."

"I am afraid I still don't know what you are talking about," Ciana says in a sweet tone before muttering, "and even if I did, it wouldn't be any of your concern."

"What was that?" Kieran leans towards her slightly to hear her better, knowing she isn't going to repeat herself.

"You've made it clear you're only here to ensure we continue providing your kingdom with food. A political movement that I reluctantly approve of. But it has been a long day for me, and I need to rest. That way we can continue tomorrow fresh and full of energy."

"See, you changed your whole personality again. I can physically hear it and it's so fake. It's like you're hiding something."

"I am not hiding anything."

"Uh huh, sure," he draws out. "You know, I was told about how kind, gentle, and perfect you are... well, supposed to be. Among other things. They were obviously very wrong, because you are none of those things."

Ciana whips around to look at him. "What do you mean you were told? No one on your side knows anything about me, as I don't know anything about you. And I am all those things. I just healed a bear for its family. I fought for the safety of my people. I'm traveling with *you*... I'd say that's pretty kind."

"I'm pretty sure you only did it so it wouldn't eat you. Doing something for your own benefit is not the same thing as being kind." Kieran laughs.

"I healed that girl in your kingdom."

"So I've heard..."

Ciana freezes, glaring at him. "And yet it sounds like you don't believe I did."

"I saw no proof."

"How can you say that? You don't trust your own people?"

"I never said that."

Ciana turns back around with an eye roll. She pushes aside a low-hanging branch; a clearing comes into view.

"Here, this will be a good place to spend the night." Ciana gathers some nearby twigs and rocks, forming a small fire pit, before she starts to rub two of the twigs together.

Kieran chuckles. "You're seriously going to try and make a fire?"

"It's going to get cold tonight, we need heat." Kieran sits on the opposite side of the pit, still laughing to himself. "Would you like to help?" she offers as he watches her struggle.

"That's not as fun. I will help you out by telling you that you're doing it wrong."

"Thanks for the advice, but I am not doing it wrong," she counters.

"If you were doing it right, we'd have a fire by now. Or if you came prepared with whatever you start fires with, you wouldn't have to use twigs."

"We use what's called an Ember Stone. And that doesn't mean I'm doing it wrong, I just haven't made a spark yet." Ciana sighs before adding quietly, "I didn't think about the need for a fire until right now, or else I would have."

"That's pretty clear. In that case, could you hurry it up then?" Ciana locks her jaw, throwing the sticks at Kieran, hitting him in the head. "Ow!"

"You do it then." She gets up then plops down on a fallen tree trunk nearby, turning her back to Kieran. The crisp crackle of flames fills the silent air a few seconds later, heat warming Ciana's back. She glances over her shoulder, where Kieran is warming his hands over the flickering red-orange flames.

"Told ya you were doing it wrong." He looks up at her.

"Whatever." Ciana sighs, turning her back to him once more. "Ow!" She whips around, rubbing her head where something small and hard hit her.

"What?" Kieran asks, digging a stick into the dirt, glancing up at her. Ciana grumbles, facing the trees again without answering, only to get hit by something again.

"Will you cut it out!" she accuses, pivoting her whole body so she faces Kieran and the flames.

"Cut what out? I'm not doing anything," he responds, focusing on the mesmerizing flames.

"You're throwing little rocks at me."

"Oh? You mean like this?" He picks up a little pebble, gently throwing it at her leg.

"Ow! Yes, like that!"

"Still don't know what you're talking about." He smiles mischievously.

"Just please stop," Ciana asks. Kieran rolls his eyes in response, poking the fire, feeding it so it grows. Ciana watches him closely as he quietly minds his own business.

*He acts as if he always does things alone. He didn't have any guards or anyone in the castle when we went. Does he live there alone? Does anyone help him?*

Ciana peers through the flames, taking in Kieran's more relaxed expression. His hair gently falls over his softened eyes as he stares into the flames as if in thought himself. A crack in the flames causes Ciana to jump. Thinking it was something in the trees behind her, she peers around. Kieran lets out a short laugh, smirking.

"It was just the fire, Princess. Scared much?"

"No. I was just making sure there wasn't anything else." Ciana continues to examine their surroundings, ignoring the fact that Kieran is still watching her.

"You've never been without one of your little guards, have you?" he concludes. Ciana's gaze flickers to him.

"They're not always around me in the palace."

"What about outside the palace?" Ciana doesn't respond, making him raise an eyebrow.

"Do you even know how to protect yourself?"

"As a princess, I don't need to. But yes. I know the minimum use of a sword."

"That won't get you anywhere, especially against more advanced weapons." He snorts. "And you still wanted to go on a trip alone with me? Do you really trust me that much?"

"I never said I trusted you, but I have to if my kingdom is to survive."

"So you do?"

"I just said I have to."

"What if I wanted to do something to you? Would that change your mind?"

Ciana locks eyes with him. Would that change her trust in him? She only has to trust him to help her people. In the end, it wouldn't matter what happened to her as long as her people were safe.

"No," she finally answers. Kieran raises an eyebrow, surprised at her response, turning his focus back to the flames.

Ciana continues to watch him. When he's relaxed, he's not as intimidating. They just had a conversation without accusation or snark towards each other. Maybe they could get along during this trip.

"Kieran?"

"What? I thought you wanted sleep, not conversation." He sighs, snapping a branch, tossing it into the flames. On second thought, maybe it'll still take time to get along.

"Do you live alone in your castle?"

"My entire kingdom lives alone. We don't need to use people dressed up in armour to play guard."

"That doesn't answer my question. What about any maids or siblings or anything? Or what about your mother?"

Kieran's eyes shoot up, darkening. "That is none of your business," he snaps. "What about you? You have a whole parade of people by your side! Can't you do anything yourself? What about the heart? Why is it so important?" he drills back at her.

Ciana avoids his eyes, laying down on the tree trunk, resting her head on her arm. "I'm tired. I'm going to sleep. I ask that you don't wake me, please. Since you wanted to continue through the night, I'll let you keep watch."

"There's nothing here. There's no need to keep watch."

"Kieran, we already came across bears. Who knows if they will come back or if there will be something else."

"Still no point. If we're asleep. They won't bother us."

"Kieran—"

"Go to sleep, Princess." He waves her off, annoyed. Ciana was getting the feeling perhaps she was annoying him as much as he was to her. Kieran's voice drops to a whisper that barely carries over the crackling of the flames. "You'll be safe."

Ciana frowns, looking at him through the fire. "Goodnight, Kieran."

# Chapter Eight

"Who are they?"

"Not sure. They're strangers."

"I told you not to wake me," Ciana mumbles to two high-pitched voices, still half asleep.

"The female is waking up."

"She can hear us?"

"No, she's just dreaming. No one can hear us."

"Kieran, please stop!" Ciana repeats, sitting up on the trunk. She rubs her eyes as she looks around at the smoking fire pit, sunlight streaming through the trees; Kieran is laying next to the fire pit, his chest rising and falling slowly. Ciana stands, confused, her headache slightly increasing.

"She's awake," the high-pitched voice narrates. Ciana looks up in the trees and around the bushes.

"Hello?" Ciana calls.

"She *can* hear us!" the other high-pitched voice gasps. Ciana notices it's slightly deeper than the first.

"Who's there?"

"Princess, no one is there. It's just you and me. I was considerate and didn't wake you up, but of course you had to wake me," Kieran growls, sitting up himself.

"Sorry Kieran," she says, eyes scanning through the trees. "Can't you hear them?" she asks, voice low.

"Hear who? I heard you being loud and talking to yourself. You could have warned me you were going to go crazy."

"I'm not crazy. There are two other people here."

"Oh great, not just one voice, but she's hearing two." Kieran shakes his head.

"Ooo, she's a smart one," the first high voice compliments.

"See there it was again!" Ciana points towards the sky,

Kieran raises an eyebrow. "I didn't hear anything. You're imagining things."

"I am not." Ciana kneels next to the smoking fire pit, grabbing a few nearby twigs.

"If you're going to attempt to make another fire, I would just let me do it." Kieran reaches for the twigs, but Ciana pulls them out of his reach.

"I'm not." She places the twigs in the ash, focusing so a light tingle runs through her fingers to the twigs.

"What are you doing?"

"Shh," Ciana shushes, imagining the twigs as a big tree with red fruit. The twigs begin to grow, reaching towards the sky, transforming into an enormous tree.

"You're kidding me, there are already plenty of trees here. We're in a forest!" Kieran slaps his hand to his head.

Ciana climbs up the tree to the middle of the branches, where bright red fruit hangs within. She grabs one, throwing it down so it hits the top of Kieran's head.

"Hey!" he shouts up at her.

"Whoops, sorry," Ciana smiles, gathering another fruit before she climbs back down.

"What is it? A poisoned apple? You already trying to kill me, Princess? We just woke up," he snickers, twisting the fruit in his hands, examining it.

"They're not poisonous, it's breakfast. You're welcome." She takes a bite of the red fruit.

"Hmmm, not a chance." Kieran tosses the offering into the thickets.

"Why not?"

"I still think you're hiding something. I don't trust anything from anyone who is fake."

"Your loss." Ciana dissolves his words.

"Tsk tsk tsk. The boy should eat the food," the deeper squeaky voice comments.

"It's his choice," Ciana answers, walking away from Kieran, whose eyes look like they're about to pop out of his head.

"He's pretty stupid," the high voice concludes.

"He's not stupid. Don't say that."

"Why are you defending him? He's been nothing but rude to you."

"That's how he is. He's just being himself."

"I wouldn't waste your time with him. Dump him."

"I can't do that."

"Why not?"

"If you could keep your pretend conversation in your head, that would be much appreciated." Kieran pinches the bridge of his nose.

"I'm not having a pretend conversation."

"He doesn't even have the decency to believe you. How rude." The higher voice scoffs.

"If he can't hear you, then I don't blame him," Ciana answers.

"So? He shouldn't be saying you're crazy."

"No, but that's his opinion, even though it's wrong."

"Do you *always* have these types of conversations back at your palace?" Kieran huffs. "I can only imagine what your staff must think—the princess walking around talking to yourself."

"I *only* have conversations with real people."

"Well, then you must be in shock from this journey because *no one is there*! Maybe you *think* you have conversations with real people, but they're actually all fake."

"I'm not hallucinating if that's what you're getting at," Ciana says through her teeth.

"It *is* what I'm getting at. I'm glad you were able to know that at least."

"I think I would know if I was, Kieran." Ciana clenches her fists, eyes narrowing.

"You're hearing voices! That's not a good thing! I think it would have been better if you had just stayed in your little palace where you could kiss and cry with all your delusional people." A smirk grows across his lips. "It all makes sense."

"Take. It. Back." She locks her jaw.

"Take what back? The truth? You and your people are so weak; that's why the pact was made in the first place. *You* put the white flag up because you knew you couldn't win against us. We're just better. Your 'light' and 'happiness' were nothing against real strength and power, and your imaginary friends you talk to weren't any help. My people and I live in the real world, not fantasy land like *you*."

"That's not true."

"Yes, it is. Wasn't it your mother who came crying to my father for him to stop the war? Begging on her knees to save her people and you. Broken and defeated because you are all too weak to stand up and do anything yourself. That's how your father and siblings died, right? They were too weak against us, fighting with useless weapons," Kieran starts.

Ciana's breath quickens, her fists clenching. *Keep it together, Ciana,* she reminds herself as Kieran continues.

"No wonder you're hearing voices. It's probably the only comfort you have to hear your family again. To have a glimpse of what it would be like to have *real* advice and a *real* conversation with someone, but it's all in your head. How would your mother feel knowing this?"

"Stop it, Kieran." She grits her teeth.

"No wonder the balance broke. You're all too weak to handle anything, and the voices aren't being very helpful." Kieran exaggerates a pout. Unable to contain herself any longer, Ciana slaps him across the face. He grabs Ciana by her shirt, slamming her against a nearby tree, his eyes darkening. "Don't *ever* do something like that again. Believe me, it'll be the last thing you will ever do," he threatens through clenched teeth.

"I'm not scared by your threats. It's only fitting that the Prince of Darkness would have the darkest heart," she breathes back.

"Aw snap. She gave it to him," the high voice giggles.

Ciana and Kieran stare each other down, both breathing heavily, waiting for the other to break first.

*He has no right to say such things. He doesn't know what I've gone through,* Ciana argues in her mind. The darkness inching over her kingdom comes to mind when Ciana looks into his deep brown eyes.. *I need him to finish this journey with me. We can't waste time arguing.*

*Who knows how much the darkness has spread by now. Even if we kill each other along the way, we have to get to the fortress.*

Ciana sighs. "I'm sorry." She relaxes, hanging her head as her chest tightens in regret, her headache intensifying. "Please forgive me. I didn't mean to slap you."

Kieran lets out a short breath before Ciana continues.

"Listen, we don't even know each other. Can we just start over and get to know one another since we will be with each other for a while?" she offers softly, looking back into his eyes. Kieran's hard expression doesn't change as he stares her down for a moment more before letting her go, walking ahead without a word.

"The girl apologizes, but he doesn't return it. How rude."

"Please stop," she whispers to the voices, straightening her shirt again as she follows behind Kieran at a safe distance.

They continue through the forest, neither of them talking until they reach another fork. "Which way?" Kieran asks bluntly. Ciana pulls out the map, carefully looking at it before answering.

"Right this time." She walks past Kieran, re-pocketing the map. The trees thicken, grabbing hold of the other branches so they block out the sun. A twig snaps nearby, bringing Ciana to a stop. It feels like someone is watching her... Kieran brushes past her.

"Are you coming or what, Princess?" He sighs when she doesn't follow. Ciana fixes her eyes on one of the large bushes next to her. Kieran comes next to her, looking at the bush. "It's probably just a squirrel. There's nothing there, come on."

"No."

"You've got to be kidding me!" He hangs his head back. "Why not? Scared? If you want to go back, we can."

"I'm not scared. There's something in the bush. It's watching us."

"There's nothing there. Just more of your imagination."

"It's a feeling, Kieran. Something you wouldn't know about," she shoots at him as she nears the bush, carefully separating the leaves to see nothing within. "I swear there was something there," she whispers.

"Like I told you, there isn't. Now may we go?"

"No, I still feel like there's something watching us."

"Look, Princess," Kieran grumbles, nearing the bush. With a touch of his finger, the bush goes up in black flames, dissolving to the ground, revealing nothing but a stone spearhead next to a pile of black ash. "See, nothing. Now may we go?"

"I guess." Ciana eyes the spearhead next to the burned bush, starting her way ahead when the bushes around them rustle as a swarm of small green men, no taller than Ciana's waist, with pointy ears waddle out. Leaf clothing blends in with their skin. Black sticks of what is supposed to be hair, stick up from the green bald heads. Their long green fingers wrap around spears. They hiss and grumble, showing off their yellow pointy teeth as they surround Ciana and Kieran, some jumping down from the trees above.

"Great, now look at what you did. This is why you don't snoop around," he snaps.

"I didn't snoop, but I was right, wasn't I?" she snaps back, comparing the spears to the one next to the ash. "*You* were the one that burned the bush and I think you killed one of their friends!"

"Silence!" one of the little men orders with a surprisingly deep voice.

"Listen, we didn't mean any trouble. We are just passing through and—"

"I said silence! Or you both die right now!" The man threateningly points his spear at Ciana.

"These are goblins, Princess. Something *you* wouldn't know about. They don't care about why we're here, they just care about eating us for lunch," Kieran explains as if she were a child.

"I don't see you doing anything, just kill them. You already killed one."

"Oh, now that's a little dark coming from you." Kieran lets out a fake gasp. "I wouldn't think you'd want anything innocent to be killed."

"I don't, you're right. Any other ideas?"

"I. Said. Silence!" The goblin raises the tip to Ciana's neck while another comes around, taking their bags from them, and tying their hands in thick rope. Kieran eyes the spear at Ciana's neck. "Now move!"

The goblins lead them deeper into the forest. The trees fill the sky above them, blocking out the sun. A cold breeze blows through the shade. Ciana wrinkles her nose as she gets a whiff of a stench. The trees encircle each other until they reach a clearing, holding a small village, easily indicating where the filthy stench was coming from. Taking as few breaths as she can, Ciana looks at the little houses made from the trees, entwined with vines as they walk through. Goblins line the sides, gleefully watching and sneering. Ciana looks over at Kieran, who once again appears relaxed, despite being a captive. They approach the largest building in the middle of the village; vines hang over the entrance like a curtain.

"In!" A couple of goblins draw apart the curtain of vines, while the others push Ciana and Kieran into the house's big room. Ciana examines the room, reminding her of the heart room in the palace, only slightly smaller and more nature-like. Green leafy vines snake up the side of the bark walls, tracing around the few open holes that allow light into the room. A large green goblin sits on a throne of roots and vines across from them; two smaller goblins fan him with giant leaves from either side. The large goblin snaps his long fingers, allowing the two goblins to drop the leaves and untie the rope from Ciana and Kieran's wrists before going back to fanning. Ciana and Kieran exchange confused looks as they wait for further instructions.

Kieran rolls his wrists, gently rubbing them. "Well, this was a valiant welcome, but I'm not interested in staying with you filthy goblins," he sneers, turning to leave. Guards thrust their spears at him, points pressing against the fabric at his chest. "If I'm no longer a prisoner, I suggest you let me go, unless you want to become homeless." Black flames flicker in his hands as a warning before they disappear.

The goblin king chuckles, but it's far from humorous, more vile and condescending. "You think you can simply walk away? After trespassing on my land?"

Kieran eyes a small goblin that's binding him in rope once more. "Seriously? More rope? Just because I'm bound doesn't mean I still can't burn this place down."

"The Prince of Darkness may be able to create flames, but we live in the trees and almost always make our own fires. We Goblins are not idiots, we've fireproofed almost all our items with blazeguard to avoid any accidents. Your flames won't even leave a mark, but by all means you're welcome to try."

"Blazeguard?" Ciana questions.

"A gift from our ancestors. They brought it from their home planet when they were forced to leave. We are familiar with creatures, such as yourselves, holding power so we have no fear," the goblin briefly explains, keeping challenging eyes on Kieran.

Ciana watches Kieran, who looks as if he wants to take the goblin's challenge and try to burn the place, but decides against it by staring at the ground in front of him.

"Then why live in the trees when you have to fireproof everything? Seems kinda pointless." Kieran scoffs, meeting the goblin's eyes once more. The goblin snaps his fingers, causing one of the smaller goblins to drop their fan, scurrying to a nearby tree trunk. The small goblin presses against the trunk, opening a hidden compartment to reveal colorful tangled wires. The large goblin snaps his fingers again, ordering the smaller one to close the compartment and go back to fanning.

"We've hollowed out a few trees around us to supply our needs for living. The trees make quite a scenic home, which is why we've chosen it. Now enough questions!" The goblin gives Ciana a sardonic smile which only sends worry fluttering through her. "You!" he grumbles, pointing one of his long green fingers at Ciana.

"She's no one of importance. Just a foolish child," Kieran quickly answers, whipping his head up towards the goblin.

"On the contrary, the Princess of Light is very important. However, regardless of *who* you are, you're still trespassing. What are you doing here?"

"Me?" she squeaks, pointing her own finger to her chest, looking between the goblin and the prince.

"Yes."

"We were brought here against our will. We were just passing through, I promise we didn't mean to intrude."

"We don't like trespassers." The goblin licks his rotting teeth

"I'm sorry," Ciana pleads. "We didn't mean to. If you let us go, we will continue on our way and—"

"Too late! You should have thought of that before you wandered here."

"Is there any way we can leave? We're kinda on a time limit regarding an important matter, so we need to be going." A small gasp escapes her lips. The goblin looked big on his throne, but his size is nothing compared to when he stands on his wart-covered legs. He's almost three times the size of the two goblins next to him, his head barely bushing against the ceiling. His eyes gaze over her, a smile forming on his lips. Ciana's insides churn under his gaze, his smile sickening. She glances over at Kieran, watching him struggle to free the rope binding him, his eyes locked on the advancing goblin.

Mere inches from her, the goblin reaches a hand out, teasing a lock of her blonde hair between his long fingers. Ciana tries to step away from his touch, only to stop when a sharp point from one of the spears presses between her shoulder blades.

"My, you are beautiful," the goblin whispers, twirling her hair. Ciana gives another quick glance at Kieran; she notices him pressing forward, the blades at his chest pressing dangerously far into his clothing. His arms gently move under the rope as he continues to try to free himself, but his eyes, they're solely focused on her.

"I'll let you go," the goblin says, glancing at Kieran himself.

Ciana's heart jumps, returning her focus back to the goblin. "Really?"

He nods, but the smirk curling at his lips crushes any hope Ciana had at potential freedom. "Of course." He turns his attention fully to Kieran, his smirk deepening. "If you win against my strongest warrior, you'll be free to go."

"Okay. He fights, he wins, we both leave?" Ciana confirms looking at Kieran who shakes his head.

The goblin's wicked chuckle returns as he places his gaze back on Ciana. "No. *You* will fight." he runs his long finger against the side of her face. "You win, you both leave."

"And if she loses?" Kieran asks.

"Then you both stay here as slaves." The goblin pulls Ciana close. "You'd make a great personal slave. I can see it now, the great princess in rags."

"Why can't he fight?" Ciana pulls away.

"He's the bargaining chip. If you refuse to fight, he dies."

Ciana looks over at Kieran. *Why couldn't I be the bargaining chip? Kieran can kill anything in an instant, he doesn't care what dies. Realization hits Ciana as she looks back at the goblin. They know who we are. They know he'd kill without hesitation and I wouldn't want to hurt anything or anyone.*

Ciana lets out some air, looking at the goblins around her.

*The goblins are small... it can't be that hard to fight one right? It's not like I'd have to kill anyone. Zomo and my guards all use weapons, and I've seen them use them and it didn't appear to be difficult. Zomo told me the basics of using a sword, but I've never held one. If I had brought the voidcaller gun, all I would have to do is press a button and it'll hit my target to tranquilize them. No skill required. But... perhaps I won't have to use a weapon at all.*

She glances at the big goblin. *I could refuse and have a chance to leave alive, but I can't risk Kieran's life. I can't be responsible for his death if for some reason he couldn't save himself, not when I'm the one who dragged him out here in the first place. It wouldn't be fair. I still need him to fix the balance.*

"Fine. I'll fight," Ciana agrees.

"What? Are you crazy, Princess? You've probably never held a weapon in your life! You're going to die!" Kieran counters.

"It'll be fine, trust me. I can do it."

"You? Fight a goblin? Really? How? By smiling nicely and saying, 'please go easy on me, please let me win, I mean no harm,'" he imitates her voice. "This is a fight to the death, not a leisure stroll in a garden."

"I'm quite aware of that, Kieran. However, I'm hoping it won't end up that way. I've seen weapons used multiple times, I've got this. Have some faith in me?"

"Yeah, I'll have faith. Faith that you'll die and we've hardly gone anywhere!" The goblins take him away as the big goblin leads Ciana to a smaller room in the house, holding only a single leaf and vine bed.

"Wait here. You will be fetched in a few minutes when we're ready."

"Now? We're doing this now?"

"Of course. We do our fights right away, less time for you to back out or try to escape. Now stay." The goblin leaves with one of the smaller goblins, leaving the other one with her in the room. Wringing her hands, she begins to pace around the bed.

*I can do this. There's always a solution that doesn't involve killing an innocent person. If it does come to the point that I need to use a weapon, I'll just injure him. Or hope Kieran can free himself and come assist me if I distract them long enough, but this fight can't be hard. The goblins are half my size. What could go wrong?*

# Chapter Nine

After pacing for what seemed like hours, a goblin enters the room, chuckling. "We are ready for you."

He leads her to an underground chamber. Ciana looks at the metal chains weaved together, protecting the onlookers from the action that happens within; vines run up the sides of the cemented dirt walls behind the audience, matching the dark spotted, cement floor. A hint of copper and iron adds to the stench in the air. Chatter from the goblins fills the chamber as they wait expectantly. Ciana scans the room, finding a bored Kieran, along with their bags, on one of the vine and root chairs next to the big goblin in the front. Looking back, Ciana notices gaps in some places in the chains. Freshly gleaming weapons of different types hang on the left side, waiting to be used.

A deafening cheer arises from the onlookers as a goblin twice the size of Ciana struts into the chamber, a large, glowing, hazardous green sword in hand. Ciana's mouth drops to the floor as she stares at her challenger, her limbs frozen in place.

*There is no way,* Ciana repeats to herself.

"These are the contestants!" the big goblin announces from his chair, "Let the fight start... now!"

"What about the rules?" Ciana shouts over the cheers, forcing her frozen feet to move backwards, away from the advancing behemoth goblin.

"Goblins don't have rules besides winning! Don't lose and don't die, Princess!" Kieran yells back at her.

"If I lose, I will die!"

"Just grab a sword and fight!"

"Do you see the size of him?" The goblin swings his weapon down, nearly hitting Ciana as she jumps to the side, running away.

"Grab the sword!" Kieran repeats.

"No!"

"Then you're going to die!"

"Shut up, Kieran!"

"I'm trying to—" Kieran's cut off as a goblin covers his mouth with its hand.

The goblin swings his sword again, hitting the ground with a sharp *chink* as Ciana dodges, running in the other direction. Frantic, she looks around the chamber for something that would be useful. Her eyes fall back to the weapons hanging up.

*I can't kill him. It's not right. There's got to be something I can do to beat him without him ending up dead.*

A goblin's shriek blends with the cheers as Kieran bites its hand. "Grab the sword!" Kieran yells again, watching her freeze in thought, before a rag is shoved into his mouth to keep him quiet.

Ciana sighs internally, trailing the chains holding the weapons to the ceiling, where they all connect to one hook in the middle of the dirt and vine ceiling.

*A single hook. Of course this whole place would be held up by a single hook with sixty pound chains hanging from it. It's a miracle they don't fall.* Ciana dodges another blow from the goblin. With a quick glance at the warrior, she returns her focus at the hook with a smile. *On second thought, it would be a miracle if they did fall.*

"Grab the perfectly good sword and fight with it!" Kieran orders over the cheering goblins after successfully spitting the rag from his mouth.

"No!" Ciana yells back. She runs to the chains, peeking back at the advancing goblin. Finding her grip in the chains, she begins her climb to the top. Ciana swings to the side, narrowly missing the giant goblin's hand as she climbs higher out of his reach.

"Princess!" Kieran yells as she slips on the chains.

Ciana ignores his yelling as she struggles to climb further up the chains. Her muscles burn as she nears the center, her arms and legs exhausted. The cold metal digs into her soft palms as she fights against the pain to get to the hook.

*I'm almost there. Training with Zomo on weapons and body strength is a must when things are back in order because this is ridiculous. The chains are heavy enough to pin the goblin or at least entangle him. No harm. No foul. He lives. I live.* Ciana risks a look at the cement floor far below her, her breath quickening slightly. *I'll hopefully live. I just have to outsmart him.*

Ciana lets out a shriek when her hand slips from the chains she was grabbing, nearly dropping her to the ground.

"Princess!" Kieran yells again, panic filling his voice.

Heart racing, Ciana regrips the chains, making sure her hands are secure before shifting her body weight to climb the rest of the way to the hook. She glances back down at the goblin, who's struggling to climb after her, unable to fully grip the chains with his massive hands.

Her hands tremble with fear as she tries to unhook the chains, her arms failing, forcing her to switch her attention to getting the hook loose instead.

"Stop her!" the big goblin orders, shoving from his seat.

"Look out, Ciana!" Kieran warns. Ciana peers at the smaller goblins entering through the chains, climbing up towards her. Getting a good grip on the hook, she yanks with all her might.

"Come on," she mutters, digging at the cement dirt around the unmoving hook, breaking some of the vines. Finding a loose chain, she wraps her hand around it for more support as she yanks the hook again.

"Princess!" Kieran yells, trying to get out of his binds once again.

"This is the only way, Kieran!" Ciana yells back at him.

"Then hurry!"

A spear whizzes past Ciana's head, landing in one of the vines. Breaking off the end, she uses the point to help cut the vines and jab at the dirt, loosening it. The stench from the goblins grows thicker, and she knows they're closing in.

"Ciana!"

She hears Kieran, the biting fear in his voice, but she has no energy—no time—to yell back. There's only one vine left on the hook, and she yanks on it with everything she has. Over. And over. Dirt falls onto her face, into her eyes, her hair, down her clothes with every tiny movement.

"Beneath you!" Kieran warns. Ciana flickers her gaze down, noticing a small goblin who is almost in reach of her.

*It's almost free.*

A sweaty, heavy hand grabs hold of her leg, tugging her down. Ciana slips, kicking at the creature who refuses to let go.

"Use your other leg!" Kieran offers. Ciana groans in frustration. She'd only have her arms keeping herself up, but there's no other option. Clenching her hands around the chains, she lifts her free leg and shoots it down, knocking the goblin on the head. He slips, giving her the small break she needs to keep tugging at the hook.

"To your left!"

Ciana risks a glance, seeing a goblin with a spearhead between his yellow teeth, clambering closer.

*There's no time,* she thinks, panic rising, urging her arms to tug harder.

Yanking with everything she has left, the hook finally pops free. A sigh of relief escapes her, but it catches in her throat as she looks at Kieran. Horror fills his wide eyes, and he's straining against the ropes binding him.

The seconds after seem to happen in slow motion. Turning her attention to the chains, dropping and bringing the goblins with them, a weightlessness washes over her, the realization of what's happening hits her. She was falling.

Ciana squeezes her eyes shut, knowing there's nothing she can do to prepare for the impact. Just as she thinks she's about to hit the hard ground below, something softer grabs her, wrapping her body in a sort of hug, holding her close, cushioning her against the ground as they land, slightly rolling, but saving her from imminent death.

Panting and heart pounding out of her chest, she flutters her eyes open and rests her head to look next to her. Kieran. He sits up, freeing his arms from around her, moving one of his free hands to a bleeding gash on his left arm. Ciana takes him in in a heart beat, noticing the red rope burns on his arms.

He saved her. He hurt himself—*freed* himself—to save her.

Silence fills the chamber as the goblins check on each other, helping each other get up, the majority helping the tall goblin who's tangled in the fallen chains.

"You're crazy, you know?" Kieran breathes, standing up with Ciana.

"Everything was under control." She shakes a chain off her leg.

Kieran scoffs, running his fingers through his already messy hair. "Yeah, sure seemed like it. Plummeting to your death and all."

"Rematch!" the big goblin orders, his voice echoing through the chamber.

"No, no rematch. I won!"

"You cheated!"

"Says the one who sent hundreds more goblins to get me in the middle of my fight! No rules were given, so I won fair and square!"

"He's still moving, you haven't defeated him."

"He's tangled in the chains. You just said I had to *beat* him, which I did. There was no mention of fighting to the *death*." She sucks in a breath, still shaking from the fall. "Now we are leaving." Stepping over the chains, Ciana and Kieran walk to the closest door.

"Fine! You can go! But if you ever step back on our territory you will not get another chance to be free!"

"Trust me, we won't be back. Good day!" Ciana leads them out of the chamber and into the forest. Kieran chuckles. "What?" Ciana glances at him.

"Nothing." He smiles to himself.

"Well, it must be something."

"It's just... I never thought you'd be able to win. I thought you were dead when he came out."

"Thanks for believing in me." She rolls her eyes. "I told you I could do it, even without a sword and fighting, thank you very much."

"Still, the sword would have been a better option."

"Maybe for you, but not for me." Ciana eyes his bleeding gash. "What cut you?"

"What? Oh, nothing, the chain came down and nicked me. It's just a scratch."

"I can heal it for you. It is bleeding pretty good." Ciana reaches for his arm only for Kieran to move his arm away from her.

"No. You should save your strength."

"What? It'll only take a second. Trust me." She reaches for his arm again, but he bats her hand away.

"No."

"Will you stop arguing with me? I can heal you, and then we can be on our way," she grumbles.

"It'll heal on its own," he says through his teeth, avoiding her eyes.

"Kieran, just let me—"

"I said no!" The harshness of his words forces Ciana to take a step back. "It will be fine."

"You don't trust me..." It isn't a question, Ciana can see it all over his face. How he practically flinches when she reached for him. "Why?"

"Why, what?"

"Why don't you trust me?"

"Because."

"Because why?" Ciana folds her arms across her chest.

"You haven't done anything to show me that I *can* trust you. You keep changing from nice to not so nice. I know all too well not to trust someone who puts on a face, my people do it a lot, and believe me, it's never for a good reason. Besides, why should I trust someone who doesn't trust themself? That's a recipe for disaster."

"I do trust myself."

"Do you really? Let me ask you, who do you trust more right now, me or you?"

"That's irrelevant."

"Just answer the question." Ciana bites her lip. "Silence always means guilty, Princess. Give me one good reason why I should trust you when you don't even trust yourself."

"I do not have to give you a reason. I do trust myself, otherwise, I wouldn't have beaten the goblin. You are just being skeptical since you don't know me."

"I'm skeptical because of how you're acting. Changing between two different personalities. Tell me, if you trust yourself, are you being your *real* self, right now?" Kieran asks her sincerely. Ciana stares at her folded arms, dropping them to her sides as she takes a few deep breaths before answering with a smile.

"Yes."

Kieran shakes his head, walking ahead of her. "Princess, I don't care if you pretend in your kingdom, but if we're going to trust each other enough to get through this journey, then you might as well stop pretending with me. Otherwise, we'll never get anywhere, and this journey will be more miserable than it already is. You want to know more about me and my kingdom? If I were to tell you everything right now, would you believe me or think I was making everything up? I certainly wouldn't believe anything you tell me about you and your kingdom. Just like I don't trust what apples you grow and the healing you can do. You say it's food and that it'll be quick, but you've nothing that makes me know I can trust those words. I'll leave it up to you to try to show me which side of you is the real one. Maybe then we will have a little more trust towards each other to survive this mess."

Ciana stops walking, taken aback by the sincerity hidden in his voice. This couldn't be the same Kieran who had pinned her against a tree that morning, threatening her life. The same Kieran who had been nothing but mean to her, throwing her insults. The same Kieran who was yelling out warnings and broke her fall just moments earlier. Could it be possible that he wasn't heartless after all? That there was good in him like she had originally thought?

Ciana catches up with him. "I will. But you'll see I haven't been faking anything."

"By all means, I'd love to see that." He stops, bowing mockingly at her.

"Good."

# Chapter Ten

Sunlight streams through the trees as they leave the thicker part of the forest. Ciana watches Kieran from behind as he continues to try and stop his bleeding arm.

"Are you sure you don't want me to heal that? Putting pressure on it with your hand isn't going to do anything."

"Yep, I'm sure."

"Alright." She sighs, kicking a pebble, rubbing her temples. "So, Kieran, tell me a bit about yourself."

"I'm sorry?"

"I'm trying to get to know you."

"You're kidding me, right?"

"You said you'd get to know me if I'm being myself. I am, so we can get to know each other. Truth be told, I'd actually like to know more about your side of the border."

"I never said that, and there's nothing you need to know about my side. We aren't supposed to know much about each other and our sides for a reason." He sighs.

"I know that, but I don't see why we can't. It can help us get along better. I mean, it's not like we're going to use the knowledge and take advantage of the other." Kieran doesn't respond. "I see... you *would* take advantage."

"I told you, we aren't supposed to know for a reason."

"So for the rest of our lives we're supposed to just hate each other and not try to find peace between our kingdoms?"

"There is peace between us, Princess. We don't need to change anything."

"Doesn't seem very fair."

"Our sides are complete opposites; it is fair that we don't interact with each other. If we did, we'd kill each other. As someone who lost everyone in her family except her mother in the war, I'm surprised you're even trying to change what the queen put in place to help protect you."

"How *do* you know that?"

"We have the same history books, just different views and opinions."

*Different views? What would be different other than the fact that they might think they were in the right? Our history should be the same. Unless they added things in their books to support their opinions. Or... we're missing things from ours. Could that be possible?*

"Still." Ciana shrugs.

Kieran pushes away a tree branch, revealing a meadow. The bright colors reflecting off multiple wildflowers in the afternoon sun contrast against the dark forest. Ciana stops walking, entranced by the sight, taking in the view.

"It's beautiful," she whispers to herself, covering her parted mouth. Kieran pauses, turning his head as if to look back at her, but then continues walking. Ciana gently touches the wildflowers as she walks after Kieran, taking in all the plants.

*The colors are breathtaking. It reminds me of home,* Ciana thinks, smiling at the thought, before her smile falters. *It's so opposite to Kieran's kingdom. It was so dark and cold. No feeling of life, joy, or beauty at all, just a bunch of dull colors, no green. I wonder…*

"Kieran?" He doesn't say anything. "Kieran?"

"What?" he mumbles.

"Do you have any live plants on your side of the border?"

"Why do you ask?"

"I'm just realizing, even though I wasn't on your side for very long, I don't recall seeing any living plants. The trees in the forest within your borders were all dead."

"What do you expect? We bring death and darkness. We really just have weeds and dead trees."

"I suppose…" she muses, wondering how someone can live in a world without a rainbow of hues. "There's never any greenery? Nothing *alive*?"

"Nope."

"No wonder you guys are all miserable and gloomy."

*But it explains his melancholy and careless behaviour.*

"It's just how we are. That's the life we were given. We don't get the sunshine and rainbows like you."

"I don't believe that's necessarily true. Yes, it makes sense, but I think you can change and make the most out of your life and enjoy it like we do."

Kieran turns around, intrigued. "What do you mean?"

"Just because you're the Prince of Darkness doesn't mean you have to *live* in darkness. I go back to what I told you before about there being good in everyone. I know there's good in you, too; you just have to choose to live that life."

"I'm still not following, and I can't tell if you're messing with me."

"I'm not, I'm serious. Okay, umm... here, I'll compare it to this flower." Ciana plucks one of the nearby blooms, holding it up. Kieran watches, raising an eyebrow.

"You're not seriously going to compare my life to a flower, are you?"

"Just hear me out."

He rolls his eyes. "Okay, I'm listening."

"Good. So this flower is growing, but there is bad weather, storms, snow, all these things, the flower petals fall off and it bends over. Now, the flower could just take all that bad stuff and die or grow to be an annoying weed that no one likes. Instead, it toughens up; takes in the sunlight and grows into something beautiful, making the most of its life."

"Uh, huh." He nods slowly.

"So, if you dwell on all the bad and dark of things, you'll always be gloomy, but if you focus on the good and try to make the best of what you have, even if you are the Prince of Darkness, you can live a beautiful happy life."

"I think I understand what you're trying to say, but that was a horrible explanation," he says honestly, beginning to walk away.

"Yeah, I know, but I try. As long as you get the point of what I'm saying."

"I do, but like I said, there's nothing good to focus on, even if we wanted to.. What about you, Princess? You live in a world of greenery and light, why are you so in awe with this meadow when it's similar to what you have back at home?"

"Sure, our kingdom is filled with living plants, but they're nothing like these," she says, gesturing to the meadow. "The flora within our borders was never naturally there; we grew it, tended to it, urged it to spread and bloom. But these... This is here all on its own with the freedom to grow and thrive without aid. Each bloom is... free."

"I see," Kieran replies, his voice soft, almost as if he's lost in his own thoughts. Ciana glances at him, noticing his gaze locked on the colorful petals around them, as if seeing the hues for the first time.

"This is also just a rare sight for me." Ciana smiles, but it's full of longing. "I don't get to see much of my kingdom outside the town."

"How come?"

"It's the best way to keep me protected; keep me safe."

"From what?"

"You know, people, disasters, et cetera."

"People? Like your *own* people?" Kieran's eyes widen, his surprise filling every inch of his face. Ciana nods. "You're the Princess of Goodness, why would anyone on your side want to hurt you? I mean minus what's-his-name, he seems like he would hurt you."

"His name is Zomo, and he would never hurt me. You shouldn't assume that about someone you don't know. There's always those people who don't approve of those in a higher position." Ciana stares at her feet.

"You mean to tell me that there's been attempts on your life?"

"Yes, that's usually what happens when others don't like the ruler. They don't trust me, especially right now, people don't think I'm spending the town's money wisely, when really, it all goes towards them."

"They don't trust you? Really? It's probably because they think you're hiding something from them." He coughs into his hand, looking around as if he didn't say anything.

"No one is perfect, Kieran."

"Pfft, as if. There is one person who's perfect."

"Who?"

"Me." He smiles.

"I should have seen that one coming." Ciana rolls her eyes, unable to keep from laughing.

*If my people don't like me, could it be possible that Kieran's people don't like him? Do they treat him like my people treat me? I have my guards to protect me, Kieran mentioned how he doesn't have anyone... if someone did try to overthrow him, no one would be there to defend him, but himself. If that has ever happened, he really must be quick to stop them or he has their respect and his people don't even try.*

A patch of flowers moves a little ways away, catching her eye. "Wait, wait. There's something over there." She points to where she noticed the movement.

"Probably just a rodent of some sort."

"Let's check it out."

"Hey, remember what happened the last time you investigated? We were taken captive," Kieran reminds her as she nears the flowers.

"It all worked out though, didn't it?"

A small growl comes from the patch of flowers as Ciana gets closer. A small furball jumps onto her face, knocking her to the ground. Ciana laughs as a cold, sandpaper tongue begins to lick her face. Gently grabbing the little body, she pulls the furball away from her.

"Awww, what a cutie."

"What did you find?" Kieran asks, racing over.

"It's a cypup."

"A what now?"

"A cyclops puppy. See, it only has one eye." She holds up the small black dog with brown patches so Kieran can see the one blue eye in the middle of its head, its pink tongue hanging out as it wags its tail.

"I didn't know they actually existed."

"Look how cute he is!" she coos, petting the pup. "What should we name him?"

"Hold on now, we can't take him with us. You know the rules."

"But he's so cute and is probably all alone out here."

"We can't bring him, Princess. You were so strict with Fobo not coming with us. You'll get both of us in trouble." Kieran turns to leave.

"*Zomo*," Ciana corrects. "He's just a pup. Where's your mom, puppy? Is she nearby?"

"I hope not. Who knows what she'll do if she sees you holding her baby. Wild animals get very protective of their young."

"He's not wild, but we need to make sure he gets back home."

"No, Princess, just put him back on the ground. We don't need a whole pack of dogs attacking us just because *you* tried to be helpful."

Ciana considers his words. "He's right, little pup. You can't come with us," she apologizes, gently setting the puppy on the ground, then following Kieran. The puppy barks happily, running around her feet, his body rubbing against the bottom of her shins, tail wagging. "No, you can't come with us. Stay." The pup barks again, trotting behind Ciana as she walks. Giving up, she picks the puppy up once again, his body fitting perfectly in her arms. "I'm going to name you Patches."

"Did you not hear me? He needs to stay," Kieran counters, hearing her name the dog.

"He was following me. You know they're very loyal once they like someone, so for all we know he could have followed us the whole way anyways."

"What about—"

"We'll leave him outside when we get to the fortress."

"If you're going to leave him outside, why did you refuse Hazo from coming?"

"*Zomo!*" she corrects harshly. "And Patches isn't a person. The only two *people* who can go are you and me. The king and queen said nothing about creatures."

"Fine," Kieran groans, eyeing Patches carefully.

"Thank you."

"But if he starts to slow us down, he'll have to go."

"We won't have to worry about that, will we, Patches?" Setting him down, Patches runs off, coming back with a stick. "Fetch?" Ciana grabs the stick from him, throwing it ahead, nearly hitting Kieran.

"Are you trying to hurt me?" He whips around.

"Sorry, I didn't mean to." She laughs, taking the stick again when Patches returns with it.

Kieran eyes the pup as he comes up to him with the stick, tail wagging. "I'm not going to throw you the stick," he tells him. Patches drops the stick at his feet, sitting down, making Kieran stop. "I said I'm not going to throw it." Patches continues to wag his tail, waiting expectantly. "Ugh, only one time." He picks up the stick and throws it ahead. Patches watches as it lands, standing up, his tail wagging faster as he looks back at Kieran. "Well, go after it!" Patches doesn't move. Kieran gently nudges the pup with his foot, which Patches gently paws at, rolling over onto his back. "Crazy dog," he mumbles, a smile tugging at his lips as he squats to rub Patches's stomach. Patches jumps back up, running to the stick to bring back to Ciana. She watches as Kieran looks at her, the smile that was forming disappearing.

"See he's not that bad." She smiles.

"Don't get attached to him."

"Why not?" She throws the stick, trying to ignore her headache that hasn't gone away.

"When you have to part ways from him, it'll break your heart."

"That won't happen. He likes me."

*And you.* Ciana picks Patches up when he returns with the stick, laughing as he licks her face. "Huh, puppy?" She throws the stick again, setting Patches down, who runs after it only to get distracted with a butterfly that flies in front of his nose. Ciana smiles as she watches him chase the butterfly around, her body relaxed and weightless for the first time. She sits down in the flowers, closing her eyes as she lays back, focusing on her headache.

"What are you doing? Aren't we on a time crunch?" Kieran comes over, kicking her feet, annoyed.

"It'll only take a second. When was the last time you took time to enjoy the moment around you?"

"Never."

"Well then, come here, come sit next to me." Ciana sits up, patting the ground next to her. Kieran stares at her, crossing his arms.

"Okay, fine." He reluctantly sits.

"Now close your eyes."

Kieran huffs. "Isn't sitting here enough to satisfy you?"

Ciana shakes her head, grinning. "Just trust me." Kieran raises an eyebrow. "Please?" she adds softly, watching him deflate in defeat, closing his eyes. Inside, she cheers at her small victory, closing her eyes.

"Okay?"

"Pay attention. Focus on what's around you. What do you hear?"

There's a moment of silence before he answers, "I hear birds singing, the flowers rustling against each other, you talking, me talking."

"Okay, now what do you feel?"

"The light breeze, the coolness from the ground, the sun beating down on me," he drones.

"How does it make you feel?" Ciana opens her eyes. She looks at Kieran, whose straight posture relaxes; his hands are lazily resting on his knees; his breathing slow and calm; his face neutral. "Do you feel calm? Peaceful? Relaxed? Maybe even happy?" The corners of his mouth twitch before his body shakes back into his rigid posture, his eyes opening to meet her gaze.

"Like I'm going to answer that." He stands back up.

"We never get a chance to take time and enjoy the moments that come up in our lives. We always just think about what lies ahead blind to the moment we are currently in." Ciana looks up at Kieran. "We need to enjoy the little things in life; who knows what lies ahead, because we may never get a chance to later."

His face falls slightly. "When was the last time you enjoyed a moment?"

"Too long." Ciana kneels, running her hand along the ground where she had destroyed the flowers, growing new ones in its place. Plucking one as she stands up, she carefully pulls away the petals so she can see the middle, where it's an unhealthy black. Her breath catches in her throat.

*No. It can't be possible. I can't be— but how?* Letting out a trembling sigh, she shakes her head, not wanting to think about black in the flower. "We can continue on now," she tells Kieran, throwing the flower to the ground.

Ciana examines the map as they continue walking through the meadow, the sun beginning to set on the horizon. Patches barks a few times, before running off.

"Patches, come back!" Ciana calls after him.

"Let him go. He wasn't supposed to stay anyways. We're almost to the river, if he catches up, let him; if not, then it was never meant to be."

"Your caring nature is too much." Ciana rolls her eyes, looking back at the map.

The sound of rushing water fills the air as they walk up a hill. They look down at the roaring blue river at the foot of the hill, an old rickety bridge leading across it to the flower-filled meadow on the other side.

"Oh good, we found the bridge too. That'll save us time, now that we don't have to walk along the entire river to find it," Kieran acknowledges as they start down the hill.

*Thump. Thump.*

The ground vibrates when they're halfway down, small pebbles jumping at their feet. Ciana looks at Kieran, trying to keep herself steady as the ground jumps.

"Earthquake?" she questions.

"No, it almost feels like giant footsteps." Kieran shakes his head. Patches comes running to Ciana, barking.

"Come here!" a deep voice bellows from behind.

# Chapter Eleven

The thundering footsteps grow louder—the ground trembling, threatening to crack from the power. Ciana freezes, scanning the top of the hill where an enormous green and very bald head appears.

With a gasp, Ciana steps back, watching as the creature's form crests the hilltop, revealing a troll, at least seventy feet tall, wearing nothing but a pair of worn leather shorts.

"Oh, my—" But there's no time to finish her thought, because the troll picks up his pace, running right towards them.

Patches snarls, baring his teeth as if trying to threaten the large being. To the troll, the cypup would be a delicious snack.

"What did you do?" Ciana accuses the puppy as she swipes him up into her arms. At the same time, Kieran begins walking backwards, grabbing her elbow as he moves.

"Run!" he orders.

They dart down the rest of the hill towards the rickety bridge, barely staying out of reach of the large troll. Running across the bridge, relief washes over Ciana, knowing the troll can't follow them without going into the rushing water. She tightens her grip on the pup, trying to catch her breath, readjusting her bag.

*We're almost safe. It wouldn't be worth it for the troll to tread through the water to follow us.*

Kieran suddenly stops, causing Ciana to bump into him. His heavy breathing seems to quicken as he stays frozen.

"What are you doing? We're halfway across the bridge." Ciana tries pushing him, but he doesn't budge. He glances back at her, his face mixed with worry and annoyance.

Ciana peers past him to the other side of the bridge, her relief quickly vanishing when she sees another troll waiting; blocking their only escape. This troll is slightly larger than the other and a lighter shade of green. Warts and whitish, possibly scar-like spots mar his bald head. His belly protrudes out over his filthy pants. Ciana gulps, trying to steady her breathing as dizziness starts to settle in, her limbs trembling uncontrollably.

"What do we do now?" Ciana panics over the roaring river, clutching the side of the bridge with her hand that's holding the map, squeezing Patches close to her chest with the other.

Kieran's eyes dance around, looking for an escape or anything that could be helpful, before they fall back onto the trolls. "How am I supposed to know? I didn't think we were supposed to come across any danger on this trip!"

"We weren't!"

"Get baby one!" the smaller troll in the shorts snarls.

Ciana looks behind her at the troll. *Whatever Patches did, really made them mad, unless it's a misunderstanding. I've read that they're usually good with negotiations. I wonder if there's something I can work out with them that doesn't require us getting eaten.*

Gathering all her courage and strength to keep her limbs steady, Ciana straightens her posture, turning towards the troll behind her. "Mister troll? Is there some way we can work out what happened? Maybe come to some sort of agreement?" Ciana calls up to him, hopefully.

"Get all!"

"Or not." Ciana sighs in defeat. Out of the corner of her eye, she sees something big move. Ciana whips her attention to her right where a third troll, one who's much shorter, more boulder-like, is bending his knees. Swinging his arms back, using the forward momentum to press off the river's edge, tucking his legs up to make himself into a ball, and plummets into the water.

Ciana watches, paralyzed, as the growing wave rushes towards the bridge.

There's no time to form a plan as the water rages closer, sweeping the bridge, and them, downstream.

Ciana spins under the water, her grip around the map and the pup both forced loose by the momentum, before she manages to come back above the water. "Kieran!" she gasps before being submerged again, her bag weighing her down. Flailing her arms, she tries to get back above the surface. The rapids slam her against a rock, hitting her head and making her headache almost unbearable. Fighting the pain, Ciana quickly grabs the rock, hands slipping as she struggles to pull herself to the top for air. "Kieran!" She coughs once she's above the water, looking around.

"Ciana!" She looks behind her where Kieran is on his own rock. Ciana smiles, relieved that he's okay. "Look out!" He points behind her. She turns around, sliding back into the raging water just as one of the trolls reaches for her. She fights against her bag and the current tugging her down, tumbling with the undertow making it impossible to find her way up. A pair of strong arms wrap around her, forcing the bag off her, and pulling her to the surface for air.

"Kieran," she gasps, wrapping her arms around his neck, "I can't swim."

"Really? I didn't notice," Kieran says sarcastically, despite being out of breath.

"You took off my bag! My things were in there."

"Forget about it. The weight you packed wasn't helping you. If you would rather drown, by all means you can find it."

"Come here!" the troll huffs. Kieran pulls them both under the water once again, swimming with the current, keeping them out of reach from the trolls. Resurfacing for air, Ciana notices how close she is to Kieran. His soaked brown hair sticks to the side of his face, water streaming down his strong jawline. She pays attention to how he's holding her; strong and firm enough to keep her in place, but loose enough that if she wanted, she could easily move out of his grip. Kieran looks at her, his chocolate brown eyes standing out against the blue water. His eyes flicker over her face, his hand around her waist twitches slightly as if he's debating on letting go. His gaze meets hers for a heart beat before he looks ahead, eyes widening as he notices where the water is flowing.

"Uh oh," he whispers.

"Don't say that. What now?"

"Just know, I've got you."

"What's that supposed to mean?" Kieran tightens his grip around Ciana with both his arms. "What are you—" her words turn into a scream as they fall over the edge of a waterfall, plunging into the pool of water below.

Kieran never let her go. Not when she sunk so far down her feet hit the rocky bottom of the pool. Not when she flailed her arms as panic seized her. He held firm, swimming them both to the surface and then to the river bank. Climbing out of the water, Ciana lies down, curling into a ball, coughing and shivering, trying to catch her breath with her pounding head.

"You okay?" Kieran heaves, bending over.

"Uh, huh."

"You were never taught to swim?"

"Nuh uh."

"Noted," he pants, but there's a genuineness to his tone.

Ciana files that away to unpack later, adding swim lessons to her to-do list for when she gets back then remembers the pup. "Do you see Patches anywhere?"

"No," Kieran answers, watching Ciana look around.

"We need to find him to make sure he's alright." She starts to get up, but Kieran stops her.

"No, no, no, you've got to make sure you're alright and catch your breath first, then we can see if we can find Patches."

"I am fine, and my breath is caught."

"Show me then." He extends his arm out in an invitation, before crossing both arms across his chest. Ciana huffs, but gets her feet under her and presses to standing. Once up, her headache overwhelms her, pounding against her skull like a knife. The pain makes her dizzy, and her knees give out, but Kieran is there, catching her before she has a chance to hit the ground. Carefully, he lowers them both to the ground.

"You're not fine, Ciana. You need to rest." He gently lays her on her back.

"Will you go look for Patches then?"

"No."

"Why not?"

He scoffs, running a hand through his wet hair. "He's not even your dog. And for all we know, he made the trolls mad in the first place so they may have him."

"I know, but—" Ciana tries, but Kieran continues.

"He was swept into the river with us. If the trolls don't have him, then he could have ended up anywhere."

Ciana hates that he's right, but it didn't diminish the fact that she felt responsible for the poor pup. She was the one who let him go when the wave hit—not purposely, of course. The wave... she jerks up causing another rush of dizziness to hit her.

"The map!" she squeaks. "I was holding the map too when we got dumped in the river! I lost the map! We'll never make it now!" Tears well in her eyes, her bottom lip trembling.

"Hey, hey, hey," Kieran quickly comforts her. "Don't worry about the map. When I told you I had it memorized, I wasn't kidding. I do. We don't need the map. We'll still make it to the fortress and fix the balance. Don't worry." He gently helps her lay back down.

"You sure?"

"Yes." He runs his hand through his hair again as she calms down.

"Okay."

"Now the sun is almost gone, and since you like your beauty sleep, I suggest we just stay here for the night."

"What about Patches?"

"He may find his way back to us. And if not, we can look for him in the morning."

"Okay." Ciana closes her eyes, readjusting herself so she's comfortable. "What about our bags? I noticed you lost yours too."

"We didn't *lose* them. It was either sacrifice our things or our lives. They're probably at the bottom of the water, but I'm not going to get them. We can manage without them."

"*You* can manage. I had brought a self-heating blanket that could dry everything for us."

"You brought a heated blanket but not a fire starter? You definitely had your priorities off. No wonder your bag weighed so much. I'm sure you'll be able to survive without it."

"Still, would be nice to have," Ciana mumbles. Crackles from the flames fill the air, heat warming her cold body. "And faster than a fire. Better hope the trolls don't see the smoke," she teases Kieran, opening her eyes a crack.

"They won't, otherwise, I wouldn't have made it. Now hush and rest."

# Chapter Twelve

A searing pain runs through Ciana's right palm, forcing her to shoot up into a sitting position. She places both hands on the ground, causing the pain to intensify.

"Ow!" she seethes, looking at her bloody hand where a deep cut runs from the bottom of her pinkie to her thumb. Looking around for Kieran, she only sees the smoking fire pit. "Kieran?" she calls. No answer.

*He's got to be around here somewhere. After yesterday I don't think he'd just leave... I think.* Head still hurting, she crawls to the water's edge to wash the dirt and blood from her hand, her clothes dry from the previous day's events.

"Feeling better?" Kieran's voice comes from behind her.

Ciana jumps, placing a hand over her racing heart. "Don't scare me like that!" she accuses, huffing out some air. "I guess. My head is still killing me."

"Still?" His eyes narrow. "Did you hit your head on something?" Moving closer, he presses his fingers to the back of her head searching for a wound.

"Ow!" Ciana wacks his hand away. "Yes. Clearly."

A hint of annoyance crosses Kieran's face. "Sorry." He shrugs. "What are you doing back by the water? Wanting to almost drown again?"

"I was just washing dirt off my hands." She flicks the water off her hands, careful that Kieran doesn't see her cut.

"Hmm," he hums in response, studying her. "I have some good news," he goes on, a single blink the only inclination he's moved on from what was being discussed. "I found Patches—"

Ciana lights up. "You did? Good. Where did you find him? Where is he? Did he get hurt from the river?" Her eyes scan around them, searching for the pup.

Kieran shrugs. "He's around here somewhere and I didn't find him. He found us. Tough dog. And no he's not hurt in any form."

"Good. We can continue on our way, assuming you really do have the map memorized." Ciana stands only to bend over as the world starts to spin. "Dang it," she mutters under her breath.

"You think you can continue today? If you need another day to rest by all means, I'd rather we do that than you collaps—"

"Shh, I'm fine." Slowly straightening, Ciana takes a few slow steps forward, holding her injured hand close to her chest.

"Okay, but I'm not carrying you if you pass out." Kieran scratches the back of his head, before raking his fingers through his hair, following behind.

"You won't have to. I wouldn't let you anyways."

"Good."

"Patches!" she calls out. Patches barks, running to her from a patch of flowers, his tail wagging, something silver hanging out his mouth. "What do you have, puppy?" Crouching, Ciana pulls a small silver locket from his mouth with shaking hands. "Where did you get this? Is this what made those trolls chase us?" Patches barks as she pockets the locket. Ciana straightens, holding both hands to her chest, shivering.

"Are you cold?" Kieran asks, watching her with curious eyes.

"No."

He frowns. "Then why are you shaking? What is it?"

"Do you always have to question everything? Perhaps I'm just hungry!" she bites back, feeling lightheaded.

"Well then grow another apple tree."

"I don't want to and it wasn't an apple tree."

"Well, they were red fruit, what else was it?"

"I don't know."

"How do you not know what fruit you can grow?"

"I just don't, okay? If you want to know what I *think* it is, I think it's a haw."

"Calm down, Princess. We're still in the meadow so there's probably gophers or something around here."

"Patches, can you hunt?" Ciana asks, looking down at the pup who jumps ahead, excited.

"He's a dog, he can't understand what you mean."

"No, I think he does." Patches runs off ahead to some tall grass.

"Or he's finally leaving us."

"He came back once, he'll do it again." Ciana runs her fingers through a patch of flowers, bees and butterflies fluttering around them.

"You sure about that?"

"Yes. I trust him. Just give him a bit."

"You can't trust a stray puppy that looks like a cyclops. Who knows what's going on in his head. He could turn on you." Kieran crosses his arms, watching as a butterfly lands on Ciana's finger, a smile forming on her lips.

"You've heard of them, you know he wouldn't. Why do you have such a problem with trusting others?"

"Why do you have such a problem with not being yourself in your own kingdom?"

"I don't." She frowns, the butterfly fluttering away.

"Don't lie, Princess. I know you've acted more like your real self out here, it's different than how you were in your kingdom."

"And how could you know that?" She raises an eyebrow at him.

"I can see it on your face."

"Oh wow, like that's proof."

"No really. You've almost looked happier, more relaxed, being out here than back in your kingdom. What are you hiding from? What are you scared of?"

"I'm not hiding from anything. I'm not scared of anything either. Stop suggesting that I am!" she says, waving a threatening finger. Kieran smiles as if he was expecting her reaction and snatches her hand. "Stop it!" she scolds, tugging her hand back, but he holds firm, flipping her hand over to examine the still bleeding cut.

"I thought you looked a bit pale this morning. Why didn't you tell me you were hurt?"

"I did."

He rolls his eyes. "Why didn't you tell me your *hand* was injured?"

"I'm fine, it's just a cut." She shrugs.

"A cut that's bleeding." His eyes flicker up to hers. "Why don't you just heal yourself?"

Ciana holds his stare for a breath more before letting her gaze drift to the gash on his arm and the burns that are still a bright red. "Why don't you let me heal you?" she retorts.

"I'm fine. But this... you should heal before it gets infected."

"I can't."

"What do you mean you can't? You can heal everything, even bring people back to life."

"Fun fact. My people and I can't use our powers on ourselves."

"You're messing with me, right?"

"I have a bleeding cut on my hand. If I wasn't kidding I would have healed it before you even knew it was there."

"Can't you wrap it in something?"

"Did you have anything to wrap your cut with?"

"No."

"Then there you go." Ciana looks back at Kieran's hand around her wrist. With his light grip, she can feel how soft his palms are, with subtle roughness as if he's worked hard despite being a prince. There's a gentleness in the way he's holding her wrist and in the way he's looking at her. And the hint of concern in his voice... Ciana must have been imagining it. She pulls her hand from his light grip, walking away with her other hand against her forehead, rubbing her temples, sickness settling in her stomach.

Kieran runs up next to her. "Wait, so if you can't heal yourself, then what do you do if someone breaks a bone or something?"

"We have a designated 'doctor' that is medically trained who people can go to if they're sick to determine if it'll pass on its own or need some medicine, but really they would just have to go to anyone else to be healed. We try not to just heal everything so our autoimmune can still build up to whatever sickness comes around. We'll only instantly heal broken, sprained, or fractured bones."

"So does that mean no one dies on your side? Like, you know someone is dying, so you just heal them or bring them back to life?"

"No."

"Really? Why not?"

"Well, everyone on your side can kill someone instantly, right? So if someone is sick or injured, do you just kill them to take them out of their misery? Or do you heal them with whatever you guys do?"

"No. Well, not unless it's really necessary. We have ointments and things that help with wounds. The basics made with some of the things you send over in our weekly food deliveries. But if that doesn't do anything, then they either die or deal with the pain since our doctors are limited."

"Okay, so we will heal wounds and stuff, but if someone is dying, we let them die. We all have our time. Besides, I'm the only one that can actually bring things to life; everyone else can only heal."

"Wait, so what happens if *you're* dying? You just die because no one can heal you?"

"Yes. Wait, why am I even telling you all this? You said we weren't supposed to know about each other's sides!" Ciana throws her hands in the air.

"Yeah, but I'm intrigued now. Following that, don't you basically keep your kingdom alive, so if you die, everything else dies?"

"In a sense, yes."

"So what would you do if you're dying?"

Ciana eyes him. "Are you planning on killing me or something?"

"No, I'm just curious. Remember, you wanted to share things in the first place."

"If I was dying, the queen would give my power to someone else so the kingdom wouldn't die. Happy?"

"Almost, so if the queen gave your power to someone else, wouldn't they be able to heal and bring you back to life?"

"Yes, but they wouldn't."

"Why not?"

"They just wouldn't."

"Okay, but why would the queen give *your* power away? Aren't yours and hers the same or something, especially since she's your mother?"

Ciana glances at Kieran before looking away, hesitating to answer. "They're not the same."

"How can they not be the same? You share the same bloodline."

"They just aren't, Kieran. Now, are you done interrogating me? You're making my head hurt more than it already does," Ciana says tiredly.

"For now."

"Good."

"I think you should still wrap your cut in something though, to avoid any infection."

"You didn't wrap yours in anything. Besides, since when do you care?"

"I—" Kieran hesitates, shaking off what he was thinking. "I don't. I just don't need you dying in the middle of this journey, making this trip pointless."

"We have nothing to wrap it in. It'll have to wait until we reach the town."

"There are no towns on the way."

"Yes, there is."

"No, I told you I have the map memorized, there is no town," Kieran reminds her.

"The town is the only thing on this journey that I know we'll come across."

Kieran smirks. "An imaginary town? Fits perfectly with your imaginary people."

Ciana shakes her head, giving him a glare as she walks ahead.

The colorful meadow gently fades into grassy fields. Patches finally returns to them, his mouth barely keeping hold of two gophers and a fish, dropping them at Kieran's feet, sitting down to look up at him with his big blue eye.

"Oh, good boy! See, what did I tell you?" Ciana gives Kieran a smug smile, rubbing Patches's head.

"You don't have to rub it in. I'll make a fire."

Kieran builds a fire, skins the gophers and fish, and cooks it over the hot flames. Ciana sits next to the fire, entranced with the dancing orange flames, Patches curled up next to her.

"Ooo, that smells good," a high-pitched voice sighs.

"I know," Ciana agrees, distracted.

"What?" Kieran raises his eyebrows at her.

"Oh sorry, nothing, just—nothing," she apologizes. Kieran shakes his head looking back at the food.

"Hehe, he still can't hear us," the voice laughs. "You know, he's still mean to you. You should still leave. Not respecting you and accusing you of things."

"You guys are still here?" Ciana asks. Kieran looks at Ciana again, mouth slightly open, his eyes widening with concern. Knowing what he's thinking, she stands and walks a little ways away.

"We never left! Your victory against the goblins impressed us, and that river ride was quite an experience. Now, back to that boy, he's been accusing you and thinks you're crazy."

"Don't get on that subject. If you're going to stay, can I at least see you?"

"Suppose so."

Two people, no bigger than a hand, appear in front of her feet. One of them is wearing a flowery purple dress with matching purple shoes adorned with a flower on top, with short black hair. The other has short brown hair and is wearing a suit made of rich green leaves; both have pointy ears.

"Are you... are you gnomes?"

"We're pixie gnomes!" the gnomess explains.

"What are your names?"

"I'm Iris and this is my husband, Liko."

"Nice to finally meet you both."

"Are you still talking to yourself?" Kieran interrupts, coming over to her.

"No, I found the source of the little voices."

"Let me guess, it's your hands?" He smirks.

"Oh, shut up. Meet Iris and Liko."

Kieran does a double take at the pixie gnomes, showing no emotion. "You're full of it."

"Am not, you see them."

"They're puppets."

"Who ya callin' a puppet, slimeball?" Liko sneers, walking up to Kieran's foot. Kieran glances at Ciana as if something interesting is supposed to happen.

"Be nice," Ciana tells Liko.

"What did he say?" Kieran asks Ciana, gently pushing Liko back with his foot.

"You still can't hear them?"

"I saw his puny lips move, but no sound."

"The big doofus here can't hear us. Only you can," Iris explains.

"I said to be nice," Ciana reiterates. "Why can't he hear you?"

"We're not sure. We're surprised you can even hear us. It may have something to do with you being nice and him being mean. Don't know."

"He's not mean."

"How can you say that after the way he's been treating you! Look at what he's put you through. He almost made you drown!"

"He didn't. He saved me! Plus, I haven't been all that nice to him either."

"Saved you? When did I save you? Like I would ever do that," Kieran interrupts again.

"Shush. I'm not talking to you."

"See, he doesn't even know when he saved you!" Iris crosses her arms, her face turning a light pink.

"He's just... not used to doing good things."

"What are you talking about? I'm used to doing good things," Kieran counters.

"Will you stop interrupting my conversation? How do you know we're even talking about you?"

"Who else would you be talking about? I'm the only other person here!"

"You're so touchy. Now please stop interrupting me. I won't ask you again." Ciana and Kieran roll eyes at each other as Ciana turns her attention back to Iris. "So, why have you two been following us?"

"There's something different about you two compared to the others we've seen."

"Really? What others?"

"Yeah, there are others who come through occasionally."

"I'm interrupting again. I came over to tell you that the meat is cooked." He backs away, heading to the fire, tired of the one-sided conversation he was hearing.

"Okay, I'll be right there," Ciana tells him. "Now who—wait, where did they go?" She looks around for the two pixie gnomes, but they've disappeared. "Now look what you did; you made them leave!" Ciana accuses Kieran as she heads over to the fire herself.

"Good riddance! I didn't like not being able to hear them."

"They could have been helpful. They said there's been others that have been through here."

"Okay? Maybe it's just travelers." Kieran hands her a stick of meat.

"Who'd be traveling? No one has left our kingdoms."

"Speak for yourself."

"So some of your people have wandered out here when they aren't supposed to?"

"No."

"Okay then." Ciana takes a bite, thinking about what the pixie gnomes said. "I wonder if it could be... no, they wouldn't."

"Who wouldn't?"

"No one. Never mind." She shakes the thought from her head, tossing a few pieces of her meat to Patches, the sickness from her stomach taking over the rest of her body, drowning out her hunger.

*Who else could it be, though? I trust that no one on Kieran's side has left and nobody in my kingdom has wandered out here. Unless there are others that came to this planet without us knowing, the only other explanation would be the—*

"Listen, I'm sorry for thinking you were crazy and hearing voices and whatnot," Kieran says, breaking her trail of thought.

Ciana gasps, giving Kieran a dazed look. "Are you apologizing?"

"Me? Apologize? Never. I don't do any of that mushy stuff. I'm just... correcting myself. Which I hardly do, so don't get used to it."

"Ah, I see. Well, I accept your correction." She smiles with a giggle. "I'm sorry for how I've been acting towards you."

"I guess I can accept your apology." Kieran exaggerates a sigh with a roll of his eyes, making Ciana laugh.

"I will admit... you were right. I am happier out here. There's no pressure from the kingdom, from my people... the pressure to be kind and perfect all the time."

"So you admit you've been putting on an act? Why?"

"I've needed to. I can't let all she's built go to ruins because of how I think and act. It would all be for nothing." Ciana stares at the flames, sniffing as her nose begins to get stuffy.

"She? Who's she? The queen?"

"What? Oh, nothing."

"Tell me, if you enjoy being yourself so much out here, why don't you in your kingdom?"

"I can't be myself *and* be the princess." Ciana stands and walks away before he has a chance to respond. A light breeze blows the grass around Ciana as she sits on the cool ground, pulling her knees to her chest. Scrunching her nose, her eyes water as she tries to prevent a sneeze.

Kieran slowly joins her on the ground, plucking some of the grass to fiddle with. "Why not? Being the princess *is* who you are. As the Prince of Darkness, I don't do all that royalty stuff, as you could probably tell. I do things my way and that makes me the prince. I'm my own person, I don't need anyone telling me what to do and how to do it. I shaped the title around who I am, not who I am around my title. I don't see why that wouldn't be the same for you. I'll ask again, why can't you just be yourself?"

"I have to li—achoo!" Ciana sneezes before shaking her head and standing. "Forget it. Let's go. Come on, Patches," she calls, wiping her watery eyes. Kieran carefully studies her as she walks ahead, her skin a shade lighter than before. Patches runs up next to Ciana, tail wagging as they tread through the grassy field.

Kieran glances at Ciana periodically. "You did eat the food, right? You didn't give all of it to Patches?" Kieran verifies after another glance towards her.

"Yeah. Why?" Ciana sniffs, her congested nose not helping with her headache.

"You're still shaking, and you sound a little congested."

Ciana holds her hands out in front of her so she can see them shake slightly. "It just hasn't gotten into my system yet. I'm—fine—achoo!" She sneezes into her shirt.

"You're sick."

"No, it's just allergies."

"Uh, huh."

"It's all the pollen in the air—achoo!" She wipes tears from her eyes again. Kieran watches her almost as if he's debating something.

"If you're sure... I just think—"

"Kieran, I'm fine. Let's just keep going. We're wasting time."

# Chapter Thirteen

The grass grows higher the further they walk until it's nearly as tall as them. The wind picks up, rustling the grass, cooling the air from the hot afternoon sun. Head pounding and nose burning, Ciana sits, resting her head against her knees, too exhausted to call out for Kieran to stop.

"Princess?" Kieran calls, realizing she was no longer behind him. "Princess? Where are—oh, there you are." He pushes aside some of the grass, locating her within. "In the future, if you're going to take breaks, then can you at least tell me? I thought you were kidnapped or something."

"Sorry," she apologizes breathlessly. "I didn't think you'd care if I was kidnapped."

"I wouldn't, but then *I* would have come this far for nothing."

"Right."

Kieran paces around Ciana, not sure what to do while he waits. A few barks come from Patches nearby, causing Ciana to look up, eyes wide with worry. Kieran sighs, "I'll go make sure Patches isn't getting into trouble." He walks off through the grass.

The grass rustles in front of Ciana. Confused, she looks up, a pair of glowing yellow eyes staring back at her through the grass. Heart racing, she straightens, placing her hands down on either side of her, ready to stand. A gray wolf eases out of the tall grass.

"Kieran?" she whispers in a shaky voice, knowing he's probably too far to hear her. The wolf sticks its nose in her face, sniffing. Ciana leans back as far as she can without lying down. The hairs on her arms and neck stand from the wolf's hot breath; a sudden warm sensation fills her body as she stares into the wolf's eyes. The fear she was having immediately disappears, forming an instant trust towards it. The grass to her left moves as Kieran returns, stopping short.

"Don't. Move," he instructs. The wolf narrows its gaze at Kieran. "What did you do?"

"Nothing," she barely manages to say, a sneeze trying to escape. The wolf backs away, transforming into a man with dark eyes and rich brown hair, nearly standing a head taller than Kieran. His shirt is dusty, but pristine looking while his pants are much dirtier. Ciana's mouth drops, not believing her eyes. The man offers his hand to her with a smile, which Ciana cautiously takes.

"I didn't mean to frighten you. Sorry about that," he apologizes in a deep voice. He places a light kiss on the back of her hand, sending a warm tingle up her arm and through her body. Ciana takes her hand back, still in awe. Kieran grabs her arm, carefully drawing her back and away from the unknown man.

"Didn't mean to frighten? You stuck your nose all up in her face! Who are you?" Kieran demands, sizing him up.

"My name is Olcan."

"And?"

"And what? You asked who I am, and I told you." He smiles mischievously.

"Smart mouth. What are you doing here?"

"This is my territory that you're trespassing on, so if anyone should be asking the questions, it'll be me."

"Oh, I see. Werewolves are very territorial, big surprise." Kieran rolls his shoulders back as Olcan walks closer.

"I didn't think I'd ever come across the Princess of Light way out here, let alone with the Prince of Darkness. Your heart really is as dark as they say. What are you doing out of your cave?"

"Funny, you're the one who lives in a hole. Now excuse us, we've got to get going." Kieran pushes Ciana forward gently.

"Achoo!" Ciana sniffles. "Sorry."

"Come on, Princess, we're leaving." Kieran continues nudging her forward towards the grass nearest them, away from the man. Olcan runs in front of them again.

"I don't think so. The princess here is sick; she needs rest in order to get better. Or are you so heartless you don't realize that?" Olcan reaches for Ciana's hand, but Kieran wacks it away.

"I am perfectly aware she is sick. She's the one who thinks it's just allergies. Plus the princess herself agrees that we need to keep going, isn't that right?"

"It is allergies, and yes, we do. We were just taking a short break," Ciana answers.

"See? Now, if you excuse us, we'll be going." Kieran tries to push Ciana forward, but she doesn't move. "We are going," he reiterates.

"It wasn't much of a break. I'm not quite ready to go yet."

"Give the princess a rest. I'm sure it's been a long journey." Olcan smiles.

"She's rested enough for her... allergies," Kieran says through his teeth. Ciana shivers, a cold rush running through her body. Light-headed, she stumbles backwards. Kieran quickly grabs her, giving her enough support to stay on her feet, her head resting against his shoulder. "Ciana, do you think you'd be able to wait to rest longer until we're out of his territory?" he asks, noticing a small sweat on her brow.

"No, I need rest," she huffs.

"We need to—"

"I know we need to keep going, but I'm sick. Alright? I lied. I just need to rest, *then* we can continue."

"I understand, princess, but regardless, I think it's better if you rest outside of his territory. Who knows what he'll do to us if we stay here any longer." Kieran eyes Olcan.

"I don't think he's going to harm us. He did apologize."

"Don't you remember what happened with the goblins? We can't trust anyone we come across. Especially a werewolf."

"We escaped the goblins, but what could one werewolf possibly do?"

"Uh, a lot of things. They supposedly can do weird things that others can't. I don't know the specifics."

Ciana examines Olcan. Kieran was right; they couldn't trust anyone they meet, but she can't help but feel that Olcan was indeed there to help. "We can trust him."

"I do believe I can be of assistance." Olcan raises a finger in the air.

"See? He's offering to help. Now let him talk." Ciana straightens on her feet.

"Pfft, yeah right. I can't believe I'm hearing this right now!" Kieran plops down in the grass, lips pursed, arms tightly crossed against his chest.

"You know if you had a heart, you would understand and be more open to trusting me," Olcan tells him snarkily. "Now, Princess, I know something that'll help you feel better."

"What is it?" she questions with a small smile.

"It's an herbal mixture. My place isn't too far away, but you shouldn't exert yourself more than you need to. You stay here and rest. I'll go grab some things and be right back." Olcan transforms back into a wolf, disappearing in the tall grass.

"I don't trust him," Kieran huffs darkly.

"You don't trust anyone, Kieran."

"He's a werewolf, Princess. I know you've read about them, so you should know he can't be trusted. I wouldn't drink his herbal mixture."

"If it'll make me better, I'll take it so we can continue. Now where's Patches?"

"Don't change the subject."

"I'm not. Where is he?"

"He was off rolling around in the grass not that far away." Kieran waves a hand towards the grass behind him.

"Good. Thank you for checking on him."

"If I hadn't, you would have thrown a fit. I was avoiding that, not doing you a favor."

"I wouldn't have gotten upset, but I would have convinced you to go check, anyway." Ciana crosses her arms.

"Same thing. It saved me the trouble of having to hear you argue."

Olcan comes back a few minutes later with some water in a little wooden bowl, hands filled with nuts and berries, Patches trailing behind him, quietly baring his teeth.

"Patches, come here, pup." He runs up to Ciana, rubbing against her legs.

Olcan clears away some of the grass, giving him enough space to make a small fire, placing the water over the flames, and grinding up the nuts and berries in his hand.

"Where'd you get the bowl?" Kieran quizzes.

"I told you, this is my territory. I have kitchen utensils, ya know." Olcan rolls his eyes, sprinkling the crushed ingredients in the water, swirling it around to make sure it mixes, before offering Ciana the bowl. "Here, this will help."

"I'm warning you, Princess, do not drink it. He could have poisoned the water. Besides, how will nuts and berries make someone feel better?"

"Unlike you, I can actually make things so they can heal. The berries and nuts are nutritious in and of themselves. Crushing them brings out that nutrition and goes into the body faster. Heating it on the flames takes out all the unhealthy parts. Now, regularly we have it simmer for a few days to really let the healing properties sink into the water, however, in your case I used my powers to speed up the process."

"You're a werewolf; you don't have powers."

"You obviously know nothing about us. 'Cause we do. Now drink up, Princess."

"Don't refer to her like that. Only I can."

"Ooo touchy." Olcan smiles.

"Watch it, hairball."

"Cut it out! Both of you!" Ciana stops them, taking the bowl from Olcan. He watches eagerly as she drinks the mixture. A cold sensation trickles through her body as she finishes the last drop. "That's disgusting." She looks at Olcan with a pained expression. A sense of relief washes over her body as her strength gradually returns, her congestion loosening although the tightness in her nose remains.

"But it'll help you," he reassures her.

"You shouldn't have drank it." Kieran turns away.

"Come on, Kieran, now we can go. I'm feeling better already, thanks to Olcan." Ciana starts making her way through the tall grass, Kieran following behind.

"Can I tag along? I think you need someone who can help you medically in case something more... major were to come up on your journey. I doubt the Prince of Darkness would be of any use. Plus, the mixture tends to vary from person to person, and I want to make sure it helps as it should."

"Sure!"

"No!" Kieran counters the invite, fists clenched tightly, eyes narrowed.

"Why not?" Ciana looks over her shoulder at him.

"We already have one mutt with us; we don't need another one."

"He's coming! Come Olcan, don't listen to him." Olcan walks past Kieran to Ciana, giving him a smug smile as he passes.

"You said so yourself that we're the only two people that can go."

"He never said he was going to come the whole way."

"He pretty much did."

"He's right about us needing someone with medical knowledge. He's also part wolf, so I'm sure it'll be fine."

"Where are you two headed anyways?" Olcan asks, clasping his hands behind his back.

"That's none of your business," Kieran hisses.

"We're on our way to fix a problem," Ciana answers, throwing Kieran a brooding look of her own.

"Must be some problem if you have to bring him along with you." Olcan throws his thumb over his shoulder toward Kieran.

"In a way, yes."

"How did you get that cut?" Olcan holds up her injured hand.

"I think from a rock."

"And not-so-prince-charming back there didn't even try to heal it or wrap it for you? *Tsk tsk tsk,* you're some gentleman."

Kieran sniffs hotly. "For your information, furball, I can't heal. I'm the Prince of *Darkness,* not the Prince of Medicine. Do you really think using my power on her would have *healed* her? I didn't even bring any of my medicinal ointments. We're out in the wilderness as well, if you didn't notice, where there's nothing to wrap her hand in. I also have some cuts and marks on my arms, so she's not the only one suffering."

"Good thing I'm here then, and exactly why I should come along. Since the princess here is feeling better, let's stop at my place real quick so we can get something for your hand, then we can continue."

"Oh, that would be wonderful!" A grin spreads across Ciana's face. She was right to trust Olcan. In just the short time they've met, he's already been so helpful.

"She'll be fine," Kieran remarks. "Besides, you didn't want *me* to help with your hand. Why are you letting him?"

"Kieran, he's trying to help. You just admitted that you can't heal and didn't bring anything to help with wounds, so what would you have done? If he has something that'll help, I'll take it. I offered to heal your wounds, but you refused. This is what kind looks like. You could learn a thing or two from him."

"I know what being kind is, and he is not kind."

"How can you say that? You don't even know him!"

"Listen, Princess, you are kind... mostly. He is not. I told you he can't be trusted, especially if he really does have a few inferior powers, and I don't need to get to know him to know that he isn't a good person."

"He is trying to help. We're stopping by his place. Show us the way, Olcan."

Olcan leads them through the grassy field to a small hut made of wood. A stream burbles right next to it. Olcan opens the wooden door, letting Ciana walk in with Kieran close behind into a little room with wooden furniture and cupboards. Olcan opens one cupboard full of medical supplies, searching through the items until he finds what he's looking for.

"This should do it!" He walks over to Ciana with a gauze and a bottle of ointment.

"What's in the bottle?" Kieran takes the bottle from his hand, examining the label.

"It'll help prevent infection from any dirt that may still be in the wound." Olcan soaks the gauze in the ointment, carefully wrapping it around her palm.

"Ow!"

"Oh sorry, it might sting a bit." He secures the gauze, putting the items back in the cupboard. "There you are. Now we're good to go."

"Don't you want to pack a bag or bring anything that may be of help?" Ciana questions.

"That won't be necessary. Believe me." Olcan bumps into Kieran's shoulder as he walks by with Ciana.

"Watch it, hairball," Kieran warns. "Come on, Patches." Kieran closes the door behind them as they continue through the grassy field.

The tall grass shortens as they approach another forest; the trees towering over them, blocking most of the late afternoon sun. Slightly lightheaded, Ciana leans against a tree, still sick in her stomach. She rubs her temples once again to try to help her pounding headache. Kieran watches her carefully as she takes some staggering deep breaths.

"Princess, are you okay?" he finally asks.

"Yeah, I'm fine, just still have a headache," she answers, her voice tired.

"This is your doing, furball!" Kieran whips towards Olcan.

"No, it's not, Kieran. Headaches are normal, and I've had it since we started this journey."

"Don't defend him! You don't look any better! You almost look worse since he's given you that mixture!"

"I'm not. You're jumping to conclusions. He never said it was going to help right away or that it would last long-term."

"That's true, I didn't say that," Olcan sides with Ciana, defending himself. "The medicine is probably still working its way into your system. It takes longer to kick in for some people. In the meantime, I can whip something up to help your headache, if you'd like?" he offers.

"If you could, I would appreciate it."

"You shouldn't, Princess. It'll go away on its own," Kieran counters once again.

"Kieran, will you please stop?" She didn't want to hear what he had to say. He isn't the one who's been trying to be helpful this trip. Olcan, on the other hand, was. Kieran had no right to try to tell her otherwise. He isn't the one needing the medical help, so how would he know that Olcan wasn't being helpful?

"I'm trying to warn you, Princess. I don't trust him and his... medicines. I want you to hear what I'm saying. To trust me," Kieran tells her strongly. He couldn't believe she was choosing to trust a complete stranger over him. He's shown that he can be trusted, even a little, but not a werewolf. He knows how they can be, so why was Ciana denying everything that she should know? Why was she not listening to her own instincts?

"Olcan, what can you do for my headache?" Ciana ignores Kieran.

Olcan smiles, gathering some pines and leaves, breaking them into little pieces before crushing them with a rock and mixing it with dirt in his hand. Covering his hand with the other, he pulls away his top hand, thick brown paste now in his palm.

Ciana scrunches her nose. "I'm not eating that."

"You don't have to. All you do is put it on your forehead."

"Ew!"

"It doesn't have to stay on for long, just at least two minutes, then you can take it off."

"It's just mud, nothing special," Kieran mumbles.

"You don't have to if you don't want to."

"No, I'll try it." Ciana presses from the tree, allowing Olcan to put some of the paste on her forehead. "It's not going to stain or anything, right?"

"Nope." Olcan smiles, wiping the rest on his pants. Ciana glances at Kieran, who looks like he wants to say something, but doesn't. Ciana becomes very somnolent as her headache slowly disappears.

"I still don't see how mud is going to help," Kieran finally grumbles.

"I'm not surprised. Let me see if I can explain it simply enough for your small brain to understand." Olcan smirks, watching as Kieran holds back from barreling into him.

"Go on." Kieran leans against his own tree, arms folded tightly across his chest.

"The pine needles and leaves hold an oil that helps relieve headaches. Crushing these items up allows me access to the oil, which I can then amplify with my powers so it can be effective. It works best when absorbed into the skin compared to being digested, so by making it into a paste, it'll remain in contact with the skin long enough for a good portion of the oil to be absorbed."

"Assuming that's true, wouldn't you have had some of that mixture stored? Why did you make it from scratch?" Kieran raises an eyebrow.

"I ran out of my supply a few days ago and haven't had a chance to make more. Otherwise, I would have. Now do you understand how I'm helping?"

"I understand, but I doubt it's actually doing anything helpful."

"That's because you don't trust me like the princess here does." Olcan turns his attention to Ciana. "Ready to take it off?"

"Yes, please," she answers.

Olcan covers his hand with his sleeve, gently wiping the paste off her forehead. "Feeling better?"

"Yes, thank you." She smiles up at Olcan, who grins back, offering his arm to her.

"You're welcome."

"Oh, you've got to be kidding me!" Kieran slaps his palm to his forehead, looking down at Patches, who stares back, tail wagging.

"Shall we continue?"

"Sure." Ciana takes Olcan's arm.

"Gross, she's gone mad," Kieran tells Patches, following behind Olcan and Ciana.

Kieran, lagging slightly, observes Ciana and Olcan's playful laughter ahead, his lips tight. Ciana glances over her shoulder at him; Olcan frowns at her action.

"How long have you two known each other?" he inquires.

"Only for these last few days," she answers truthfully.

"You two aren't close then?"

"Ha! No." She laughs at the thought. "We're complete opposites and can't wait until we can go back to our separate worlds."

"Is that right, Prince Charming?" Olcan calls back to Kieran.

"I'm not talking to you, hairball." Kieran shoots daggers at him with his eyes.

"He really is the Prince of Darkness." Olcan looks ahead, rolling his eyes. "Or more like the Prince of Grumpiness."

"He's not always grumpy," Ciana defends Kieran.

Olcan shrugs. "Then perhaps he's just heartless."

"You would know all about that, wouldn't you, *furball*?" Kieran sneers.

Ciana grimaces over her shoulder. "What is that supposed to mean?"

"Oh, don't you know, Princess? Werewolves have no hearts. They were born without them, so they don't feel remorse when they pick on innocent people to take theirs," Kieran shoots at Olcan, who whips around, pulling Kieran into his face by the front of his shirt.

"I can bite your head off in a second, princey. I'd watch what you say to me," he growls.

"Don't forget that I can take all the life out of you before you can even *think* about harming me." Kieran's lips curled into a joyless smile.

"Is that a challenge?"

"It is if you feel like dying today." Clenching his jaw, Olcan lets Kieran go, backing away. "Smart choice."

"If you two are done arguing, can we continue on our way?" Ciana sighs, fighting to keep her eyes open. She wraps an arm around Olcan's, dragging him away from Kieran. Dropping his shoulders, Kieran furrows his brow and shakes his head, disbelieving.

"You hardly know him!" he calls after her.

Ciana ignores Kieran, focusing on Olcan. "How did you come across us?"

"Well, I saw smoke and thought maybe the grass was on fire, so I went to check it out and saw the both of you. I followed you for a bit to make sure you weren't going to set the field on fire or destroy my beautiful home," he explains.

"How did you know who we are?"

"Who else has a natural light emanating from them? I've heard of you and what you look like, so once I saw you, it was not hard to figure out."

"So why did you want to come with us again?"

"To provide any medical help that may be needed and to make sure the mixture was working like it should. Speaking of which, how are you feeling?"

"Pretty good, I haven't felt congested or sneezed for a bit."

"And your headache?"

"Gone for now. Thank you. Although I am tired." She yawns, making Olcan chuckle.

"Glad I could help. You're probably just worn out from your trip. Which is normal. Where *are* you guys going and what is the problem that you have to come clear out here to fix?"

"Well... we're going to the fortress."

"You mean the fortress where the Queen of Light and King of Darkness are?" Olcan's eyes widen, mouth dropping slightly.

"That's the one."

"That clears up why you had to bring *him* with you."

"Yep, we have to go together or else they won't help us. It's all part of keeping the balance."

"That's stupid."

"It makes sense, though, to have both of us take responsibility for anything that happens to the balance. We've been lucky not to need their help until recently." Patches runs in front of Ciana, jumping against her legs so she picks him up. She laughs as he licks her face before turning towards Olcan, growling. "Patches, be nice. He's a friend."

"He is *not* a friend. He's hardly an acquaintance," Kieran corrects, forcing his way between her and Olcan.

"He's not *your* friend, but he's mine. Here, you take him." Ciana shoves Patches into Kieran's arms.

"No, no, he's your pup. You're supposed to take care of him."

"Well, I can't if Olcan's here. You both don't like him, so you take care of my pup."

"Princess, I am not your caretaker, nor the dog's."

"I never said you were, now hush, I'm talking to Olcan." Kieran stops, allowing the two to go ahead of him a few feet before following behind once again, closely examining Ciana; her skin a shade paler than before; her attention solely on Olcan; ignoring Patches and Kieran; the instant trust towards Olcan. Something wasn't right, and Kieran knew it. Ciana knew it. But the feeling is drowned out within her.

The warm air grows colder as they walk deeper into the forest, the trees thickening above them, hiding the sun that's almost gone over the horizon they no longer can see. Forcing her eyes to stay open, Ciana rubs her hands against her goosebump-covered arms. Patches begins to snarl and bark in Kieran's arms, trying to wiggle free.

"Patches, be quiet. There's nothing here but us. Kieran, make him stop," Ciana pleads through her numb lips.

"Me make him stop? He's your dog, and he's probably trying to tell us something, which I agree with. We shouldn't be this far into the forest. This isn't right. We should have reached a clearing by now." Kieran examines the surrounding trees.

"We're going the right way. Olcan says he knows where to go."

"Wait, we've been following *him* this whole time?" Kieran gapes. "No wonder we haven't gone anywhere! I should have guessed that since *you* don't know where to go. *I'm* the one with the map memorized."

"He knows where to go; he's part wolf, remember?"

"No, he *is* a wolf. A werewolf, to be exact. What makes you think he knows where to go when he can't even control when he turns into a hideous monster?"

Olcan glares at Kieran, straightening his posture, puffing his chest out slightly. "As a matter of fact, no, we can't control when we turn into our hideous werewolf form from the full moon, but we can control when we turn into a normal wolf," Olcan corrects through his teeth.

"That doesn't mean anything; it's the instincts," Ciana continues.

"So we're going off his instincts? Great, that means we're dead in my vocabulary book. How would that tell him where to go anyway? Is he feeling the wind for direction? Thinking it's coming from the fortress? *We're* the only ones with the maps. If he were going based on smell, that would be more believable." Kieran throws his hands in the air.

"I'll have you know, *princey,* that we're taking a shortcut. I've been in these woods for a long time and know the fastest way to get you to the fortress," Olcan explains.

"Have some trust, Kieran," Ciana urges.

"I do have trust, just not in *him.*" Kieran glares.

The darkened forest casts dancing shadows in the moonlight as they continue on. Ciana slows her pace, feeling like she weighs a ton. Unable to go on, she collapses, rubbing her heavy eyes.

"I'm sorry," she says through heavy breaths. "I'm just so tired. We need to stop for the rest of the night." Patches runs up to Ciana, rubbing against her. "Go away, Patches!" She shoos him away. Tail drooping, he sulks to Kieran, who rubs his head.

"What is wrong with you, Princess? He was trying to comfort you!" Kieran snaps at her.

"I told you. I'm tired. Just let me rest."

"The Princess is right; we're all tired. It's been a long day. We should rest here until morning," Olcan agrees anxiously.

"Cork it, furball. She's only tired because of you." Kieran's eyes darken.

"Nonsense. It's all in your head. By morning, the medicine will have reached her system well enough."

"Oh! Speaking of which, have you heard from your little gnome friends recently, Princess?"

"Who?" Ciana lifts her head slightly so she can look at Kieran.

"The pixie gnomes, or whatever they were called."

"Still not following you."

"You know, the little people that popped up that you can only hear. One had a purple something, and the other had a green whatever on?" he tries to explain.

"You're not making any sense, Kieran."

"You know who I'm talking about. One was named Iris and the other Liko?"

"Kieran, you're talking nonsense. You should definitely get some rest. There's no such thing as little people." Ciana lays her head back down.

"What did you do to her?" Kieran pushes Olcan away from Ciana, eyes darkening even more, his breath quickening.

"I've done nothing. All I did was give her mixtures to help her headache and make her feel better!" Olcan pushes him back, clenching his fists into tight balls.

"And wiping her memory with it!"

"I've done nothing of the sort!"

"Kieran! Olcan hasn't done anything to my memory. Stop accusing him of things. Now I'm going to sleep. You two better not kill each other in the meantime." Ciana lets her eyes fall shut. Kieran and Olcan exchange death looks before laying far from each other.

A stabbing stomach pain wakes Ciana. Her skin feels as though it is on fire despite being drenched in sweat along with a cool breeze. With difficulty, she rises, finding a tree to lean on while she breathes heavily, bent at the waist, clutching her abdomen, and feeling sick to her stomach.

"Princess? Are you alright?" Kieran's concerned voice comes from behind.

"No, I'm not okay," she barely manages to say, her voice shaking with her weakened body.

"Princess! You're awake!" Olcan's voice trembles slightly.

Kieran slowly turns to face him. "Say that again?"

"I said she's awake." Olcan clears his throat, voice cool and calm, yet a speck of fear haunts his eyes.

"What were you expecting?" Kieran slowly advances on him, cracking his knuckles.

"She was very tired yesterday, I thought she'd still be asleep. That's all. It is very early in the morning." Olcan backs away from Kieran, shaking.

"I probably would be, but I feel like crap. Your mixture isn't working," Ciana includes.

"And I don't know why. It might be because of your natural healing ability within the power you hold. It could be fighting against it."

"Are you scared, furball?" Kieran's smile is ominous.

"Never." He straightens. "Princess, would you like me to see if I could make some more?"

"No!"

"Here, let me take a look at you to see if I can determine why it's not working." Olcan runs around Kieran to Ciana, who starts to turn, but Kieran steps in between them.

"She isn't going to, not after you've been poisoning her," he spits.

"How can you say that? I've been trying to help. Tell him, Princess," Olcan tries, desperation in his tone.

"No, Olcan. I will not tell him off. You said you could help me, but I've only gotten worse. Plus, I hate that feeling that keeps running up my arm and body every time you kiss my hand." Ciana's legs start to tremble from her weight.

Kieran's eyes widen, turning to Ciana. "The what feeling? No wonder why..." He faces Olcan again, jaw locked and understanding hitting him. "Poisioning *and* entrancing her. No wonder she's been so trusting towards you."

"Princess, I promise I can make it go away; it just takes some time," Olcan reasons, taking another step away from Kieran.

"No, Olcan. You had your chance; you can go back home now."

"Please, Princess, give me another chance."

"You heard her, hairball, you've had your chance. Now get lost before I make you!" Kieran rolls his shoulders back, chest out, spine stiff. Olcan sneers, turning away.

"She wasn't supposed to wake up. I shouldn't have done the mixtures, should have just taken care of her myself," he murmurs under his breath.

"What did you just say?" Kieran grabs the back of Olcan's shirt, forcing him to turn, clenching his fist into a tight ball.

"Nothing, I'm going home. I'll let you deal with the Princess of Death over there since that's your specialty." Kieran lets his fist fly, colliding with Olcan's face, knocking him down before the almost-assassin attacks back. The two wrestle on the ground, holding nothing back.

"Kieran, stop fighting, please, before you kill him," Ciana pleads, grimacing as she collapses, resting her head against the tree trunk.

"Would that be so bad? He was trying to kill you." Kieran shoves Olcan off him, wiping blood from his lip with the back of his hand.

"It's not right." She takes a big, staggering breath, her body heavy. Olcan transforms into his wolf form, running off.

"Not right—He deserves it!" Kieran exasperates. "I get you're sick and not feeling great from whatever he put in your system, but how are you not even the slightest bit upset about this?"

Ciana stares into the distance, not wanting to say anything as Kieran waits for an answer. She was upset. Too many times has her life been on the line in her own kingdom, but it's come to the point where being upset won't change anything. Something she's now become used to.

Kieran calms, remembering what she had mentioned towards the beginning of the journey. He gently kneels next to her. "Your people don't trust you." He speaks softly. "You have to be protected from people. There's been attempts on your life. You told me yourself, but

I didn't think you were telling the truth. Even if I did, I wouldn't have guessed... there's really been that many attempts to not surprise you anymore?"

"My palace is the only safe place for me. I've had to give some of my guards or servants some duties I would normally do, because it's not safe for me in town or at our farms. My own people have made me shut myself out from them, because they'll try to do something to me at any given chance."

"And you didn't execute any of them?"

"I punish them, but if I were to kill them, there'd be an even bigger uproar with my people."

Kieran shakes his head in disbelief, feeling her forehead, seeing sweat fall down her face. "You're burning up. I told you that you shouldn't have taken anything from him," he reiterates gently.

"Oh, don't rub it in." Ciana closes her eyes.

"Just saying. Patches, come here." Patches trods up to Kieran. "Go find a nearby body of water for us, please?" Patches gives a little bark before running off.

"What'd you do that for?" Ciana coughs, making her stomach pain worse.

"You have a high fever, Princess. We need to cool you down."

"Isn't that why I'm sweating?"

"Funny. Just relax."

Kieran fans his hand over her, trying to keep her cool until Patches comes barreling through the bushes barking. He jumps up and down in front of Kieran.

"Did you find some, buddy? Show us." Patches runs off a ways, then stops to jump in place, looking back at Kieran and Ciana. "Can you walk, Princess?"

"I think so." Leaning against the tree for support, Ciana pulls herself up, hunching over slightly as she takes a couple steps before her knees give out completely.

"Okay, you can't walk. That leaves only one other option."

"We stay here?"

"Uh, no." Kieran wraps an arm around her shoulder like he's going to pick her up.

"Wait, wait, wait, no, nuh uh, no thank you," she refuses, trying to push him away, but her arms hardly move.

"I wasn't asking." He scoops her up bridal style, following Patches through the forest.

"This is embarrassing. This is never going to happen again, so don't get used to it." Ciana rests her head against his shoulder, closing her eyes once again.

"I'm not the one getting comfortable," he jokes, smiling down at her.

"Shut up, I'm not comfortable. I'm being carried against my will, and I'm too weak to do anything about it." Ciana feels Kieran's chest vibrate as he chuckles. "Don't laugh at me."

"I'm not laughing, I'm chuckling."

"Same thing," Ciana mumbles. The bare skin of his arms feels refreshingly cool against her warm body, like a cool breeze on a hot day. As Kieran shifts his grip on her and she repositions her head, she notices his delicate hold, like she's a fragile vase. There's a small scent of dirt from his shirt, masking another scent of what Ciana thinks is Vanilla Bean. There's a comfort in the way she sits in his arms, the way he's holding her. It makes her feel... safe. That she's home and nothing bad will come to her. A feeling she hasn't felt in a long time.

The sound of a rippling stream grows louder as they reach a clearing in the forest. Kieran gently lays Ciana next to the water, carefully resting her head on a smooth rock. Not wanting to open her eyes, Ciana slowly readjusts herself into a more comfortable position. Patches jumps onto her chest, licking her face until she opens her eyes. She turns her head, laughing, which quickly turns into a coughing fit.

"Sorry, Patches," she apologizes between coughs. Patches jumps off. She waves him to her so he can curl up next to her, rubbing his soft black and brown fur. Her eyes gradually get heavier until she falls asleep.

Something cold and wet drips down the side of Ciana's face, waking her up with a start. Kieran jumps back, startled himself from her sudden movement, something balled up in one of his hands. Furrowing her eyes, she wipes water off her forehead.

"Why are you putting water on me?" she asks, her voice a little rough.

"I'm trying to cool you down. You're burning up, remember?"

"Mmm."

Kieran moves to put what's in his hand back on her forehead, but she weakly rejects it. Ciana looks around in a daze; Patches is curled up next to her, sleeping, the hot sun shining brightly in the middle of the sky. Her eyes fall on Kieran, who's watching her patiently. His right eye is slowly turning black, with scratches and bruises all over his body, his gash from the goblins bleeding once again. Looking closer at what's in his hand, she realizes it is the shirt he's no longer wearing.

"Don't worry, it's clean. I know better," Kieran explains, following her gaze to his balled-up shirt.

"Good." She gently places her hands on the ground on either side of her, trying to hoist herself up.

"What are you doing?"

"Getting up."

"No, you need to rest."

"I'm too hot in the sun. I need some shade."

"Okay." He sighs, helping her up and over to a nearby tree. Ciana leans against the trunk, sighing in discomfort.

Kieran frowns as he turns to re-soak his shirt. Ciana looks at the bruises on his back, frowning until her eyes fall on a long scar running almost the entire length of his back, nearly hidden under the bruises.

"How did you get that scar?" she asks when he returns with the dripping shirt.

"That's not important." He gives her a small smile. "Just rest. I'll try to not wake you this time." Ciana pouts slightly, before going back to sleep, Kieran carefully dabbing her forehead with his shirt-made washcloth.

# Chapter Fourteen

A tickle creeps into Ciana's throat, waking her up as she lets out a deep, cruddy cough. Her eyes water as she tries to sit upright, struggling to take breaths in between coughs. Kieran rushes over, helping her sit up.

"Put your arms up," he instructs.

"What?" she hacks.

"Put your arms up, like this." Kieran raises his arms above his head. Lungs burning, Ciana raises her hands over her own head. Her coughs continue but stop shortly after. "There." Kieran goes back over to a nearby fire with something cooking over the flames. Ciana looks up through the tree she was under at the starry sky.

"How long was I asleep for?"

"I don't know. At least six hours or something."

"That's terrible! We wasted a perfectly good day."

"No, we didn't. You're not in any shape to continue. You need more rest."

"There is a thing as too much sleep, you know."

"Not if you're sick."

Ciana sighs, moving closer to the fire, knowing he's right. Warming her hands, her eyes flicker over to Kieran. "Will you tell me about the scar on your back now?"

"Why do you care?" Kieran glances up at her, his face lit by the flames.

"I don't. I'm just curious. I know Olcan didn't give it to you. It looks old, so how did you get it?"

Kieran sighs, poking a stick in the fire. "The scar is a reminder of why I can't be good."

"Okay, that's ridiculous. What do you call helping me then?"

"I call it a temporary forced alliance. Necessary until everything is fixed."

Ciana huffs. "Well, I call it being good. You're not an entirely bad person. There's goodness in you. Otherwise, you wouldn't be here right now. If you weren't good, you'd let your kingdom go to ruins despite the circumstances, but you're not."

Kieran pokes the fire logs, giving the flames some more air, remaining quiet.

"Okay," Ciana goes on. "I'll be quiet and let you continue. What happened?" Kieran gives her a side eye. "You don't have to tell me, but I'm just trying to understand you more."

After a lengthy pause, he deflates, giving in to her request. "203 years after our parents left for the fortress, there was a riot amongst my people—a misunderstanding about an exchange of money. One thought he was getting jipped so naturally he caused an uproar. They had gotten the people to divide into two groups, based on who they believed was right. Usually they just yell at each other and protest, but this time it got more violent. They started setting houses on fire and beating each other up..." His voice trails off, as if falling into the memory. "I tried to calm them, reason with them, but they refused to listen. One of the houses they set fire to was a daycare; a child got trapped inside, but no one knew until it was too late. From this, I'd had enough. I called the leaders of both groups to me. As their ruler, it was my job to dispose of them, to get rid of the problem; we don't give second chances, but I decided to give them one, anyway. Both had families so I wasn't going to leave them fatherless. They were dismissed, but as I walked away, one of them came at me from behind with a knife."

"Oh no!" Ciana gasps.

"He nearly killed me, but the King of Darkness, my father, intervened. Aware of how dangerous the situation had gotten. My father disposed of the man and the other. He turned to me and told me I couldn't afford to show mercy to anyone, especially my own people. As Prince of Darkness, that isn't how I should be, otherwise, it would result in my undoing. He gave me this potion that showed me this sort of vision of what would happen if I chose to continue to show mercy. The outcome was terrible, and I vowed that I would live up to my title to continue my rule. He helped heal the wound but left the scar as a reminder."

"He can heal?"

"Not really. He made a potion to make sure I wouldn't die from it, so nothing like you can do."

"Oh, but that's not fair. If you vowed to be dark and ruthless, why bother helping me?"

"You said yourself that if we don't fix the balance, we both die. I'm just doing what's necessary for my people to ensure we live."

"So you're being selfish, not nice."

"I'm being a good ruler. Making the sacrifice to risk my life with you so my people can be semi-happy. Sacrifice is something a good ruler must do, even if it means eliminating the source of the problem."

"You just admitted you're a good person. The same reason as I said a little bit ago."

"Being a good ruler doesn't make me a good person. It just means I'm doing my job correctly and as I should."

Ciana shakes her head. "Still. And there's more ways to fix a problem than just killing."

"Yeah, but killing is the easiest." He shrugs.

"Still." Ciana eyes Kieran's black eye in the firelight. "Come here."

"I'm not going to let you heal my scar. I know you can do that." He shakes his head.

"I won't, but I can at least heal your black eye and other wounds."

"We've been over this, I'm fine with letting my wounds heal on their own."

"It won't hurt."

"No thanks. Now, are you hungry at all? You've hardly eaten anything today."

"Not really."

"I wasn't really asking. Here." Kieran brings over a wooden bowl filled with liquid.

"Where did you get this?" Ciana examines the bowl.

"I found a good-sized log and carved it. I tried to make some sort of soup. It's not great but not completely terrible."

"What's it made from?"

"Water, nuts, flowers, berries, anything edible I could find. I didn't make it to try to heal you, only for sustenance. Now eat."

"How do I know you're not going to try to poison me or something by just saying it's for food purposes?"

"I would have just let Olcan do it if I wanted to poison you, Princess. Besides, I don't have any influential powers like he presumably does. I'd eat some first, but I already ate." Ciana looks at the soup in the bowl. "You don't trust me?" Kieran frowns, tilting his head slightly.

"No, I do, I'm just not hungry, like I said."

"And you should eat, like *I* said. Eat, then go back to sleep."

"How many times do I have to tell you that you're not in charge of making decisions for me?"

"How many times do I need to tell you that I don't have to listen to you either? Now eat." He jabs a finger towards the bowl. Ciana carefully sips the soup, wrinkling her nose and pursing her lips. "I told you it wasn't good."

"Well, you're right about that, but it's surprisingly better than whatever I took from Olcan and his friend."

"That is actually reassuring for me because I am a terrible cook."

"I can tell." She laughs. "In the future, don't cook anything except fish and gophers, I'll do any other cooking."

"Wow, thanks." Kieran laughs with her.

She sips some more soup. "Kieran?"

"Yeah?"

"Did you know that there were werewolves out here?"

Kieran adjusts his position next to the fire. "Yeah, I knew they were here somewhere, but I didn't bother to listen to what all they could do. Didn't think we'd run into them. Did you?"

"No." She shakes her head. "I remember you mentioning how I've read about them and should know not to trust them, but... I didn't even know they existed. The Queen of Light can create plants, animals, and other things like that, not people, so how did they get here? How did they know who we are? How do you know about them but not me?" She looks at Kieran, searching his emotionless face for answers.

"I don't know, Princess. I can't give you those answers," he responds, looking at the flames. "But be glad we're done with them. Now finish eating and get some more sleep."

Ciana takes another sip, a question she's been wanting to ask forming at the tip of her tongue. "Kieran?"

"Yes?"

"How old are you?"

Kieran whips his head in her direction. "Where's that question coming from? Why do you want to know?"

"It was brought up the day the balance broke. I don't know much about you and your people, so I thought I'd ask since this is probably the only time we have to get to know each other. I know for us, our power makes it possible for us to live for a long time without looking our age. It's been so many years since the pact was made. Your father must still be alive, so do you guys age like us, or are you just a generation ruler from the King's first son?"

She watches Kieran stare into the flames, waiting for his answer, not wanting to push it. He finally lets out a sigh. "I'm four hundred and ten years old. That is the one thing our people do have in common; we age the same, funny enough."

"And to think we've never even tried to find a better peace between our kingdoms in all those years. And you never bothered to learn how to cook." She laughs.

"Very funny." Kieran chuckles. "We didn't have a need to. We weren't allowed to either. Still aren't."

"I know, but sometimes I wonder what things would be like if our sides did get along."

"It would never happen. The result would be the darkness overrunning your light like it is now. Finish your food and go back to sleep."

Ciana finishes her bowl, setting it beside her as she lays back down. Her eyes fall on Kieran's lit up face, smiling at her as her eyes close.

A cool, misty breeze stirs leaves across the ground. Ciana sits up, shielding her eyes from the early morning sun streaming through a light fog. Headache still gone and not feeling as sick as before, she stands up, crouching over for a second, lightheaded. Carefully treading through the fog, she finds her way over to the calm stream; cupping her hands to collect some water, she sees her cut on her right palm, her skin beginning to scab over it, the bandage from Olcan no longer around it. Shaking her head, she collects some of the cold water, splashing it on her face.

"Well, morning, sleeping beauty, you're up and moving! Feeling better?" Kieran greets, walking next to her, his eye a dark purple.

"A little."

"Let me feel your head."

"No, I'm fine. There's no need for you to."

"Okay, but if you start dying from the heat later, let me know."

"Don't worry, I won't." Ciana stands up slowly, making sure she's not going to get lightheaded again, holding her hand out for a shake. "Thank you." She smiles.

"You're welcome?" Kieran hesitantly shakes her hand.

Ciana focuses on Kieran's wounds, watching as his purple eye fades back to its normal color, the rest of his wounds disappearing. Kieran yanks his hand from hers, realizing what she's doing.

"Sneaky Princess, that's not right, you know. I said I didn't want you to heal my wounds."

"I'm sorry, but I couldn't let you walk around with a black eye and all that," she defends. "But I did let you keep your scar, don't worry."

"Next time, ask for my permission and wait until I say yes." He rubs his face. "Now, do you feel like you can continue our trek today or do you want another day to rest?"

"We've already wasted time; I can continue. It just might be slow."

"Whatever you say, Princess." Kieran whistles to Patches. "Come on, pup. We're leaving." Patches jumps up from his curled position, barking. "Good boy." Kieran starts through the forest ahead of Ciana.

"Oh, there they are! Oh, the miss looks terrible." Ciana hears the familiar high-pitched voice of Liko.

"What do you expect? I'm sick," she answers. Kieran raises an eyebrow over his shoulder towards her. "Iris and Liko."

Kieran stops, letting her catch up. "So you do remember them?" he questions, hopeful.

"Of course I do. Why wouldn't I?"

"Why wouldn't she?" Iris appears on a branch in front of them.

"Do you remember anything from our little encounter with Olcan?" Kieran asks.

"Yeah, he gave me something that was supposed to help my headache and make me feel better, but it didn't work. He just made things worse and wrapped my hand in a bandage, and by your definition, he was poisoning me."

"His poisoning was also affecting your memory."

"He what?"

"He was somehow messing with your memory, like wiping it or something. I mentioned the pixie gnomes and you thought *I* was going crazy. You didn't remember them."

"I don't remember that." Ciana frowns.

"Miss, how could you forget us? That's very rude." Liko crosses his arms, popping up next to Iris.

"It's not her fault, it was Olcan's. He was the one causing it," Kieran answers him.

"It was my fault, Kieran. I was the one who trusted him to—wait, did you just respond to Liko?" Her eyes widen. Kieran glances between her and the two pixie gnomes, shrugging.

"It wasn't your fault though, Princess. You were just doing your duty of being the nice Princess trying to see the good in everyone, and he took advantage of it, even though I think part of it was him entrancing you in some way."

"I felt something was off when he showed up, but then my fear and everything went away when I was watching him. I should have listened to my gut and ran before he got close to me; besides, I wasn't expecting the wolf to turn into a person. You're right though, it is the princess thing to do, I probably would have tried either way. I know she would have, and she would have probably succeeded too, but of course it wouldn't for me."

"You're referring to someone again. Who is this she?"

"What?"

"You said 'she'. Who are you talking about? Your mother?"

"My mother?" Ciana looks at Kieran almost as confused as he is. "I didn't say 'she', I never said that." A rush of heat runs up her body, making her sick again. "I need to sit down." She carefully lowers herself onto a nearby rock.

"Oooo, she's hiding something. Was not expecting that." Liko laughs.

"I'm not hiding anything," Ciana denies.

"But you are and are just not admitting it! What bad thing have you done?"

"She hasn't done anything bad. She's the Princess of Light; it's nearly impossible for her to. But I'd be careful what you say or else *I'll* do something bad," Kieran warns Liko.

"You *can* hear them!" Ciana points towards Kieran.

"Yeah, but I don't think I want to."

Liko sticks his tongue out mockingly, spitting in Kieran's direction.

"Liko, don't do that. Be nice. Now where did you two disappear off to?"

"We had to. Them werewolves eat us. We sensed Olcan near-by and had to skadoodle, otherwise we would have been food. We didn't mean to leave without saying goodbye," Iris explains, sitting on Ciana's knee.

"Do you live near werewolves?"

"No, we live far from them, but they track us down, even somehow managed to when we came to this planet. They pretend to be normal mortals, but we know better."

"Are they the ones you were referring to when you said we're different from the others you've seen?"

"No, those dogs are a norm in our lives. We meant the other ones of you." Iris points to Ciana.

"Uh, don't you mean us?" Kieran interrupts.

"No, only her. Although they're still different."

Ciana bites her tongue, knowing who Iris is referring to.

"Come with me, Iris." She gently picks Iris up in her hand, walking a few trees away from the boys.

"Are you going to hurt me?" Iris panics.

"What? No, of course not. I just want to talk to you without the boys." Iris lets out a breath of relief. "These others, what are they doing in the forests?"

"They take trips. They walk through the forest back and forth from the town to where you're from."

"What?" Ciana gasps.

"Yes, they're a stubborn bunch and are always complaining about something when they walk through. They come through, are gone for a few days, then come back. Then they do it again."

"How often?"

"Like once or twice a month or so. Pointless if you ask me."

"It is who I thought then. It's the only thing that makes sense."

"Hey gossipers! Are you done talking about us yet?" Kieran calls over to them.

"He's so impatient," Ciana whispers to Iris, walking back over to Kieran.

"Haha, I agree!" Iris laughs.

"Tell me, Princess, since you were able to walk a few feet away, does that mean you're ready to continue?" Kieran asks, pulling a sniffing Patches away from Liko.

"I suppose. The sooner we get this over with, the sooner I can move on to the next problem." Ciana gently sets Iris down on a tree branch, before continuing her thought. *She never had problems, but of course I would, and it might get worse.* She walks ahead of Kieran. "Iris, how far is the town from here?"

"It's just on the other side of the forest. I'd say you'd reach it by nightfall," she chirps.

"Thank you."

"There's no town, Princess," Kieran counters, following behind.

"Didn't you just hear Iris answer how far away it is?"

"Yeah, but I told you it wasn't on the map. You're both crazy for thinking there is one."

"No, they're right. There is a town," Liko chimes in.

"I'm sure I would remember if there was a town way out here."

"It's three against one, how can you not believe us?" Ciana pushes back a branch, accidentally slapping it back into Kieran's face.

"Ow! Hey, that's not very nice. There's no town because other than the werewolves and pixie gnomes and whatever other creatures are out here, there is no other civilization of people like us. I've been educated and done my homework of this world. The goblins and trolls were a surprise, though, but I know what I'm talking about. "

"I didn't know there were werewolves out here, and yet they are. So just because you *think* you know everything, doesn't mean you do."

"Yeah, yeah, whatever," he rolls his eyes.

"Can you at least be nice enough to believe me about something for once? You don't see me going around thinking you're crazy, do you? You thought I was crazy about the pixie gnomes, but I was right. Believe me when I say I'm going to be right about the town, because I sure as heck do not want to go through it, even though we have to. It wouldn't hurt to trust me for once, you know."

"So what if one person doesn't trust you one time? It's not the end of the world. You don't have to get all upset about it. We wouldn't even be out here if it wasn't for you, so excuse me for going off what I know."

"This isn't my fault! I wasn't the one who broke the balance. *Your* darkness is coming into my kingdom! If anything, your side did something to mess up the balance!"

"It's not *my* darkness. I didn't create it or do anything to upset the balance, nor did anyone on my side!" Kieran breaks off a low-hanging branch, shriveling it up. "You're *weak*. Just like your kingdom, which is why the balance broke so easily. I've done nothing but save your butt so many times, without a thank you, I might add, and you go and try to make excuses for everything because you can't handle the simple truth."

Ciana takes a deep breath, caught off by his statement. Iris and Liko look between them intently.

"Mister, you need to not say those things to her. It's not nice," Iris speaks up.

"It's Your Highness or Prince Kieran to you, *pixie*," Kieran spits, throwing the shriveled branch to the ground near them.

"Don't speak to her in that tone," Liko confronts.

"I do what I want."

"You two should go," Ciana whispers to the pixie gnomes, silent tears rolling down her cheeks. They disappear without another word. Ciana lets another branch snap into Kieran's face.

"Will you cut that out?"

"No. It serves you right." She wipes her tears away, straightening her posture.

"No wonder no one in your kingdom likes you. You aren't a very good Princess of Light and Goodness like you should be."

"I never said they didn't like me."

"Didn't need to. I put it together. It's the only reason you'd pretend to be all nice and goody-goody there but not out here. You aren't as nice as you should be."

"Congratulations, I'm so happy you figured that out. I'll be sure to add you to the list so I can be extra nice and cheerful the next time we ever see each other. Which won't happen after we fix the balance." Ciana smiles, sarcasm in her voice.

"Good, I can't wait until I don't have to see you anymore. I'm sick of everything about you. We better not see each other again once we're back."

Patches runs up to Ciana, whimpering slightly from Kieran's upset tone. Picking him up, she holds him close. "Don't worry, he won't hurt you either, puppy," she reassures him in a hushed tone, scratching behind his ears.

Neither speaks again until the sun is high in the sky, beating down through the trees. Coughing and sneezing again, Ciana sits in one of the tree's shade, curling into a ball, resting her head on her knees as her headache begins to pound. Kieran throws his head back, making fists in the air.

"Again? We've already had to stop ten other times this morning. We'll never reach our destination at this rate!"

"What's wrong with you? I'm still sick, remember? Yes, I'm going to stop again. My headache is coming back as well, thank you very much. I'm weak, and it keeps getting worse. Luckily for me, Olcan's poison side effects have worn off some, so I'm not suffering from stomach pain anymore, and I'm not as bad as I was earlier, but I'm still not improving," she reminds him. "You were so considerate before, why stop now?"

Kieran gives her a sharp glare. "I just want to get this stupid thing over with, but can't with you stopping every single minute. Besides, I just have to make sure you live long enough to get to the fortress to fix everything."

"Right, I forgot. I can die after the balance is fixed, so you don't have to worry about anything." Ciana glares. Kieran leans against an adjacent tree, crossing his arms over his chest, examining her.

"You're still pale," he says bluntly.

"It's just my light."

"No, you're pale. Paler than you were before. You shouldn't be; you're not bleeding anymore. I made sure of that before I took off Olcan's bandage."

"I just told you I was still sick. Yeah, I'm still going to be pale—achoo!" She sniffs.

"No one gets pale just because you're sick. I know that much. It's not normal, and I know it's not from Olcan and his friend. You can't just be sick. What else is wrong with you?"

"Nothing. I'm just sick. You don't care."

"You're right, I don't. Sorry for asking. Can we go now?"

"Do I look like I'm ready to go?"

"No."

"Then there's your answer."

"Ugh!" Kieran kicks the trunk of the tree. Ciana steadies herself, standing.

"Fine. Let's go."

"Thank you. Now, I ask that we don't stop again except to sleep and eat."

"Whatever."

The sky changes to a deep blue, painted with streaks of red, orange, and pink as the sun slowly sets behind the horizon. Ciana's feet grow heavier with every step as they reach the edge of the forest. Patches barks, running into nearby bushes, followed by Kieran, leaving Ciana to straggle behind. A short distance away, near the base of some mountains, a proper town with brick and stone houses, similar to those in Ciana's kingdom, comes into view. Ciana gulps at the sight, half smiling as she looks at Kieran, whose mouth is a thin line.

"What did I say?" She coughs, sitting on the ground. "Now I can't go on today."

"We're a few minutes' walk from the town, you can make it and we can stay in a proper room for once," Kieran tells her, continuing ahead.

"No, Kieran. I can't go on today. I'm tired and feel worse than I did before. We stay here for the night, then tomorrow we can get clean clothes, good food, and deal with everything that may happen and go from there."

"Wouldn't Your Highness rather sleep in a bed for once instead of on the ground?" Kieran turns around.

"I've survived this long. Now, build a fire for us."

"Nuh uh, I'm going to the town."

"I said we're staying here."

"No, you said *you* were staying here. I'll see you in the morning in the town if you manage to survive the night." Kieran leaves hotly. Patches looks between the both of them, before curling up to Ciana.

"You trust me, right Patches?" He wags his tail. "At least someone does—achoo! I thought he was letting his real side come out, but I guess I was wrong. I shouldn't be too surprised."

"Why put up with him?" Iris's voice rings, popping up in front of Ciana with Liko.

"I need him to help bring back the balance between our two sides. Once that's over, we won't have to deal with each other anymore."

"He's just pretending. Pretending to be nice to you," Liko comments.

"You don't know that."

"But I do; it's obvious. Especially since he changed on you so quickly. He was tired of being nice."

"Sorry Liko, but I don't think that's it. I don't think he's that bad. He must have something on his mind or is just worn out, which is why he snapped."

"Miss, you've got to start trusting your gut."

"I am. I can tell he's not as mean and heartless as he seems to be, despite what he says. Whatever, some people can't change anyway, even the Prince of Darkness; it is his title. Now, do either of you know how to build a fire?" They shake their heads. "Great. It better be a warm night."

Patches shoots up barking, running around gathering sticks, piling them up.

"Patches, I can't make a fire. I've tried." Patches inhales deeply, breathing out flames towards the sticks, catching them on fire. Ciana's jaw drops, watching the flickering flames. "What the—?"

"Cypups are amazing creatures. They have many a power." Iris smiles.

"Well, I knew that, sort of, but I didn't think fire breathing was on the list."

"You've got one special pup."

Patches curls up next to Ciana again, tail wagging with his tongue out.

"Thanks Patches, you're such a good boy."

"You look terrible, miss. You should get some rest."

"Achoo!" She sniffs, laying down. "I will, thank you. You guys get some rest too."

A drop of water falls on Ciana's face, followed by another and another. Waking up, she shields her eyes as she looks up at the foreboding rain clouds overhead; the rain falling harder, quickly putting the fire out. She grabs Patches, moving under the most shaded tree. Placing her hand on the trunk, she concentrates on the overhead branches, growing them thicker to fully block out the rain. Goosebumps running up her arms from the cold, Ciana curls into a tight ball, falling back asleep.

# Chapter Fifteen

Bird songs fill the crisp morning air, sun rays stream through fluffy white clouds. A cold, rough tongue licks Ciana's face, waking her up. She rubs Patches head, sitting up to avoid any more kisses.

"Morning, miss!" Iris yawns.

"Morning, Iris." Ciana smiles, looking down at the town, taking in a deep breath filled with the refreshing smell of rain. "Let's get this over with—achoo!" Ciana stands, making her way to the town.

She looks around at the brick buildings, the quiet air sends a chill up her spine as she ventures down the deserted street. A clothing store comes into view with an open sign flashing in the door. Ciana swallows a lump in her throat as she opens the door with her shaking hands. Besides the cashier, who has their back turned towards her, the store is empty. Ciana rummages through the clothes, glancing around her every so often.

"Oh look, you didn't melt last night," a voice laughs from behind. Ciana whips around, nearly slapping Kieran in the face with her hand, but he dodges her blow. "Hey, watch where you're smacking, Princess, it's just me."

"I know. Still would have slapped you. How'd you find me?"

"You're a female. All females are the same. You're always in need of a new outfit. I came here first yesterday myself, so I just figured you would too."

"Of course. We haven't had a change of clothes since you lost our bags. You're lucky I kept my money in my pocket."

"I kept us from drowning. I think that's a pretty good reason."

Ciana shakes her head, grabbing a set of clothes, setting them on the counter where the cashier's back is still turned. She rings the desk bell to get his attention.

"What can I help you—" The cashier turns, his green eyes darken when he sees Ciana, a smirk forming on his lips. "Well, well, well, look who we have here."

"I'd like to buy these clothes, please." She pushes the clothes towards him. *If you don't start anything then there won't be any problems. We can be in and out of here without a scene,* she reminds herself.

"Yes, I can see why," he says slowly, running a hand through his long blonde hair. He looks her up and down, taking in her dirty, worn out clothes. "Such a shame, we don't serve imposters here. You'll have to go to the next town. Sorry, not sorry." Ciana grabs the clothes off the counter, rolling her eyes. Kieran stops her as she tries to walk away, turning his attention to the cashier.

"She's not an imposter. She can buy the clothes, she has money."

"Oh, who's this you've got with you?" The man eyes Kieran. "A bodyguard? Very unlike you, Ciana. I don't care what you say, bud, she can't buy anything here in town. She's not welcomed."

"I'll buy it then."

"No can do. You're with her, so that automatically means a no for you too."

"You sold me clothes yesterday."

"I didn't know you were with *her* then. Be lucky I'm not asking for your clothes back."

"Let's try this again, shall we?" Kieran slams his hand on the counter, causing heatless black flames to shoot up on it. The cashier pales, jumping back. "She's going to buy the clothes or you and your whole store go up in flames, capisce?" Ciana looks at Kieran bewildered.

"She can take the clothes for free; I don't want her filthy money!" The cashier's voice raises an octave. "Just put the flames out!"

"Fair enough." Kieran waves his hand over the flames, extinguishing them, leaving the counter perfectly intact.

Ciana closes a dressing room door and rips the tags off the clothes. Changing out of her worn-out pants, the locket falls out; opening up as it hits the ground. Ciana stares at the picture secured inside, quickly picking it up and stuffing it into her new pants pocket along with her money. Leaving her old clothes in the dressing room, she returns to Kieran, who's waiting patiently, eyeing the shaking cashier.

"Good, now let's get some food." Kieran holds the door open for Ciana, letting her exit first. "How did he know your name?" he questions as they walk down the barren street.

"That's not the important thing right now," she whispers, looking up at the building they walked to, the loud chatter from inside seeping through the doors.

"'The Outkasts' Hash House', what a dumb name for a place. They even put the apostrophe in the wrong place." Kieran laughs, reading the sign out loud.

"No, they didn't." Ciana watches Kieran head up to the door, about to go in before he realizes she's not with him.

"Aren't you hungry?"

"Yes."

"Then come on, if you want food."

"I can't go in there, Kieran. You get us both food and bring it out here. I'll wait," she requests calmly, walking over to a bench under a window.

"You're kidding me, right? Are you really going to let what that doofus says bother you? You can buy things here."

"It's not that; it sounds full in there. If I go in, I probably won't come out alive."

"Don't be so dramatic."

"Please, Kieran?" Ciana gives him a pleading look.

"Fine, I'll get you food and bring it out here for you." He sighs, not wanting to argue.

"Thank you."

Kieran heaves a heavy sigh, pushing the doors open. Patches follows behind him. Ciana sits on the bench, fiddling with her hands in her lap. Laughter from inside grows louder as the door opens. A group of boys exit, spotting her. Ciana tries to avoid eye contact, but fails when the group surrounds her, forcing her to look up at one of the boys with short curly blonde hair and blue eyes.

"Well, well, well, what a sight. Never thought I'd see you way out here, Ciana." The boy laughs, forcing Ciana to her feet.

"I'm just passing through, Hamill," she answers, trying to release his grip on her shirt.

"You aren't anymore."

"Hamill, let me go, please. I'm not here for any trouble," Ciana begs.

Hamill drags her into the middle of the road, throwing her to the ground. One of the other boys runs into another building, coming out with more people, and then racing to the next establishment. He repeats the routine until all the doors from every building slam open; everyone files out to watch. Over Hamill's shoulder, Ciana sees Kieran shake his head as he makes his way towards her.

"Look who decided to join us, everybody! Her Royal Highness Princess Ciana!" Hamill announces to the onlooking crowd. "What happened, Princess? Get kicked out of your own kingdom?"

"Back off!" Kieran shoves Hamill back, helping Ciana to her feet.

"Who's this? I've never seen him before?" Hamill circles Kieran, a hand on his chin.

"You don't just go around and bully anyone you can find," Kieran shoots at him.

"She's not just anyone. She's a *nobody*."

"Kieran, don't!" Ciana pulls Kieran's arms down as he prepares to punch Hamill. Patches runs up to Hamill, growling at his feet.

"Get away, mutt." Hamill kicks Patches aside. Kieran swoops Patches up into his arms. "Kieran, huh?" The cashier from the clothing store runs up to Hamill, whispering something in his ear before rejoining the crowd. "Oh, I see, the Prince of Darkness," he mocks. "Now, how would you be so unlucky to wind up with Ciana?" Hamill walks up to Ciana, circling around her. "You wouldn't be out here for kicks and giggles, not with the prince. The only reason would be to save the kingdom. What mess did you get yourself into this time, decided to try to make friends with an enemy that backfired?" Everyone laughs. "You know you can't do things the way she did."

"The kingdom is dying, Hamill." Ciana straightens; he smirks.

"Are you sure it's the kingdom that's dying? Or you? 'Cause by the looks of things you might want to worry about yourself, not like you don't already. You're a very unusual pale, Ciana."

"Achoo!"

"She's sick," Kieran intervenes.

"She's dying, *Your Darkness*..."

"I wouldn't mock me unless you wish to lose your tongue," Kieran seethes, eyes narrow.

Hamill smirks. "I doubt you'd actually do that. I'm not scared of your threats." He scoffs a laugh. "Besides, the 'princess' here is the one who can't do anything right. She never could. She never will."

"That's not true, Hamill," Ciana shouts. "You know it's not. You've known me long enough to know that." Tears threaten to spill, but Ciana desperately blinks them away.

"How do you know him, Princess? How do you know these people?" Kieran shifts to better see Ciana's face, his gaze hard.

"I—"

"She's no princess!" Hamill interrupts, then juts a finger in her direction. "You stole the title! Took it because you wanted the power, and now look at you. You're paying the price for it."

"I didn't take it!" Ciana urges, her voice on the edge of pleading. "She got sick all on her own. I did nothing to her!"

Hamill steps closer, nostrils flaring with rage. "She never had a sick day in her life!" As he speaks, spit hits Ciana in the face, but she refuses to wince. "She took you in, Ciana. She treated you like a sister! But you betrayed her!" His words hit like venom, burning into her.

"What is he talking about?" Kieran asks.

Ciana shakes her head, refusing to look at Kieran. She knows if she does, if she sees the look of distrust in his eyes, she may break completely. "I did *not* betray her," she replies, ignoring Kieran's question. "She got sick on her own. Died on her own."

"Ciana," Kieran begins, voice soft with a hint of uncertainty. Ciana sniffs, daring a glance in his direction.

"The queen offered me the position," she goes on, holding Kieran's gaze. "I took it to try and help everyone."

The harsh scoff from Hamill forces her attention back to him. His brows raised accusatory. "Help? Really? Then why did you kick us out? That's the opposite of helping." Hamill advances on Ciana, forcing her to stagger backwards.

Ciana pants, searching for an escape. The only thing she happened to remember from the map was they *had* to go through this town. There was no way around it. But this is what she wanted to avoid. This is what no one was supposed to find out. She was cornered, just like when she first took the position of princess. She was the princess. She shouldn't be treated this way.

Lifting her chin, she glares at Hamill. "I didn't kick you out; the *queen* did."

"For you, Ciana!" Hamill shouts, startling everyone. "She did it for you. But why?"

"You know why," Ciana replies through clenched teeth.

"No, she did it because you wanted your new life to be perfect, no problems from us or anything else. A fresh start. It looks like it's not working for you now, is it?"

"I didn't want her to kick you out, but we needed to. To avoid any problems, but not because I wanted her to. We didn't need a riot to arise. It hasn't been easy trying to do things the way she did."

"Oh please." Hamill rolls his eyes.

"No, really."

"The two personalities," Kieran whispers, although no one hears him as Hamill continues.

"Ciana, you are not the Princess of Light. You never will be. You aren't worthy of the title. Heck, it isn't even your title! It's still Princess Leora's! You never had a proper coronation because you and the queen were too busy banning us from the kingdom. Nothing you do is right because you aren't the real princess! You can't even hold her power! That's why everyone's memory had to be erased, so we wouldn't know you were a fraud. The kingdom is dying because of *you*, Ciana. You're killing it by making things worse for everyone. We've been to the outskirts of the kingdom, we know how bad things are for everyone. We've heard their plans and thoughts with you ruling. You think you're helping it, but you're not!

"You know, you wouldn't even be here if I hadn't found you. I wish I could go back and change that, knowing what kind of person you'd grow up to be. You came out here to fix the balance you broke, but the king and queen won't help you. Why should they? I don't get why Olcan didn't get rid of you when he had the chance. He mentioned he was going to the last time we went to visit the kingdom. You are a disgrace to everything you try to stand for," Hamill lays out for her. Tears stream down Ciana's cheeks, biting her lip as she looks over at Kieran who looks at her, confused yet as if everything was making sense.

Kieran whips his direction back to Hamill. "You know Olcan?" Kieran questions, trying to wrap his head around all this information.

"We accidentally wandered into his village one day. As outcasts, we got along quickly. We have lots in common, compared to our own Princess here," Hamill answers, keeping his eyes locked on Ciana.

"Forget the food, Kieran," she swallows. "We're going." Ciana turns on her heels.

"You don't want to go with her, Your Darkness. She's taken you on this long journey for nothing. She's not anything special I'd waste time with."

The crowd thins, everyone glares and spits at Ciana as she walks past them down the street. A scuffle forces Ciana to pause, shifting to look over her shoulder where she sees Kieran, nose to nose, with Hamill.

"Kieran!" she calls, hoping he hears the desperation in her voice for him to back down, to let it go.

Kieran sneers, chest rising and falling rapidly. "*You're* not anything special. *You're* a waste of time and a waste of a life. A life that could have been given to someone who's actually worth something."

Hamill's face reddens. "Why you—"

"I'd choose your next words and move carefully."

"Kieran," Ciana tries again, softening her tone. Holding her breath, she watches as Kieran finally blinks out of his rage-induced haze and brushes by Hamill, setting Patches back on the ground.

Ciana sniffs, wiping her tears in silence as they reach the end of town at the bottom of the mountain. Kieran looks at the ground in front of them before he glances back at the town.

"May I ask what happened?" he requests in a soft voice.

*I can't keep the truth from him now. Not after what was said in the town.* Ciana sits against a boulder, curling her knees to her chest, patting the ground next to her. Kieran understands and sits down.

"How much do you want to know?"

"Everything."

Iris and Liko appear at Ciana's feet, sitting to listen too; Patches curls up next to Kieran.

Ciana rubs her legs, gathering her thoughts as she digs her foot into the dirt. Kieran patiently waits as she takes a few deep breaths. "I was abandoned when I was a baby, left for dead in a dumpster. Hamill found me and took me to the orphanage, where I grew up with him and the others. Having nothing, I wanted to work at the palace so much. The queen's daughter, Princess Leora, was the nicest person one could ever meet. She'd visit everyone in the town, especially us orphans. You could say I wanted to be her when I grew up. She was the image of perfection. She loved everyone, and everyone loved her. She never lost her temper or anything with her people. When I was finally old enough, I got a job as a maid in the palace. It was a dream come true. The princess treated everyone as family; she treated me as if I was her own sister, even making me her personal lady's maid."

Ciana takes a shaky breath. "One day she got sick. She was coughing, shaking, fever, all of it. She looked terrible. Everyone tried to heal her, but nothing was working, and she kept getting worse. The queen even came to try to help heal her daughter—she was all she had left for family, but even she couldn't fix her. She got so sick she eventually passed away. It devastated the kingdom. Heartbroken, the queen offered me the crown since I was closest to Leora. I knew all the things she did and how she did them. I knew how she behaved and interacted with her people. I knew her schedule and just... everything since I was always there with her. The offer surprised me. I thought she was joking, but after careful consideration and contemplation, I agreed. It would be easier for me to fill in since I knew what and how to do everything compared to trying to train someone else. Everyone was furious, thinking I had poisoned and killed the princess, knowing I would take her place. I didn't. I loved her; I could never betray someone I cared so much for. She was the sister I never had. The kingdom was on the verge of rebelling, so to prevent any damage, the queen created a potion and distributed it to everyone as a new drink. It wiped their memories of Princess Leora, so I was the only princess they knew.

"For some reason though, not everyone was affected by the memory spell. Hamill and many others still remembered and were even more furious. The queen banished them from the kingdom to avoid any contention and such. We couldn't kill them—they had every right to be angry—but we couldn't just lock them up either. If one were to somehow escape or get a message out to someone who'd believe them, we would be back at the beginning. That's why the queen put them out here. Far enough not to cause trouble, but if they were to step foot back in the kingdom, they'd be killed. She couldn't make another potion either. For us, if one potion doesn't work, then it means almost no potion will. We're not sure as to why, but we suspect it may have something to do with their healing power, making them immune to any harmful or altering substances."

Ciana takes a staggering breath. "Fearful for my safety, the queen made a potion for me to help protect me, but it was only strong enough to protect me from one person. Unsure how the King of Darkness would react to the new contention, the queen made it so the potion protected me from him, so he couldn't lay a hand on me. I've tried so hard to do things and be like Princess Leora, knowing things had been perfect under her reign. The laws, distribution of food among my own people, funds to provide better living conditions and roads, the school system for the children. But no matter how hard I try, everyone still doesn't trust that my intentions for all of those things are for them. They think I'm changing and providing funds for what I want, when I want, instead of listening to what they need. They don't even think I spend their money to help them when that's all it goes towards. They think I spend it on myself, buying things to add to my 'luxurious collection'. I haven't bought anything for myself since I've been in rule. Nothing seems to work right for me, and I don't know what to do. My own people don't come to me for help. A few have even tried to assassinate me just so someone else can be in power. Wanting someone who they know will listen to their needs. 'One of their own,' as they say. They just don't remember that I *am* one of them." Kieran's eyes stay locked on Ciana, taking in every word she says.

"I'm so sorry, Ciana. I can't even begin to imagine what you've had to go through," he whispers, careful not to interrupt, his eyes saddening.

More tears roll down her cheeks. "Since I wasn't born in the royal line, I can't even hold all the power that the princess held. You asked what was different between my power and the queen's? Technically, the queen's power and the princess's are the same, but since I had to be given their power, not born with it, I can't do all the stuff the queen and Princess Leora could. I never will. There is so much they can do with their power, like creating life all at once. I can't do that. I can only bring life to singular things. If I held all that power in me, I would die. That's what the heart is for, Kieran. It helps hold and regulate my power so I can keep the necessary ability to separate myself from everyone else."

"The power to bring life," he whispers.

Ciana nods. "The queen gave it to me, but in return, I had to have my life intertwined with the heart. That's why it's so important. I don't keep the kingdom alive, but I hold the power that helps our kingdom flourish with ease. If the heart dies, I die. If something happens to the heart, it'll affect me. I think that's how I knew something was wrong to begin with. The heart somehow felt the darkness and was triggered by it, but it's gotten worse, Kieran. Something is happening to the heart; I can feel it. It's affecting me. Whatever it is, it's killing the heart. It's killing *me*. That's why I'm pale, sick, and weak. I'm dying, Kieran, and there's nothing I can do to save myself or the kingdom." Her voice chokes, tears flowing freely.

"Why do you think we're on this trip in the first place, Princess? To save your kingdom." Kieran rests a hand on her shoulder. "We'll make it to the queen and my father, and they'll help us fix it, so things go back to normal. That hasn't changed."

"Don't call me Princess. I'm not worthy of the title. Like Hamill said, I was never properly crowned; I've just been filling in. You know neither of us can enter the fortress unless it's both the prince *and* princess. We just have you. They won't help us because I'm not the princess. Hamill was right. I'm nothing special. I don't know why I thought any of this would work." Ciana buries her face in her knees, crying. "I'm sorry I took you on this worthless journey, Kieran, but it's over. You should head back home."

"Princess—"

"Just leave, please. All of you."

"Ciana I—"

"Just leave!" she yells in his face, a sob overwhelming her. "It's over. Everything is over. Go away. Go home. Leave me be." She turns her face back to her knees, shoulders trembling, distraught.

Ciana begins to calm down, forcefully slowing her breathing after a few minutes. Ignoring the set of footsteps coming over to her.

"No, I'm not going back yet," Kieran says firmly. Ciana looks up at him through her blurred vision and red, puffy eyes.

"Why not? You couldn't wait for this whole thing to be over with, and now it is."

"It's not just your kingdom that will die if we don't fix this, Ciana. My people will suffer too. I won't let either of our sides die. There will be even bigger problems if the darkness consumes your side, completely getting rid of the balance. That's why we're out here in the first place—it's not over until we finish what we came out here to do and that's what we're going to do, Princess."

"I told you not to—"

"No, who cares if you weren't properly crowned? The queen knows, and you've been ruling as such for who knows how long; that makes you the princess."

"You know that's not how—"

"It doesn't matter."

"Kieran, I haven't done anything right since I've ruled. Ask the people, they'll tell you."

"Because by the sounds of it, you've been trying to do exactly what the previous princess did."

"Well, yeah. Everyone loved her and the way she did things was flawless. I couldn't get rid of what she was doing, but it's not working for me because—"

"Because you aren't her. Listen, Ciana, the only reason nothing is working and everyone doesn't like you is because you're trying too hard to be someone else. I saw it from the very beginning; it made it seem like you were hiding something. Sure, you were hiding that you're not the first princess, but no one else knows that, so you trying to keep things how they were, is making everyone think there's a bigger secret that you're hiding. Of course everything worked out for the other princess and everyone loved her, but part of that is because that's who she was and the perks of being born in the royal family, so nothing went wrong with her being the Princess of Light. You're trying to do things the way she did, but you can't because that's not your way. It's hers. You just need to be yourself, and when you do, things will work out like they're supposed to. You even admitted to me that you've enjoyed being able to be yourself."

"I know, but I can't be myself and rule the kingdom as the Princess of Light."

"Yes, you can! Your title doesn't define you. Just because you have the title of the Princess of Light doesn't mean you have to be all nice and friendly like it sounds. It just gives you the respect you need for being who you are. Especially if there was someone before you. You may know how she acted and was like, but your people don't, so for all they know, the princess doesn't have to be so jolly and perfect. You aren't her, Ciana, so don't act like it. You get to do things your way and make things better for your kingdom in your own way. Ways the previous Princess would never be able to do."

"We still can't finish the journey though."

"Yes, we can." Kieran crouches in front of her, gently grabbing her shoulders. He lifts her head so she's looking into his determined brown eyes. "Ciana, you've come this whole way to fix the balance, and without any doubts along the way! Goblins, trolls, werewolves—anyone else would have given up, but you... you never faltered. So what if that one boy thinks it won't work because you're not the 'real' princess? You've made it this far, so what's to say it won't work? The queen knows what happened and chose *you* to fill in for her daughter. You have the title and the heart of a princess, which is good enough for me. If it doesn't work, then we'll find our own way to get things back to normal without their help." Kieran stops, catching his breath as he holds Ciana's gaze. Keeping her locked on every word. As he exhales, his lips curl into a determined smile.

"We're almost there, Ciana. It's just over the mountains, and then we'll be at the fortress, but we're losing the daylight. I can't go alone, you know that—you've been reminding me all along we need to do this together—and even if we want to kill each other along the way, we're the only ones that can fix this whole mess. We started this together, and that's how we're going to finish it." Kieran gently wipes away her tears; standing up with a warm smile, he offers her his hand.

"Thank you," she sniffs, taking his hand.

"Of course. Now, let's start the climb. Come on, Patches."

"What a guy," Iris cries to Liko, dabbing the corner of her eyes with a little handkerchief.

"He really is something, huh," Liko agrees, wiping his own tears.

"Come on, you two!" Kieran calls to them.

"Coming!"

# Chapter Sixteen

The air thins the higher they climb up the mountain. An icy cold wind blows, causing Ciana to shiver and sneeze more than she already had been. Kieran grabs her hand, helping her up the last part of a ledge.

"This c-cold weather u-up here isnnn't doing anything to he-help me," she comments through her chattering teeth, wrapping her hands around herself, rubbing her arms.

"Oh, that reminds me!" Kieran pulls out a roll of gauze from his pocket.

"Wh-where did y-you get that?"

"I might have snuck it from the hotel I stayed in last night. Now gimme. This will give your hand extra protection until it's fully healed."

"You mean you s-s-stole it?" She gives him her hand with the cut.

"I'm borrowing it."

"Y-you can't steal things, Kieran."

"Pfft, so? Those idiots won't even know." He carefully and tenderly wraps the gauze around her hand, making sure it's secure. "As for keeping you warm, there's nothing I can do about that. We should have realized where we were headed and gotten something from the clothing store."

"Achoo!" Ciana sneezes in agreement.

"I'm sorry for pushing you. I didn't realize you were dying. I thought you were just sick, otherwise, I would have been more lenient and understanding to let you rest."

"Yeah, w-well, you didn't, s-s-so..."

"Hey, I'm trying to be nice and apologize here."

"I know. I a-appreciate it."

"Good. You were also right about the town of idiots. I'm sorry I didn't believe you, but now I know why you were so hot about it."

"I a-accept your apology."

"I am confused about one thing though. Our kingdoms couldn't expand past the forest border to help keep the balance, so how did the balance not offset when the outcasts were... well, outcast?"

" I th-think it m-m-might have to do with your power being able to easily overtake ours. S-so the amount of people that were cast out wasn't enough to s-set it off. I-I don't know a-all the details w-with that, but it's as if th-the town doesn't exist, magic wise."

"I see. That would also explain why it's not on the map."

"Th-the map was also m-made before th-the town was created. Now h-h-how far up do we have to g-go?" Ciana looks up towards the top of the mountain where snow glistens in the sunlight.

"All the way. Apparently once we're up the top of this first mountain, it's supposed to be flat. Not sure how that works or what that means, but okay." Kieran climbs higher in front of Ciana.

"Ugh, okay."

"Ciana, we're f-freezing!" Iris shivers. Ciana looks down at her and Liko, both turning a light shade of blue.

"O-oh, I'm s-sorry, guys. I d-don't have anything to wr-wrap you in. K-Kieran, do y-you have any pockets innn your sh-shirt?"

"What?" Kieran looks down at Ciana, his eyebrows squished together.

"Ne-never mind! Here." Ciana carefully picks up Iris and Liko with her shaking hands, setting them on Patches's neck. "Ho-hold on to Patches f-f-for now. His f-f-fur should give you a l-little extra warmth."

"Th-thanks, Ciana!" Iris forces a smile on her frozen face.

Ciana trails behind Kieran up the mountain. Her hands and fingers go numb from the biting cold air, causing her to lose her grip a few times. Kieran reaches the top of the mountain, disappearing from view.

"Kieran?" she questions after he doesn't come back into view. "Achoo!" She gasps in fright as her fingers slip from the rock. Kieran quickly grabs her frozen hands, pulling her the rest of the way up.

"You know, you shouldn't mountain climb when you're sick," he jokes.

"It's not ideal, n-no." Ciana sits, curling into a tight ball, rocking back and forth, shivering uncontrollably. "H-how are y-you not cold?" She eyes him enviously.

"I dunno," he shrugs, sitting next to her. Picking up a nearby stick, he starts to poke the snow.

"Can you m-make a f-fire?"

"The sticks up here are too wet from the snow, or else I would."

Ciana's face lights up as she watches Patches jump in and out of the snow, Iris and Liko shouting in disapproval. "P-patches! Come h-here, puppy." Patches jumps through the snow over to Ciana. She grabs the soaked pixie gnomes, setting their icy bodies on her leg. "C-can you m-make a f-fire?" He lets out a yelp, jumping back through the snow, digging around with his nose, putting together another pile of sticks, even taking the stick Kieran had.

"He's a dog. He can't make a fire, Princess."

"He's a special pup."

Patches takes in a deep breath, exhaling fire once again, drying out the sticks enough so they catch fire. Kieran's jaw drops open.

"How in the—?"

"P-pretty impressive, huh." Ciana picks up Iris and Liko from her leg, moving closer to the warmth, carefully setting them down next to her.

"Th-thank you, Ciana," Liko shivers.

"You're welcome."

"How did you find that out?" Kieran joins her, warming his own hands.

"L-last night."

"Ah, cause you don't know how to make fire."

"That's r-right." Ciana grabs her stomach as it growls. "A-any of you happen t-to have food?"

"No, we left town before we had a chance to grab anything," Kieran reminds her.

"Do y-you think there's anything up here w-we could cook?"

"Who knows. I'll go look. You stay here and don't die."

"Ha ha, thanks." Ciana laughs sarcastically while Kieran lets out a short chuckle, leaving. "Mmm, this feels so nice." She holds her hands out towards the dancing flames.

Kieran plops a couple of rabbits by the fire a short time later. "You know, couldn't you just grow an apple tree again?"

"You didn't eat the fruit last time, and I already told you it wasn't an apple tree."

"Well, I know, but it's food."

"Watch." Ciana grabs one of the sticks that didn't catch fire, growing it into a little tree with red fruit.

"See? Why couldn't you do this before?" He grabs one of the fruits, about to take a bite.

"Wait! Don't eat it!"

He lowers the fruit from his mouth. "Why not?"

"Break it in half."

Kieran does as she says, breaking the fruit in half, revealing a black withered inside. "I didn't do it."

"I know you didn't. I'm dying, so anything I bring to life won't be healthy on the inside."

"So, if you're dying, then why is your light that you emanate not dimming?" Kieran tosses the fruit into the fire.

"That's not how that works. Our light only goes out once we do."

"Well, how was I supposed to know?" Kieran starts to skin the dead rabbits. He's about to toss the skins in the fire, but Ciana stops him.

"Wait, give me those." She yanks the skins from his hands.

"What do you want rodent fur for? A purse?"

"Rabbits aren't rodents, and you'll see. Patches, do you think you could find me some vines or something similar?" Patches wags his tail, running off. "Can I borrow your knife?"

"What knife?"

"The knife you've been skinning all these animals with. What other knife would I be talking about?"

Kieran hands over his knife, allowing Ciana to break off a stick from the tree, carving it into a small needle.

"There's not enough fur to make you a coat or a blanket, you know."

"I'm quite aware of that, thank you."

"Where are you going to get vines or whatever, anyways? We're up in the mountains, covered in snow, with no trees that would carry vines. We're not in the jungle."

"Don't underestimate me and my puppy."

"Does he even know what he's looking for?"

"He can breathe fire. I'm pretty sure he knows what to look for."

Ciana walks over to a nearby snow pile, submerging the skins so they get wet from the snow, scrubbing them as best she can before bringing them back over to the fire to dry out. Patches comes running back, mouth full of brown roots that have the consistency of a vine.

"Awww, good boy!" Ciana coos, taking the roots from him, scratching his head. "Yes, you are. You're such a good boy. Thank you." His tail becomes a blur as it wags back and forth.

"Oh, please. You're making me sick."

"Good."

"Can I have my knife back?"

"No, I'm not done with it yet. You've already skinned all the rabbits, so you can start cooking them for us."

"I still need to gut them."

Ciana glances between the skinned rabbits and Iris and Liko. "Well, then it'll have to wait until I'm done."

"I thought you were hungry!"

"I am, but Iris and Liko will probably freeze to death before we starve."

"Fine."

Ciana turns her attention to the pixie gnomes. "Iris, Liko, do you have any powers?"

"W-we do." Iris chatters.

"Do you think you can speed up the tanning on these skins?"

"Anything for you, Miss." They climb up the skins, rubbing their hands against the coarse hair. In a waterfall effect, the skins become dry and ready for use within a few minutes.

"Thank you." Ciana smiles, setting Iris and Liko back by the flames, grabbing the rabbit fur and cutting it into smaller pieces. Kieran dully watches Ciana, following her delicate cuts through the skin.

"If you go any slower, *I'll* starve to death." he mumbles as she repositions the knife for the third time in the same spot.

"There," she tosses the knife in his direction after finishing her last cut. "Now you can gut the meat and cook it for us."

"Finally." Kieran slices a rabbit open while Ciana begins to sew.

"There, the meat is all cooked," Kieran tells Ciana, turning the meat on a stick.

"Hold on, I'm almost done." Ciana finishes her last stitch. "There! Iris, Liko, come here for a second, will you?" They walk over to her, still shivering. "See how these feel." She hands them the little winter clothes made from the rabbit skin.

"Oh, these are perfect!" Iris compliments, sliding the clothes over her head. "So warm, thank you!"

"You're welcome." Ciana looks over at Kieran, who's smiling at her before he quickly looks back at the food. "What?"

"Nothing, I just didn't know you could sew," he adverts.

"Uh huh." Ciana draws out, knowing he's not telling the whole truth. Not wanting to cause a disagreement she brushes it off. "You said the food was ready?"

"Yes, here you go." Kieran hands her one of the sticks with meat on it.

"Thank you." Ciana takes the stick, blowing air on it. Liko wanders over to her with Patches.

"May we please have some?" he requests. Patches tilts his head sideways, his eye growing big and cute.

"Of course you guys can. You don't have to beg." She laughs, tearing off some of her meat for Liko, Iris, and Patches.

"Thank you!"

"What are you doing? I thought you were hungry?" Kieran questions her actions.

"I am, but so are they. I can't let them starve."

"No, I guess you're right." He looks at his food thoughtfully before taking a bite with a shrug.

Patches finishes his portion of meat, whining as he goes up to Kieran.

"Nuh uh, you already got food, you're not getting any of mine. Look what you're making him do, Princess."

"I did nothing." Ciana consumes the last of her meat, tossing the stick in the fire. "I'm going to look around." She wipes her hands on her clothes as she stands up.

"What for? There's not much up here. I already looked. Besides, you should save your strength."

"I want to see for myself. I've made it this far and my strength isn't gone yet. I can manage."

"Wait, I'll come with you." Kieran sighs, throwing the rest of his meat to Patches, following behind Ciana.

"You guys stay here, we'll be back," she instructs Iris and Liko, rubbing her arms as she leaves the fire's heat, down a carved pathway in the snow.

"Oh, wh-what's down this path?" Her teeth chatter, pointing to another path breaking away from the one they were on.

"Are you cold already? Maybe we should head back so you don't freeze to death out here. The sun is getting ready to set anyways, we don't need to be lost in the dark."

"I-I'm fine. Let's go this w-way—achoo!" Ciana steps onto the path, her foot slips, causing her to fall back into Kieran. He grabs under her arms, helping her back on her feet.

"Princess, that's nothing but pure ice. We're not going that way. Let's head back before we get too far."

"We're not that far, let's just go down the other path."

Ciana yanks her arms out of his hands, turning around. Her feet slide on the ice again; she reaches towards Kieran to regain her balance, but she falls backwards. Kieran grabs her hand, attempting to pull her back up, only to fall down the path with her. Ciana screams as Kieran pulls her closer to his feet as they slide down the ice. Trees and rocks fly past them in a blur.

"Look what you did!" He scowls.

"I didn't do it on purpose!" she panics.

"You're more in the front, try stopping us!"

"What do you think I'm doing?" Ciana tries to dig her heels into the ice, but it's too smooth.

"Look out!" Kieran yanks Ciana up to his side, pushing her head down as a low tree branch passes over them.

"That hurts, you know, yanking my arm like that!"

"I'll let the next branch hit you then!"

The icy path twists and turns as they gain momentum. Ciana glances around, her eyes focusing on the never ending white in front of them as Kieran looks around for anything that could help.

"Are we going to the bottom of the mountain?"

"How should I know? I haven't been here before." Kieran reaches into his pocket and pulls out his pocket knife, stabbing it into the ice to slow their momentum. "Come on," he grunts, the knife freezes before it shatters. "Dang it!"

"You shouldn't have done that!" Ciana's eyes widen.

"I was trying to stop us, or at least slow us down! What are you doing to help?"

"Look what you did!" Ciana yells, gesturing to a long crack, created from the knife, breaking the ice down between them and up ahead.

"It's just a crack, what's the big deal?" A loud snap echos up ahead as the ice breaks, caving in slightly to create a hole. "Oh," Kieran breathes.

"We're going to die!"

"No we're not." Kieran randomly taps the ice next to him, creating another crack.

"Wow, another crack to help kill us. How helpful." Heart pounding, Ciana squeezes Kieran's hand as they slide towards the hole. The additional crack from Kieran breaks just right creating a little lip that slides them into the air, jumping them over the hole.

"You nearly killed us!" Ciana huffs, releasing her grip on Kieran's hand, nudging him slightly.

"Hey, but we're still alive!"

The icy path abruptly turns to snow as the mountain around them shifts into a field of white.

"That's not good," Kieran looks around them once again, digging his feet into the snow. "Dig your feet into the snow!"

"I'm trying!" Ciana tries to help, but the snow slides with them.

Kieran's face lights up. "A tree!"

"Where?"

"Up ahead!"

Ciana looks in the direction Kieran was watching. A baby tree barely peeks out of the snow.

"Don't you dare!" she warns.

Not listening, Kieran grabs her hand, grasping the little tree with the other as they slide past it. Heart racing in her numb chest, Ciana looks up at the little tree, Kieran struggling to keep a grip on it.

"It's not big enough to hold us."

"Yes it is, trust me," he grunts, focusing on his hand.

"Can't you let go? We've stopped sliding."

"Princess, do you see how steep this side of the mountain is? Even with ten feet of snow, we would still slide down."

"Okay, okay." Ciana wrinkles her nose, eyes watering slightly.

"You better not sneeze," he warns, adjusting his grip on the tree without letting go.

"I'm trying not to." Ciana looks at the glistening snow around them. They had just fallen, who knows how far, down the mountain. She'd hate to admit it, but was glad she was with Kieran right now and that he was keeping them from falling any further. He was keeping them safe. The thought alone helps her calm down.

Ciana's heart jumps at the sound of a small rip; looking up at the tree she sees it starting to uproot. "Kieran, let go of the tree!"

"No."

"We're going to fall anyways, let go!"

"No!"

A snap echoes, the tree breaks from the weight, dropping them down the mountain once again. Ciana squeals at the sudden drop. Kieran lets go of the broken tree in his hand, digging his hand through the snow, catching it on a small rock hidden underneath.

"Kieran!" Ciana panics out of breath, trying to keep her feet above a ledge. "Whatever you do, don't let go." Tears well up in her eyes.

"Okay, just don't panic." He looks down at the cliff ledge.

"That's a little hard to do right now." Ciana tightens her numb grip in his hand as her palm starts to slide. Kieran tightens his hand in return.

"I've got you, Ciana," he tells her in a tight breath. "I won't let you fall. We'll find some way out of this." His voice shakes slightly, struggling to hang onto her and the rock, sweat sliding down the side of his face.

"Achoo!" Her grip relaxes, nearly sliding out of Kieran's grip. She grabs his hand with her other frozen hand, unable to regain a good grip.

"You shouldn't have sneezed!"

"I tried not to!" Her hands slide in his palm. "Kieran?"

"Don't worry," he carefully moves his hand, trying to get a solid hold on one of her hands.

"Kieran?" She looks into his fear-filled eyes, tears streaming down her cheeks.

"Try grabbing hold of my wrist."

"That's a little hard to do when I can't feel my own hands." Ciana slides one of her hands up to his wrist.

The snow under her feet breaks off, falling over the ledge, nearly taking Ciana with it as her hand slips from Kieran's wrist.

"Careful! I won't let you go," Kieran repeats, trying to grab her wrist. "I can feel your hand slipping, grab hold of my wrist!"

Ciana tries to adjust her hand again, slipping out of Kieran's. She extends her arm to grab Kieran's outstretched hand, hardly touching his fingertips.

"Kieran!" she screams, falling over the cliff. The sound of Kieran calling her name echoes from the cliff above.

"Ciana!"

# Chapter Seventeen

Ciana's eyes flutter open, seeing the 100-foot cliff she fell from in the setting sun. Sitting up carefully, her numb body trembles in her wet clothes as she gazes at the white snow. Her head throbs as she struggles to stand up in the knee high powder. Tears well in her eyes as she looks towards the top of the cliff once more.

"Kieran?" she calls, her voice catching in her throat as the tears escape down her face. He was still on the top of the cliff. She was alive, but alone. She had no way of knowing if Kieran would look for her, if he thought she was alive. Rubbing her frozen, pink hands against her arms she looks around. The icy air stings the inside of her nose with every breath. She couldn't just stay here, she had to try to find some way back to the top, or at least somewhere warm; taking a chance, she forces her frozen limbs to move, staggering through the snow as she decides to follow the bottom of the mountain.

Ciana fights back her tears, a lump forming in her throat, not knowing where she was or where she's going, no sense of direction.

Lost and scared, she takes in her surroundings, hoping to find something that's familiar or helpful.

In the distance, a small cave comes into view, illuminated by the last ray of sunlight. She lets out a sigh of relief, reaching the little cave as the sun disappears. Looking for signs of life, she slinks slowly to the back of the cave and curls into a ball to warm up.

*Thump. Thump.*

The ground shakes violently, before settling down again, only to shake once again. Ciana moves further into the cave as a ginormous foot steps down in front of the cave entrance.

"Mmm, smell something," a deep voice bellows as if talking to someone.

"Bear?" an even deeper voice asks.

"No. Can't put finger on it." The ground shakes as the foot moves away, replaced by an enormous nose, sniffing the cave loudly. "Come from here."

"It bear. Cave small. Forget bear. We go or be late."

Ciana tries to stand as the ground shakes violently from the two beings walking away. Once they're far enough away, the ground no longer shaking, Ciana pokes her head out of the cave, examining the giant footsteps. They're easily wider than she is tall, very similar to the size of the trolls she encountered. Looking ahead, she notes each step is at least 20 feet away from the previous.

*Wherever they're going must have some sort of shelter and heat, right?* she convinces herself, venturing through the snow after the footprints.

A faint glow bleeds into the night sky from what looks like inside one of the mountain peaks with a chatter of deep voices. Relieved she doesn't have to walk much further, Ciana fights her frozen limbs, creeping up toward the peak, hiding behind a boulder.

At the edge of the crater, Ciana looks down where a large blazing fire radiates heat up to her, lighting up the faces of trolls and giants sitting and chatting around the basin as if waiting for something to start. Compared to the trolls, the giants—although standing two heads taller than the trolls—seem almost human; their hair neatly combed against their tanned skin; their clothes plaid and lumberjack looking, making it very obvious they were all males, and their shoes worn and torn, a few with a hole to let their big toes breath.

Yearning for more heat, Ciana sneaks closer, being sure to stay hidden. She peers around the rock, covering her mouth to hold back a gasp as she sees what's fueling the fire. Large green and blue bulbs periodically flash around the base of the flames, a silver-like dish slightly elevating the fire from the snow underneath. Ciana has only seen one of these in her life and it was located in the antique room back at the palace. One of the large green trolls nearby sniffs the air loudly, turning in her direction.

"Smell again," he informs the troll next to him, who sniffs as well.

"No smell. Puny brain tricking."

"No. Me smell too," a third troll agrees next to him, about to peek around the rock.

"Feo! We had dinner, stop sniffing about!" one of the giants calls. The troll backs off with a pout.

"Something here, Bergelmir!" He points to the rock.

"Unless it's a threat, I don't care. Now sit so we can begin." Feo takes his seat again.

"Nice, Feo," one of the other trolls grumbles. Ciana examines him, recognizing his bald head and worn leather shorts. Studying the other troll, she recognizes the multiple warts, his belly protruding out over his filthy pants. They were the trolls that had chased her and Kieran.

"Shut mouth, Kabandha. I no lost locket," Feo shoots at him.

"Cypup stole to magic peoples. Locket I get back. Peoples no need locket."

*That's why they chased after Patches. They were trying to get the locket back. It must be very important to them.*

"Quiet, you two!" Bergelmir yells, ending Ciana's thought; the ground rattles from the force of his voice. Ciana grabs the rock to help keep her balance, a loud crash echoing in the distance.

"Nice going, boss, you made another tree fall," all the giants laugh, making the ground shake even more.

Ciana loses her grip on her rock, sliding into the crater, trying to prevent any noise. She looks up at the trolls and giants near her, easing to her feet, not wanting to draw any attention to herself. Her already pale face drains further, turning her almost as translucent as frost as her eyes lock with the giant Bergelmir's. Forgetting how tired and weak she is, Ciana begins to run.

"Get her!" the giant orders, pointing at the fleeting Ciana.

Ciana looks around before sliding down a narrow opening in the crater to the peak's bottom. A stampede of trolls and giants chase after her, pushing and shoving each other in the process. The ground heaves so much, Ciana can hardly keep her balance. A hand grabs her wrist, pulling her into a nearby bush, covering her mouth before she has a chance to scream, the other wrapped around her waist.

"It's just me," Kieran whispers in her ear. Ciana quiets her breathing. She feels Kieran's heart beat rapidly against her back as one of the trolls stops in front of the bush, sniffing the air. Ciana twitches, wanting to run, but Kieran holds her in place.

"There!" The troll smiles, reaching a large green hand towards them.

Kieran lets go of Ciana, grabbing her hand and leading her away from the bush, narrowly avoiding the troll's grasp.

"Back here!" The ground vibrates again as the trolls and giants see them running away, fighting each other so they can grab the intruders. Kieran somehow manages to keep his balance, practically pulling Ciana along with him as he weaves through the trees.

"There's a cave up ahead somewhere!" Ciana informs him.

"I know, we're not going there, though!"

"Why not?"

"Just trust me." Kieran looks behind them, pulling her closer to his side as a rock lands where she would have been. "Over here!" He pulls her to the bottom of one of the mountain peaks. He touches the side of the mountain moments before the ground shakes more violently than the giant footsteps, a rumbling sound in the distance. "Hurry, this way!"

Ciana topples over, struggling to stay on her feet. Kieran grabs her hand, helping her back up and through the snow.

"What did you do?"

He smiles. "With darkness comes destruction."

"And?"

"Escape first, explain later," he says panting, glancing behind them. Kieran's eyes widen, pushing Ciana aside and to the ground.

A giant green hand wraps around Ciana's body before she has a chance to get up, binding her arms to her sides.

"Finally," the troll breathes in her face. Ciana holds her breath, wrinkling her nose as the troll talks to her. Lungs screaming for air, Ciana releases her breath with a cough as the hand holding her begins to tighten. She peers around for Kieran. Her eyes land on him, clutched in a giant's hand.

"Kieran!" she calls, using the air remaining in her lungs. Taking an agonizing gasp as she tries to take a breath. The hand is too tight, and only growing tighter as she fights. Her vision darkens around the edges, her insides feeling as if they're about to collapse. The rumbling in her ears must be her heart urging to survive. But then, the rumbling grows louder... and louder still. Dizziness rushes over her, her body fighting for life but wanting to give up all the same, but Ciana manages a heavy blink to focus her fading sight as the giant beside her falls onto his back, motionless, and Kieran wiggles free from the large hand.

"Kieran," she says his name again, pleading for him to help her, but there's not enough air to project it.

"What do?" the troll bellows.

"The same thing I'll do to you if you don't let her go right now!" he threatens.

Another giant approaches, falling to his knees beside the one who held Kieran. He touches the motionless giant's neck, then releases an anguished cry. "Bergelmir is... dead."

The tension around Ciana vanishes, and the troll staggers back. Ciana inhales a breath of relief, before releasing a scream; plummeting to the ground. Kieran catches her in his arms, breaking her fall.

"We've got to go." He smiles, setting her on her feet, grabbing her hand once more before running away from the trolls and giants.

"They're not following us, why are we still running?" Ciana asks through her breaths. "And what is that rumbling sound?"

"That's what we're running from."

"Okay, but it sounds almost like..." Ciana's heart pounds. "Oh, you didn't!"

"Oh, I did, now, more running, less talking."

"We can't outrun an avalanche! We need to move to the sides!"

"There are no sides!"

The avalanche gets louder, the ground jumps like it's ready to break apart. Kieran glances behind them, quickly wrapping his arms tightly around Ciana.

"Hold on tight!" he instructs.

"Why?" Ciana looks behind just in time to see the rolling snow nearly upon them. She wraps her arms around Kieran who tucks her head close to his chest. The snow pulls out from underneath them, rolling them under the sea of white, burying them alive.

# Chapter Eighteen

"Is she okay?" a mousy female voice asks.

"She's fine."

"It's been a long time, and she hasn't woken up yet."

"She just needs to stay warm." A male sighs. If it wasn't for the deepness of the voice, Ciana would have thought it was Liko talking.

"You sure she ain't dead?" Another male voice, more high pitched. She was sure that it had to be Liko.

"She's not dead. Her light is still glowing and she's breathing," Kieran's voice whispers, almost as if he's reassuring himself.

"Then why hasn't she woken yet?"

"She's been through a lot and she's already been dying. It's going to take her some time. Now give her some space."

"We're hardly taking up any space. We're pixie gnomes!" Liko scoffs.

"Right, I'm sorry."

"No, you're not, you big lump of coal!"

"Be nice," Ciana mumbles, listening to the voices. She hears Kieran's familiar chuckle before a cold tongue runs up her cheek, waking her up. "Awww, Patches." She opens her eyes, tilting her head up so she can see her puppy, scratching the top of his head. Her eyes fall on Kieran, who gives her a relieved smile, a raging fire next to him. "How did we survive?" She hoists herself into a sitting position.

"That pup of yours is quite amazing," Kieran answers with a nod towards Patches.

"What did he do?"

"Once the avalanche settled, he managed to sniff us out and dig a hole to us, allowing me to pull us out the rest of the way. Then he led me back to the top of the mountain."

"Told you he wouldn't slow us down."

"No, you were right. He still shouldn't come the whole way with us, you know."

"He just can't come inside, we can still leave him outside of the fortress. How did you find me after I fell off the cliff? Let alone know I was still alive?"

"It was actually Patches again there. He must have sensed something was wrong, because not too long after you slipped out of my hand, he came and helped me get somewhere safe, then immediately went looking for you. I followed him and came across you running from the trolls and giants. He ran off when I went to you and must have found somewhere safe until the avalanche settled."

"It's amazing." Ciana sighs, moving closer to the fire.

"Not as amazing as you."

Ciana holds back a laugh. "I'm sorry?"

"Ooooo," Iris and Liko breathe.

"I mean in the sense that you're dying, yet there's so many things we've come across that would've, could've, should've killed you, yet you're still here... still alive. That's pretty amazing for someone who is dying. Someone must really want you alive," he quickly adds, his red face hard to distinguish from the flames.

"Or someone really wants me dead," Ciana counters.

"Why do you say that?" He looks back at her.

"We weren't supposed to come across any danger, yet every day there's something that comes up trying to kill us, or me, since you seem immune to everything that's happened."

"Well, either way, it's been quite the adventure, and you should get some sleep." He changes the subject, watching her yawn.

"I will." She lies next to the fire.

"We'll reach the fortress tomorrow, and then everything will go back... to normal," he trails off.

"I hope you're right. Goodnight, Kieran. Thank you."

"Goodnight, Princess."

# Chapter Nineteen

Ciana wakes up the next morning to the birds singing, the morning sun reflecting off the snow. Sitting up, she warms her hands next to the fire which managed to stay burning through the night. She looks over at Kieran, who's sound asleep, Patches curled up next to him with Iris and Liko leaning against his fur in their new clothes. A smile spreads across her face as she watches them; pulling her knees to her chest, the locket digs into her leg, reminding her that it's there. Reaching into her pocket, she pulls out the pendant, tracing the silver floral carvings engraved around it. Her heart sinks as she runs her finger over the locket's small latch. Opening it like a book, she admires the picture inside of the Queen of Light, Princess Leora, and a baby troll.

*It's starting to make sense. They came after us to retrieve what they have of the Queen and Leora. The fire plate must have been given to them from the Queen or her daughter. To provide them endless heat against the cold.*

Her eyes settle on Princess Leora's beautiful blue eyes looking back at her. Her arms gently wrapped around the baby troll sitting on her lap. The queen's eyes look lovingly at her daughter, her own arms wrapped around her. Tears well in Ciana's eyes as she thinks back to when Leora told her when she had this photo taken and how much it meant to her to help the trolls. It reminds her of how amazing the princess was.

"You were so perfect, Leora. You never had problems. Everything worked out for you, even when you made a mistake," Ciana whispers to the picture. Her gaze drifts to the beautiful queen. "My queen, why did you think I could rule in place of her? I'm nothing but a mere commoner, a simple maid. What made you think I could be a princess? I haven't done anything right. Everything's been worse since I've been in rule. My people don't trust me like they did with Leora. I shouldn't have agreed to take the title. I'm not fit to rule. I'm not a princess. I'm nothing like Leora."

*Of course you're not.* Leora's warm, soft voice comes to mind. *You're not me. You're Princess Ciana.*

"Same thing. I don't want to get rid of your ways, they worked perfectly. I want to do everything you did."

*You can't. You know this.*

"Yes, I can. I have been for 200 years. I have been during this journey."

*Have you? What have you done on this journey that would be in my way?*

Ciana thinks back to the beginning of the journey. There were the bears; they wanted her to heal their cub. Ciana had pity for them, she had an idea of how it feels to lose a loved one. There were the goblins; she couldn't risk Kieran's life, so she fought and won. Then there was Olcan; yes she was under an enchantment, but she tried to be friends and prevented Kieran from killing him. Then there's... Kieran. She's had to trust him this entire time.

"I've done everything you'd do, Leora."

*Think again.*

Ciana goes back through the events. She was wrong. Leora was deathly afraid of bears after an incident happened to her when she was younger. Ciana recalls a time where a stray bear found its way into the town. Leora had her guards shoot it in an instant. She would have had Kieran kill the bears on sight on this journey. Yes, Ciana herself was scared, but she didn't want them dead. Leora would never have the bears lead her, let alone revive a cub. She would have left it dead. She wouldn't have compassion towards them like Ciana did. Leora wouldn't have been able to fight the goblin. She was given sword training but never had to use it. If her life was at stake, she would have mindlessly killed the goblin. Ciana fought and figured out how to overpower the large goblin through her own thoughts and instincts. In her own way without the loss of an innocent life. Leora would have willingly befriended Olcan, she would have given him another chance if he had entranced her. If he tried to poison her, Leora would have him tried for murder even though he's not part of the kingdom. Ciana wouldn't and she didn't. She wouldn't let Kieran kill him. Then... Kieran. Leora had always talked about Tenebris and how she hoped nothing would come up that required her to work with them. She would say she would never ask for their help and would figure out the problem herself. She said if the balance broke, she wouldn't take the journey with the prince. No matter what her mother said. She would never trust them. Not after they killed her family and forced her mother to leave her. Ciana had no choice. She was brave enough to ask and to go on this journey with the Prince of Darkness himself. Ciana had to make that trust, and she knew she would trust Kieran repeatedly after all they've been through.

"I have done everything in my own way," Ciana verifies.

*So why haven't things worked out in the kingdom?* Leora's voice gently presses.

"Because I've been trying to be you instead of myself."

*Kieran is right. Nothing's gone right because I've been trying to do it Leora's way. Not mine.* Ciana thinks to herself as she wipes away her tears.

"Will I be able to fix everything when I get back? Will my people listen to me? Even if I do do things my way, will I help the kingdom or still make things worse?"

*All things will work out. Just be yourself.* Ciana closes the locket with a snap, stuffing it back into her pocket.

Kieran stirs, sitting up with a yawn. He looks at Ciana then, at the fire. "Are you hungry?" He stands up.

"No." she answers, a hint of sadness in her voice.

"Hey, are you okay?"

"Yeah, just trying to wake up," she lies, avoiding his gaze.

"Okay. We can leave whenever you're ready."

"Patches!" she calls. He jumps awake, wagging his tail.

"Ow!" Iris rubs the back of her head.

"Sorry, Iris, I didn't know he would jump up like that. We're heading out if you're still planning on coming with us."

"Of course we're coming!" Iris and Liko jump up, clambering onto Patches, who trots after Kieran. Ciana follows after them through the mountains.

"I heard what you were whispering to yourself this morning," Kieran admits.

"Did you n-now?" She shivers, rubbing her arms.

"I did, and if I'm being honest, I think if anyone were to rule over a kingdom, you would be the perfect person for the job."

"You're j-just saying that—achoo!"

"I'm serious. You're thoughtful and caring of others, but also know how to stand up for yourself and not be a pushover; every good ruler should be that way. The queen saw that in you, which is why she asked you to take over."

"Y-you don't know i-if I'm like that."

"And what if I do?"

"It s-still wouldn't make a difference. It doesn't m-matter if you think I'm a good ruler; my people have t-to think that."

"And they will when we go back. I've honestly enjoyed this version of you. With you being your natural self. Not forcing yourself to try to be the goody-goody princess you think you're supposed to be, always being nice and proper. If you rule as yourself, I know your people will know what a good ruler you are." He gives her a warm smile, which Ciana returns. They hold their gaze with each other before Ciana turns away, her cheeks flushing.

"Gasp! Did you see that?" Iris whispers to Liko from behind.

"I did!" he whispers back. "This is why we stuck around." They giggle. Ciana turns to look at them, shaking her head.

*He likes this version of me? He knows that my people will see I'm a good ruler? He was right before, he can't be wrong about this. If the Prince of Darkness can like me, then what means my own people won't? I believe him.*

The snow sparkles in the sunlight. Everything looks clean and beautiful despite the bitter cold air. Ciana looks around, memories of when she used to play in the snow with the other orphans comes to mind. Smiling at the thought, she slows her pace, allowing Kieran to walk ahead a little ways. With his back turned, she scoops up a handful of snow in her frozen hands, forming it into a ball; she throws the snowball at Kieran, hitting the back of his head.

"Hey!" He whips around laughing, scooping up his own snow, warily forming it into a ball as Ciana hurriedly forms another snowball.

"Get him!" Liko cheers.

"You wouldn't h-hit a p-princess would you?" She smiles.

"You threw one first, so it's only fair," he replies, gently tossing his snowball in the air.

"How a-about I apologize and w-we call it good?"

"That's not how it works."

"Okay, but I'm dying, so you w-wouldn't throw a snowball at me."

"Wanna bet?"

"No." Ciana throws her snowball first, hitting Kieran once again. Ciana tries to run away, but Kieran's snowball hits her in the back.

"Running away is cheating!"

"No, i-it's not!" Ciana darts behind a boulder, forming another snowball. She comes back around, arm up and ready to throw it at Kieran, but he's no longer there. "K-Kieran?" She walks out a little more, searching for him. Cold snow hits her in the back, where Kieran is coming out from the same boulder.

Ciana runs towards him, throwing her ball so it hits his arm, running away to gather more snow in her cold, pink fingers. Kieran comes back from behind the boulder, throwing his ball at her. Ciana turns her body so it hits her side; she raises her arm up, breathing in too much cold air, triggering a coughing fit. Kieran stops making his next snowball as he watches her crouch over, hacking into her arm.

"You good?" He jogs over to her. Ciana nods in response, her cruddy cough straining her stomach. "Arms up, remember. It'll help."

Ciana listens, raising her stiff arms above her head, relieving her cough. "There, better?"

"Yes," she says on a strained exhale. "Th-thank you."

"I think we should stop before you have another coughing fit. Besides, you're shivering non-stop from the cold."

Ciana throws her snowball in his face with a laugh. "A little cold and cough n-never hurt anyone. It's all part of th-the fun."

"Good, cause I've got to beat you at this little snow war." He gives her a pleased smile, picking up some more snow as she backs away.

"Hey, there's n-not a p-point system."

"Yes, there is."

"S-since when?"

"Since now." He throws his snowball, hitting her square in the face. "That makes five points for me." He laughs. Ciana starts to pick up her own snow, dodging Kieran's next throw.

"Ha! You m-missed!" She taunts, throwing her ball at him before running behind the boulder once again, gathering more snow in her numb hands. She peers around the boulder to locate Kieran, but once again he's not there. Hand raised, she turns around to where Kieran is sneaking up on her. She quickly throws her snowball at him first, running back around the boulder, laughing. He throws a snowball at her back, and as she turns around, he slips on ice hidden by snow. Sliding into Ciana, he grabs her to catch his balance only to cause both of them to fall and roll down the mountain a little bit.

Kieran turns them both over at the last second when they stop rolling, so he lands on his back with Ciana landing on top of him, both laughing.

Calming down, they catch their breath; Kieran tucks a loose strand of Ciana's hair behind her ear, so it doesn't cover her face, causing Ciana to unintentionally lean into his warm hand, closing her eyes for a second. She looks back at a smiling Kieran; his soft expression gives Ciana butterflies in her stomach.

The cold air around them seems to warm slightly as everything nearby quiets like the world is holding its breath. Ciana's breath quickens as Kieran searches her eyes, the sparkling snow reflecting within them, before he glances at her lips. Kieran gently cups her face, making Ciana's heart jump. Both start to lean in towards one another. Kieran's warm breath dances with Ciana's, consuming the bitter air between them. The princess's chest tightens, shortly followed by her throat when they're inches away, Kieran's breath traces her lips. Ciana quickly turns away, getting off of the prince as she begins another coughing fit, walking a few steps away.

"Aww, come on! You're not supposed to cough! You were so close!" Iris exclaims from on top of Patches, throwing her hands in the air as they head down to them.

"What?" Kieran looks at her confused, hoisting himself up.

"Nothing!" She hides her giggle.

Ciana raises her hands over her head to stop coughing, but doubles over in pain.

"Ow," she whimpers, grabbing her aching stomach.

"No, don't bend over, straighten back up," Kieran instructs, walking over to help. Ciana shakes her head.

"It hurts," she strains to say through painful coughs. With every breath, the icy air digs into her throat, and the coughing that follows is shattering it, sending shards of ice ripping through her.

"I know," Kieran says, placing a hand on her back. "It'll help, though. I promise."

Ciana straightens, forcing her spine to stiffen as another cough erupts from her. Gasping for breath, her body shivers, the only warmth from the tender pressure of Kieran's hand on her.

"Now raise your arms again, but keep them up this time," he instructs. As Ciana raises her arms, his fingers trail the movement, guiding them until they wrap around her wrists to offer support. That touch alone brings on another coughing fit. But Kieran holds strong, not letting her bring her arms down. He's right once again. The extra space the posture provides makes the coughing less violent. Finally, the pain and annoyance in her throat eases; the coughing finally gone.

"Thank you," she says, her voice hoarse.

"Your coughing is getting worse. No more messing around," he replies, his hold on her wrists lingering before releasing them gently. Without his strength to hold them, Ciana's arms drop to her sides. Exhaustion settles over her limbs, but the soft smile Kieran is giving her—a mix of sympathy and concern—forces her to push through.

Kieran must have noticed her fatigue because he seems like he's going to reach for her, but then pulls away. "We're almost there," he says instead. "Just one more peak to climb, then the fortress will be at the bottom. We will be there by late afternoon."

Ciana nods, fighting against the tremors rolling over her as she follows behind Kieran. They climb the final peak, breathless and cold. Kieran offers her his hand as they ascend the last bit, helping her reach the top. Kieran takes his other hand and rubs it over her icy fingers. The gesture of warming her knuckles sends a rush of heat to her cheeks. Kindness from Kieran is rare, but when he shows it, something about his face changes. He almost brightens. As if the darkness in him is waning ever so slightly.

Another shiver wracks Ciana's body, jerking her hand from his grasp. She sniffs, drawing her palms to her chest to keep them warm, averting her gaze to take in the view from the top of the peak.

"It's a beautiful v-view from here. T-too bad it's s-so c-cold."

"Look! There's the fortress!" Kieran points to the bottom of the mountain at a pearly white mansion; ivy running up the tall pillars, looking barren and deserted. Despite being surrounded by trees and dirt, the whiteness of the building looks fresh and new, like no one's ever touched it.

"I-I don't unders-stand why they c-call it a f-fortress. I-I was expecting s-something more f-fortress-like."

"Who knows, but at least we found it. Come on, let's head down so you can warm up before you turn into an icicle." Kieran starts down the snowy path, Ciana following close behind.

"Achoo!" Her foot slips from her sneeze, sliding her forward into Kieran. "S-sorry," she apologizes, sniffing.

"You're alright."

They continue down the path, only for Ciana to slip again, sliding into Kieran once more.

"Ah s-sorry, sorry, sorry. A-apparently me and snow d-don't mix." Ciana laughs. Kieran joins in, taking her frozen hand so their fingers interlock.

"Try walking sideways. Like this." He turns to demonstrate. Ciana follows suit, holding his hand tightly.

The icy air warms the further they descend, the snow melting into green grass and flowers. Ciana lets go of Kieran's hand when the path dries out, the mansion growing bigger until it's towering over them at the bottom.

"We made it," Ciana breathes, holding her shaking hands out in front of her.

"Are you still really cold or are you nervous?" Kieran eyes her hands. "Both—achoo!"

"There's nothing to be nervous about. We made it to our destination! We'll go in, get things sorted out and go from there. Back to our lives." His voice fades as he looks at the mansion, a frown replacing his smile.

"That's w-what I'm worried about." Ciana plops down in the grass, exhausted, taking in the marvelous structure in front of them. Kieran joins her.

"Everything will work out. I know it will, and everyone will love you. And if they don't, then I can always come over and threaten them too," he jokes.

"You can't do that." She nudges him.

"I know, but if they ever need a push, you know who to call."

"I'll keep that in mind, but I doubt I'll ever need to."

"Whatever you say."

They sit in silence as Ciana continues to stare at the mansion. Her heart races, knowing this will be the first time she'll see the queen since becoming ruler. Kieran watches her breath quicken, following her gaze to the building. He gently places a hand on her arm, almost instantly calming her down.

"Are you ready to end this whole mess?" he asks, gently.

"Let's get it over with."

# Chapter Twenty

Kieran helps Ciana up, hesitating to follow behind her. She glances over her shoulder, trying to read his face as she stands before the two wooden doors.

"Are you scared?" she asks.

"No, I'm not scared. I'm just... preparing myself." He struggles to smile, meeting her at the front doors.

"Okay," Ciana turns to Patches. "Patches, you need to stay here with Iris and Liko." He whines. "I'm sorry, but only we can go in. We'll be back out. That goes for you two as well," she points at Iris and Liko.

"The last time you said that, you almost died. We can come," Iris insists.

"That wasn't planned, this is different. I promise we will both be back. Just wait here."

"Fine," Iris pouts, crossing her arms.

Kieran holds his breath as Ciana knocks. When no one answers, Kieran almost seems relieved. He steps back like he wants to leave, hesitating before he grabs the door handle. It glows a midnight black at his touch, and the door swings open. They look inside at a tene-brous open space, holding nothing but a staircase leading to a second floor. Even in the dark, Ciana can tell that the inside is just as clean and pure looking as the outside of the building. A looming sense of unsuspecting stillness causes the hairs on Ciana's neck to stand. She hears Kieran take a staggering breath before stepping in, his expression darkening slightly. Ciana takes a few steps after him, stopping short, looking around the room. A shiver runs down her spin, an uneasy feeling forming in the pit of her stomach.

"Something's not right," she comments.

"How so?" Kieran cocks his head, turning to look at her.

"I don't know. This just doesn't feel right. Something's off." Her eyes follow faint lights leading up the edge of the stairs.

"Maybe we should go, we can find our own way to fix the balance." Kieran heads back to the door, pulls on Ciana's arm for her to follow as he passes by.

"No, Kieran, we can't leave now. We've made it this far."

"Are you sure?" he asks, disappointment hidden in his eyes.

"I'm probably just overthinking things and tired from the trip. Let's go upstairs."

Ciana heads up the marble stairs, Kieran at her heels. A single pair of doors greets them at the top. Ciana stares at the white polished doors, hesitating to open it.

"Whenever you're ready, Princess." Kieran lowers his head.

Ciana puts her hand on the doorknob. It glows a bright white at her touch, triggering the door to slowly swing open. Ciana scans the room. Circular lights line the edge of the floor, gently illuminating the polished room. A trail of subtle wires run along the ceiling to the far end of the room where the Queen of Light sits on a cushioned, metal throne; the light gray metal is lined with lights, glowing a deep red, except two bulbs next to her shaking hands that are glowing yellow. Her long white dress elegantly drapes to the floor, wrapping around her feet gently; her long glowing white hair blows around her fair-skinned face in an invisible breeze, her blue eyes bright against the white surrounding her. Next to her sits the King of Darkness on a throne made of rich black wood; his jet black hair messy like Kieran's, a midnight cape wrapped around him, shadowing his already tanned complexion. His dark eyes, somehow managing to darken as an unusual smile widens on his lips. Ciana stares into the room, the uneasy feeling intensifying as she looks at the queen's face. From the distance, it seems as if the queen is concentrating on something. Looking back at her hands, she sees them shaking slightly.

"Kieran, I can't go in there," she whispers to him. "It doesn't feel right. It doesn't... look right."

Kieran grabs her shoulder, turning her so he can look into her eyes. "Trust your instincts, don't go in if you feel like you shouldn't. Please," he whispers back with pleading eyes.

"Kieran!" the King of Darkness yells across the room, his smile faltering slightly. "Come in, my son! Don't keep us waiting! It's rude!"

Head high, Kieran walks into the room, leaving Ciana frozen outside the door.

"Ciana, my dear! Please come in! Join us!" the Queen of Light offers sweetly. Kieran looks over his shoulder at Ciana.

"Kieran, eyes on me!" the king yells again, forcing Kieran to turn back around. Ciana takes a deep breath, pushing away the uneasy feeling.

*I don't know what I'm so worried about. I'm just walking into a room to get a problem fixed. I've survived goblins, trolls, and giants... werewolves, an avalanche, vindictive people. This is nothing compared to that. I can do this. This is all for my kingdom and the people,* she reminds herself, filling her lungs with a brave breath, following after Kieran. The door closes behind her with a subtle click once she's far enough in the room.

Ciana looks at the king, noticing a small trail of black leading from him toward the opposite throne. Her eyes follow the path as it branches across the queen's dress. She hadn't seen it from the doorway, but now, up close, it stains the ground like a curse.

"My queen?" She swallows, stopping her approach.

"Everything will be alright, Ciana. Don't worry," the queen reassures her through a pained smile. The king jumps to his feet, his cape whipping around him with the sudden motion, causing Ciana to stagger back a step.

"Well, that's enough reunion, let's get this party started!" He hoots and hollers. "Kieran, my boy! You somehow managed to hold up your part of the deal, bringing the 'princess' to me so we can finally rid this world of them and take their power. I was a little worried when I had to convince you to go with her after she had come to get you, but you pulled through. Well done."

Ciana turns to Kieran, opening her mouth, trying to say something, but can't as her chest tightens. She can't have heard correctly. In her mind, she replays his words, shaking her head at the realization that she had, in fact, heard right. Kieran was on a mission of his own. Not to help save their kingdoms, but one to bring her to her own assassination.

How could she have been so stupid, so naïve, to believe he had any good inside of him? Kieran himself said she was kind and caring, and now she sees how right he was. She has been too trusting, too occupied with getting to the fortress to save her people that she was completely blinded by the hope of him being different than she had thought. But she was wrong. All those questions he had asked, especially about her powers... he was trying to understand them before he took them. He's just as wicked and selfish as she should have believed. Like Leora would have. And that sends her mind spiraling.

A cold sweat breaks out on her forehead, her breaths coming in quick pants. Kieran was going to kill her! After everything... his care he had shown for her—Ciana's stomach knots. He was only caring for the power. Making sure nothing happened to her before he could take it. He was looking out for his own interests.

This entire time, Kieran was leading her death march, and she fell, with an open heart, right into the parade.

Fighting every nerve in her body, Ciana clenches her fists, forcing her eyes to meet Kieran's, but he can't even look at her. Instead, he looks away, and that makes her wonder if anything between them had been true.

"Father—" he starts.

"Shush, I'm complimenting you. I feared you would break our deal while rescuing her from my orchestrated mishaps—goblins, Olcan's poison, the river, and other unexpected dangers. Except for the trolls and giants, those were a nice surprise for me, too. Anyways, it didn't help that her goodness over here"—the king nods his head towards the queen—"was giving her life to keep Ciana alive longer either, but it would have been easier if she had died along the way, but you pulled through. Making sure I get to be here with you for this momentous moment. I'm very proud of you, son."

"Father—" Kieran tries to speak again. Tears burn Ciana's eyes. The whole journey was to get rid of her. She was right. But Kieran knew. He had to have known. He said himself that he just had to make sure she stayed alive long enough to get to the fortress. Ciana's heart quickens as new thoughts come to mind.

*But if the whole trip was to get rid of me and Kieran knew, why did he still help? He saved me in the river. He was worried about my cut and was so insistent that I didn't take anything from Olcan. And if the trolls and giants weren't planned, why would he still help me escape from them. He came looking for me after I fell off the cliff. Wouldn't it have been easier to say I had died on the journey instead of saying I died at my destination? The fear in his eyes on the cliff, did he really—*

"I'm not done yet!" The king's voice breaks her thoughts. "Now what was I going to say next? Oh yes, and how when she lost all hope, you got her to believe your good words of encouragement to keep her going to get here—brilliant! You had me thinking you were actually telling the truth!"

"They were—"

*No, he doesn't care. He lied to me. Lied to keep me going, just so his father can witness him fulfilling his duty as the Prince of Darkness.*

"STOP INTERRUPTING! You know what, let's just get this over with. Ciana, my favorite fake princess, look up at your dear queen for me, will you?"

"No," she spits between tight teeth.

The king's fists clench at his side. "I said, LOOK!" His voice echoes off the walls, vibrating through Ciana. With a fluttering blink, she obeys. The king forcefully pulls the queen to her feet, circling around her with a giddy laugh.

"My dear Queen of Light! For years we have kept this ridiculous balance between our sides, but no more! I'm tired of my power being limited, and now, once I kill you and the *princess,* your power won't have a body to cling to, allowing me to take possession of it and rule this world. Any last words for your non-daughter here? Not like any of it will matter."

"Ciana—" She smiles, holding back her own tears.

"Too long, goodbye, old enemy," the king interrupts, stabbing the queen in the side with a black dagger, pushing her to the ground.

Ciana cries out, collapsing to the ground as a sharp pain sears through her body. Her body falls limp for a moment as her energy and strength disappear, her emanating light flickering out as it does, before she gasps for air. Kieran runs to her, but she pushes him away.

"Don't touch me," she cries, laying down, taking staggering breaths. He nods, stepping back respectfully.

"One down, one to go," the king celebrates.

"Father, I can't—"

"First time jitters? Don't worry, it'll get easier. I haven't been so happy in my life! We've been waiting for this moment our entire lives, and now it's finally happening! Can't you just feel the power we'll have? We're one step away from ruling the world!" The king wraps an arm around Kieran, encouraging him. "She's even more vulnerable now than ever! I mean, look how weak she is! She almost died when the queen died! Just remember, the queen is dead so all her power went to Ciana, she's the last thing tied to it, so all we have to do is kill her and then the queen's power will be ours for the taking and our reign can begin. Make me proud, son. Show me that you are the Prince of Darkness."

"She's the strongest person I know," Kieran finally manages. Ciana's heart jumps at his words.

*He doesn't mean it. He just doesn't want my blood to be on his hands. He lied to me. He put me in danger. He wanted to get rid of me himself. He was just pretending to care, got me believing he was trying to help.* Ciana thinks back on their journey together, hoping to find all the times he lied to her. She takes a staggering breath. When she was in the arena with the goblin, he could have kept his mouth shut and let her battle on her own, but he didn't. Kieran offered her words of guidance and support. When the trolls were chasing them, he never let her falter. When Olcan poisoned her, Kieran was the one warning her not to trust the wolf; not to drink the tonic. He stood up for her in the village. He came for her when she fell down the mountain. Kieran had every opportunity to let her die, but he didn't. He *saved* her time and time again.

Ciana's dizzy mind floods with realization. *He didn't lie; he was telling the truth. He's a good person. He even tried to warn me not to come into the room. He knew what would happen. What he would have to do.* Her vision blurs with tears, but she blinks them away, looking toward the man she'd grown to know and trust over the last few days. *He never wanted me to die, even from the beginning.* She thinks back, remembering how he refused to go anywhere with her, threatening her life if she came back into his kingdom, how he even came to make sure it was actually the balance and not something else. *Even then he was protecting me, knowing how the journey would end for me.* Then, her gaze flickers to the king, a man who could only be filled with wickedness—not a single speck of goodness within. *The king made him do this. This wasn't Kieran's choice.*

"No matter, now do it!" The king backs off, clapping his hands and startling Ciana from her daze. Kieran approaches her slowly, turning her face towards him as he squats down next to her.

"I'm sorry, princess," he apologizes, his eyes sharp and cold. He grabs her neck with his hand, hoisting her to her feet. She puts her hands on his, trying to release his grip.

"K-Kieran," she gasps, her voice strained. "You... don't have... to do this." Tears stream down her face, Kieran's grip tightening.

"Yes, I do. I'm the Prince of Darkness; this is something I have to do."

Ciana searches his eyes, finding the pain he's hiding behind them.

"No... you don't. You are... better than this. This... isn't you, I... know it's not. You told me... yourself," she gasps, struggling to breathe in more air. "Your title doesn't... define you. Just 'cause you're... the Prince of Darkness doesn't... mean you have to be dark... and bad. You are such a... good person, Kieran. Or was..." her voice starts to air out, "everything you told... me a lie?"

Kieran watches as her pale face turns a ghostly white, loosening his grip slightly, but not enough.

"No, I never lied to you. Everything I told you was true." He keeps her gaze, his eyes watering slightly.

"What are you waiting for? Finish her, Kieran!" The king bites his hand anxiously. Kieran shakes his head, tightening his grip, hardening his expression once more. A stray tear escapes, rolling down his cheek.

*He's scared,* Ciana gasps in her mind. *He said he's never scared. But he's scared now, just like he was scared when I fell off the cliff. He's scared of losing me. He knows we need each other and the balance.*

"Kier... an... please," Ciana pleads, hardly able to get any words out. Black spots threaten the edges of her vision, her lungs on fire, begging for air. "I know... you know he... can't... hurt me. If you... kill me and... t-take... the queen's... p-power, he'll... just k-kill... you himself... so he... can... have the... pow...er."

"She's lying, son."

"I've... never... lied," she counters. His fingers fumble slightly, allowing her to take a small gasp of air in, but the blackness is hazing her vision and her limbs feel heavy. Ciana knows she only has seconds left. "No one... is supposed... to have... both... powers." Another swallow of air. "It doesn't... work... like that."

"She's messing with your head, Kieran. Why would I kill my own son?"

Ciana softens her grip on his wrists as a numbness settles over her. With a final tiny inhale, she tells him, "Do what... you choose, Kieran... Just know... I forgive you."

Kieran looks at her misty eyes, tears forming in his own. He releases his grip from around her neck. Ciana falls to the floor, coughing and gasping for air as he falls to his knees, trying to catch his own breath he didn't realize he was holding.

"What are you doing? She's not dead yet!"

"I can't kill her, Father," Kieran tells him firmly, standing back up to face him.

"Oh, don't tell me you've actually grown to care for her!" The king snatches Kieran's collar, jerking him to his feet. "You have gone back on our agreement! I'm ashamed of you!" he spits.

"Maybe I did start out wanting to rule the world and have their power, tired of the balance, but after spending time with Ciana, I realize that I just want to live my life the best I can with the balance. They help us so much by providing us with food; we can't live without them, Father! I don't want to get rid of them and reign over everyone. That's what *you* want."

"But once we have the queen's power, we won't *have* to rely on them for food!" He releases his hold on Kieran, using his hands to emphasize his point. "We could grow our own! Don't you remember the last time you decided to be nice and show mercy?"

"I do."

"Then I suggest you finish the job or I won't hesitate to kill you right here, right now, with or without you holding the queen's power," the king threatens.

"Go right ahead. I will *never* kill her."

"Have it your way then."

The king grabs the front of Kieran's shirt, throwing him across the room into a wall. Once Kieran hits the floor, the king stomps his foot, sending a crack through the floor up to the ceiling, causing a section to fall on top of Kieran.

"Kieran!" Ciana screams through her agony watching the dust settle; the debris unmoving. Her heart sinks. She didn't care that he had led her here to die. He had changed. He was good regardless and didn't deserve to die himself. The king turns his attention to her, a big smile on his face. "You can't hurt me. The queen made sure I got that protection when I became the princess," she reminds him.

"Oh, I'm quite aware of that potion she made you. She was smart to do so, knowing I'd try to harm you. However, Kieran wasn't going to just kill you himself, I made sure he had help on the inside to make things easier for him. He didn't know, of course, and neither did you. So I'll just wait until they finish killing you. Ta-ta!" He whips his cloak around his body, disappearing in a black smoke. Heartbroken and weak, Ciana curls up and cries.

A warm hand lightly rests on her shoulder. "I am so sorry, Ciana. I really truly am," Kieran apologizes, shaking slightly. Ciana turns her head, her eyes widening as she looks up at an unharmed Kieran.

"You're alive?" she squeaks.

"Well, yeah. I broke the floor beneath me just enough for me to fall through, before the ceiling completely fell on top of me. I'm never going to fall down a floor again though, that's for sure." Kieran rubs his neck. Ciana musters up as much strength as she can, sitting up, wrapping her arms around Kieran. Caught off guard slightly, Kieran wraps his arms around her, hugging her tightly in return. "I know I led you into this. I am so sorry."

"Did you know Olcan was going to poison me?"

"No! No, I didn't. I didn't know my father had set him up. I didn't need you dying before we got here, but I also didn't want him... to hurt you either. I swear I only knew what he and I were going to do. I didn't know he was going to send things our way to try and kill you. I am so, so sorry. Please forgive me, Ciana."

"I already did," she sniffs.

"Why didn't you trust your instincts and not come in? I was really hoping you would listen so I wouldn't have to... you know."

"I wasn't thinking about myself. I was thinking about my people. No, it didn't feel right, but I didn't know what was going to happen. I still had to try to fix the balance for them."

"Spoken like a true princess."

"Why didn't you tell me about your plan?"

"You tell someone that you're going to kill them. But I didn't know how you were going to react if I did tell you or if you'd believe me. Besides, I made a promise with my father, so I wouldn't have been able to straight up tell you anyways."

"Why not?"

"When he came to convince me to go with you, we drank to it. He doesn't trust anyone fully, not even me. He secretly gave me a potion to prevent me from telling you outright in case I did change my mind. I wasn't aware he had given it to me until I found the bottle he had accidentally left behind."

"There was nothing you could do but give me hints."

"No."

"Kieran, we need to get back to my kingdom." Ciana pulls out of the hug, wiping away her tears. "He said he had someone on the inside helping kill me."

"How do you think we do that? The only way we can get back is the way we came, but I don't think you would make it that long. You are way worse than before."

"I have an idea, help me outside, please?"

Kieran glances at the queen's motionless body. "What about Her Majesty?"

Ciana follows his gaze, tears welling in her eyes as she looks at the queen; her white dress and hair covering her ghostly pale skin. She carefully watches the body, half expecting the queen to take a breath and stand, but Ciana knows all too well that she won't. "I'm... not sure. We can't just leave her, but we can figure out what to do in a minute. One thing at a time. Help me outside?"

"Permission to carry you?"

She smiles, meeting his gaze. "Granted."

Kieran carefully picks her up, carrying down the stairs outside where Patches is running after a butterfly, Iris and Liko watching in the grass.

"What happened?" Liko questions as they come over, Kieran setting Ciana in the grass.

"Kieran! What did you do to her?" Iris accuses, shaking a finger at him.

"No, no, he didn't do anything to me other than save my life," Ciana explains, exhausted. "Patches, come here." Patches runs over, licking her pale face a few times. "I need you to find the troll Kabandha, the one in worn leather shorts, and bring him here, please," she instructs. Patches yelps, running off towards the mountain.

"Your plan is to bring a troll to us? You do know they will eat us, right?" Kieran laughs, sitting next to her.

"I have an idea." She pulls the silver locket from her pocket.

"The locket? How's that going to help?"

"I have a feeling."

"Alright. I trust you."

"Now... the queen." Ciana sighs, rubbing her eyes. "She needs a burial."

"What do you usually do for those?"

"I'm not actually sure. Not for a royal at least. I've never seen it done."

"What about Princess Leora? Didn't you hold a funeral for her?"

Ciana shakes her head. "No, we couldn't. There was too much of an uprising at the time and then memories were wiped. The queen took her daughter's body and held her own funeral for her."

"In that case, we can do it our own way," Kieran offers.

"She's the queen, Kieran. It needs to be special. She was the one who created this world. Without her, none of us would be here."

"That's true, but we can make it special in our own way. I'm sure she'll appreciate it, regardless."

"Like what?"

"I'll let you decide what that is. In the meantime, would you like me to go grab her body and bring it out here?"

"Yeah."

"I'll be right back." Kieran walks back into the mansion. Ciana looks around her, trying to figure out what they could do for the queen's burial. Her eyes fall on the multicolored flowers scattered through the grass, sparking an idea.

Kieran comes back out, carefully holding the blackened body of the queen in his arms. Ciana gasps, pointing to the grass in front of her, showing Kieran where she wants the body. Crawling closer, Ciana can clearly see the stab wound, but the rest of her was not engulfed in a dark black before. Her hair, which was pure white only a few minutes ago, was now an unhealthy black; her white dress looked as if soaked in ink, as well as her skin. She looked as if a single touch would cause her body to dissolve into ash.

"What happened? Did you do this?"

"No. It was my father. When he stabbed her, he sent a surge of his power into the knife. Killed her in an instant internally, but just now finished making its way through the rest of her. Her entire body is dead and dry."

"That's terrible." Ciana reaches to touch the queen, but pulls away, afraid she'll cause the body to shatter.

"We hold a terrible power." Kieran frowns.

Ciana stares at the queen. *Leora's mother came to the fortress with the king. The King of Light died in the war. If Kieran's mother isn't here with him... what happened to her?*

"Kieran, if you don't mind me asking, what happened to your mother?" she whispers. "We don't have anything on her after the pact was made."

Kieran's brows furrow, looking over the queen's body. "She passed away."

"What happened?"

"She died... when she gave birth to me."

Ciana gasps. "I'm so sorry, Kieran. I didn't know."

"It's alright. It's just one of those things that happen in life."

"It's still an awful thing to grow up with. Thank you for telling me."

A silence falls between them, both looking at the queen until Kieran speaks up. "Did you figure out what you wanted to do for the burial?"

"I did. I'll need your help for one part though."

"Name it."

"You can control what and how much you can destroy, right?"

"Yes."

"Good. I'll let you know what I need from you when we get to it." Ciana runs her hands in the grass, feeling the cool soil beneath.

"What did you come up with?" Kieran sits beside her.

"You'll see." Ciana closes her eyes. Taking a deep breath, she focuses on the grass around the queen, imagining it reaching towards the sky. She feels the familiar warm sensation run through her fingers into the ground, the grass growing at her will.

"Ciana, you're—"

"Sshh," she hushes Kieran, picturing the grass folding and weaving with each other over and around the queen's body, creating a casket. Ciana's body begins to shake, exhausted. Fighting against her lack of strength, she pictures white flowers decorating the grass-made casket. A warm hand rests against her back. The gentle support from Kieran is all she needs to push through her tired body. Opening her eyes, she gently leans against Kieran. He wraps an arm around her, giving her enough support to not completely collapse.

"It's beautiful," he whispers, admiring the green casket. The flowers spotted around it, a few clumped together near the head in the shape of a crown. "I thought you couldn't grow things because you're dying?"

"Everything I create or grow won't be healthy," she breathes. "The grass and flowers may look healthy, but inside they're the same black like in the fruit from the tree."

"So what do you need me to do?"

"Can you cause the ground beneath the casket to sink or something? That way she can still be buried underground."

"Of course." Kieran rests his free hand on the ground. Nothing happens at first, but the casket suddenly begins to lower, stopping roughly six feet under.

"Thank you." Ciana rests her hand back in the grass. Growing the grass together above the casket, making it seem like nothing happened, before sprouting white tulips and roses right above the queen.

"Any words you'd like to say in memory?"

Ciana ponders his question. There was so much she could say, so much she wanted to say, but none felt like the right thing. She recalls the locket, to what the queen was going to tell her before she died. The words come to her, so fast and clear in the queen's voice as if she was sitting right there with her. She smiles, feeling a surge of courage and confidence. "The power is within yourself, not in anything nor anyone else."

# Chapter Twenty-One

*Thump. Thump.*

Patches comes running back, barking like mad. Giant footsteps shake the ground as the seventy foot, bald troll runs after him. Kieran helps Ciana to her feet, getting in the troll's line of sight.

"You!" he bellows, eyeing Kieran. "Kill leader!" He stops running.

"Hi, Mr. Kabandha!" Ciana yells up to him with all her strength, leaning against Kieran for support.

"What want?" he grumbles.

"I have something you want!" She waves the locket in the air.

"Give back!"

"I will give it back, but only if you take us to where we need to go."

Kabandha glares down at Kieran. "No."

"Why not?"

"He killed!"

"Yes, I know, and he shouldn't have. How about, you take us where we need to go *alive* and quickly, and in exchange we will return the locket, and when I'm able, I will revive your leader?" she offers. Kabandha sits down, tapping his chin.

"Tricks?"

"No tricks!"

"Promise?"

"I promise on my life as the Princess of Light."

"Deal."

"Thank you, Kabandha!"

Ciana sighs, resting her head on Kieran's shoulder, worn out from the yelling as Kabandha lowers his hands. Patches jumps into the big green palm with Iris and Liko on his back; Kieran gently grabs Ciana's waist, lifting her up.

"Where?" Kabandha stands up.

"My kingdom, Luxregnum, please."

"Tell me, Kabandha, why is the locket with the picture of the queen and the princess so special to you trolls?" Ciana wonders, laying down in his big palm.

"Giants too."

"Why is it special to both of you then?"

"Light Queen gave. Reminder that in world of turmoil, always good. Never harm queen. Never harm princess."

"In a world of turmoil, there is always good," Ciana repeats. "I like that. But I'm the princess and you tried to hurt me."

"No princess. Princess picture."

"Can't disagree with that."

"Don't say that. You're the princess now," Kieran pieces together the sentence, lightly hitting her arm.

"He's right, though."

"I strongly disagree, but whatever."

Ciana turns her attention back to Kabandha. "Did you see the princess often?"

"Visit a month with queen. Check on," he continues, stepping over some trees. Ciana looks up at the gray clouds folding across the sky as she listens. "Princess sick. Stopped. Had died. Queen no see. Must busy."

"How can you understand what he's saying? He's making no sense." Liko scratches his head.

"Kieran?" Ciana tilts her head to look at him, not hearing Liko.

"Yes?" Kieran carefully looks over the troll's hand to the ground.

"Did you notice the black on the queen's dress? Those branch-like marks?"

Kieran sits back down next to her, rolling his eyes slightly. "Those weren't branches. Those were holding roots. It's basically a trail show-ing where the holder is sending some power to hold someone as—" he stops, nodding slowly. "Oh, I see where you're going with this."

"How long does—"

"It takes time, especially if the captive holds a decent amount of opposite magic," he answers, reading her mind.

"So he must have—"

"Started the process shortly after they made the truce."

"Will you let me finish my questions?" Ciana crosses her arms.

"Sorry." He laughs, combing a hand through his hair.

"So how does it work?"

"Basically, the king must have been working on making the queen a captive. He made holding roots and used them to threaten her life, ensuring her compliance and taking away her free will, lest the king have her killed. She was basically magically chained to my father."

"I didn't notice it when she came to the kingdom when Leora died."

"It probably wasn't showing yet, but I wouldn't be surprised if that was the last thing she did without my father threatening her life."

"Do you think that is what broke the balance?"

"Not likely. Anything the queen and king did to one another wouldn't affect the balance. The king was just holding the queen captive; he wasn't really killing her or anything. Something else must have set it off."

"Hey, Kabandha?" Ciana sits up, gently patting his palm.

"Yes?" He glances down at her.

"I don't know how to tell you this..." she begins, twiddling her thumbs. "Uh... the queen is... dead."

Kabandha stops walking, eyes bulging out of his bald head. "Can't. How know?"

"I saw the King of Darkness kill her."

"Impossible. Queen no heart!"

"The queen... heartless? Well, that's harsh." Kieran laughs.

"Uh, Kieran?" Ciana whispers, shaking her head at him when he looks at her.

"What? She was the queen of happiness, of course she had a heart." Kieran's smile fades as Ciana shrugs, giving him a half smile. "Wait, you're serious? You don't actually mean..." She nods. "Really? How?"

"Queen gave good cause," Kabandha answers, walking once again. Kieran's eyebrows knit together as he looks at Ciana, not following.

"The heart that's oh so important to protect?" Ciana smiles weakly, holding in her laugh.

He snaps his fingers. "Oh! You mean the heart you had Zipo watch over?"

"Zomo and yes."

"That's the queen's?"

"Yes."

"Ah." Kieran nods his head slowly.

"You're still a little confused, aren't you?"

"Maybe, just a little."

"The only way to ensure the kingdom survived was by physically giving us her heart. I told you I couldn't hold all the princess's power since I wasn't born a royal and that Leora and her mother had the same gifts. The only way to allow me to hold her ability was to give us her heart, tying me with it so it could regulate the power to me."

"So since the queen is dead, so is the heart?"

"No." Ciana shakes her head. "The heart was still connected to the queen and her physical body and her powers, but since it wasn't physically in her when she died, it wasn't harmed. I was inadvertently connected to the queen through the heart so if anything, the heart is barely keeping me alive and vice versa since..." her voice trails off.

"When she died you collapsed because she was the only source guaranteeing you life since something is happening to the heart," Kieran finishes for her.

"Her life was still connected to the heart, but since my life was also connected to it to regulate my power, instead of dying with her body, it had another life force allowing it to keep beating despite its real owner being gone."

"Really gone?" Kabandha sighs.

"I'm sorry, Kabandha," Ciana whispers, laying back down, curling into a ball.

"Who replace?"

"I'm... not sure who'll replace her. I don't think there's anyone who would be able to. No one on my side was born a royal, so they wouldn't be able to hold the power. She's been here since the very beginning so—" Ciana buries her face, coughing.

"Kabandha, can you get us to the kingdom faster?" Kieran requests, helping Ciana sit back up.

"I fast. Only listen her."

"Incompetent troll," Kieran mutters.

"Kieran!" Ciana wacks the back of his head. "Be nice to our transportation. He's already going faster than we would on foot!" Iris and Liko roll around laughing.

"Okay, okay, you're right. I'm sorry," Kieran apologizes. "Sorry for insulting you, Kabandha."

"Kabandha?" Ciana looks up at him when he doesn't respond.

"Accepted," he grumbles.

"Thank you." She rests her head, no longer coughing. "Iris, Liko, stop laughing, please."

"Sorry." Iris wipes away a tear, calming down. Ciana looks up at the dreary sky, thunder rumbling in the distance.

Lighting streaks the sky, rain pouring down. Patches curls up next to Ciana, licking her already wet face. Ciana smiles, wrapping her arm around his little body, pulling him close.

"Hey, puppy," she whispers, sniffing, wiping rain from her eyes. Thunder roars, causing Patches to shake, snuggling closer to Ciana. "Awww, you're scared. Don't worry, it's not going to hurt you. I've got ya."

"But who's got us? We're soaked!" Liko complains.

"Come here, you two." Iris and Liko walk over to her, climbing under her arm. "Better?"

"Yes, thank you!" Ciana closes her eyes, the cold rain dripping onto her skin.

"There midmorning," Kabandha announces over the thunder. Ciana opens her eyes again, watching Kieran look ahead, before he sits back down, facing towards her. His wet hair falls over his eyes slightly, water caressing his face.

"How are you holding up?" he asks, seeing her eyes open.

"I'm still here, but..."

"I know. We're almost there, and we'll fix everything and get you better."

Thunder rumbles again, and Patches lets out a yelp.

"It's okay, puppy. The thunder can't hurt you," Ciana soothes him, her eyes getting heavy.

"Get some rest, Princess. You need it."

"I'm fine."

"You're tired. Go to sleep. When you wake up, you'll be home." Ciana allows her eyes to close, listening to Kieran talk to Kabandha amid the thunder and rain. "So, Kabandha, how is it that you can travel to the kingdom in like a day and a half while it took us like four?"

"I big. Larger leg span."

"Still don't get it."

"Don't think it."

"Okay, but if you're able to travel so quickly, why weren't you able to catch us when we ran?"

"Kieran, don't question the technical stuff. It's hard to run and grab something as small as us when you're seventy feet tall. Plus, it took us a week to get to the fortress, you have to remember we had interruptions and slight detours along the way." Ciana laughs, keeping her eyes closed.

"I was just wondering," Kieran defends himself. Ciana smiles, falling asleep to the sound of the pouring rain.

"Hey, Kabandha, you sure you took us to the right side of the border?" Kieran's voice asks.

"Yes."

"How about the right kingdom?"

"Yes!"

"I don't know. It looks a bit dark."

"What?" Ciana jolts awake at Kieran's comment; holding onto him for support, she looks up ahead.

The rain has stopped, but grim clouds loom over her kingdom; the plants dark or withered; dim lights illuminate the town, reflecting off smoke. Her eyes water as she looks at her shadowed palace, hardly any light or life left in anything.

"Oh no! Kabandha, you need to get me as close to the edge of the town as possible without anyone seeing you. They'll kill you if they see you."

"Okay."

Kabandha reaches the outskirts of the town; close enough for Ciana to walk, but still far enough so no one will see him. He carefully lays his hand on the ground, letting them get off. Kieran helps hold Ciana as she takes the locket from her pocket, placing it in Kabandha's palm.

"Just as promised, here's the locket. Once I get my strength back, I'll come and heal your leader."

"Thank, Princess." Kabandha closes his hand around the locket, stomping away.

"Let's go," she tells Kieran who wraps an arm around her for more support, walking towards the town.

Ciana looks around the dull, barren streets, the buildings looking unfamiliar in the darkness. Fighting fills the air as they near the center of town. Following the shouts around a corner. Ciana and Kieran's eyes widen in horror as men and guards from both sides of the border fight with anything they can find, some lying motionless on the ground. Ciana pushes away from Kieran, mustering all her strength, clambering through the people towards the middle of the fighting.

"Stop!" she tries to order through her exhaustion, heat beginning to rise in her face. No one notices, ping-ponging her between bodies as they continue to fight. "I said to stop!" She forces her voice louder, though not by much. "Listen to me!" She grabs one of her guards by the back of his armor. Unaware that it was Ciana, the guard shoves her to the hard ground. Ciana curls into a tight ball, feet kicking and trampling her. Tears stream down her face as she lays helpless.

The sound of flames crackling causes Ciana's heart to jump. She wasn't being trampled on, but now she was going to burn? Looking up, black flames surround her; Kieran stands over her, his hands engulfed with the same black flames. A furious expression is plastered on his face as he looks at those fighting. Those closest turn to fight against Kieran, but quickly lower their weapons, realizing who it is. They take a few steps back when their eyes fall on Ciana. In a ripple effect, everyone stops fighting, staring at Kieran and Ciana.

"That's better," Kieran mumbles, putting out his flames. Everyone watches as he helps Ciana to her feet. "Are you okay?" he asks, looking her over.

"I think so." She looks at her hands, unwrapping the bandage Kieran had placed over the cut. Fresh bright red blood seeps through as the cut somehow reopened in the chaos. Her eyes fall on a small pile of her guards. Wide-eyed and confused, everyone watches as Ciana and Kieran walk toward the fallen, searching for a pulse. After searching the bodies, a rage of fury brews inside Ciana, bubbling like hot water, overpowering her exhaustion and sickness.

"What happened?" she demands loudly enough for all of them to hear as she straightens. All her people look at the ground, some glancing back up at her occasionally while Kieran's people glare in her direction. "What happened?" she demands again, her legs weakening, the fury burning out just as quickly as it came. Silence.

"Someone answer the princess's question. What is going on here?" Kieran commands.

"It's both our fault," one of Ciana's guards speaks up, stepping forward.

"It is not!" one of Kieran's men counters.

"How so, Ritesh?" Ciana urges, leaning against Kieran for support.

"The darkness reached our crops, limiting our viable produce. We were barely managing for our own people, let alone sending some over for them. We've been keeping it all for ourselves. They came fighting to try to steal some for themselves, breaking down the border gate," he explains, cautiously watching her.

"It was instructed that you would continue to give Tenebris food, regardless of how much was being produced. What made you think you could go against orders?"

"With the weekly deliveries we didn't have enough, even with our storage, the darkness was consuming everything. We wouldn't have enough for both sides," another guard adds. "You had us keep food from them when we were low just the other week. We assumed we could go off that again until we had more produce."

"We were not low on supplies when I initiated that order. There was a reason as to why I withheld the delivery, but the order was reversed right away. Under no circumstances are you to assume and go off a past order, especially if it has been withdrawn."

"You took away our food either way!" one of Kieran's men growls. "Leaving us to starve!"

"Watch your tone," Kieran warns.

"No!" he spits. "The king told us you were dead! That the princess managed to kill you. That we were on our own and had to fend for ourselves. No ruler. No food. He told us they wouldn't give us food, so the only way to get justice is to fight. And that's what we're doing. Fighting to get our justice for what these despicably disgusting people are doing to us! Breaking their part of the pact!"

Kieran's eyes narrow, his hands engulfing in black flames once more. "I said to watch your tone," he grits through his teeth.

"Or what? You can't possibly be anything but a ghost. A trick from these people to have us back down." The man's eyes narrow.

"Would you care to prove that I'm not real?" Kieran challenges.

"With pleasure. I'm not scared of a mere hologram."

"Then come here." Kieran points to the ground in front of him. The man scoffs, walking up to Kieran, a smug look on his face.

"And? How are you going to prove you're the real Prince of Darkness? Put your holographic hand through my heart?"

"Oh, you'll know in the quickest second of your life." Kieran places his hand on the man's shoulder. Sure enough, in a split second, the man's face changes to horror before his body is engulfed in black, similar to the queen's, except his body dissolves into ash crumbling to the ground.

"Kieran!" Ciana gasps.

"He deserved it," he tells her. "Anyone else doubting our authority?" he calls to everyone. They take a collective step back in response.

Ritesh cautiously steps forward, adding to the previous conversation. "Zomo told us you went to fix the balance, so we were planning on giving them food once you fixed it."

Ciana nods. "Thank you for telling me the truth, Ritesh."

"If you went to fix this mess, why is it not fixed yet?" one of Ciana's townspeople shouts.

"There was... a setback, but that's why I'm back. I can move on to plan B."

"Pfft, yeah right. Some princess we have. There's nothing you can do to save our kingdom." Ciana's guards unsheath their swords, aiming them at the man.

"Stand down!" Ciana's knees buckle, Kieran grabs around her waist, helping her stay up. "Ritesh, where's Zomo?"

"He's in the palace, Your Highness," Ritesh answers, sliding his sword back into its holster.

"Thank you. Now, I want half of you to give half of whatever food we have to the other side of the border; they need to eat just like us. The other half take care of the bodies. Anyone else can go home." Ciana faces Kieran's people as her side disperses. "You will go back to your side of the border; we will send over food. It may not be as much as before, but it will suffice for now."

"Why should we trust you?" one of the men sneers.

"Because I'm telling you to do as she says, and if you have a problem with that, you'll suffer the same fate as your friend. Death," Kieran warns. "I'll be back over once I'm done with things on this side, guaranteeing there will be no problems."

They head in the direction of the border, without saying another word. Ciana slides out of Kieran's hold, collapsing to the ground.

"Your Highness, are you alright?" Ritesh rushes over. "You look terrible and very pale."

"I'm fine," she breathes. "I'm just tired. It's been a long journey, I just need rest."

"Would you like me to escort you back to the palace?"

"No, no, it's fine. I already gave you a job. Do that."

"Of course, Your Highness." He bows, leaving to help the others.

"Kieran?"

"Yeah?" Kieran crouches next to her.

"Where's Patches and the pixie gnomes?"

"I don't know. I thought they were with us, but I wasn't paying much attention to them."

"They'll show up again. You shouldn't stay over here too long; we don't need things to get worse, but help me to the palace? I need to find Zomo." Kieran helps Ciana up, wrapping one of her arms around his neck for support.

🌿

"Ciana! Thank goodness you're back!" Kuma cries, running into Ciana's arms as they enter the front door, not realizing Kieran is there as he lets go of Ciana.

"Kuma? What's wrong?" Ciana looks into her puffy red eyes.

"I'm scared. Everything is so dark, and the people were fighting, and you weren't here. I didn't know what I was supposed to do or could do and..." She bursts into tears.

"Hey, everything is going to be okay." Ciana gently strokes her hair. "I'm back, and the fighting has stopped. Did anything else happen while I was away?"

"No," she sniffs. "Zomo has been watching the heart nonstop; he's hardly ever not around it. We've tried to figure out a way to stop the darkness from spreading, but we couldn't. We're just glad you're back." She breaks from the hug, taking a double look at Kieran, stepping away, her red eyes filling with fear. "Y-you?" she stammers.

"It's okay, Kuma. He's not going to hurt anything or anyone. I promise."

"But—"

"I know... he'll go back to his side. There won't be any more problems. He's helping me fix this mess, so don't worry."

"I–I..." She scampers off, nearly running into the walls.

"Poor girl. She hasn't worked here that long and already has to deal with all this." Ciana holds onto Kieran for support again.

"I don't know why, but she reminds me of someone..." Kieran ponders, tapping his chin. "How old is she?"

"Kieran, please. Not now." Ciana rubs her temples, exhaustion weighing heavily. "We have to find Zomo."

Kieran nods, pushing the thought aside. "Right. Where would he be?"

"By the sounds of it, probably the room that holds the heart. This way."

Ciana directs Kieran through the palace, up to the observatory-type room. Opening the door, they find Zomo next to the heart, putting drops from a silver and pearl white vial onto it.

"Put that down!" Ciana orders. Zomo jumps, nearly dropping the vial, stepping back to look at them. "Zomo, what are you doing?"

"My Princess, I didn't know you were back. You scared me." He places a hand on his heart.

"What are you doing with that vial?" she asks again.

"Are you alright, Your Highness? You look really sick. Did this idiot do something to you?" Zomo charges towards Kieran, but the princess raises a hand to stop him.

"No, he's done nothing to me. If anything, he's saved my life on multiple occasions. Now, I would like you to answer my question."

"Sorry, Princess Ciana." He lowers his head slightly. "With the darkness spreading and killing everything, the liquid in the vial is supposed to help keep the heart strong and not be affected."

"When have we *ever* put anything onto the heart, Zomo? We never have—achoo!"

"We never had a need to. You told me to look after the heart, so that's what I'm doing, making sure the heart stays alive."

"Zomo, you're killing the heart with whatever that is, not making it better."

"How do you know, Your Highness?" He sighs, rolling his eyes as he crosses his arms against his chest.

"Watch your tone with me, Zomo. Since you've been using the vial, did things get worse quicker?"

"I can't give you a definite answer on that, Princess Ciana, as nothing like this has happened before, so we can't be sure how fast the darkness could spread." He straightens his posture, relaxing his tone. "I will admit the heart light has dimmed slightly."

"Where did you get the vial in the first place?"

"I'm not sure. It was delivered here with a note saying it'll help with the heart. I assumed it came from you since it came after you had left."

"Was there a return address?"

"No, and the address for here was printed."

"Give me the vial, please." Zomo hands over the vial. Ciana takes a small sniff, nearly collapsing and getting lightheaded. "Get it away from me!" She holds the vial as far from her body as possible. Zomo takes it back as Kieran helps Ciana sit down.

"You alright?" Kieran whispers softly.

"Yeah." She takes a breath. Kieran grabs the bottle from Zomo, sniffing it with no reaction. Dumping some into his palm he examines the clear liquid.

"Princess, who knows if the heart dies, you die?"

"Only those who work here. I don't need the public to know in case... you know. Why? What is it?"

"Whoever is trying to kill you knows their poisons and where to find them. This is Lumenocinide. Very hard to come by, and should not be over here on this side of the border. This will literally suck the life and light out of anything. Not so dangerous in small portions, but if all of it is taken, then it'll kill you within minutes. As for inhaling it, it won't kill you but it'll have its effects," Kieran explains.

"When it came, it said to put a couple of drops onto the heart twice a day," Zomo adds.

"So the heart's been absorbing the poison in little bits, slowly killing it?" Ciana verifies.

"Yes. Just be glad Zigzag here didn't put the whole vial on." Kieran points a thumb at Zomo.

"Hey! What's your problem?" Zomo challenges.

"Don't start, you two—achoo! Zomo, do you have any idea who could have sent this?" Ciana curls her knees to her chest.

"Yeah, Prince Uncharming here."

"He didn't send it."

"How do you know? He knows so much about it."

"Um, excuse me, Zippy. I wouldn't go that low to kill someone. If anything, it was probably my ex-father," Kieran snaps, pointing a finger in Zomo's face.

"Kieran, there's no such thing as an ex-father." Ciana gives a soft smile, shaking her head.

"Well, I don't want to be related to him anymore. I'm disowning him, so he's an ex-father to me."

"Okay, whatever. Zomo, is there any evidence on the package of where it came from?"

"No, and if there was, it's long been destroyed, so we can't look at the packaging," Zomo answers. Ciana lets out a heavy sigh, rubbing a hand over her face before giving Zomo a long stare. "No, Ciana, you can't seriously—" Zomo reads her thoughts.

"I'm sorry, Zomo. I know you're innocent, but I found you with the vial, putting it on the heart, making you guilty until we find any evidence to prove your innocence." A knot forms in her stomach as she speaks.

"I understand, Your Highness. As long as you know I would never intentionally hurt you in any way."

"Come on." Ciana forces her weak body to her feet, hanging onto Zomo as they walk out of the room, Kieran trailing behind.

Ritesh and another guard meet them at the bottom of the marble staircase. "Your Highness, we've finished. The food has been sent over and all the bodies taken care of," Ritesh updates Ciana with a bow.

"Good. Now, I need you two to escort Zomo to one of the prison cells."

"Your Highness?" Ritesh's eyebrows disappear under his hair as he looks between her and Zomo.

"I know, but that's an order. Ritesh, you'll be the head guard while Zomo is out. Is that clear?"

"Yes, Your Highness." They bow respectfully, taking Zomo by the arms, leading him away.

Ciana plops onto the floor, out of energy. Kieran reaches to help her back up, but she puts her hand up, stopping him.

"You put the poison in your hand, so unless you're wanting me dead, by all means," she reminds him.

"Oh, right. Sorry."

"You need to leave now. You've been over here long enough. I don't need another fight starting with my people."

Kieran's eyes sadden at the thought. "You're right. But what about you?"

"What about me?"

"You're still sick and dealing with an imposter. If it really isn't what's-his-name, whoever it is can easily take advantage of you. I'm taking the vial with me, so they can't use it on you anymore, but that's not to say they'll do something else. You can hardly walk."

"I have my guards. I'll be safe, but the poison is already killing me, so it's not like they haven't already succeeded."

Kieran shakes his head. "The bottle isn't even halfway empty. Yes, it was and is slowly killing the heart and you. Fortunately, it won't completely kill you since hardly any has been used. The bad part is, you will just remain sick like you are now." Kieran begins to walk away.

"Kieran?" she calls after him. He turns back around. "Is there an antidote?" He lowers his head so he looks at the ground, turning back around, disappearing from sight without a word.

# Chapter Twenty-Two

Ciana curls under her warm covers in her dry pajamas, shivering and sneezing, trying to sleep. "Come in," she sighs at a small knock on her room door. Kuma slowly opens the door, carrying a silver bed tray over to Ciana, a steaming bowl of soup and orange juice on top.

"I brought you some soup for dinner. Hopefully it'll make you feel better." She smiles.

"Thank you, Kuma, but I'm not hungry right now."

"No problem. I'll just set it on your nightstand for when you're ready to eat."

"That's fine. Thank you."

Kuma curtsies, quietly closing the door behind her when she leaves. Ciana closes her eyes, just to be woken up by her door opening once again.

"Princess!" a voice exclaims, shaking her shoulders vigorously. Ciana groans, sitting up and glaring at Kieran, who's darting his glance from her to the bowl. "I'm glad you're still alive."

"What does a girl have to do to get some rest? You should also know better and knock next time and not just barge into my room! What are you even doing over here? You're not supposed to be here!"

"Sorry, grumpy pants. One, I don't knock. Two, I saw the food and thought you ate it and were dead, so I had to make sure you weren't."

"Kieran, someone here is trying to kill me; I'm not that stupid and know better than to take anything from anyone, even those I trust, including my food testers. Besides, my light is still emanating from me. I told you that if I'm dead, my light would literally go out, so you didn't have to shake me awake just to make sure I was alive."

"I know, but waking you up sounded more fun." He shrugs.

"You didn't answer my third question: why are you here? You shouldn't have come back, unless you found a cure for the Lumen-whatever—achoo!"

"Lu-men-ah-cin-ide," he enunciates. "And no, there isn't a cure for it, princess. Once it's in the system, it stays there, whether it's enough to kill you or not."

"Great," Ciana groans, rolling her eyes. "So either way, I'm dead." With a weighted sigh, she focuses on Kieran. His tan color has come back, his cheeks not as hollow. But his eyes still have slight bags under them. "You never answered my other question: why are you here?"

"I'm here because we still have to fix the balance. You can't do it alone."

"So you decided to break the rules?" Ciana tsks, goading the tiniest smile from Kieran. "How'd you get past my guards?"

Kieran rocks back on his heels. "Technically, I'm not breaking anything since we've already broken them. All those rules would be out the window right now anyways since we *have* to work together to get things back to normal. After everything is fixed, we can go back to how things were. And the gate is still broken, and there are no guards watching it."

"You're right, and I forgot to station guards there before I came up to bed. I'll do that." Ciana rubs her eyes, trying to decide if she has enough strength to call for Ritesh. "Ritesh?" she tries, the force of air from her lungs turning into a cough.

Kieran frowns. "What do you need, Princess? I can get it for you."

"I need Ritesh. He should be nearby. Will you call him for me?"

"Of course." He walks over to the door, sticking his head out. "Riptush! Her Highness requests your presence!" he calls into the hall, coming back to Ciana's side.

"It's *Ritesh*," she corrects him. "If you call him by his name, he might actually come."

"He'll still come." Kieran shrugs. The door swings open, Ritesh nearly running in with his sword in hand. His face hardens at the sight of Kieran.

"I thought I heard *your* disgusting voice. What are you doing here?" he demands.

"Sword away, Ritesh. You are in no position to question His Highness like that," Ciana warns.

"Forgive me, Princess Ciana." He resheaths his sword, relaxing his posture slightly. "Was there something you needed?"

"Yes. I need guards stationed at the gate. Have the number of guards tripled since the gate is still down."

Ritesh nods. "It will be done."

"After which, please escort Zomo up here to me."

"Yes, Your Highness." He bows, leaving the room.

"Why do you want him up here?" Kieran kneels beside her bed, his eyes falling on her newly bandaged hand.

"I want to talk to him again. I'd go down to him, but I'm not in any shape to do so."

"Do you honestly think he's innocent? We saw him put the poison onto the heart; he probably sent it to himself." He gently grabs her hand, holding it up so he can look at the bandage.

"He wouldn't kill me. If he wanted to, he wouldn't try so hard to protect me from everything."

"Do you really believe that? What about our whole journey?"

"What about it? We went so *you* could kill me, but you still protected me because you didn't want to."

Kieran opens his mouth to counter, but closes it again. "No, I guess you're right. I can see your reasoning." He sets her hand back on her bed. "Why is your hand wrapped again? I would have thought you'd have had someone heal it for you by now."

Ciana looks at her hand. "Just like everything else, it was the last thing on my mind when I came up to rest. I just haven't gotten around to it yet."

"The sooner, the better. You don't need to be losing any blood right now."

"I'm aware of that, Kieran, but it's stopped bleeding. It's not a priority right now."

"Come in," Ciana answers a knock on her door. Ritesh enters, guiding Zomo. "Have a seat, Zomo." She motions from her bed to a nearby chair. Ritesh moves it closer to her bedside, standing guard next to the door. Zomo eyes Kieran as he sits down.

"Princess Ciana, what is *he* still doing here?" he questions.

"Being more helpful than you, Zebro," Kieran replies, folding his arms across his chest.

"Will you two ever get along?" Ciana interrupts.

"No," they huff, looking away from each other.

"Well, learn to." She holds her bandaged hand out to Zomo. "Will you heal me and my hand, please?"

"Heal?" He gently takes her bandaged hand.

"Yes, the poison, among other things, has made me unable to heal myself."

"Of course, Your Highness." Zomo unwraps her hand, cupping it. A warm sensation runs through her palm and body as her wound disappears.

"How are you feeling?" Kieran asks, nearly ripping the bandages from Zomo's hold, throwing them in a nearby waste can.

"The same—achoo! I was hoping I was still partly suffering from Olcan, but I guess not." She lies back on her pillows, propped up so she can still see Zomo and Kieran. "Thank you, Zomo. Now, has anyone here in the palace been acting strange or unusual? Or has anyone come into town that you didn't recognize?"

Zomo frowns. "I'm sorry, Princess Ciana, but no. Everything and everyone has been normal, well, as normal as it can be with the darkness."

"I'm telling you, Princess, he's guilty. He just doesn't want to admit it," Kieran states. Zomo grips the arms of the chair, holding himself down.

"I'll gladly admit to anything I do wrong, unlike you, but I did not intentionally poison the heart."

"I'll admit anything too, like I'll admit to killing you." Kieran rolls up his sleeves, standing up with Zomo. Ritesh rushes over, pulling Zomo back as Ciana quickly gets up, pushing Kieran away from him, standing between the two. She grabs onto Kieran's arms, bending over as the room starts to spin.

"Forget the poison. You two are going to be the death of me. Now, as long as I'm alive, I want you two to *try* to get along for my sake." She hears Kieran's heavy breathing, reluctantly shifting so he's no longer facing Zomo.

"Now, Zomo…" Ciana lowers herself back onto her bed. "There has got to be something that is unusual. You somehow were in possession of the poison. You say you aren't behind this, so is there any indication as to where it came from? You said the address for the palace was printed, did you try to compare it to our printing devices?"

Zomo releases his shoulder from Ritesh's grip, his eyes locked with Ciana's but refusing to answer.

"Answer me," she orders.

"I'm afraid I didn't," he answers shortly.

"Didn't what?"

"I didn't compare the print to our printing devices throughout the kingdom."

Ciana raises an eyebrow, hearing the bitterness on the edge of his voice. "Watch your tone with me," she warns. "Why didn't you?"

He takes a few deep breaths, composing himself before answering, choosing his next words carefully. "I didn't see the need to. As I said before, I thought it had come from you. You know the heart best, so I naturally assumed. I didn't know it was poison, or else I would have. The darkness was only getting worse, so I figured I'd do as the note said to try to help things. I was looking out for the heart and the kingdom."

"Zomo, you are my most experienced guard. Why, in *any* circumstance, would you have thought I'd send you something to put *on* the heart? You know it just as well as I do."

"I'm sorry, Princess Ciana. But I couldn't consult with you about it. It came after you left, so I figured you came across something or were keeping something from me that would, in fact, help. I followed the note, out of good intentions to help."

Ciana rubs her eyes, glancing at Kieran who looks like he doesn't believe a single word Zomo had said. "Kieran?"

"Yeah?" He meets her gaze.

"Tell me your instinct," Ciana requests. Zomo's eyes furrow.

"I don't trust him. His story isn't adding up. There's no hard proof that he didn't do it intentionally. Regardless of what you may think of him, he was found with it. Not to mention, he wasn't even a part of the fighting that took place. As a guard, he should have been fighting with the others, unless he's working with my father and wanted the fight as a distraction so he could do the poison."

Zomo's eyes widen in fear. He drops to his knees next to Ciana's bedside. "My Princess. I swear to you on my life, I am *not* working with the king. I'm innocent! Being framed! I would never harm you."

Ciana nods. "Kieran makes a fair point. As head guard you should have been fighting for the safety of my people with the others. Not staying cooped up in the palace. I told you to keep things in order."

"Ciana, I promise you I didn't do anything. I know I should have helped fight, but I wanted to make sure the heart stayed safe. All the guards were out of the palace. Someone had to stay here and guard it in case someone from the other kingdom found a way in."

"While a valid point, it isn't enough. Any guard would have been sufficient so you could be where needed most; fighting, taking charge."

"Princess—"

"No more, Zomo. Unless evidence is found to prove your innocence, you are to be tried for attempted murder."

"My Princess..." Tears well in his eyes. "I would never harm you. You *have* to believe me."

"This conversation is over. Ritesh, escort him back to his cell please. Then I would like you to oversee that everyone in the kingdom is getting fair portions for their families."

"Yes, Your Highness." Ritesh grabs Zomo's arms, pulling him to his feet and out the door. Ciana turns to Kieran.

"I'm knackered, so I'm going to sleep. You need to get back to your side of the border to prevent any more trouble. Because if anyone wakes me up this time, they will regret it," she tells him, having no energy to deal with anything else. "Am I clear, Kieran? No trouble."

"I won't cause trouble so you can rest," he confirms.

"Because you'll be back in your kingdom," she restates.

"Right." Kieran slowly nods, heading to the door. Quietly closing it behind him as he leaves.

Ciana rubs a cold washcloth across her warm forehead, eating a bowl of oatmeal she made herself. The dining room doors open, closing behind Kuma.

"Good morning, Your Highness." She curtsies.

"Morning Kuma." Ciana smiles, her voice soft.

"How are you feeling today?"

"The same as before but with a new fever. I probably won't be getting better anytime soon."

"I'm sorry, Ciana. I hope you will."

"Thank you—achoo!"

"I know you need space to heal, but I came to tell you that Prince Kieran is here for you." Her voice rises slightly. On cue, Kieran enters; Kuma squeaks, running into the kitchen. Kieran watches, eyeing her closely as she darts past him.

"Kieran, what did I tell you about knocking?"

"I already told you I don't knock. Besides, you said that for your room. This is the dining room." He grabs the seat next to Ciana, sitting in it backwards, looking towards the kitchen doors. "That maid still looks so familiar and it's starting to bother me."

"You saw her yesterday and before we left on our trek, she's going to look familiar."

"No, because I noticed it the first time too. I just can't put my finger on it. It'll come to me eventually."

"What are you doing here? You need to stay on your side." Ciana stirs her oatmeal.

"Not until we fix the balance. I can't let you try to heal your kingdom alone."

Ciana looks him over. Kieran has admitted that he doesn't want to get rid of the kingdoms, but she can't help but wonder if he really means it. His father could show up and offer him what he wants most, causing him to turn against her. He could still be pretending to care for her and is in her kingdom to, not help it, but gather more inside information.

"Have you seen your father yet?" she pries, not completely sure if he'd tell her the truth.

"I haven't and hope I don't. Have you figured out who might be trying to kill you over here?"

"No. I talked with everyone this morning and nothing. I hate not being able to trust anyone, even my own staff right now. The only person I can semi-trust is... you, believe it or not."

"That's a first." Kieran laughs. Even if he were to potentially switch sides, Kieran was still trying to help her right now. His actions so far give Ciana enough trust in him. Trust that he really would stand by her to the end. But then again... only time would tell. "I still think Gizmo is behind it."

"Zomo can't be guilty."

"Who else would it be? Plus you agreed that—"

"I know, but I still don't think he's behind the poisoning—achoo!"

"I'm telling you, Princess, he's just playing dumb, knowing you'd think he's innocent."

"I won't believe it." She sighs, setting her washcloth down, pushing away her bowl. "Come with me." Kieran helps Ciana up, giving her support as she directs him to the only balcony that overlooks the lightless city and dreary sky.

"You're warm, Ciana," he mentions, feeling her forehead.

"I know, but don't worry about that right now. Now tell me what you see."

Kieran stares at what once was the kingdom of light and life; a place of color and joy. But now, it's overrun in darkness, overwhelmed with fear and wariness. Gloom filling every corner. "It looks like my side of the border," he replies softly, eyes still scanning.

"What do you hear?"

"Silence, but not the good kind."

"Kieran, without the queen, I can't save my kingdom. She was the only one who could heal everything and fix the balance. As soon as I die, everything else will follow unless I give the power to someone else, but I can't do that. No one is a royal. Zomo is well aware of that and is the only person who everyone will listen to. My own people won't even listen to me; you saw that yesterday. He would never kill me—he's helped me through so much since I took Leora's position. We saw him with the vial, dumping the contents. That's the only reason I have him locked up, but I can feel that he isn't the real perpetrator. I'm listening to my instincts, Kieran."

"Was he head guard with Princess Leora?"

"Yes, actually. I kept all the guards she had. To help ensure my and the heart's safety, his memory wasn't wiped. He was the only other person who knew about the past. He became a crutch for me whenever I struggled, giving me support."

"You said she got really sick, right?"

"Yeah—achoo!"

"Describe her sickness to me."

"Well…" Ciana puffs out her cheeks, racking her brain. "Now that I'm thinking about it… it was basically how I am now. That's how it started at least, then she got even worse, becoming bedbound eventually."

"And nothing you or anyone did helped? Not even the queen?"

"That's right. Wait!" She puts a hand to her mouth, eyes widening. "You don't think—"

"Not even the queen can heal someone poisoned by Lumenocinide."

"Why would he though?" she whispers, coughing into her arm.

"Doesn't the head guard take over when the royal ruler dies, at least until a new ruler is in place?"

"Yes, how did you know?"

"It's the same thing on my side, which is why I don't have any guards. My people are selfish. That's beside the point, though; he probably killed Princess Leora, thinking he'd take over, not thinking the queen would ask you right then. So when you were crowned, he probably waited until the right time to kill you. Plus, with the queen gone, she can't anoint another ruler after your death."

"He's always been so protective."

"Probably to make sure you didn't die before you were supposed to. My father must have been in touch with him, letting him know when to start the poison, so it would weaken you on the journey."

"Would the poison have set off the balance then?"

"I guarantee it did; it's the only thing that would have weakened this side enough to set things off."

"But Zomo said he got the package after I had left, the balance had broken before that."

"We never saw the package, for all we know he's had it before we left and he was just saying that."

"But why would he—"

*Bang!*

# Chapter Twenty-Three

Ciana and Kieran whip their heads towards the town, searching for the source of the loud bang. The princess watches as her guards run from the palace towards the edge of town. "What now?" she sighs, trying to look over the buildings.

"It's not my people," Kieran says, but Ciana shoots him a look of uncertainty. It was just the other day his kingdom raided hers. "Trust me. If they value their lives, they won't go against my orders."

Ciana watches him a breath more, studying the sureness of his face. A wolf howl echoing through the air draws her attention back.

"Oh brother, I can't deal with this right now," Ciana stresses, running a hand through her hair.

"I'll take care of the dogs," he offers, but Ciana shakes her head.

"I can't let you—"

"Yes, you can." Kieran faces her. Slowly he reaches for her, as if to caress her cheek, but his hand lowers, and a single finger traces down her arm. "You need to stay here where it's safe."

Ciana's breath catches at his touch, his words, his concern. "I need to do my part, Kieran."

"You're part is to stay safe." His eyes glisten with determination. "There's only one reason why they're here."

Turning her face away from him, Ciana stares at her kingdom. "I know. But it's all the more reason why I need to help."

"You're not going to listen to me, are you?"

Ciana glances at him, seeing a half-cocked smile on his lips. "No," she tells him.

"Fine," he says with a sigh. "But I'm coming with you."

Kieran helps Ciana through the marble hallway out to the hay and wood stables. Horses fill the large stalls.

"Moondust!" Ciana calls. Her beautiful black and silver mare whinnies, sticking her head over her stall door at the sound of her name. "You can come out, it's okay—achoo! You won't get in trouble this time." With a snort, Moondust unlatches the door, letting herself out, and trots to Ciana. "Good girl." Ciana presses her head against her mare's nose. "I've missed you. Kieran, will you help me up, please?" Kieran carefully grabs her waist, lifting her onto the horse. "You can get on too; I'm not going to make you walk," she offers.

"I'm good. I'll meet you there."

"You sure?"

"Yeah."

"Okay then. Let's go, Moondust." She clicks her tongue, trotting down the stone streets, following the sound of the howling wolves to the edge of the town.

Her guards are lined up, swords out, threatening a large group of unfamiliar men. In the front, Olcan and another man are staring the guards down. Ciana slides off her horse when she reaches the line of men, leaning against Moondust as she heads to the front.

"Your Highness, I wouldn't—" Ritesh begins, silencing when she puts her hand up. Olcan smiles mischievously at her sight.

"My, Princess Ciana, you look much worse than when I last saw you. You should try more of my mixture." He laughs.

"We both know you were poisoning me yourself, Olcan."

"What can I say? I was only trying to help a friend."

"What are you doing here—achoo!"

"We saw that big ugly troll carrying you this way and thought we'd pay you a visit."

"And you had to bring your entire pack? Are you that weak by yourself?"

"Ooo you are quite different from when we first met."

"Answer my question."

"Of course I brought my pack! I told them about you and they were all very worried." He bows mockingly.

"There is no need for you to be here, Olcan—achoo! Just leave and we won't have any problems."

"I'm not leaving until I get what I came here for. I left empty-handed the last time you came across my path, it will not happen again."

Kieran joins Ciana's side. "You might want to think again, furball."

"You're still here?" Olcan raises an eyebrow. "Rumor has it you died."

"That's why you don't trust rumors."

"No matter." Olcan moves closer to Ciana, Kieran stepping in between defensively. "Go home, princey. This doesn't concern you, it's between me and the princess."

"I'm not going anywhere, hairball." The man next to Olcan steps forward, grabbing Kieran's arm. "You too hairball junior, hands off and leave unless you and your whole pack feel like dying today." He lets go of Kieran, stepping back.

"You're full of it, Prince Kieran. You can't take on my pack all by yourself," Olcan sneers.

"Who said I was alone?" Kieran motions behind him, where his men have joined Ciana's guards, who defensively aim their swords at them.

"What are you doing?" Ciana hisses to him. "They shouldn't be over here. You told me that you ordered them to stay in your kingdom. If you want a war, do it on your side."

"Princess, they won't leave until they kill you themselves. I will not let you die. I commanded them to help. You and your guards aren't a match against Olcan."

"Kieran, I don't want any bloodshed; I can't afford to lose any more of my men."

"Lucky for you then, we don't spill any blood."

"You know what I mean."

"There won't be a war. If these mutts are smart enough, they'll go back to their filthy holes. We can kill them all within seconds and they know that."

"Olcan, is there some way we can work something out?" She turns her attention back to Olcan, whose smile grows when she sneezes into her shirt.

"Why, of course. If you willingly give me your power, we will leave peacefully." He bows again.

"I won't do that," she sniffs.

"I'm well aware you won't. I made the mistake of going with the king's plan to kill you slowly, but that won't happen this time. Instead, I'll kill you outright and give him the power myself. It's the least I could do in return for his hospitality of bringing us to this beautiful pixie gnome-filled planet."

Ciana steps back, gently pulling Kieran with her behind her guards, Moondust following closely. "Ritesh?"

"Yes, Your Highness?" He nears.

"Why don't you have your guns?"

"Prince Kieran's people destroyed them all."

"What about our other weapons? The bows? Tasers?" she lists.

"All unusable. We only have our swords."

Ciana sighs. "For that reason, take your men and protect my people, in case things get out of hand. Leave Olcan and his pack to Kieran and his men."

"But, Your Highness—"

"Do as I say. I know what these intruders are capable of. Trust me, please."

"Princess, you need protection back at the palace," Kieran intervenes.

"Not if you take care of them."

"Not if one gets by us. If I'm here and all your guards are here in town, no one is there to protect you. Have a guard or two go back with you."

"I don—achoo!"

"Please, Ciana. I want you to be safe," Kieran pleads. Ciana looks between him, Ritesh, and Olcan.

"Ritesh, ensure all the guards are in place then report back to the palace. You'll be at my side until the intruders are gone."

"Yes, Your Highness." Ritesh bows, taking all the guards into the town. Olcan fixes his eyes on Ciana, watching as Kieran helps her back onto her horse.

"Kieran?" she coughs.

"Yeah?"

"As much as you don't like me, you've got me?"

Kieran meets her eyes without hesitation. "Always. Just get back to the palace and stay there. Your guard should be there soon. I'll take full responsibility for anything that may happen." Kieran whacks Moondust's hide, sending her and Ciana back towards the palace, turning his attention back to Olcan.

"Get her!" Olcan orders.

Moondust stops a few feet into the town, rearing on her hind legs as one of the brown wolves jumps in front of her, almost knocking Ciana off.

"Easy girl, just get me home." Moondust attempts to go around the wolf, before deciding to jump over him instead. Ciana's eyes widen as she sees the wolf preparing to pounce. "No!" she cries. The scene before her unravels in slow motion, and there's nothing she can do to stop the wolf. He jumps, extending his claws to Moondust's underbelly. The mare squeals as the claws make contact with skin. "Moondust!" Ciana gasps, feeling the unsteady landing.

Her mare takes another step only to falter and collapse. Ciana rolls off her horse's back as they hit. "No!" Ciana's breath quickens, trying her best to crawl back to her horse. "Come on, Moondust. Get up." She nudges her with the little energy she has; Moondust snorts. "Please, you need to get up for me." Ciana crawls around to Moondust's stomach, a long scratch bleeding to the ground. Moondust lets out a sigh. "I can't heal you, girl. I'm too weak. I'm sorry," Ciana cries, laying her head on a section of Moondust's chest that's not bleeding, feeling her horse let out her last breath.

A low growl snarls from behind.

Ciana locks her jaw, turning to face the wolf. Mustering all her strength she stands, fists clenched as tears stream down her cheeks. The fighting of Olcan's pack and Kieran's men engulf the air. A shrill shriek escapes through the fighting, echoing through the air, making Ciana's heart pound. She locks eyes with the wolf slowly stalking towards her. The noise around her disappears the closer the wolf gets. She's alone... no protection from inevitable death. While she waits for it to pounce, she hopes he'll end her quickly. But what was he waiting for? He had her defenseless.

"Do it already!" she seethes. The wolf snarls, rolling his shoulders back, getting ready to pounce. She keeps her eyes locked on him, with a push from his hind legs, he's in the air; jaw opened, teeth bared. Ciana stands her ground, breathing faster. This was it. At the last possible second, the wolf drops to the ground in front of her with a yelp. A sword sticking out his side. The sound of fighting fills the air once more as Ciana sways, her body no longer strong enough to hold her up. Knees buckling, she falls into a pair of strong arms. She looks up at Kieran, who's staring at her with every bit of concern.

"Did he hurt you?" he nearly demands.

"No," she mutters through a cough, following Kieran's gaze to her horse.

"You still can't heal the dead or dying, huh?"

"No."

"I'm sorry, Ciana," Kieran whispers, supporting her on her feet as he pulls the sword from the wolf, guiding Ciana away from her horse, towards the palace.

"I can't leave her."

"You'll have to, Princess. You need to go where it's safe."

"I thought you guys could take them out in seconds?"

"Yeah, well, it's a bit harder when they use their so-called powers to mess everything up. Stupid wolves. We'll take care of them, though. Right now, just worry about getting back home."

Footsteps shuffle behind them before Olcan's strong voice yells, "You have something of mine!"

"No, I don't think so," Kieran dismisses. Olcan runs in front of them; Kieran points his sword towards his chest. "Watch it furball, I'm not afraid to use this."

"Oh please. The princess here didn't want any bloodshed, so we both know you wouldn't kill me in front of her." Kieran lowers the sword slightly. "Told you. You know, I think the princess made you go soft. That's not good for the Prince of Darkness. What would your father say about that?"

"I haven't gone soft and I don't care what my father would think. He already tried to kill me."

Olcan takes a step towards Ciana, making Kieran raise the sword back up. A pair of hands grabs Ciana from behind, ripping her away from Kieran, a sharp knife pressing against her neck. Kieran's breath quickens as he looks between the knife against Ciana's neck and Olcan.

"Drop the sword, Kieran, or she dies right here, right now," Olcan bargains. Ciana inhales sharply as the man presses the blade more forcefully. The sudden intake of air stirs a cough, but she holds it in, wanting to prevent getting cut if she were to let it out. Kieran drops the sword, raising his hands above his head. The pressure lessens against Ciana's neck, giving her a chance to cough. "Smart choice, Kieran." Olcan smiles, grabbing the sword. Kieran looks at Ciana apologetically.

"I still have my own power, you know. I don't need a sword," Kieran reminds him.

"Oh, I'm quite aware of that, but you still have to touch a part of us for that. If you even try to touch us, we'll kill her in an instant." Olcan smirks, before pouting his lips. "I don't think you could live knowing you caused her death, so I wouldn't try. For your best interest of course." Kieran lets out a frustrated puff of air, crossing his arms, a hint of realization crossing his face as he uncrosses his arms to gently pat his pockets. "Smart boy." Olcan grabs Ciana's arms, exchanging the sword for her from the other man, pushing her back down the street. "So, Princess," he spits, "any last words? Now's your chance."

"If you're going to kill me, why not just do it?"

The other man snickers, following behind as Olcan lets out his own laugh. "I want to share your death with everyone. So they can watch as I bask in the glory of holding your power before giving it to the king."

"Still seems pretty pointless if you ask me."

"Are those going to be your final words before I silence you for good?"

"No—achoo!"

"Then what are they? I won't give you another chance." Olcan's eyes narrow.

"You're so dumb." She lets out a single laugh. "Never turn your back on the Prince of Darkness."

"He wouldn't dare try to get you back from me now. So don't count on it. And for the record, those are pretty lame last words."

"Ah, but you see, those aren't going to be my last words." Ciana smirks.

"Maybe you're the one who's dumb, Princess." Olcan begins to laugh, only to stop as he stumbles forward, nearly tripping over Ciana, his eyes watering as he rubs the back of his head. He whips his head around, tightening his grip around Ciana's arms as he stares Kieran down, who is swinging a silver chain in the air.

"No one is allowed to insult the princess, except me," he states, coming closer.

"Oh, I'm so scared," Olcan laughs, shoving Ciana into the other man's hands once again. Ciana's mouth drops as she watches Olcan's face slowly start to bubble with blisters. "We're not scared of a little silver."

"Who said anything about silver?" It's Kieran's turn to smile. Olcan's eyes widen as he looks down at his blistering red hands.

"What's happening? What did you do?" he demands, voice shaking as he touches his face.

"I'm the Prince of Darkness and Death. I know how to kill anything in this world whether they were born here or not."

"Olcan, are you alright?" the man questions in horror as the rest of Olcan's skin begins to blister. Olcan changes into his wolf form, running off. The man releases Ciana, letting her fall to the ground, chasing after Olcan in his own wolf form.

Ciana rolls over so she can look up at the dreary sky. Kieran walks over to her, tilting his head so he can look straight at her.

"You aren't allowed to insult me either," she coughs.

"We'll see about that." He smiles, throwing the chain away from him, offering his hand.

"What did you do?" She takes his hand, standing up, wrapping her arms around his for support, starting their way back to the palace.

"I just found the chain in the blacksmith's nearby and may or may not have dipped it into Grimmist. Touch it and it'll instantly start to burn blisters into your skin and may kill you if not taken care of. Fatal for a werewolf, harmless for anyone else." He pulls a small black bottle from his pocket.

"We don't have Grimmist."

"I never said you did."

"Then how did you get it?"

"You're forgetting who you're talking to."

"Okay, but you can't just magically make poison appear."

"No, sadly. That would be cool, though." Ciana raises an eyebrow at him. "Hey, for me it would be!"

"Then how did you find it?"

"When I was staying in the hotel in the Outcasts town and found the bandages, there was a bottle of it just sitting on the counter, unopened."

"It was just—sitting there—achoo!"

Kieran gives her a sheepish grin. "Okay, maybe it wasn't just sitting there. There was a cabinet next to the medical supplies that had a very secure lock on it. My curiosity took over, so I opened it and saw it."

"Kieran, you can't just break into others' belongings."

"They lived out in the middle of nowhere, I was confused as to why they would keep something locked up in a very public space. Then I was even more confused as to why they would have such a thing, but once blondie boy mentioned Olcan, it made more sense. Despite being friends, they must not completely trust them."

"Blondie boy?" Ciana's eyebrows furrow together. "Oh, you mean Hamill," she connects. "You stole two things from them? What else did you take?"

"I only stole two things, I promise. Not like they'll notice."

"Still! You better not have stolen anything from me." Ciana coughs. Her body grows heavier with each step, feeling like she could collapse at any moment.

"Why would I do that? I have no use for anything from over here."

"Your Highness!" Ritesh runs toward them and stops, trying to catch his breath.

"Yes, Ritesh?" Ciana and Kieran stop walking to listen.

"Those men are retreating. Permission to carry out normal duties?" he requests.

"Only once they're completely gone and Kieran's people are back on their side of the border."

"Still don't trust me, Princess?" Kieran wonders.

"It's them I don't trust. You're not exactly there to watch them to make sure they don't try anything. They shouldn't be over here anyways—achoo! You all need to get back over the border before you get too comfortable here."

"You're right. But I'm not leaving until we fix the balance. You still need me."

"Your Highness, how can you trust him? Zomo told us what happened, are you sure he's not the one killing you?" Ritesh pulls Ciana away from Kieran.

Kieran's eyes darken. "I could say the same thing about you, Riptush."

"Watch it, buddy." Ritesh places a hand on the hilt of his sword.

"Ritesh, Kieran, *please* just stop. Kieran, from now on, please don't pick a fight with any of my guards or staff. Ritesh, I'm following my instincts. You are dismissed." Ciana releases herself from Ritesh. The guard bows, eyeing the Prince of Darkness as he leaves. Kieran's expression softens once he's far enough away, wrapping Ciana's arm around his neck for support, seeing her begin to sway.

"I can see why you've tried so hard to have everyone like you. Everyone is such a doubter." Kieran shakes his head.

"What can I say? It's been hard—achoo! You can't blame them though; to them you are the Prince of Darkness. They have no reason to trust you like I do." Ciana leans against his side, tired.

"But, as their ruler, they should trust you and your decisions. They should trust who you trust."

"Not for me." She frowns.

# Chapter Twenty-Four

Kieran opens the palace doors, helping Ciana to the dungeons. Goosebumps prickle on Ciana's arms as the cold air hits her, her light bouncing off the shadowed stone walls. Kieran guides her to a barrel next to the thick metal bars of Zomo's cell.

"My Princess?" Zomo walks over to the bars from his bed. "Why are you here? I heard there was another fight happening."

"There was, but everything is alright now." Ciana touches her hot face. "Zomo, I know you've been loyal to me, but there's been new insight."

Zomo's eyes widen. "What do you mean new insight? What has this... what has *he* been filling your head with?" He gestures to Kieran, throwing daggers with his eyes.

"He's been helping me realize some things."

"Yeah, realizing what he wants."

"He isn't brainwashing me. He can't do that." Ciana sighs, feeling a rush of heat despite the cold air. She wanted to go back to bed. To rest. She couldn't keep exerting herself like this. Not right now at least.

"You wouldn't know!" Zomo fights.

"Zomo! Just because you're in a cell does *not* mean you can disrespect me!" Ciana's voice echoes against the stone walls as Zomo drops to a knee, bowing his head at her authority. Kieran smiles with pride at the sight. "You've been the only person who's ever trusted and listened to me. Why are you failing to do so now?"

"I'm sorry, Princess Ciana, please forgive me. I meant no disrespect. I do trust you, I'm just stressed being down here. Please forgive me," Zomo finally apologizes, keeping his eyes fixed on the ground.

"I accept your apology, Zomo. Now please listen to me." Ciana calms herself.

"Of course."

"You were the head guard for Princess Leora before me. You know very well that her sickness was the same as what I'm currently experiencing." Zomo looks back up. "I have reason to believe that you poisoned her knowing you would run the kingdom if she were to die, but the queen anointed me in her place right away. Now that the queen is dead, she can't anoint anyone else in my place if I die." Zomo's lips purse.

"My Princess—"

"Wait, wait, wait, Freedo. You didn't react to the queen being dead," Kieran stops him. Zomo looks at him, before looking back at the ground.

"You knew she was dead?" Ciana gasps, which quickly shifts into a cough.

"My Princess, please let me explain," he pleads, looking back up, meeting her eyes as he stands.

"I think your silence was enough." Kieran crosses his arms.

"Kieran please." Ciana shakes her head. "Go ahead and explain, Zomo, but it better be the truth—achoo!"

"Of course, my Princess. You see, during Princess Leora's reign, I got greedy for power and was tired of taking orders from others. The King of Darkness visited me one day in private and told me that if I killed the princess, I would be able to take her power and rule over everyone. He gave me Lumenocinide and told me that I just had to put it in her meals and drinks and it would slowly kill her and no one would suspect a thing. After the princess died and you took her place, the queen talked with me, knowing what I had done. She was furious. Even had me detained, was going to have me killed. But then the people started to rise against you. The queen was going to come out and tell everyone that it wasn't you who killed Leora, but with the way everyone was acting, she knew they wouldn't believe it."

"Why?"

"To them, it made more sense for the handmaiden to kill the princess than the guard. There was no physical proof to tie me to it. With the hatred they had towards you, even with my confession, they weren't going to believe it. They would have thought the queen and I were trying to protect you from the wrong thing you had presumably done. And if the queen went along with my execution, the people would be even more furious, thinking I would have been killed innocently even though I wasn't. That's when the queen wiped the memories. Looking out for you, however, she wanted to ensure you'd be safe and not have any trouble. Since she and I knew the truth about Leora, she reluctantly gave me another chance to redeem myself with you. To make sure things stayed in order and didn't fall apart like it was. It was also a punishment for me to see what I caused within the kingdom. What trouble I had brought upon you. No words can describe how terrible I felt for what I had done, and I vowed that I would protect you and the heart, never to be greedy again."

Zomo takes a breath. "The king came to me later, saying we could try again, but would get rid of the queen first to prevent her from ruining our plans. I declined, giving him the poison back. Furious with me, he left. Over the years, seeing the way everyone has been treating you, broke my heart. It still does because I caused it." Tears well in his eyes. "I didn't know the queen had died, but I knew the king was going to kill her at some point, so I'm not surprised he's done it. I'll admit to killing Leora, but I promise you, Ciana, I did not know I was poisoning you."

"If you dealt with the poison before, why didn't you realize what was in the vial?"

Zomo bites his tongue, not answering.

"It was different from the one you had last time?" Kieran asks. Zomo nods. "There's two different types of poisons. The ones that you can see and smell and the ones that are clear and odorless. Lumenocinide can be either depending on how it's brewed," he explains to Ciana. "The one in the vial was clear and odorless, but I bet the one last time smelled almost sweet and a light pink color?"

Zomo nods. "I even checked what was in the vial before I put it in the heart, but I didn't realize it was the poison," he adds.

"So why were you not affected by it?" Ciana questions.

"Gift from the king. He made it so the poison wouldn't hurt me when I was using it on Princess Leora." Silence falls again. Ciana stares at her hands before looking up at Zomo, trying to hold back her tears. "No, Princess, you can't—"

"I'm sorry, Zomo, I really am," her voice shakes, tears rolling down her cheeks. "As Princess and based on your testimony and the events that have happened both in past and present"—she takes a deep breath—"I'm declaring treason."

"Ooo," Kieran breathes, raising his eyebrows.

"Unless further evidence can be presented to prove your innocence of recent events, you will be scheduled to be executed at the nine o'clock hour, tomorrow morning. The method of carrying this out will be revealed prior to the event."

"Your Highness—"

"I'm sorry, Zomo. I really don't want to, but you know I have no choice. I hope we can find evidence before then. Please forgive me," she cries.

"I do."

"And after the execution, at noon, I will be renouncing my position as princess, naming another as queen."

Ciana gathers all her strength, despite the room starting to spin and her limbs shaking from exhaustion, she leaves the dungeon without the help of Kieran, clinging to the stair rail as she ascends them. At the top, she collapses; from down the hall, Kuma runs over to her.

"Ciana, are you alright?" Kuma helps her up.

"I'm fine—achoo! Just tired and stressed," she tells her out of breath. "Help me to my room, please, Kuma."

"Would you like to eat first?"

"No, I'm not hungry. I just need rest."

"Okay, let's go." Kuma wraps her arms around Ciana, helping her to her room.

Ciana leans against her balcony railing, looking over her blackened garden. She hears footsteps approach her from behind. Kieran leans on the railing next to her.

"You can't give up your title," he tells her softly.

"What did I tell you about knocking?"

"We've been over this, I don't knock."

Ciana rolls her eyes. "I told you that I was never actually crowned as the princess, so technically it's not my title, but I need to give it up."

"Why? Because your people don't believe in you?"

"No, I have to give it up to *save* my people."

He scoffs. "That's ridiculous."

"Kieran," she begins, shifting to face him. "Only the queen would be able to fix the balance."

"But she's dead, so we have to find another way to fix it."

"There is no other way. That's why we're still in this mess!"

"We just haven't figured out another way yet, we've been occupied with other important things."

"Kieran, listen—achoo! The queen is dead, but her power isn't." She rests a hand on his arm, looking into his eyes.

"I know that. It went to you, but you said you couldn't use her power because you aren't a royal."

"Her power went to the heart, not me, and you're right, I can't. However, when the queen gave me Leora's power she gave me what I needed to set me apart, tying the rest to the heart. The queen's power is the only one that can bring life from your darkness. I can give someone the queen's power, just enough to fix everything, but not enough that their body can't handle all the power. The rest will go with me."

"She gave you the power to bring life though and what do you mean *with you*?"

"She only gave me what I needed so I can bring life, but not enough so I can bring life from *your* darkness. That requires much more power than I have. All of the queen's power is in the heart. One can take her power by killing me, as you know—achoo!"

"Right." Kieran nods, following. "Because you're connected to the heart holding it. In the process of killing you, the power would transfer from the dead heart to the killer through the physical touch they have on you. I'm aware of that. Right now you're a walking gateway to it."

"Exactly. But I can access the power if I choose to, opening the gate that keeps it from all filtering into my body. I can possess all her power. When I do so, my power will be overrun by the queens—achoo! Disappearing. My body still can't handle all that power, so it'll kill me shortly after, but not before I can give the new queen what she needs to fix everything." Ciana's eyes fill with tears, keeping them locked with Kieran. Trying to see that this is what needs to be done.

"Then wouldn't someone else take the rest of the power?"

"Yes, but no one would be able to live with all that power, none of our bodies can't handle it unless we were born as a royal. Yes, we're all descended from her, but since the queen never remarried and Princess Leora never married, the power stopped with them. The rest of us are so distantly related that we aren't able to hold that much power anymore. I'll have Ritesh make sure no one takes it."

Kieran blinks away his own tears, shaking his head. "Just use the queen's power yourself."

"I can't. I may hold it within the heart and have access to it, but I can't use it, not unless someone took the princess's power, giving me the queen's. I can't just pick and choose what I use from her power; it has to be given to me. The queen gave me the power to bring life, just like I'll give the new ruler the power to bring life, especially from your darkness."

"So have someone give you that power."

"I'm the only one who can do that now. I'm the only one with access to the queen's power—achoo!"

"Then give yourself that power," Kieran reasons.

"I can't. If I wanted to have a chance of living long enough to try and give myself what I needed from the queen's power, I would have to get rid of my own. But I can't get rid of my power without killing the heart, because my power is also connected to it via my life."

"Mmhmm," Kieran nods.

"I can transfer my power to someone else, but as soon as I do, it'll break that connection with the heart, killing it instantly, which would cause the queen's power to automatically come to me as I'm the only thing left it's connected to. And even if that wasn't the case, our powers are what keep us alive. If we lose it, we die. So as soon as I'd start to transfer my power, I'd have no choice but to start taking possession of the queen's power in order to live—achoo!" Ciana looks back over her garden, taking her hand from Kieran's arm. "Even then I'd be taking on both powers at once, despite transferring my own power, it'll result in killing me almost instantly."

"What are you saying?"

"You know what I'm saying," she sniffs, taking staggering breaths as tears stream down her face.

"Ciana, I won't let you."

"It's the only way."

"No, it's not. We can find another way," Kieran nearly pleads.

"Yes it is, Kieran. The only way for my kingdom to have a chance of survival is to use the queen's power to restore everything. I can give the new ruler just enough to do so, but not without sacrificing myself. I have to die in order for things to get better."

She buries her face in her hands, sobbing. Kieran gently places a comforting hand on her shoulder.

# Chapter Twenty-Five

Ciana grips the side of her sink, forcing herself to stay standing despite the room spinning. Once she finishes her hair, she'll be ready for Zomo's execution, and then she can relax until it is time to head down. She forces her mind to focus on her image in the mirror instead of the room spinning behind her. Raising her hands, she goes back to doing her hair, reflecting on everything she's been through the last few weeks.

*I took the title of princess to help everyone. I made things worse by trying to do things the way Leora did. In just the week I've been gone... so much has happened. I've grown so much.* Ciana coughs into her arm, then quickly grabs the edge of the sink as she begins to sway back. Tears fill her eyes. *And now I have to execute the one person I thought I could trust... the person I confided with for everything... who betrayed me.*

Grabbing a tissue, she gently dabs her eyes so she doesn't mess up her makeup. *I only want the kingdom to be happy. To be how it was when the queen ruled. When Leora ruled. I don't want to die.* She wipes away new tears streaming down her face, taking staggering breaths. *There's so much I could have done, but there's no other way. I have to give my life for my people. Things will be better once I do.* Ciana's breaths turn into a coughing fit. Raising her hands above her head, she collapses to the ground, her body out of strength. Looking up to grab something to hoist herself back up, the room spins faster, overwhelming her, so she lays back down.

"Princess Ciana?" Kuma's voice calls from her bedroom.

"In here," Ciana coughs. Kuma peers around the bathroom door, then rushes to Ciana's side, helping her up.

"Are you alright?" she asks once Ciana's coughs die down.

"Yes, I'm fine. Thank you. Perfect timing." Ciana sighs, motioning for Kuma to help her to a nearby chair.

"I was bringing you some breakfast." Kuma nods to the silver tray on the bedside table.

"Thank you, Kuma. But I don't have an appetite right now."

"You need to eat. It'll give you strength."

"I know. I had some fruit earlier, but I'll eat a better meal after Zomo's execution." Ciana sinks into the chair. Kuma fiddles with her fingers.

"Are you really going to kill him?"

"He's guilty. I saw him poison the heart, and there's no evidence to prove he's innocent."

"How is his execution going to be carried out?"

"He's to be electrocuted."

Kuma gasps. "That's horrible!"

"Let the punishment fit the crime." Ciana shakes her head, glancing at the clock on her wall. "I should be getting to the arena. Will you help me over there, please?"

"Of course, Your Highness." Kuma helps Ciana to her feet, then wraps an arm around her for support.

They hobble outside, towards the back of the palace, where a stone arena towers over them. Low whispers fill the air from the onlookers inside, guards stationed at every entrance and exit. Kuma helps Ciana to her box on the floor of the arena, straight across from Zomo, bag over his head, cords hooked onto him from the metal chair he's been seated on, the hooded executioner next to him. Ciana lets go of Kuma, leaning against the wood of her box.

"Thanks Kuma."

"You're welcome, Ciana." Kuma looks around at the crowd, fiddling with her fingers. "Your Highness?"

"Yes?"

"Is it true you're going to give up your title?"

"It is." Ciana smiles warmly, wrapping Kuma in a hug. "But the next ruler will be perfect for the job."

"It's not going to be the same. I don't want to work for anyone else."

"Don't worry, things will be just fine. Have I ever let you down?"

"No." Kuma smiles.

Ciana breaks the hug, leaning back against the wood. Kuma looking around. Ciana watches as her maid fidgets even more, frantically glancing around the arena.

"You alright, Kuma?"

"What? Oh yes, I just don't... do good with executions."

"Aww, Kuma, I'm sorry, but this is something that I need everyone to witness. Is there anything that will make it easier for you?"

"Yes, I have something that would help keep me calm, but it's back in the palace."

"There's still some time before the execution. You can go grab it."

"Oh, thank you, Princess Ciana." Kuma curtsies, rushing out of the arena, running off faster when she nearly runs into Kieran as he enters. Ciana watches Kieran as he makes his way to her box.

"You have a great turnout for an execution, I'm surprised," he comments, standing beside her.

"What are you doing here?"

"Same as everyone else, I'm here for the execution."

"Why?"

"You'd be surprised how interesting they can get, at least on my side of the border. I've always wondered if you guys did them, too."

"Only if absolutely necessary, so don't get too excited."

"I'll try not to." He smiles. "Have you figured out who you want to take your place?"

"I believe so. She's perfect for the job."

"Who?"

"Kuma."

"Your handmaiden?"

"Mmhmm, she's so sweet and on top of everything, she'd be great. I'm going to tell her later. Ritesh is aware of what is to happen and will make sure no one is there but him, Kuma, me, and you."

"Why invite me?"

"As Prince of Darkness, it's only fitting for you to be there and see who the next queen is in case something were to happen again, although nothing should, but also so I can say goodbye." Ciana looks up at Kieran who frowns. "What?"

"Do you have to?"

"You know I do. You haven't seen Patches or the pixie gnomes by chance, have you?"

"No, I haven't. I don't know where they've disappeared too."

"That's too bad, I was hoping to see them one more time. But, if Patches does happen to show up, will you look after him for me?"

"Only if he shows up and doesn't make a mess. He is your cypup after all." Kieran lightly nudges her.

"Thank you."

"Anytime."

A horn blows, silencing everyone as all the doors close. The hooded executioner rips off Zomo's bag. Ciana glances around for Kuma, her heart beating faster as the executioner stands next to a metal box holding a bright red button.

"Zomo Thadious Finx, a royal guard to the princess, is sitting here before us now on a count of treason." The judge's voice rings through the arena. Ciana's heart skips, hands shaking more than ever. "Treason for poisoning the princess for his own gain as ruler of our kingdom. Pleading innocent, there has been no evidence to say that he is not behind the plot to kill the princess. He was found poisoning the heart that keeps our kingdom alive. The accused will be electrocuted at exactly nine o'clock, with the current time being eight fifty-eight with thirty seconds."

"Kieran?" Ciana whispers, placing a hand on her racing heart, struggling to catch her breath.

"Eight fifty-nine. On the hour at my command."

"Kieran?"

"Yeah?" He looks over at her, just as she collapses into his arms.

"Stop the execution," she gasps, black dots appearing in her vision.

"What?"

"Thirty seconds."

"Stop the execution," she orders. "Now!"

"Five, four, three, two..."

"Stop the execution!" Kieran yells as the clock strikes nine. The executioner steps away from the button; one of the guards storms over.

"You have no power over here, Your Highness. Only the princess can stop an execution," he snaps.

"I did. I told him to stop it. It's not him," Ciana tells the guard, fighting for breath.

"Your Highness, are you alright?" the guard asks, eyes darting between Ciana and Kieran.

Kieran tightens his grip around her, keeping her on her feet. "Ciana, what's going on?" he whispers.

"Zomo is to be released and regain his position as head guard." Ciana shrinks slightly as her light flickers. "Immediately."

"Yes, Your Highness." He leaves with a bow, commanding orders as he approaches Zomo in the chair.

"Ciana..." Kieran's voice is soft but tinged with alarm and worry. "Your light."

"Take me to the heart," she tells him, clutching her chest. Without another word, he scoops her up and races towards the palace.

Kieran runs the best he can through the palace, up the marble stairs to the double doors. Kicking the doors open, they look wide eyed at the short, blonde-haired girl, dumping the remains of the silver and pearl white vial into the heart. Kieran walks in further, setting Ciana on her feet, keeping her upright.

"Oh, that was quick, I thought it would have taken you longer to get here. How was the execution?" The girl smirks, pocketing the vial.

# Chapter Twenty-Six

"Kuma?" Ciana squeaks, sliding out of Kieran's grip to the floor, weakening by the second.

*Kuma? Out of everyone... Kuma? This can't be possible. She's too sweet. So nice. There's got to be a mistake. A misunderstanding.*

"You know, it was just chance that Zomo killed the last princess. I didn't realize he had a record when I sent him the vial after you left, but after overhearing his confession to you in the dungeon, it made framing him even better. Too bad you had to kill an innocent man, but what's done is done."

Ciana can't believe her ears. There was no way Kuma was saying this. "Why, Kuma? I was nothing but nice to you."

"That made things easier! You're so vulnerable and trying so hard to be nice, it was so easy to get on your good side. But it was sickening all the same, putting up the charade. I just want the queen's power; I can do so much with it. I felt it when the king made her save my life after I had almost died."

*Sickening? My being nice to her was sickening? But wait...*

"What do you mean... you almost died?" Ciana rests her head on Kieran's leg, eyes getting heavy.

"Prince Kieran here should know, since he was a part of it." She glares at him.

Ciana struggles to lift her head to look up at him.

"I've never been on this side of the border until recently. How could I have been a part of almost killing you?" he questions, confused himself.

"I never said it was on this side of the border."

Ciana looks at Kieran as his eyes narrow and fists tighten at his side. But slowly, his features soften as recognition crosses his face.

"You're..." he exhales sharply, shaking his head. "I knew you looked so familiar."

"You really do know her?" Ciana asks.

Kieran nods, considering. "The daycare... the fire." His eyes never leave Kuma's. "You were the child trapped inside."

A wicked grin splits Kuma's face. "Took you long enough."

"What?" Ciana gasps. "But how could you—"

"You left me for dead!" Kuma spits. Her words cause Kieran to flinch. "If you weren't so hesitant in doing your duty, I would have never been trapped and almost killed."

"I... I..." Kieran grasps for an explanation. "How did you survive?"

Kuma scoffs as if the answer were obvious. "The king got me out and then had the queen heal me. I despised living in the kingdom since then. Wanted to escape. Leave everyone. No one would have noticed anyways. A few years later, the king came back to me, offering me a deal. He told me how someone by the name of Zomo had failed him and needed a new recruit for his new plan. Knowing my hatred with Tenebris, he thought to ask me. I agreed. With the queen's help, the king took away my power of darkness, forcing the queen to replace it with the power of light, making me one of you. The queen had no choice and couldn't tell anyone because of the holding roots. The time finally came. The queen had to wipe the memories of everyone in your kingdom for whatever reason. That's when I was put into place at the orphanage. No one even knew."

"Kuma—" Ciana tries to speak.

"I'm not done!" Kuma snaps. "I worked my way into the palace, getting close to you; that way when the queen was finally at her peaking point with the king's holding roots, I could start the poison, setting off the balance to send you both off where you would kill her. The king would take the power and make me his new queen."

"Kuma—"

"Quiet Prince of Nothing," Kuma spits. Ciana curls up on the floor. "I waited, keeping the king updated with facts about you." Kuma sneers at Ciana. "Anything that would help with your downfall. Such as your kindness, how perfect you try to be. I even intercepted the letters from the prince to help ensure that you would leave for the fortress. He was so insistent that nothing was wrong, but finally you crossed to his kingdom to get him to go, but that still didn't help. I finally reached out to the king for help to convince him to go with you."

*I was told of how kind and perfect you are supposed to be.* Kieran's words from the beginning of their trip come to her mind. *He was told by someone. The king had gone to him to go on the journey. Kuma was updating the king, who then told Kieran what to expect. And the letters... No wonder Kieran was so surprised by her accusation that he was ignoring the problem. He was, and he tried to tell her, but... Everything was starting to make sense.*

"The king finally told me it was time," Kuma continues. "I started the poison. I almost got caught the first day when Zomo came to tell me the orphan children were here, but he didn't see the vial. After you put him in charge of the heart, I sent the package to him, letting him do my work for me without even knowing. Once the princess here dies, I can take the power, and the king and I will rule over this pathetic world."

*Used. I can't believe she used me. She's working with the king, but so was Kieran. He's not a bad person—Kuma can't be either, right? The king could be using her like she used me.*

"Kuma," Ciana wheezes. "He'll kill you for the power. The king will kill you and just take it for himself."

"Of course you'd say that, Princess. He's been nothing but nice to me; he's the only one that cared for me."

"So have I."

"That's your problem. You cared for me, but I never cared for you. No one could. All those sweet things you'd say to me made me want to hurl. I almost killed you sooner because of how nice you were acting. Bleh."

*Because of how nice I was acting? I wasn't acting. Of course I cared for her, she reminded me of me when I first started. But... no one could care for me?* Despite saying them in her mind, the words still catch in Ciana's throat. *No one?*

"I took the poison back to my side of the border. How did you get it?" Kieran changes the subject, seeing Ciana's face overwhelmed with hurt.

"While you were over here doing who knows what, the king got it back for me. He's anxiously waiting for me to return, and then you're next. Some Prince of Darkness you've been. Your father thinks you're a disgrace."

"Kieran?" Ciana coughs, her energy leaving her body. He kneels, cradling her in his arms.

*No, there is one person who cares.*

"Say your goodbyes now, time's a ticking!" Kuma laughs maniacally.

"Kieran?" she whispers, taking one of his hands, looking into his tear-filled eyes.

"You can fight it." He tries to smile.

"You know I can't—the king can't have the queen's power."

"I won't let him." Tears roll down his cheeks, falling on her ashen face.

"I know you won't. I know you'll do the right thing." Ciana takes a deep breath, a cold rush washing over her body as her hand grows warm.

"What do you—" Kieran stops and looks down at his hand that's starting to illuminate.

"NO!" Kuma shrieks, running towards them, stopping and stumbling backwards when a sword points to her chest, eyes bulging from their sockets as she looks at the once again fully armored Zomo.

"No, Ciana. You can't." Kieran's bottom lip trembles.

"Kieran, you're the only one who can hold all of the queen's power. You're a royal. The only one I can trust to have it," Ciana whispers.

"But I have my dark power. You said—"

"I know what I've said. But you have to trust me."

Kieran tries to pull his hand away, but Ciana tightens her grip. "It'll disappear."

"I'm trusting my instincts. Please trust me."

Kieran tightens his grip on her hand, allowing the warm energy to flow through his body. His arm illuminates. "I will always trust you, but... you'll die."

"I'm already dying." She shivers, shrinking in his arms. Her body starts to numb.

"We can find another way."

"There is no other way. I'd have to give up my power either way. We've been over this."

"I can't lose you, Ciana." He tucks back her hair, his voice cracking. The rest of his body illuminates as he wipes away her tears.

"Kieran, thank you for believing in me." She smiles, closing her eyes. Her hand falls limp in Kieran's, her body darkening as her light disappears.

## Kieran

"No," Kieran whispers, holding her lifeless body close to him in a hug. He shivers from the warmth the power is providing in his body, not realizing how cold he felt before. He waits for the warmth to disappear, but it surprises him when it doesn't. His body nearly feels at peace. Feeling both his and the queen's power flowing together, not raging against one another like he was expecting.

"Z-Z-Zomo?" Kuma finally finds her voice. "But your execution?"

"The princess called it off at the last minute." He smiles at her. "Ritesh, Eyal!" he calls, and the two guards enter. "Take her to the dungeon. We'll deal with her later."

The guards bind Kuma's hands behind her back, pushing her out of the room. Zomo sheaths his sword, squatting next to Kieran.

"You two became close, didn't you?"

"No. We couldn't wait to be away from each other."

"Perhaps it started out that way, but I see how she is around you. And I see how you've changed too."

Kieran's head sways, fighting to keep his voice steady. "You're wrong."

"Why else did you return to this side to help her?"

"I don't know what you're talking about."

"Yes, you do. Prince Kieran, Ciana was never herself after she obtained the throne. You somehow got her to show it."

Kieran pulls Ciana away from his chest so he can look at her face. Gently tucking more of her hair behind her ear. "She wasn't herself because everyone thought she had killed the previous princess. She was trying to have everyone love her like they did Leora. No thanks to you, I might add."

"I didn't mean for everyone to turn on her. I honestly didn't think they would accuse her. Even then she was so kind."

"Why didn't you try to keep her from hiding herself?"

"I knew what she was doing, but was too worried about redeeming myself to the queen to try to make her stop. It was her decision anyway."

"She did it because of you," Kieran nearly spits.

"I know. She knew she didn't have to pretend."

"You never gave her that chance. You made everyone doubt and hate her so much that even with their memories wiped, she had to try to be someone else to be loved. I don't even know why she's gone through all this trouble to save you all after the way she's been treated." Kieran holds Ciana close to his chest once more.

"She did it because that's who she is. That's the one thing she did do as herself. She always puts others first. Which is why I became so overprotective of her—she cared for them first even if they tried to take her life. She's the most selfless person one could meet; Princess Leora wasn't even as selfless as Ciana. I couldn't let something happen to her."

"You failed."

"No, I didn't. Yes, I contributed unintentionally, but she didn't die from the poison. She died because she gave you the queen's power, getting rid of hers in the process. She gave her life, giving you the power to prevent it from getting into the wrong hands."

"Same thing. She's not here."

"Listen, Your Highness. She trusted you. I've never seen her trust someone as much as she has with you, not even with me. She trusted you enough to give you the power of life and light along with your own powers, which no one should have. You could easily take all of us out and use the powers for your own purpose, but she trusts you enough to know you won't. Since I'm skeptical, I don't trust you, but I have never doubted Ciana and her judgements. I voiced them, but I know she knows what she's doing. If she trusts you that much, then I have complete faith that she made the right choice. If she trusts you, so will I, Your Highness." Zomo straightens before falling to one knee before Kieran.

"Wait a minute, I'm not in charge here, you are." Kieran shakes his head.

"She gave you the queen's power; technically, that means you're in charge. We don't have to tell anyone that, but your word will be my command. You know more of what is going on than me anyways."

A gust of wind blows into the room, spinning dirt around in a tornado. Kieran shields Ciana with his body, squinting through the debris to see the source of the power, but the air is too thick, blocking his view.

"Aww, I love seeing two people who hate each other become friends!" a deep voice thunders through the space. The dust devil pulses with the declaration.

Zomo presses to his full height, withdrawing his sword and taking position before Kieran.

A low laugh greets them, and with a final rush, the wind ceases, revealing the center of the storm. "Is that any way to greet an old friend, Zomo?"

# Chapter Twenty-Seven

"You are not a friend," Zomo seethes.

The King of Darkness tsks. "How about you, son? You managed to surprise me once again. You know, I thought you were serious when you said you wouldn't kill the princess, but you proved me wrong. Here you are with her dead in your arms, glowing with all that power. Although I have to give credit to my dear Kuma for weakening her for you. Now together we can rule the world, and darkness will prevail!"

Kieran gently sets Ciana on the ground, reluctantly letting go of her cold hand to stand next to Zomo.

"I will never rule with you, Father," he tells him firmly.

"Oh, come now, Kieran. I know you can feel the strength of the queen's power."

"So what if I do? It's not going to change my mind to rule with you."

"We can do so much with it! We can even split the power between us, so we can both create *and* destroy life. We'll be unstoppable."

"Not going to happen."

"Then give me the power. You are much younger; I doubt you could hold it for long." The king clenches his fists, forcing a smile onto his face.

Kieran lets out a single laugh. "I'm pretty sure I'm stronger than you."

"My son, I can give you your own planet to rule over. Your own people. Your own... love." The king glances at Ciana. "One that won't die because she's pathetically weak."

Kieran's jaw locks, black flames engulfing his hands. "I don't need my own anything," he seethes. "I already have everything I need."

"Do you? It doesn't look like it. We can change that!" The king's nostrils flare.

"I don't want to change anything."

"Then don't. Just give me the power and I'll leave you to the kingdoms."

"You're not getting it." Kieran's eyes narrow.

"Give it to me!"

"No!"

"I order you to obey me!" the king commands.

"You will not get the power from me," Kieran tells him strongly.

"If you won't give me her power freely, I'll just have to kill you again."

"Not going to happen."

"We'll see about that," the king spits, before breaking into a mischievous smile. "You'll change your mind after I've killed everyone else."

"Don't—" With a wave of his cape, the king disappears in black smoke. Kieran sighs, extinguishing his hands, wiping his dried tears. "It's between me and him, not anyone else."

"Just say the word, Your Highness."

"I can't make you and everyone else risk their lives because of something I won't do."

"Not giving up the power is the right thing; we will stand by your side for that. He can't have the power, and you're the only one who can give it to him."

"He'll kill all of you."

"Prince Kieran, we will protect you and the power. You can't do it alone, not even with your men. If there is a good time for our sides to fully work together, it would be now. Who knows what the king has in store, but we won't make it through unless we work together. Think of Ciana. She said you'd make the right choice."

"She'd—" Kieran looks at Ciana's lifeless face, trying to imagine what she would tell him. "She wouldn't want a war."

"No, she wouldn't."

"She would try to negotiate. But she would let me fight. To save her people, she'd do anything, allow anything if it meant her people would be safe, even if some lost their lives. She'd even risk her own life if it meant her people would be safe."

"She would."

"She is so selfless and caring, she needs to stop." Kieran chuckles, smiling to himself.

"That's what you love most about her, isn't it?" Zomo smiles, watching Kieran admire Ciana.

"No, that's just what she did throughout our whole journey. She watched over Patches and made the clothes for Iris and Liko. She tried to heal me, before she managed to heal me. She thought of anything and everything else but herself; she cared for all life. Even the ones that threatened her own. It was sickening." Kieran shakes it off, turning towards Zomo, who raises an eyebrow at him. "Don't get any ideas, you mention this to anyone, I know where to find you."

"Mention what to whom?" Zomo asks, furrowing his brows with a smile.

"Zomo." Kieran holds his hand out. "Prepare everyone to fight. My father will be coming over here since this is the Kingdom of Light, so I propose all the women, children, elderly, anyone who can't or shouldn't fight, come over to my side of the border to hide and be safe. I will round up my men and bring them here. Without the light, we can't survive, so we can't let it get into the wrong hands."

Zomo firmly shakes Kieran's hand. "It shall be done, Your Highness. The best place to gather will be the town square in the center of town."

"Perfect." Zomo puts a fist to his chest, bowing. He turns on his heel, exiting the room.

Kieran looks back down at Ciana's dark body, gently picking her up, carrying her to her room. Placing his hand on the handle, he stops.

*What did I say about knocking?* Ciana's voice enters his head.

"You said for your room," Kieran whispers before he knocks, opening it. Throwing back her covers, he carefully sets her down on her bed, tucking her in. He makes sure none of her hair is covering her face, then gently placing a kiss on the back of her cold hand. He walks over to the balcony and windows, locking them and closing the blinds, darkening the room. Taking one last glance at her on the bed, Kieran leaves the room.

# Chapter Twenty-Eight

Returning to Tenebris, Kieran orders everyone to gather. They needed to know what was happening; with the kingdoms, with his father, with the princess. His throat tightens remembering how pale Ciana had turned, how dim her body had become, how fragile and cold she felt in his arms. Tears sting his eyes, threatening to flow, but he blinks them away and shakes off the emotion. Now is not the time to fall apart. Not only did the Kingdom of Darkness need him, but the Kingdom of Light too.

Around him, his people murmur softly to each other as they wait. A few men shout profanities, setting Kieran off. The princess is dead, and all these idiots care about is wasting a few minutes away from their work to listen to their prince.

"People of Tenebris," Kieran begins, stepping up onto a stone platform to address everyone. The crowd quiets. All eyes turn to him. "We are fighting against the king!" A feeling of unease spreads, and then, some are shouting in protest. These people only know the way of darkness, but it was time Kieran showed them there is more to life than living in the shadows.

"The Princess of Light is dead," he continues. Clapping ensues, only fueling Kieran's anger. He clenches his fists at his side, glaring at a woman cheering. "Her death is not a cause for celebration," he seethes. "The king is after the former queen's powers. Powers the princess protected to keep both our kingdoms balanced. And now, that magic flows within me. We can't survive without them, they are the only ones that can provide us with food on which we live. We must work together with the other side in order to win against the king; we can not afford to lose. We're assuming he's going to strike on their side of the border, but that's not to say he may come over here. The women, children, and all those who will not be fighting will take shelter in our bunkers. And the people of Luxregnum will be sheltering with us." Everyone shouts in protest.

"Why can't they stay on their side of the border?" a man yells. "We don't need them wasting our provisions!"

"They will be safer on our side. Away from the fight."

"Bunch of wimps, can't even fight their own battles!"

"Tynan put yourself in their position. Would you want *your* wife to die in battle? How about *your* children? You want them to fight beside you and expect them all to live? If that's the case, I can make their deaths quick rather than the tortuous demise they'll face by my father's hands." An unsettling quiet falls over the crowd. "I thought not. They will be safer over here along with your loved ones, protecting them from whatever awaits in the coming battle. The rest of us that will be fighting will meet in Luxregnum's town square. Get things squared away quickly and report within the hour to either the bunkers or the Kingdom of Light."

Kieran sits on the platform as everyone disperses in a low rumble. He grips his hands together, feeling the warmth from the queen's power disappear, his new light flickering slightly as his power tries to overpower the queen's, before they flow together once again. When some of his people halt to observe the forest, Kieran glances up. Standing on the platform, Kieran smiles when he sees Zomo make his way through the town, followed by a large group of people, escorted by guards.

"Your Highness." Zomo bows, reaching Kieran. "All of Ciana's people have been informed of what is to take place. These are all of them who will not be fighting, minus Kuma and... Ciana. I couldn't find her."

"Thank you. Kuma should stay locked up; as for Ciana, I put her in her room."

"She'll be safe there."

"Come; the bunkers are in the forest." Kieran extends his arm, leading Zomo and the people through town into the thick black trees.

Kieran opens a hidden trapdoor in the dirt, a wooden stairway leading deeper into the earth. Blue lanterns flicker on as Kieran walks down first. The lights illuminate a large open space filled with shelves of food, large metal boxes, blankets, pillows, and other necessities. As more of Ciana's people file in, huddling close together, the blue lights are drowned out by their natural lights.

"Everything you need should be in here. There are multiple bunkers through our forest, but some of my own people will be joining you here," Kieran explains. "For your safety, stay in the bunker and under no circumstances leave. Someone will come get you once the fighting is over. We don't know how long it will last, but hopefully it will be over quickly."

Kieran climbs the stairs to the ground above, followed by Zomo and the guards.

"Your Highness?" Zomo closes the trapdoor.

"Yes?"

"What will happen if the King of Darkness does overpower us?"

"I really don't want to think about it, but believe me, you wouldn't have to worry about it 'cause he'd probably get rid of all of us first."

"How much food is in the bunkers?"

"Enough to last them roughly a week if they eat appropriately, but hopefully this fight won't be a long one."

"I know you weren't here, but if you have stored food, why did your people come fight us for some?"

"We preserve what we can, either by canning, drying, or freezing them. Those metal boxes hold a lot of fresh fruit you've given to us. We cryonic them until we need it; but they're fresh once taken out. The food is strictly for situations like this, not just because we run out. My people are aware of that and would have gotten in trouble if they started eating the stored food."

"I see."

Kieran, Zomo, and the guards make their way back over the border. Kieran frowns when they pass through the broken gate. The dense metal hanging off its hinges, dents showing where many people kicked it. His thoughts trail back to when he first came over the border.

*What are you doing here?* Ciana's voice comes to mind. He smiles, remembering how beautiful she looked in her lilac dress that day, how tired she looked. Kieran shakes his head, remembering how annoyed he was that his father had come and convinced him just a day prior to make him go on a long journey, and he showed it. The gate then was beautiful, shining in the light, but it was so bulky compared to the rest of the kingdom. Maybe it wasn't all bad that it was destroyed.

His smile turns into a frown as they continue through what once was a beautiful town. Walking past the dark stone and brick buildings, they reach the gray and black town square. Men armed with any form of weapon patiently wait. Thunder rumbles above them, rain escaping the clouds. The men eye Kieran suspiciously as he and Zomo confidently stride to the front of the group. One by one, Kieran's men cautiously walk through the town, joining the rest of them.

"Your Highness," Zomo begins, drawing Kieran's attention away from the awaiting people. "I know we haven't seen eye to eye before all of this..." Kieran scoffs, crossing his arms over his chest. "But I want you to know I believed in the princess in every decision she made. I could tell she trusted and believed in you. And I believe in you just as much." Zomo drops to a knee on the wet ground, bowing his head.

"Stand up," Kieran huffs. "We've been over this."

"I know, Your Highness, but—" Zomo stands, silencing when Kieran raises a hand.

"There's no need for you to make a scene. I'm only taking command of you and your people until this whole thing is over."

"You hold—"

"I'm aware. Holding the queen's power puts me in charge. I can't rule both my kingdom and yours. Once this battle is over, you will be the ruler until a new prince or princess is in place. At that time, I will hand over the power."

"Of course, Prince Kieran. I just wasn't sure if you'd consider combining the kingdoms with you ruling."

"I'm afraid that would be much more difficult. It wouldn't be the best idea to combine our people. In the meantime, I am honored to fight beside you. I can see that you mean well and everything you've done was to protect Ciana. Together we will protect her kingdom and her power. It's the least we can do to make up for our distrust and bickery towards one another."

"I couldn't agree more." Zomo smiles. Kieran nods, turning his attention back to all the people gathered around.

"As you all already know," Kieran finally addresses the crowd, ensuring his voice rises over the rain pounding off the ground, once everyone has made their way over, "we are fighting against the king. We are a team. In order to survive, we must work together. We cannot afford to turn on one another in this dire time. We must remain focused on our goal to defeat the king and whoever is on his side."

"How do we know we can trust you?" a man yells, waving his hand in the air.

"The princess gave her life to help save us. She trusted Prince Kieran to give him the queen's power. I trust he is on our side," Zomo answers firmly. "The king is responsible for the death of Princess Ciana, and he's the one who is going to pay for causing this whole mess."

"Why should we fight for her?" another man yells. "She's done nothing for us. All she's done is hide away in her pretty little palace while things fall apart."

"Like what? What has she not done?" Zomo strongly counters.

"Look around! The balance broke, and she was supposedly gone to fix it. It's not fixed, now is it? She never comes to town meetings to discuss problems. She uses all our money to buy her own things. She's trying too hard to keep her life perfect, like she's hiding something. What is it, Zomo? What has our princess secretly been working on? She's never where she needs to be. Like now. She's off playing dead while we're supposed to fight to fix *her* problem."

"Ciana *died* for you all!" Kieran snaps, clenching his fists, not believing his ears. "She's done nothing but try to be the best person so you can all like her. She couldn't fix the balance before, which is why she came back and now... she's dead. Did any of you even try to get to know her?"

"Why would we?"

"Why not? She was your ruler. I bet you don't even know how selfless she really was. How she hasn't had a chance to enjoy a moment since she's ruled. How she put you all first in everything she did."

"Yeah, right." The man scoffs.

"If she was so selfish, she wouldn't have left to try to save her kingdom. She nearly died multiple times on our journey, but still kept going. For *all of you*."

Zomo steps forward to address the crowd. "Ciana wasn't secretly working on anything. She tried to keep her life in order to try to keep the kingdom happy," he adds. "She was never where she needed to be because she couldn't. Not with you all throwing nonsense at her for her to take care of."

"She doesn't care about us."

"She's done nothing but care for you. You're just too blind to notice it." Kieran shakes his head. "If she didn't care, she would still be alive right now. But she's not. She gave her life to save her kingdom. She did her part. Now do yours as her people and support your princess. Protect your kingdom. For her. She's the best ruler you will ever have."

Silence fills the town square; only the sound of rain hitting the cobblestone street surrounds them. All the men either look at each other or the ground. The tension that was in the air disappears, only to be replaced with the ground heaving.

*Thump. Thump.*

"Ready your weapons!" Zomo orders, trying to catch his balance. Everyone raises their weapons, some showing fear, realization that a fight really was going to take place.

"Wait!" Kieran stops him as a bald green head peers over the town, a big grin spreading across his face at the sight of Kieran. "Stand down," he warns. The crowd freezes, weapons still raised, unsure what to expect from this large being. "Kabandha?" Kieran yells up at the troll, wiping his wet hair from his eyes. "What are you doing back here?"

Kabandha carefully steps behind the group of men, breaking a few houses. "Pesky dog came back. Heard fight from others, so came help," his voice booms, lowering his giant hand. Patches leaps from the palm, jumping into Kieran's arms, licking his already wet face.

"Thank you, Kabandha."

"Where Princess? Safe?"

"Her body is in a safe place, but the king killed her. She sacrificed her life to help save her kingdom."

"Pay!" Kabandha cracks his knuckles; the group of men stare at the troll, bewildered.

"Wait, she's dead?" the high voice of Iris chirps, appearing on Patches's back with Liko.

Kieran frowns. "Yes. She had hoped to see you guys one more time, but you also disappeared."

"We went to get our own help after we heard of the fight from the other trolls and giants. If a fight is going to happen, we want to help. Princess Ciana was nothing but nice to us, so we can return the favor by helping her kingdom!" Liko exclaims.

"We might be dealing with the werewolves again."

"Then we'll kick their little furry butts! Payback for eating us. Come on out guys!"

Pixie gnomes pop up all around the square, crying out in agreement in their high-pitched voices, startling everyone.

"Uh, Your Highness?" Zomo intervenes, curiously looking at Liko and Iris. "Sorry, Mister—"

"My name is Liko!" Liko smiles before his eyes widen. "Wait, you can hear us, too?"

"Yes?" he replies, confused. "Um... Prince Kieran, what exactly did you and the princess get into?"

Kieran smiles at the thought. "A lot happened. I'll fill you in on our adventure after this whole thing is over."

Patches barks, jumping from Kieran's arms, tail wagging.

"What is it, bud?"

Patches continues to bark, running to the end of the square. Barks fill the air from afar, and then, a family of cypups of all sizes and colors trot into the town, jumping up and down with each other, sniffing everyone. Patches scurries up to one of the larger pups, coming back to race around Kieran's feet.

"Is this your family?" Patches barks, jumping on his hind legs a couple of times. "You are loyal. All for Ciana?" Patches lets out a whine, his tail and ears drooping. Kieran rubs his head. "I know. I'm going to miss her too. I'll look after you, though. She'd appreciate all this."

Patches perks back up, quietly baring his teeth towards the side of town, the other pups following suit.

"I think they're coming." Kieran turns to all the men. "Okay, we have a lot of help here, which gives us a better chance of winning." *Hopefully*, he mentally pleads. "Stand your ground and do *not* give up!"

"For our future and for our lives! Most importantly, for the princess. We will not let her die in vain!" Zomo adds, shaking a fist in the air.

A low growl comes from the cypups as a large group walks into the town, led by the king. Everyone moves closer, ready to fight. Kieran examines the faces of the werewolves—Olcan bandaged up, but ready to fight—along with the outcasts from the village, the goblins, and many more Kieran doesn't recognize, evening out the playing field.

Zomo hands Kieran a sword, pulling out his own. "Prince Kieran?"

"Yes, Zomo?"

"I've got your back."

"And I've got yours."

Tension rises, both sides staring each other down, prolonging the fight. The king smiles mischievously and, with a snap of his fingers, they begin to charge, crying out their anger.

"FOR THE PRINCESS!" Zomo yells.

Their side shouts in agreement, surging towards the king and his men, clashing in the middle, beginning the inevitable battle.

# Chapter Twenty-Nine

Kieran pushes behind Zomo, fighting his way into the middle of the battlefield. The rain pounds against the ground and everyone, causing weapons to slide out of the grips of some. Kieran searches through the clashing weapons and bodies, locating the king hidden within the chaos and heading in his direction.

"Not so fast, princey," Olcan snarls, stopping in front of him, his bandages hanging off on some ends. "I have a bone to pick with you and will gladly take care of you for the king myself."

"I'm honored, but this fight is between me and him." Kieran side steps him, but Olcan wraps his hand around the front of his shirt before he can move by.

"Too bad, I want to deal with you first." He pushes Kieran back, releasing his grip.

"You have nothing on me, furball." Kieran raises his sword.

"Oh, really? Says the one who burned me with Grimmist," Olcan huffs. Kieran smiles. "Think it's funny?"

"Kinda, you're the one who said you have magical powers, which I've yet to see."

"Oh, you'll see plenty," he seethes.

"Then what are you waiting for? Come at me." They circle each other, Olcan breathing heavily. The sound of fighting from around, filling the silence between them. "Are you scared?"

"No."

"You sure about that? For all you know, this sword could be laced with Grimmist. Although, I don't need a sword or poison to kill you."

"You wouldn't kill me. Your precious princess wouldn't want you to shed any blood."

"She's not here, but I will most definitely shed blood for her. She had no reason to die, but you, on the other hand, tried to kill her—twice. You deserve to die."

"The princess wouldn't think so."

"I'm not the princess."

"You still wouldn't want to disappoint her."

"I'm not going to disappoint anyone. Like I said, this fight is between me and my father, no one else." Kieran raises his sword above his head, advancing on Olcan, who backs up in fear.

"Okay, okay, you fight your father, that's something I'd like to see. Only for that reason am I letting you go to him," he panics.

Kieran brings the sword down, aiming it at Olcan as he walks away, back towards his father once again. Kieran fights off some advancing men, turning around to Hamill.

"What do *you* want, goldilocks?" Kieran sighs, shaking some of his wet, loose hair from his eyes. "I'm in the middle of trying to fight my father."

"I'm quite aware of that, but you killed the princess. What did she do to you that made you decide to kill her?" Hamill's face reddens.

"You think *I* killed her? You're the one who was trying to beat her up for something she didn't do," Kieran retaliates.

"She killed Leora."

"No, she didn't. Zomo killed Princess Leora with the help of the king. I was there when he confessed to Ciana. If you were going to beat anyone up, it would be him. The king killed Ciana the same way he killed Leora."

Hamill raises his sword to Kieran's chest. "You're lying."

"If you don't believe me, go ask Zomo yourself. His memory wasn't wiped." Kieran gently pushes Hamill's sword down with his own. "You know I'm right. You knew Ciana; she would never hurt anyone."

"You don't know anything about me. About my relationship with Ciana, so don't think like you do." Hamill raises his sword, ready to strike.

"Let him pass!" the king demands over the fighting, drawing Kieran and Hamill's attention. "He's mine now."

Hamill sneers, lowering his sword once more, allowing Kieran to pass him to his awaiting father.

"I thought Olcan was going to take care of you for me, but no worries," he greets with open arms.

"Stop the fighting, Ahriman. This is between the both of us."

The king's eyes widen, his mouth falling open slightly. "Did you just call me by my name?" His eyes darken. "No one calls me by my name."

"Call off the fighting."

Ahriman grabs the edge of his cape, whipping it around him. Kieran runs to grab him, but the king disappears.

"Dang it!" He heaves before blocking an advancing werewolf, fighting to make his way to an open space. He stops in his tracks, hearing a few screams echoing through the air.

"That was the lamest fight ever!" Olcan laughs, disappointment in his voice. Kieran turns around, sword up, to be met by two swords. One in Olcan's wrapped hand, the other in Hamill's.

"Go ahead, I can take you both on," Kieran challenges.

"I don't think you can."

"Your doubt hurts my feelings." Kieran keeps his eyes locked on them, ignoring the sound of metal hitting metal and the hint of iron mixed with the smell of rain.

Olcan pulls back his sword in a charge. Kieran chops down Hamill's blade, bringing his own up in time to block Olcan's stab. Kieran turns to the side, keeping Olcan's sword down, narrowly dodging Hamill's slash towards him. Olcan wacks Kieran's sword back up, pushing him backwards. Kieran looks between Olcan and Hamill, stuck in the middle.

Together they charge towards him, swords at the ready. As they raise their weapons, swinging them at Kieran, the prince ducks, avoiding the blow, but not before one of the swords nicks his arm. The last-minute move causes the men's weapons to lance each other.

Kieran stands, pivoting to face them, catching his breath. The two men stand crumpled over, holding their sides as blood seeps through their fingers. A smirk draws across Kieran's face, raising his sword for the second round.

Hamill brings his blood-covered hand to Olcan's shoulder. Kieran watches confused, until Olcan begins to straighten, his wound healing thanks to the blonde. The werewolf tightens his grip on his sword.

With a battle cry, Olcan lunges. Kieran dodges the deadly blow, striking his hand instead as he moves. Hamill slashes his blade wildly; blood spilling down his side from the gash he cannot heal himself.

Kieran deflects the blonde's sword, grabbing his hand, twisting it behind his back until he drops the weapon. Olcan raises his sword, casually walking to them. Kieran raises his blade to Hamill's throat.

"Put the sword down, hairball. Or he dies right here, right now," Kieran threatens, out of breath.

"Don't use my words against me. Besides, I couldn't care less if he dies. Go ahead," Olcan breaths, relaxing.

"Hey! I thought we were friends," Hamill grunts.

"We are. He's not going to kill you."

"Real friends wouldn't let each other die either way. I literally just healed you!"

Olcan rolls his eyes. "I won't let him kill you. I'm calling his bluff. He doesn't have the guts anymore."

"No, that's not what friends do!"

"What do friends do?" Kieran asks him.

"They stick together. Regardless of the circumstances. They don't play and risk each other's lives."

"Oh please." Olcan rolls his eyes.

"Do you have a friend like that?" Kieran presses.

"I—" Hamill hesitates, buckling slightly from his loss of blood. "I did." His voice chokes.

"Who?" Hamill shakes his head. "Who?" Kieran nearly demands.

"Ciana," Hamill whispers, eyes filling with tears.

"I must have heard you wrong, did you say Ciana? The same Ciana who you said was a traitor and selfish?"

Hamill nods. "I was wrong. You were right. She really was the kindest person. She would never hurt anyone. All those times she stuck with me in the orphanage, when she would help me, care for me when I was upset and stick up for me when I couldn't. She was like a sister. I was so excited when she got to work in the palace, living her dream.

How she got to be with Leora, who treated her almost like a mother. Ciana loved everyone, even when she and Leora went on errands."

"You must be talking about a different person." Olcan laughs. "The princess was none of those things. She was weak and naïve."

"So why did you go against her?" Kieran brushes off Olcan's comment. Perhaps he was getting somewhere with Hamill. "Why did you cause her so much trouble when you *knew* her to be a good person?"

Tears spill down Hamill's face, mixing with raindrops, his skin growing pale. "I'm not sure. I was just going along with everyone else. Jealousy. What anyone would give to be a ruler, and she got it so easily and quickly, through no fault of her own. She got what all of us orphans dreamed of. I was jealous. I let it blind me and my judgement."

"So why are you working for the king? The person who wants to get rid of your power and take control over everything?"

"He promised we would live. He wouldn't kill us."

"He'll kill the rest of the people. Everyone Ciana fought so hard to protect. He'll kill the rest of the orphans, the families, your friends. You'd be alone in your hatred. Alone with the memory that you let everything Ciana worked so hard on go to waste. And there will be nothing you can do to bring them back."

"He knows he's fighting on the winning side. Power is everything." Olcan gives a smug smile, wiping rain from his eyes.

Hamill locks eyes with Olcan, fighting to stay on his feet. Grunts and agonizing cries surround them, blood flowing with the puddling water on the ground. "It's wrong," he finally says. "There's no need for everyone to die, just so he can rule. We all have our lives to live. We need a chance to live it."

Kieran lowers his sword from Hamill's throat, placing a hand on his shoulder. Feeling a warm energy through his hand, he pictures

Hamill's wound healed. To Kieran's surprise, he can feel Hamill's strength returning as he uses the power. Picking up his own sword, Hamill uses it against an unsuspecting Olcan.

"Hamill, what are you doing? We're on the same side here!"

"Not anymore. Ciana would never let anyone die or risk their lives. She wouldn't let anything happen to her people."

"Okay, and? She's dead now, and she killed your previous princess."

"No, she didn't. She cared about everyone. It's too late to regain her forgiveness, but I will not let her kingdom fall!"

Zomo fights his way through the battle, running up to Kieran as he watches Hamill and Olcan fight. "Prince Kieran, are you alright?"

"I'm fine, Zomo. We may be getting new recruits."

"Who?"

"Hamill." Kieran smiles. Hamill gives Olcan a forceful push, into the middle of a small group of others fighting. With a huff he returns to Kieran and Zomo, bowing.

"I will fight with you. And I'll make sure the rest of the outcasts do as well. We need to fight for our kingdom, not for the king's desires." With a swing of his sword, he runs off into the swarm of fighters.

"Now, I need to find my father. He disappeared from me." Kieran glances around.

Zomo nods. "I'll help you look."

An arrow whistles through the air, grazing Kieran's already injured arm. He whips around, spotting the archer on a building, aiming his next arrow. Kieran and Zomo run out of range of the archer, back into the middle of the fights. A wolf lunges from behind some men, burying its teeth into Zomo's unprotected arm. In a cry of pain, Zomo falls to the ground underneath the wolf. Kieran grabs the wolf's skin, prying him off Zomo; a cold, sharp rush of energy runs through his hands before the wolf's body is engulfed in black, falling limp in

Kieran's grasp. He drops the wolf, helping Zomo back to his feet as he cradles his bleeding arm.

"Thank you," he seethes.

"I told you, I got your back."

Reaching the edge of the fights, Kieran surveys the space. His breath quickens as he sees bodies motionless on the ground, others trampling over them. Goblins throw their spears, nearly hitting everyone they target. Kieran's breath catches in his throat as he remembers Ciana hanging on the underground arena. How his heart almost stopped when the spear landed next to her head. She did all she could not to kill any of them, even when they were ready to kill her.

His eyes fall to the werewolves, changing between human and wolf form effortlessly, burying their teeth into their opponents. He watches as a few wolves surround a group before attacking. Running and barreling through everyone, knocking them to the ground, causing them to be at a disadvantage. The cypups fight back, clawing and biting the wolves equally. Giving them a taste of their own medicine. The pixie gnomes disappear and reappear, teasing the wolves and others, distracting them so another can get the upper hand.

Kieran shifts his attention to Kabandha. Despite his size, he can still only do so much. As goblin ropes restrain him and werewolves attack, he grabs whoever he can. He kicks the goblins underfoot, swatting away wolves and goblins leaping from buildings targeting his upper body. Kieran's eyes linger on the wolf in the troll's hand. Ciana's pale face comes to mind—how blue it turned when the troll was squeezing her in the mountains. He wasn't going to let her die; he couldn't. She didn't have any reason to. Not then. Not now.

Lightning cracks across the sky, breaking his trail of thought, lighting everything up one, two, three times before it crashes down on the buildings, setting them aflame. Kieran pushes his way through the battle, claws and nails scratching his skin as he fights past, Zomo right behind him. He frantically looks around. Lightning illuminates the sky again, striking the fight and killing those closest to the bolts. Kieran wipes his hair from his eyes, looking towards the top of the palace in the distance.

"Kabandha!" he yells over the fighting.

"Yes?" he bellows, dropping the wolf he was squishing, stepping over to him.

"Can you lift me to the top of the palace?"

"Course." He lowers his hand so Kieran can climb on. Zomo moves to follow.

"No, Zomo. Sorry, but I need to settle this alone." Zomo steps back with a curt nod.

Kabandha lifts his hand up, stepping to the palace, holding his hand next to the only flat part of the roof. Kieran jumps off, swinging his sword in his hand. Kabandha goes back to the wolves.

"I know you're up here, Father!"

"Of course I am. Where else would I be?" Ahriman walks into view.

"Just stop the fighting and we can figure something out. We don't have to fight to settle things."

"No, I will not stop until I get the queen's power."

"Why? What good will it do?"

"We'll hold all the power. Our ability to both destroy and create would make us impossible to defeat. It wouldn't just be this world, but everywhere else as well. Everyone would bow down to me—us—at last. Everyone would be happy."

"No one would be happy; everyone would be miserable."

"They will be happy as long as they do as I say. There would be no more balance or pesky light, just the darkness and everyone living by my rules."

"We need the balance, Father. We can't survive without it. I thought you realized that when you agreed to the pact?"

"I did before I realized we didn't need the people; I just needed the queen's power, like I had wanted in the beginning. Her power is sufficient to be able to grow the food we need, which is all we rely on them for. Just think of it, Kieran. Father and son, rulers of the world and many to come. We could create new worlds and kill others, ridding ourselves of anyone who causes problems. We'd have complete control and be together once again."

"No." Kieran shakes his head. "It's not right."

"Unless you give me the power freely, I will have no other choice but to kill you to get it myself."

"Go ahead. I will not give it up." Kieran drops his sword, allowing Ahriman to get closer.

"I'd hate to kill my only family."

"Then don't. Give up your powers instead and leave here."

"I would never do that either." Ahriman picks up Kieran's sword, handing it back to him. "Let's at least make it interesting before I demolish you."

Kieran takes the sword, and immediately puts space between them. Ahriman shakes his hand, creating his own sharp, black sword.

"So it begins. No powers, just sword on sword. Man to traitor." He lunges forward. Kieran blocks the blow, throwing in his own counterattack, stepping in towards Ahriman.

The swords clash, easily slipping off one another in the pouring rain. Kieran raises the sword high, slashing it down. Ahriman blocks the blow, directing it into his arm instead by accident. Nose flaring, he grabs the hilt of his sword with both hands, raising it above his head, fiercely bringing the blade down over and over on Kieran, who blocks every blow, backing up to make distance between them again.

Kieran's foot slips over the edge of the roof. Stumbling over, he manages to grab the slick roof rim with one hand. Breathing fast, Kieran looks down at the long drop below him. Ciana's scared face when she was hanging over the snowy mountain flashes into his mind; his heart races at the thought.

"That was easier than I thought." The king shrugs, hovering his foot over Kieran's fingers.

"I won't let go," he whispers, trying to keep his grip on the roof.

"Don't worry, you won't feel a thing."

A bark followed by a growl comes from on top of the roof. Patches sprints toward them, latching his teeth onto Ahriman's leg.

"Get off you dumb dog!" He steps back, vigorously shaking his leg to throw Patches off.

Kieran throws his sword onto the roof, bringing his other hand to the edge. He hauls himself over and quickly rolls away from the edge with his sword. Patches lets go of Ahriman's leg, running in front of Kieran, protectively.

The cypup snarls, taking deep breaths in as he begins to grow in size until he's standing 60 feet tall with wings spanning out at least 30 feet long; black scales line the middle of his back; his tail stretches longer to match his body, his blue eye swirling to black. Kieran steps back in awe as Ahriman's face drains of color, frozen in place.

"You are one amazing pup." Kieran smiles. Patches inhales deeply, exhaling fire towards Ahriman, who rolls to the ground, escaping the flames.

"I won't let some dumb cyclops dog dragon thing kill me!"

Ahriman runs around the roof, dodging Patches's large jaw and fire. Kieran circles around him, putting Ahriman between them.. Raising his sword towards his chest, Kieran advances on him.

"Enough of this!" he yells. Jaw locked and eyes narrowed, Ahriman darts towards Patches's chest, Kieran running after him. Patches tries to stomp on him, but misses as Ahriman maneuvers around his large feet. Raising his hands in the air, Ahriman controls a bolt of lightning, crashing it down on Patches.

"No!" Kieran yells as the cypup howls in pain, shrinking back into a pup. Kieran runs towards him, but he's too far. The king grabs his little body before dropping him. Patches whimpers in pain, trying to stay on his feet as a black swirl engulfs him.

"No," Kieran whispers, tears welling in his eyes. Kneeling, he picks up the pup, holding him tight. This was one of the last pieces he had of Ciana. He didn't know where Iris and Liko were or if they were even still alive. But Patches meant so much to Ciana. Her laugh when Patches first jumped to lick her face echoes in Kieran's head. She was so happy. So full of light when they came across him. He promised to look after him if he came back, but failed. He couldn't lose the pup, but it was too late. Patches lets out one last bark, the black overcoming the rest of his body. "You're such a good boy," Kieran reassures him, laying him down gently, then whipping his sword up to Ahriman's throat.

"Go ahead." He laughs. "Be the Prince of Darkness you're supposed to be. Kill me."

"Renounce your title and power," Kieran growls, backing him up to the edge of the roof.

"Never."

"Then I have no choice." Kieran looks at his father, hesitating just long enough for the king to knock the sword out of Kieran's hand, aiming his own blade at Kieran's throat.

"The princess made you weak. This is what I warned you about the last time you wanted to be fair and show mercy. I gave you a second chance then, but I will not give you another." The king raises his sword above his head; Kieran barrels into him, knocking them over the roof. Ahriman grabs his cape, engulfing them in black smoke before they roll on the ground at the foot of the palace.

Ahriman stands with his back turned to the prince. Kieran grabs his father's cape to prevent him from running off, ripping it off in the process. The black sword dissolves in an instant. Ahriman looks back at Kieran, fear written all over his face as he runs. Kieran jumps to his feet, grabbing the back of his shirt and turning him around.

"Who are you?" Kieran spits in his face, eyes dark.

"Uh… I'm…" Ahriman stalls, fidgeting in Kieran's grip, trying to escape.

"Answer me!"

"Okay, okay. I'm not the king. Not the real king, at least. I killed him ages ago after he made the pact and had us, but—" he begins, talking fast.

"Wait, what do you mean by us?"

"Uh…"

"Answer me!"

Ahriman gives a pained smile, before it fades into a glare. "I'm not your father. I'm your brother."

# Chapter Thirty

Kieran's eyes narrow, burning into Ahriman's. "It's the truth! Look, you were born with all the power, and it killed our mother—somehow you took hers when you were born. But I was born with nothing, even though I was born years before you!" he spits. "I was the odd one out. Everyone in the kingdom had their powers but me. Father gave me the cape which gave me powers. It may be different from everyone else's ability, but it's mine. Father didn't want me to be left out—wanted me to be able to defend myself."

"No wonder you didn't just kill me at the mansion. You don't hold enough power to take a life." A wicked smile spreads across Kieran's face, before it changes back to a hard expression. "So why did you kill our father?"

"'Cause I could."

"Answer the question!"

"As the firstborn, I was supposed to be next in line to rule Tenebris when Father had the audacity to agree with the pact, but nooo, it went to *you* because *you* were born with all the gifts. While you were living your precious castle life, I was left to be with the commoners, not to even be considered a royal! Questions would arise if I were to stay in the palace with you. So I was cast out. Banned from the palace. From the presence of our own father because he didn't want any suspicions."

"Wouldn't the people have known who you were?"

"No. I was kept locked up in the palace until you were born. We had no guards or staff so no one knew I existed. Knowing their son lacked magic would've hurt the kingdom, and because mother was ill while carrying me, they announced I was stillborn. Father taught me how to use the cape in case they couldn't have another child. So I could pass as a real royal. But then you were born healthy, and in the night was left to fend for myself with the commoners. No one noticed of course and that was the entire point. I couldn't stand being a nobody when I was born to be a ruler, so I killed Father before he left for the fortress, poisoned him, and presented myself as the king to the Queen of Light. Fortunate for me, Father never let her see his features. Strategic move in case he were to try to find information about her by passing as a commoner. Once the queen and I met at the fortress, I started the binding roots."

"How could you have enough power to do the binding roots, but not kill a person?"

"Father couldn't give me that ability with the cape. I can't kill you, I couldn't kill the queen right off, but I could kill smaller things, such as that pesky dog of yours. Binding roots don't take a lot of power, it just takes a lot of time. Which is why no one uses it. It's a good leverage to get someone to do something for you, but it won't instantly kill them."

"So you really couldn't do much. Even with the roots. You just kept the queen captive, but she had no idea."

"Exactly. No one did. But I had to wait until her princess replacement was in a position to die. There was no point killing the queen in her weakened state if it would just go to the little fake princess where I'd have to start all over. And with you being young, I treated you as if you were my son to avoid any suspicions since everyone knew Father still needed to teach and mentor you until you were old enough."

"If you raised me, how come no one told me you weren't my real father?"

"No one knew. Like I said, no one knew I was alive. Lucky for me, I took most of Father's traits so I looked like I could be his twin. No one in the kingdom suspected a thing. I could be king, have my royal status and raise you as next in line as it should have been and once you were older, as you already know, tell you my plan to get the Power of Light. But you failed! You weren't supposed to turn soft. You were to kill that stupid princess so I could have the queen's magic and finally get the respect I deserve!"

Kieran drags Ahriman to the town square, where everyone is still fighting.

"Call it off," he orders, voice deep and dangerous, the rain dripping down his dark face.

"Or what?" Ahriman challenges.

"I'll just kill you. You've done more than enough to deserve it." Keiran's eyes narrow.

"You wouldn't kill your own brother."

"Says the one who killed his own father out of greed. I don't have a brother. Blood means nothing, to you at least."

"I'm all the family you've got left."

"You sure about that?" Kieran's free hand goes up in black flames, threateningly bringing the flames to his brother's face, who stays unfazed until he's inches away.

"Fine, you win, but only because I don't want to die." He gulps, throwing daggers with his eyes towards Kieran. "Retreat! The war is off! The white flag is up!"

Everyone stops mid-attack, relaxing as they look at Kieran and Ahriman. Zomo walks up to them, holding his bleeding arm, with a half-beaten-up Ritesh next to him.

"Your Highness?" Zomo questions. Kieran shoves Ahriman into his hands.

"He's harmless now; lock him up like Kuma." They bow, pushing Ahriman towards the palace. "Olcan!" Olcan limps forward, half his bandages off, revealing new wounds.

"What? Ready to take me on now?" He smirks.

"You and your tribe are to return home and never come back. If I see any of you again, I will kill you on sight."

"Is that a threat?"

"Or, if you'd rather die now, by all means, stay," Kieran offers.

Olcan transforms into his wolf form, running off with his pack. Hamill limps forward, raising a bloody hand.

"What about us?" His voice shakes.

"What about you, Goldie?"

"Are you banishing us, too, or can we stay?"

"If you promise to not wrong anyone again and you all work for your wrongdoings, I'll allow it. If not, then you're back in the town."

"We promise not to, Your Highness."

"The rest of you!" Kieran stares down the goblins and unknown men. "You are all to leave and go back home like the wolves. If I see any of you again, you will suffer the same fate. Now get!" They all run off after the wolves without a word. "Now, everyone else, do your part to take care of the dead and wounded, and put out any fires that are still going. I also need someone to go tell those in the bunkers they can come out."

"I can do that, Your Highness," one of Kieran's men volunteers. Kieran nods, allowing the man to run towards the border.

"Kabandha, can you lift me onto the roof again?" Kieran calls up to the troll.

"Course." He lowers his hand, taking Kieran back to the palace roof.

Kieran steps down, carefully picking up Patches's black body. Kabandha lowers him back to the ground.

"Thank you, Kabandha. You're good to go back home if you want."

"I stay little."

"Okay."

Kieran walks to the border; finding a tree, he digs a hole underneath. Iris and Liko pop up next to him.

"Oh no!" Iris cries, hugging Patches's black body.

The other cypups make their way over, tails between their legs. Liko pulls the sobbing Iris away from the pup, allowing Kieran to place the little body in the hole, covering it back up. A couple of the cypups bring over sticks, setting them on top. Kieran stares at the soil, a few tears trickling down his face. He was just a pup, but he did so many things for him and Ciana. He saved their lives multiple times. Ciana mentioned how cypups were very loyal, and Patches demonstrated that very well. Not just for Ciana, but for Kieran himself too.

"If you don't have anywhere to go, you are all welcome to stay here," Kieran tells the cypups, wiping away his tears. "You too, Iris and Liko. You and your family and friends will be safe from any wolves here."

"Thank you, Kieran. We'd like that, and I'm sure the cypups would too." Liko nods, stroking Iris's hair. Kieran gives him a sad smile, standing up and heading towards the palace.

Kieran knocks on Ciana's door before entering, kneeling at her bedside, holding her cold, gray hand. Footsteps echo down the hall, growing louder as they near the room. Kieran looks over his shoulder at a now fully healed Zomo.

"I would give anything to hear her voice again. Her laugh. Her smile. I'd even be okay with her slapping me again." Kieran lets out a small chuckle. "I wish I could bring her back. She left too early." Silent tears roll down his wet cheeks.

"You hold the power to bring life, so why don't you?" Zomo suggests.

"I can't. I already told you that there's nothing that can cure Lumenocinide. It would still be in her system."

"That's right. I forgot. I'm sorry."

"Wait a minute." Kieran perks up. "It's not in her. The poison went into the *heart*. She was connected to it, yes, but not physically in any way, so maybe..." Kieran focuses on Ciana, the familiar warm sensation from the healing power running through his body to his fingertips as he imagines if she was alive again, holding what she could of the queen's powers. "Oh, please let this work. Come back to me, Princess," he whispers, more tears streaming down his face. A chill trickles through his body, causing Kieran to feel slightly weaker as some of the power leaves him.

Ciana's hand begins to light up, flowing upward to the rest of her body. The air stands still— Kieran and Zomo wait anxiously. Ciana's chest starts to rise and fall softly. Kieran smiles, placing a light kiss on the back of her hand. He stands up, relieved.

"Zomo?"

"Yes, Your Highness?"

"Make sure she gets a proper coronation. She'll make a great Queen of Light."

"Of course." Zomo bows. Kieran leaves the room, determined.

# Chapter Thirty-One

### Ciana

Ciana rolls over, pulling her covers up over her shoulders. Sunlight streams through the curtains onto her face. Her eyes flutter open, and she squints into the light. In a daze, she looks at the sunbeams streaming into the room before taking in the rest of her room. The light makes everything seem like it's in a dream. She closes her eyes, feeling the familiar warmth of power surging through her, although it's slightly stronger than before. She opens her eyes once more, looking towards her balcony doors, hearing birds singing their beautiful, joyful songs. Turning onto her side, she faces her room door, where Zomo is standing. Fully armored, a big grin on his face.

Ciana's eyebrows furrow. What was Zomo doing in her room, and why does he look tired? Propping herself on her elbows, she looks at him, then the room. She glances back at the sunbeams. How did she get to her room? She was in the room with the heart with Kieran because... she jerks into a sitting position, her memory returning. Her heart races.

"Zomo the heart!" she exclaims, look at him. He rushes to her side. "The heart! The queen's power! It was Kuma! Where is she?"

"She's—" Zomo begins, only to be cut off by more questions.

"Where's Kieran? He has the power. Where's the king? How did I get to my room? What's been happening? What has happened? I'm so confused. Is everything alright? Is the kingdom safe? What about—" she gasps. "The balance! How bad is it?" Ciana throws the covers off her, trying to get out of her bed to look outside. Zomo gently but firmly grabs her shoulders, keeping her from standing.

"Your Highness, you need to stay in bed. You're still recovering."

"Recovering from what? I'm fine. I need to see!" Ciana tries to free herself from Zomo.

"Ciana you were dead. Your body needs time to rejuvenate. You don't want to overwork yourself as of yet."

"What?" Ciana stops trying to free herself. "I was—I didn't think I was actually—" she looks down at her wrists, turning them until she notices the black tally on her left one. "I did die." She traces the mark lightly. "But how am I alive? I thought—" She jumps out of bed before Zomo can stop her again. "I need to see what's become of the kingdom." Ciana runs out onto her balcony overlooking her garden. What was a bunch of black withered weeds was now back to its flourishing green. Flowers of every kind are blooming, with butterflies and bees buzzing around them.

A knock on her door pulls her attention away from her garden. Turning around, she sees Kieran entering her room with Patches. She smiles as the pup bounds towards her with a yelp, leaping into her open arms.

"Patches, my sweet pup. I've missed you." She hugs the pup before pulling him away to look at his beautiful blue eye. Her eyes fall to a black tally mark on one of his brown spots on his stomach. Setting him back down, she focuses on Kieran. "Did you actually knock on my room door?"

A smile spreads across his lips. "I did."

"It's about time," she jokes before her questions start rushing back through her mind. "Kieran, what happened? Where's Kuma? Where's your father? What happened with the palace? Did you fix everything? I need—"

"I'll fill you in on everything, Princess. Don't worry," Kieran reassures her, keeping his eyes locked with hers.

"I'll be just outside the door in case you need me," Zomo informs them with a bow. "King Kieran," he acknowledges before exiting the room.

"Wait, *King* Kieran? What—I'm so confused. Kieran, what happened? Start from after I gave you the queen's power and you can't leave anything out."

"I won't." Kieran begins to explain everything that happened from the moment she died to when she woke up, leaving out minor details in some conversations that had happened.

"So what are Hamill and the others doing to redeem themselves?" she asks after he mentions how he let them stay.

"Community work—rebuilding the buildings that caught fire, building new houses for themselves, the pixie gnomes, and cypups. Stuff like that."

"That's not community work, that's manual labor."

"Same difference. Anyways, I also put them in charge of the food and making sure both sides get their fair portions."

"Alright, so what happened after Hamill started fighting Olcan?"

"Ah yes, now things get interesting." Kieran continues explaining the events.

"Patches is not a dragon," she smiles, denying the fact.

"I never said he was, but it explains the ability to breathe fire."

"He really grew and had wings?"

"Yes! It was amazing, and he was incredible until Ahriman killed him."

"What happened next?"

"He hit Patches with a lightning bolt, making him shrink back to his cute pup size and then killed him. I knocked Ahriman off the roof, which caused him to teleport us to the ground. He tried to run, but I grabbed his cape, accidentally ripping it off. His sword disappeared as soon as the cape was off, which caused me to think he wasn't who he said he was. Little did I know he's my older brother."

"He's your brother?" Ciana's eyes widen. "Wouldn't he have the same powers as you?"

"Nope, he got all his power from the cape, which I have somewhere safe."

"You didn't tell me you had a brother."

"I didn't know I had one. He killed our father when I was just a little kid."

"But if he's older than you, wouldn't he be next in line for king anyways?"

"No." Kieran shakes his head. "For us, the royal line falls to whoever was born with the power, which happened to be me. So, since the real king has been dead for many years, I automatically get the title."

"This is crazy. Let me guess what happened next, you threw him in jail with Kuma, realized you could save me, did that, then healed Patches and fixed everything."

"Yep."

"How did you revive me? I thought nothing could cure the poison?"

"There isn't. You weren't physically connected to the heart, so the poison was never actually in your body, just in the heart, so I was able to bring you back."

"So, why did you bring me back?"

"Oh, you know, you looked a little dull, so I decided to enlighten you." He winks.

She laughs. "That was terrible."

"I know, but it was worth it to hear you laugh again."

"Seriously though, why did you?" Ciana lies back on her bed.

"You're the only person I want to rule with me. Plus, you deserve another chance to run your kingdom in your own way, as yourself." He smiles down at her, which she returns.

"You gave me the queen's power."

"You're the one who should have it."

"You didn't give me all of it. You gave me what my body could handle, tying the rest to yourself. You are aware of that right?"

"I am, but what else was I going to tie it to? I am getting tired of looking like a glowstick, however, so I'll figure something out."

"Kieran? Do you know why the king—your brother—couldn't have the queen's power?"

"Because he'd be able to kill and bring things to life, giving him control over everything."

"Yes, but that's not all of it."

Kieran tilts his head, intrigued. "It's not?"

"In our version of our history, when the Queen of Light was reasoning with your father, she told him that if he took her power, it would be worthless and disappear."

"I know, but it's not like that with me."

"It wouldn't be like that straight off the bat, it would take time, but eventually it would disappear. Your powers are the opposite of ours, it's impure. So if your brother had taken the queen's power, he would have had both powers for a time, but eventually his dark power would overtake the queen's pure power, making it disappear and he'd revert to only having his dark power."

"So if I hold the power long enough, it would do the same thing?"

"You know, I'd say yes, but you're a good person, Kieran. Yes, you hold your dark power, but you're not a dark person like your father or brother, so if you do continue to hold the queen's power, it may not disappear."

"You think so?"

"I do, but I guess we'll find out over time if you do end up keeping it or not."

"Let's hope I do. I don't think it would be a good thing if the queen's power disappeared completely." Kieran gives her a small smile. Ciana smiles back, eyeing his wounds.

"Will you let me heal your wounds?" She sits up.

"You won't stop bothering me until I let you, right?"

"Nope!"

"Then I guess it's fine, for this time only."

"Thank you."

She grabs one of his hands, closing her eyes, feeling the warm sensation run through her palm, healing his wounds. She opens her eyes, releasing him, but before she can let go fully, Kieran squeezes her hand, not wanting to let her go.

"Ciana?"

"Yeah?"

"What's this?" Kieran turns her left wrist over, examining the black mark, rubbing it with his thumb. "You didn't have this before."

"Not before I died. It's been there since you healed me."

"I did this to you?" Kieran gasps, letting go of her.

"You didn't do anything to me. It's not a bad thing, I promise," Ciana reassures him. "It's a price that comes when bringing someone back to life. It's there as a reminder that they've already died and been brought back once before."

"Okay, you're right, that's not bad." Kieran nods, relaxing slightly. A smirk forming on his lips. "I thought I just somehow marked you as mine."

Ciana laughs, shaking her head. "No..." she trails off.

"There's more?"

"Well... no, I shouldn't tell you."

"You have to now. I'm intrigued."

"You won't be after I tell you."

"Try me."

"You can only bring someone back once. When they die again, that's it. The mark is there as a reminder in case someone tries to bring someone back again. Which is why we don't heal the dead twice." Kieran's face becomes serious. "See, this is why I didn't want to tell you."

"Why didn't you tell me this before? That's kinda important. But why not? What happens if you do?"

"I didn't think you'd bring me back if I did die, then again, I wasn't planning on giving you the power, it just happened that way." Ciana sighs. "Nothing will happen if you do try."

"How do you know?" Kieran tilts his head when Ciana doesn't answer. "Ciana, what happens if you do?"

"They're not the same if you do."

"What do you mean not the same?"

"The queen... after the war. She went and found her husband. It's not recorded in our history books, but he had died once before. Shortly after they were married. After the war she wanted him back. So she went and revived him for a second time. Nothing happened at first, but he did come back, only... he was another person. Like he was reborn with a new spirit. He didn't know who she was or what his role was. But even then, he didn't live long. I don't know what happened, but he ended up dying again, and the queen buried him after that, not wanting to risk another revival."

"Did he also have the mark?"

"Yes." Ciana traces her black tally. "But that's why we don't. Why we don't the first time, because if they die again... that's it."

"That's still something one should be aware of."

"I didn't think I'd be revived. I thought I was gone for good."

"Not on my watch, Princess." Kieran catches her gaze, giving her a warm smile, which she returns. She runs a hand through her hair, breaking the contact.

"What did you guys do with the queen's heart?"

"Zomo took care of it. I think he demolished it? No, that's not right..." Kieran scratches his head trying to remember. "Oh! He said something about it being antique and full of history and was going to put it where a piece of the queen could be remembered. I'm not entirely sure what he meant by that."

"I think I do. It's just an empty shell. He must have put it with the rest of her family's memorial items." Ciana holds in a laugh, picturing the heart in a glass box next to clothes and weapons down in the antique room.

"Okay?" Kieran looks around, not sure what she's referring to or what to make of it.

"Did you really have the outcasts stay? Along with the pixie gnomes and cypups?" she changes the subject.

Kieran nods. "I did."

"I want to see it for myself."

"I'll be outside waiting for you when you're ready." Kieran bows, leaving her room with Patches.

Ciana gets ready as quickly as she can, anxious to see her kingdom once again in its light. Zomo escorts her to the grand hall where Kieran's been waiting.

"You ready?" he asks, motioning to the large doors.

"I am." Guards open the door, letting them exit. "Why are we going to the border?" Ciana asks when Kieran starts leading her in that direction.

"There's one thing I haven't told you yet, but I think you'll like it."

A tall silver gate sparkles in the sunlight as they near the border, two guards positioned next to it.

"Your Highnesses." They bow when they approach. "It's good to see you again, Princess Ciana."

"Thank you." She nods, examining the floral and leaf bars of the gate, looking at Kieran. "You fixed the gate?"

"It seemed fitting since my people were the ones to break it. I chose the design and everything; it complements the kingdom more than the last one."

Ciana smiles. "I agree. It's beautiful. Thank you."

"Shall we move on to the town?"

"Yes, please." Ciana admires the gate a moment longer before following Kieran to the town.

Kieran leads her through the town, pointing out the new brick buildings glowing in the sun. Cypups run past their feet; Ciana looks closer at their backs to see pixie gnomes riding on top. Her eyes fall to her townspeople, smiling and laughing as they play. Noticing some looking longingly toward the border, lost in thought.

"Kieran, why are—"

"Ciana!" a voice yells, interrupting her. She looks around to see Hamill running towards her, his eyes wide in shock and excitement. She steps back, thinking he's going to barrel into her, but he stops short. "Are you really here? You're alive?" He gasps for air.

"Hi Hamill." She smiles. "Yes, I am really here."

"How? I didn't think—"

"Kieran healed me; that's all that matters."

Hamill drops to his knees, grabbing the front of her dress as he starts to cry. "Ciana. My princess. Please forgive me. Forgive us outcasts for what we did to you. We acted out of jealousy. We were wrong. I was wrong. You are the kindest person one could have in their lives, and I betrayed you. I turned against you. We're doing what we're asked to make it up to you. Please find it in your heart to forgive us."

Ciana gently grabs his arms, encouraging him to stand. "It hurt that you would think I would have killed Leora when you and I were such close friends. Kieran has informed me of what you are all doing to make up for your actions, and I agree with his decisions. But I do forgive you."

"Thank you, Ciana." Hamill pulls her into a hug, which she returns. "Thank you." He draws away, returning to his work.

"You forgive so easily. I would have had a grudge against him and the outcasts for a long time."

"I'm not you, and based on what you told me and what they've been doing, they've shown that they're sorry. They will do their work for a while though—I won't let that go that easily."

"That sounds like you." Kieran smiles. "It's good to have you back."

Ciana returns his smile. "You said Kabandha was still here?"

"Yes, he's just outside of town in the forest. Wanted to prevent any more building damage," Kieran explains, leading her in that direction, continuing to show her everything that was new.

"Everything looks as if nothing happened."

"That's kind of the whole point." Kieran chuckles.

"I know, but there's usually evidence of a battle once it's over. There are bodies that need to be buried, but there's no blood or anything where the fighting happened."

"The rain helped with that. It was pouring so much that the blood never got a chance to settle and stain the ground."

"That does make things easier." Ciana looks at the towering trees not that far from them.

"Kabandha!" Kieran calls when they reach the edge of the trees. A big, green bald head appears over the green pines smiling down at them, moving closer.

"Ciana! Good see!" His voice booms.

"Good to see you too, Kabandha." She waves. "I told you once I got my strength back I'd heal your leader. I'm here so I can take care of that promise... "

Kieran jumps off the Kabandha's hand first into the snow reflecting in the moonlight, offering a hand to Ciana. She takes it, hopping down next to him. She looks at the trolls and giants sitting around large fires, who are cautiously eyeing them as they approach the dead giant's body laying on a bed of rocks.

Kieran stands back, letting Ciana walk ahead. She turns to look at him over her shoulder. "What are you doing?"

"Giving you space to do your thing," he answers.

A smile spreads across her lips, shaking her head. "Oh no, no, no. *You're* going to revive him."

"Me?" Kieran's eyebrows raise, pointing a finger at his chest.

"You killed him, so it's only fair you bring him back."

"You sure? It's your promise."

"You really don't want to bring back someone you wrongfully killed?"

"They were going to kill us!"

"Kieran..." Ciana raises an eyebrow, hands on hips.

"Okay, fine, yes, I didn't have to *kill* him, but still." They stare each other down, neither moving or averting their gaze. "Oh fine, I'll do it," Kieran gives up, walking over to the body, placing his hands on the large arm. "Will it even work? I mean, he's like a thousand times bigger than us."

"It'll work, don't worry." Ciana laughs.

Kieran shakes his head, concentrating on the giant, moving back to avoid getting crushed as the giant begins to stir.

"Bergelmir?" Kabandha questions, helping the giant up, the others watching eagerly as he stands up and looks around. Spotting Ciana and Kieran on the ground, he immediately reaches towards them. Kieran stands defensively in front of Ciana as Kabandha stops the giant. "No! They saved."

"He also killed me!"

"Bergelmir. Please. No harm. All frightened and protect selves. Try kill again you stay dead. He Darkness King," Kabandha explains. Bergelmir backs up.

"You can take us back now, Kabandha. We finished what we came here to do," Ciana tells him, wanting to avoid any further tension. Kabandha lowers his hand once again, allowing them to hop on.

"Thank, Princess," he smiles, walking away from the trolls and giants.

"You're thanking the wrong person." Ciana tilts her head towards Kieran.

"Thank, King."

"Don't mention it." Kieran sighs. "I don't need the idea of being good to go to my brain."

"Kieran, you *are* good," Ciana says with a giggle.

"I meant I can't just go around doing good deeds, that's your job. My job is to make people miserable."

"Not necessarily."

"Still not my job." He sighs, before sticking his tongue out at Ciana, which she does in return.

Ciana lays down, staring at the starry sky above. "Kieran?"

"Yes?"

"Thank you."

"Thank you?" He sits next to her, tilting his head in her direction.

"Yes, thank you... for everything you did, during our journey, restoring the balance and my kingdom, healing Patches and me."

"Anytime."

The sun shines brightly in the late afternoon, reflecting off Ciana's palace in the distance. Kabandha lowers his hand at the end of the forest connecting to the town so they can get off.

"Bye, Kabandha!"

"Bye Princess. See around." He nods.

"Stay in touch. We'll see you!" Ciana agrees, waving as he heads back towards the mountains. On their way back to the palace, Ciana's eyes fall on her townspeople. She frowns, slowing her pace, watching as some glance in the direction on the border.

Kieran slows to stay beside her. "What's wrong?" he asks, reading her face. "Do you not like some of the rebuildings? You can change them if you want, you're in charge."

"No, not that."

"What is it then?" His voice softens.

"You said you had those who didn't fight go to your side of the border and those who did fight on this side?"

"Yeah."

"Look around, Kieran, what do you see?"

"People, gnomes, cypups." He glances around.

"Look at my people carefully." Ciana follows his gaze from one person to the next, taking in their sad demeanor, a look of longing in their gaze towards the border wall.

"They're sad. They're focusing towards the wall instead of celebrating the survival of the kingdom," he answers, looking back at her and her hope filled eyes. "What are you thinking?"

"What if we got rid of the border? Combine the kingdoms. We wouldn't have to worry about the portions of food. They've all interacted in one way or another, and some probably connected with each other, especially if they bonded over the loss of a loved one. We can't keep them apart now that they've mingled. We only have the border because we didn't get along before."

"We still don't get along, Princess." Kieran shakes his head.

"Our people fought side by side, they went through so much together. *We've* been through so much together. How can we not get along?"

"Yes, they fought, but my people had no choice. If they didn't do as I said, they would be in trouble. There's plenty of people on my side who would love to come over here and kill you guys. I know there's some over here that would love to get rid of us as well."

"Part of that is because we were brought up being told how bad you guys are. Stuff that happened in the past. Kieran, we can change that! We hated each other at first, but look how far we've come since then. We got to know one another. Our people just have to get to know each other. No, we can't change their opinions, but if we start with the younger generation, we can start there and teach them that the other side isn't all bad. We shouldn't have to live from our past."

"How would the parents feel about that though? Teaching their children against what they know? They wouldn't appreciate it."

"We would be teaching them an updated version of our history. How we *can* work together. The battle is going to be in the books, and it's going to cause questions to arise since we have now worked together. Regardless if the people had a choice or not. It happened. We don't have to completely move everyone into one of the kingdoms, but we could get rid of the wall and let whoever wants to cross over to visit and mingle."

"Listen, Ciana. I know what you're wanting to do. It's a good idea, but we can't. Our worlds are just too different to combine them and go as smoothly as you want. That's why we have the border. To help keep our powers in balance with each other. If we combine them, the balance could just break again, and we could have another war between our people."

"You're over here, though. And you hold both powers. Kieran, you are walking proof that our powers can and do get along and work together."

"I'm not supposed to be, you know this. Once I'm done filling you in on things, I have to go back to my people and our lives will go back to how it was before." He takes a deep breath. "There's still a chance that the queen's power I hold will disappear. I'll figure out a way for you to keep all of her power on this side, and once I do, then—"

"Kieran, look at everything around us!" Ciana extends her arms out. "*You* did all this, you brought everything back. The balance is back in place and yet here we are. We don't have any problems. Kieran, we only had problems with the balance because we didn't have harmony between our kingdoms. We have it now. A little at least. We just have to do our parts as rulers to keep it! We have the chance and are able to do what the previous rulers couldn't."

Kieran shakes his head. "I'm sorry, Ciana. I know, but I'm afraid it'll be a lot harder than you think it is. I don't want to risk losing you—" he catches his words, "your power and kingdom again. It was hard enough this last time."

"We won't have to worry about it if we manage and keep the harmony our kingdoms need with each other. Please, Kieran. We have to at least try." She looks pleadingly into his sad eyes. "Will you at least think about it?" She looks back ahead when he doesn't answer. "You don't even want to consider it? We have to do *something*, Kieran. Or else our kingdoms will never be at peace and generations to come will grow in hatred. We may need each other again if another problem arises in the future."

"I don't think that would happen."

"You never know. Instead of having support in time of need we'd just have more contention."

"Ciana—"

"No, Kieran. Just think about it. Please? Do that much at least."

"Alright. I'll think about it, but I'm not promising I'll change my mind."

"Thank you." Ciana gives him a small smile, continuing ahead of him towards the palace.

# Chapter Thirty-Two

Ciana sorts a stack of papers in her study, reviewing the latest letters and requests.

"Zomo!" she calls, reading a letter from the previous day.

Zomo enters, his helmet under his arm. "Yes, Your Highness?"

"Did we pay for the repairs in town?"

"Yes, we paid for everything. All the brick, the gate, anything and everything that one could have lost if their house was destroyed. We even provided the funds for those who had died," he answers.

"Hmmm, that's what I thought." She rubs her temples.

"Why do you ask?"

"There's still distrust of me from the townsmen." She reads through the rest of the letter. "I just wanted to double check, and it looks like they're having a meeting tomorrow. I say we go. Get things squared away for good."

"I think that is a good idea. What time is it going to be?"

"Noon."

"I'll be sure nothing is booked during that time."

"Thank you, Zomo. That was all."

Zomo bows. "Of course, Your Highness." He starts for the door, but hesitates. "Princess, there is something I want to talk to you about."

Ciana sets the paper in her hand down. "What is it?"

"We need to start making preparations."

Ciana's eyes furrow. "Preparations? For what?"

"For you to be crowned queen."

"Queen?" Ciana glances at Leora's silver crested tiara in its glass box. "What did Kieran tell you?"

"He told me everything that happened on your journey. You are the only person with the makings of the next queen."

"Zomo, I can't be queen. I could hardly keep things right as the princess."

"I believe you will be able to run things smoothly as the queen. King Kieran would agree as well. He's already ordered things to be in place for your coronation."

"He what? He can't just assume I'm going to say yes. I appreciate it, but I don't think—"

"We all believe you can be the queen. All you have to do is be yourself and we'll support you. It is up to you, but whether you choose to accept it or not, you will always be the princess. Although, His Majesty may have already been informing the people to expect the coronation."

"Why would he do that?" Ciana huffs.

"I believe King Kieran is hoping to see you reign as yourself, to leave your mark on this kingdom. I wholeheartedly agree and hope you take the position."

"But—"

"Plus, I do believe it makes it easier on all of us if we have someone who already knows the ins and outs of ruling, instead of trying to train someone completely new." Zomo winks. Ciana smiles, knowing Kieran put those words in his mouth.

"You really think I'm up for it?"

"You've proven yourself worthy. Leora and the queen would be honored to have you as the new queen. The power is within you."

"I don't hold all the queen's power."

"That's not the power I'm referring to."

*The power is within yourself,* Ciana's thoughts she had at the fortress replay in her mind.

"I'll let you get back to your paperwork. The sooner you get done with it, the sooner we can plan." Zomo smiles, leaving the room. Ciana smiles at the closed door, picking up one of the papers on her desk.

"Princess!" a high chirp calls. Ciana looks to the edge of her desk where Iris and Liko appear.

"Iris? Liko?" She smiles.

"It's us! We haven't had a chance to see you since you've been back, but we're ecstatic about your return!" Iris runs over to Ciana, hugging her arm.

"Aww, I've missed you guys. How have you two been?"

"Good! We were sad when we heard about your passing, but rumor has it you're going to be queen!"

Ciana chuckles. "It looks that way."

"You're going to be great; everyone loves you. Everyone is nonstop talking about you and how you risked and gave your life to save them. They're all saying how much of a valiant ruler you are and would gladly fight for you again."

"Well, let's just avoid any more fighting. It's not ideal, and I think we've had plenty."

"We know, but it's good that they're saying things like that."

"I know."

"Where's King Kieran? I figured he would be here somewhere, but I haven't seen him." Liko looks around the room.

"He's out with Hamill, making sure he and the former outcasts are doing what he had ordered for them to do."

"Really? Like what?"

"I think he mentioned something about the crops."

"Oh! Preparing a shipment for their side?"

Ciana's smile falters. "Um, no. Making sure they were all growing healthy."

"Oh." Iris taps her chin. "I thought he would want to see your coronation since he's put so much effort into telling everyone."

"Well, yeah. He'd be there." Iris and Liko exchange confused glances. "Why do you think he wouldn't?"

"Maybe it is just a shipment of food then." Iris shrugs.

"What do you mean?"

"We saw Kieran with two horses and carts next to the gate. It looked like he was about to leave."

"What did the carts look like?" Ciana drops the papers she was holding, standing from her chair so fast it topples over.

"One looked like a prison cart. I'm assuming Kieran's brother and Kuma are in that one," Liko explains. "The other looked like it had food and supplies."

"No, no, no." Ciana runs out of the room, Zomo calling and chasing after her. She runs to the stables, looking for an available horse to borrow. Her heart drops when she nears Moondust's stall, not wanting to see it empty and full of uneaten hay, but her heart skips a beat at the sight of her black and silver mare relaxing within. "Moondust?" she whispers, opening the stall to embrace her horse.

The mare lets out an excited sigh of air, nuzzling Ciana. "But how? You—Kieran must have healed you." As excited and grateful as she was, she didn't have time to waste.

"Ciana!" Zomo calls at the stable entrance.

"Come on, girl, I'm so happy to see you, but I need to catch Kieran before he leaves." She mounts her horse, riding past Zomo, leaving him to mount his own horse and trail behind.

"Ciana wait!" Ciana ignores his calls, the wind whistling in her ears as she rides towards the gate. Kieran couldn't leave. She fights back tears at the thought of not getting to him in time. The shining new silver gate comes into view, figures on the other side.

"Kieran!" she calls, dismounting her horse, running and grabbing the closed gate, looking at Kieran next to two horses and carts on the other side, not too far away, his light contrasting against the dark trees. He stops at the sound of her voice.

"I thought you were in the middle of sorting paperwork," he tells her, not looking around.

"I was, but you can't just leave without saying goodbye. Especially when we won't see—" Ciana catches her words, correcting herself, "interact with each other again."

"I don't do goodbyes. I don't do that mushy stuff, remember." His voice shakes slightly.

"Kieran, please. There has to be some way for us to—to—" She begins to cry.

"We can't, Princess, you know we can't."

"Please, Kieran, I'm going to be crowned queen in a few days. Will you at least come to the coronation?"

"I'm glad you've decided to be queen, you're perfect for it, but I can't come. Our kingdoms can never interact with each other again.

We only did to fix the balance, which we accomplished, but it's done and over with."

"I know, but—" She tries to keep her voice steady with her cries. "We can make it so it's not like that anymore, we have to try and start somewhere."

"It's too risky, Princess." His voice quivers, his knuckles turning white around one of the horse reins.

"We can at least try. I don't think I can—I don't want to—I need you, Kieran." Ciana drops to the ground; Kieran's body begins to shake slightly to match his voice.

"I'm sorry, Ciana. It just wouldn't work."

"Please, Kieran. I need you. I wouldn't be here if it wasn't for you."

"Ciana? Do you remember when I told you not to get attached to Patches? When we—you first found him?"

"Yeah," she sniffs. "You said not to because it'll break my heart when I had to part from him."

"We should have both listened to my advice." Kieran lets out a strained laugh. Ciana takes a staggering breath, knowing he's not referring to Patches. "Ciana. Just know that I... I know if you just be yourself, everyone will see the great person and ruler that I see and they will love you just like I—just like Leora did." Kieran walks away with the horses and carts carrying the prisoners and food supply, one of his hands moving to his face like he's wiping away tears.

Ciana rests her head on the gate, sobbing. Zomo gently wraps his arms around her, having joined them, lifting her to her feet and helping her back to the palace.

# Chapter Thirty-Three

"The meeting was at the town hall, correct?" Zomo verifies as they ride down the stone streets into town on their horses.

"Yes, I see it up ahead." Ciana nods towards a large cobblestone building in the distance, white bricks leading to the black and white double doors; a sizable clock at the very top reads eleven fifty-five. "Five minutes to spare." She smiles at Zomo, who laughs in agreement.

A few men enter the building as they approach, tying their horses to a nearby rail. With a large parchment and other smaller papers in one hand, Zomo opens the door, bowing as Ciana walks in, heading down the long marble hall to a room at the end. Low voices can be heard on the other side.

"I'm here in case they decide to do something," Zomo reassures her, opening the door for her once again.

The room falls silent, all the men inside watching Ciana as she walks past to an open seat, Zomo sitting beside her.

"Princess Ciana?" a man with deep brown hair in the front of the room questions, standing up. "What are you doing here? Don't you have a coronation to plan?" A few men snicker.

"I do, but this is more important. You did send me a letter stating you were having this meeting. We have some things to straighten out," Ciana answers calmly.

"I'll say. You tell us you spend the town's money on us, but you don't spend a dime towards us." He sits down.

"I beg to differ. That money went towards all funeral services, building repairs and such. It has also gone and continues to go towards the school and education system. It's gone towards repairs needed in the town, such as roads, buildings, farms, equipment, and to families who need a little extra help during difficult times. So please tell me how not a dime is being spent towards you?"

"We've seen you spend money on those things, but how do we know it's actually *our* money that's being used?"

"Would it matter whose money it is as long as it goes towards the town to help improve it?"

"Yes. For all we know, the money you use for the town is the bare minimum so you can keep and use the rest for yourself. We know that's how you spend the money anyways. You spend it *your* way, giving us the crappy end of things while the nice part goes to you."

"Do you have an example of this?"

"As a matter of fact, yes. The new school that's to be built. We gave you our plan ideas for its structure, but you denied it, drawing up your own. Based on what *you* want. Not us."

"There's a difference between want and need. The designs you gave me were to have the school filled with fifty extra rooms that wouldn't be used, a kitchen that serves restaurant-type food and no desks, but couches for the children to sit on."

"The rooms would be for storage and to have extra rooms in case our population grew, the food now is terrible and completely unhealthy, and the kids would have a higher chance of learning more if they were comfortable."

"I respect those views and can't disagree with the idea behind it, but we don't need fifty more rooms, we can change the food so it's not what they're having now, but still be healthy and delicious, and the children would fall asleep if they were given a couch to sit on. Which I've told you all before. I didn't leave any of those out when I drew out my plans, which I had sent to you to look at, but you all refused to even take a glance at them." Ciana makes eye contact with those around the room.

Zomo hands her the large rolled-up parchment, which she hands to the man next to her. He rolls the paper out to look at it before passing it on as Ciana continues.

"If you would look at the plans for the school, you would see that we can expand the rooms. The measurements given are far too small to hold and maintain the number of children we have in the kingdom. Along with that, we can build a few larger rooms specifically for storage. I've already reached out to the school cooks and have been discussing a new menu for the children." she passes around a smaller loose-leaf paper for the men to look at. "We grow plenty of fresh foods that we can provide the children. Giving them more options to choose from that are still healthy. As for the couches, the children would be more likely to fall asleep. Instead, the chairs could have a cushion of some sort to help make sitting for so long more comfortable, and we can include more recesses for the children to stretch and relax. We can also build a large gymnasium for the children to run around in when the weather is bad."

Ciana passes around a few more pieces of paper. "I also have receipts of how much of the town's money has been used in the past leading up to recent events, including how much it would cost to build the new school. I've also included how much money I've used on myself from my own savings in the last couple of years."

The papers reach the man in the front. He carefully looks through them before passing on the school plans, keeping hold of the papers with the money count.

"You've spent more than half of the town's money on the funeral services and building repairs," he comments.

"Rebuilding and replacing everything lost from the battle and fires is already quite expensive, but all those who have passed from fighting deserve an honorary burial for their bravery and loyalty to the kingdom. Do note that those funeral costs are just the coverage for the townspeople who have died. Any funeral services for my guards come from my own savings. As you can tell, I've spent more than what would be needed to build roads, houses, and anything to help ensure they meet needs and prevent from deteriorating quickly, where we'd have to rebuild them again shortly after. I am not cheap with my people. I will buy the more expensive material if that would mean it lasts longer. I only want what's best for everyone."

"I do see that," the man hums. "What about the new border gate that was installed? It says here you used 2,000 from the town's money."

"I am aware of that. King Kieran did use that money towards the gate, while the rest came from his own pocket. But I am going to give the town that 2,000 back from my own accounts."

The man slowly nods, passing the papers on. "What about the coronation? Where's all that money coming from?"

"The money used is from both my own savings and the royal savings account, which is only used for events such as this."

"How do you expect to use our money to build a new school when we don't have the money? All of it was used for the funerals and rebuilds."

"At the moment, the plans are still under works, so we have time to save for the school build. However, if the school is needed sooner, I'll gladly pay for it from my personal accounts."

"What if we don't like your school plans or any other plans that would come up in the future?"

"Nothing is set until we reach an agreement. I'll gladly discuss options and ideas with you until we are both satisfied with the outcome."

He snickers. "But you're so busy, you wouldn't make time for us and listen."

"No, I don't always have time to come to these meetings. As ruler, I have a lot of things to take care of. To resolve this issue, I am going to put together a committee. I will let you decide who those five representatives will be from the town, and they will meet with me and my advisors once a month to discuss how to proceed with whatever issue there may be. The date of when these meetings will take place will be decided after representatives have been picked, ensuring that the day will work for all of us. In addition, I will hold a financial meeting every other month to go through what money has been used and towards what. If you so choose, a couple representatives from the town can be present to ensure that I am, indeed, using the money properly and to go over what funds the town specifically has for what it needs to be used for and what they can use freely."

Whispers rise as all the men turn to each other.

"We wouldn't have to worry about any of this if we were in charge of our own money."

"As the princess and soon to be queen, you know very well that I am to be in charge of holding all finances to avoid any robberies or misuse of the money."

"You're saying you don't trust us?" the man sneers.

"I never said that. This has always been a rule. You do have to remember that you haven't been trusting me when I have the proof that I use it for what it's supposed to go towards. I have shown that I know what I am doing, especially when it comes to the kingdom. You have to remember that I am the ruler of this kingdom and I hold the final say of *everything* that gets done. I try to get your input, but when you refuse to cooperate, then I have no choice but to make the decision myself." Ciana stands, her face serious. "I am working out a way to be able to get your input, but if you still deem that unfair, then you have no right to be upset with my decisions of where and how I spend the money. I will gladly spend the money how I see fit, without your input. It would make my job easier, but I value any thoughts and suggestions you may have, so I will willingly work with you." An uneasy silence falls at the end of Ciana's words, the men staring at her surprised.

The men exchange glances with one another, their murmurs and whispers trickling down the men as the papers go back to the man in the front. He looks at the papers as the two men beside him whisper in his ear. Ciana turns to Zomo, who smiles and nods. Ciana turns back to the man, who stands up.

"First item, all those in favor of meeting with the princess once a month to discuss any plans or problems, raise your hand," he asks the room.

Hands shoot up along with Ciana and Zomo's.

"It is unanimous." Hands lower back down. "Second item, all those who believe that the princess has spent our money wisely and in the right manner based on these receipts, raise your hand."

Almost everyone's hands go up. He nods.

"All those who wish for the princess to continue to handle our money, raise your hand." A majority of hands fill the air once again. The man passes the papers back to Ciana and Zomo. "Our apologies, Your Highness. Please forgive our skepticism."

"All is forgiven."

"However, would it be possible for us to meet to discuss the school layout as well as the menu with the cooks? Before the first monthly meeting, that is. The sooner we can get the plans sorted out the sooner it can be built to avoid any more problems we're having with our current school."

"Of course. I agree that it should be built rather soon."

"We can figure out when to meet after your coronation. You have a lot on your mind right now, I'm sure." He gives Ciana a sincere smile.

"That would be much appreciated. Send me word when you're ready and we can plan a day to meet."

"Thank you, Your Highness."

Ciana carefully stands up with Zomo. "Now if you would please excuse me and Zomo, we still have a lot to do."

"Of course, Your Highness. We look forward to your coronation."

Head held high, Ciana leaves.

"That went surprisingly well," she admits, untying her mare.

"I don't see why they thought you were spending the money wrong when they've seen you spend it towards the town with the rebuilds." Zomo unties his own horse, securely placing the papers in his horse satchel, before helping Ciana onto her mare.

"They just needed to see some proof that I wasn't hiding anything and telling the truth. Glad that's over."

***

"Would you like me to put Moondust away for you?" Zomo offers as they dismount in front of the stables.

"I've got her, thank you. I would like it if you could put the papers back in my study and make sure all the cooks are nearby so we can discuss the food."

"I will make sure they are. Where are you wanting to meet them?" He locks his horse stall.

"Just in the dining room, it'll be easier there."

"I will see that they're there." Zomo leaves the stable.

Ciana guides her horse back into her stall. Grabbing a brush, she slowly brushes her mare's black and silver hair.

"Time for more planning." She sighs, setting the brush down before hugging Moondust. She snorts, resting her nose against Ciana's back. Ciana steps out, latching the stall door, then heading into the palace.

Ciana pushes the dining room door open, all the cooks bowing or curtsying at her entrance. Zomo pulls out a chair for her, pushing her in. Papers line up in front of each cook.

"The floor is yours, Your Highness. What were you thinking of having for food?" one of the cooks inquires, readying his pencil.

"Well, we're going to have the dance afterwards, so I think appetizers with water and lemonade," Ciana says. The cooks all scribble on their papers.

"Any specific appetizers?"

"Maybe toasted bread bites with jams and melted cheese, cheese cubes, crackers and stuff for cracker sandwiches, trays filled with fruits and veggies as well. I heard the blueberries and strawberries were flourishing. Let's see what the farms have growing and have whatever is available."

"Any type of desserts or just the appetizers?"

"Umm..." Ciana looks at Zomo. "Why not? Let's have chocolate chip cookies."

"Is there anything else you would like to have?"

"Lets see, we have drinks, food, dessert... is there anything that we're missing?" Zomo shakes his head. "I think that just about covers it. If there's anything else, I'll let you know."

"Sounds great, Your Highness."

Ciana slides back in her chair, leaving with Zomo.

"Princess," he stops her in the hall.

"Yes?"

"There's one more thing. Your first dance as the queen. You will need to decide who you would like to dance with."

"Oh, that's right. I'll think about it, don't worry."

"Of course."

"And Zomo, did you invite the orphanage?"

"We invited Miss Abrie, but we can't have children at your coronation."

"I want the children there. You have to remember that they're still family to me, even though I haven't been there for years. I want them at my coronation."

"Princess, I understand that, but you have to remember that they are children. They tend to get a little rowdy, and we don't need them disturbing everyone else."

"I'm aware of that, Zomo, but they have every right to attend. This isn't something that happens very often and it'll be a good experience for them. They are to come," she instructs. "Also pay a tailor to make new clothes for them as well. They don't get much as it is."

"I will see that it gets done."

"Thank you."

"Now, I advise finishing anything that needs to be done, today. Tomorrow, you should rest and relax. I'll be sure everything is taken care of for your coronation in a couple of days."

"Thank you, Zomo."

# Chapter Thirty-Four

**Kieran**

Keiran walks through the tenebrous forest, pulling the horses and carts with him. He sniffs, trying to shake Ciana's cries out of his head. He had no choice. He had to leave. They were opposites. There was no way they could work in the long run.

The blue cobalt lights flicker at the edge of the forest, causing Kieran to push away all his emotions. He was the King of Darkness. He couldn't let his people see his weakness; they'd rebel against him. Looking over his town, his heart drops. The dark buildings... the dark light... Ciana's kingdom flashes into his mind, sending a chill down his spine as he remembers how lifeless and dreary it had become. How it was so much like his side.

His eyes fall on a few of his people walking the streets closest to him. The dull and unwelcoming demeanor they present. How very different they are compared to Ciana's people. So joyful and full of light. Making the most of everything. So happy. Tears threaten to spill as he thinks back to Ciana's cries. He knew he had broken her heart. She needed him, and he needed her, but he couldn't stay. Not if he wanted her to be safe from his people.

Kieran guides the horses into the streets, stopping a few men. "Take care of the food supplies. Distribute them equally among the people and store whatever is left in the bunkers," he orders.

"Yes, Your Majesty." The men bow, taking the horse's reins. Kieran guides the other horse and cart up to his castle. The dark stone almost whispers how different his home was from Ciana's. *Ciana.* That's all his mind could think of. He had to snap out of it. She's a thing of the past. They did what they had to do and succeeded. The cart rolls down the cobblestone ramp, leading to the dungeons.

"Get in!" Kieran spits, shoving Ahriman into a cell. A metallic lock clicking into place. "You too." He shoves Kuma into her own cell. "You'll both pay for what you did."

"Come on, Kieran. We're family!" Ahriman smiles, trying to reason.

"I don't care if you're family. You're a disgrace."

He smiles. "A disgrace to who? The darkness or the light?"

"Both."

"That princess really did make you weak. You're not as ruthless as you used to be. Such a shame."

"That princess made me a better ruler. And it'll be Queen Ciana in a few days, so I suggest you refer to her as such if you bother to speak of her."

"You still hold the queen's power. You can do so much with it! You can get rid of the soon to be queen and rule both kingdoms."

"I will not use the queen's power. It belongs to Ciana."

"You don't have to keep reminding me." Ahriman sighs, rolling his eyes as he plops onto his stone bed.

Kuma grabs hold of her bars. "We gave you all the information you needed to get rid of her. Why didn't you just kill her?" Kieran glares at her. "You fell for her, didn't you?" Kuma concludes. "You actually fell in love with that disgustingly worthless fake princess! I can't believe it." Kuma laughs. Keiran's face hardens, raising his fingers.

"Don't *ever* insult Ciana in my presence again," he warns. Keeping his back to Kuma and his brother.

"Why not? It hurts your feelings?" Kuma continues to laugh, which quickly turns into screams at the snap of Kieran's fingers. The sound of flames bouncing off the stone walls as he leaves.

Kieran sits on his throne, blue lights flickering around him, blending into the light he's emanating. Twirling a flame around his fingers, he takes in his surroundings. The room was big, bleak, and empty. Much like he felt. His thoughts trail back to when Ciana entered this room with him. He could tell she was scared, but she was so determined to get his help. To help her kingdom. Kieran shakes off the memory. He was doing it again, but he had to keep Ciana from his mind, and yet she kept coming back. Her smile. Her laugh. Her fear. Her beauty. Her warmth.

"Your Majesty?" a man calls from the doorway, breaking Kieran's thoughts.

"Yes?"

"One of Princess Ciana's guards is here to speak with you. Said it was an urgent matter with the princess."

"Let him in." Kieran jumps from the throne. His heart racing. The man bows, allowing Zomo to enter, armored and relaxed. Kieran rushes up to him. "What's wrong? Is Ciana alright? Did something happen?"

Zomo lets out a soft chuckle, amused by his reaction. "Ciana is fine." Kieran lets out a breath of relief. "She's proudly getting ready to take her place as queen tomorrow. Even started doing things her own way and standing up to her people who still think she can be disrespected."

"I'm glad to hear it. That's what she should be doing."

"I agree."

"What brings you here, Zomo? Did you come just to give me a heart attack and update me on her progression?"

"I did not. I wanted to talk to you." Zomo takes off his helmet, securing it under his arm.

"What about?"

"You and Her Highness."

"There's nothing to talk about," he dismisses.

"She misses you."

"So?" Kieran shrugs, trying to play it off, but Zomo's smile tells him that he isn't buying it.

"You really hurt her that day. Leaving."

"I had to leave. For her safety. We can't work, not with our people wanting to destroy each other."

"That's not the case right now. It wasn't the case during the battle."

"My people had no choice."

Zomo shifts, clearing his throat. "Regardless if you ordered them to or not, it was proven that both sides could work together. Ciana's people were never commanded to work with you. They followed their leader, which was me."

"Really?" Kieran tilts his head. "They were under no orders to *not* fight against us?"

"That is correct. They could have turned against you and your men at any time, but they didn't. They knew the kingdom wouldn't survive without your help."

"What are you getting at?" Kieran crosses his arms.

"The people will always follow their ruler, as long as the ruler has good intentions. Rulers once did what they considered was best for both their subjects and themselves. Resulting in the war. The queen was fighting to save her power, which your father wanted for his own gain. *That* is what caused the divide. Not the difference in abilities and lifestyles. But your father refused to make a compromise for his own selfish reasons. He only agreed when the queen was at a breaking point. Eager to do almost anything to save her people. She was weak. He had the advantage to eventually take her power and probably would have done similar things as what your brother did."

Kieran nods, following. "Okay."

"You and Ciana broke that division when the balance was broken. You had no choice but to work together. Helping each other on your journey with each other's gifts. She would not have survived without your dark power, just as you would not have survived without the help of hers. Our abilities are opposites. Our people are opposites, but we go together. We need you just as much as you need us. Just like you need Ciana."

"I don't know what you're talking about." Kieran turns around.

"King Kieran. If you didn't care for her, you wouldn't have reacted so protectively when I first came in here. I know you miss her."

Kieran looks at his empty throne. His thoughts go back to Ciana and her smile. Her determination. Tears trickle down his cheeks as the memory of the snowball fight comes to mind. She may have been freezing, but she was having fun. It was probably the first time she had fun since ruling. The sparkle in her eyes from the snow reflecting the sparkle inside her. He takes in the empty room. He'd hate to admit it, but Zomo was right. He missed Ciana. He didn't realize how much he loved her presence until she died. He didn't realize how lonely and joyless he felt until he left her. It was as if she filled a piece in him that he didn't know was missing.

*If you dwell on all the bad and dark of things, you'll always be gloomy, but if you focus on the good and try to make the best of what you have, even if you are the Prince of Darkness, you can live a beautiful happy life.* Ciana's voice echoes in his head.

"We don't get the happy things to focus on," he whispers to himself, wiping his tears. "But I found mine. I found it in her."

"Your Majesty, what would you do for Ciana?" Zomo asks.

"I would do anything. If it meant her safety. Her happiness."

"She won't be fully happy unless you're a part of her life."

"I want to be happy too. I enjoyed it. I'm not happy here."

Zomo smiles. "What would bring you that happiness?"

"She's the only thing that could." Kieran turns to face him.

Zomo nods, returning his helmet to his head. "I have a few things I need to do for the coronation tomorrow. I'll let you decide how you want to go about bringing happiness into your own life. Because if it could only be Ciana, but the kingdoms stay separated forever, then... you'll have to find something just as good." Zomo bows, leaving the room.

*There could be nothing else that would bring me happiness as much as Ciana has.* Kieran looks at the door. *Zomo, you sly dog. No wonder you're the head guard and Ciana turns to you. You've got some good tricks up your sleeve.* Smiling, Kieran heads out of the castle into town.

Coming across a jewelry store, an idea comes to mind. A broader smile spreads across his face as he enters.

# Chapter Thirty-Five

**Ciana**

From the balcony, Ciana observes the line of people waiting to enter the palace as the afternoon wanes. She smiles as she watches the orphans jump up and down in their new clothes in line.

"The dress looks beautiful on you, Your Highness," Zomo compliments, walking out next to her in a black suit.

Ciana looks down at her rose gold ballgown, delicately tracing the silver lace along her half sleeve.

"Thank you." She tosses her curled hair over her shoulder, looking back at the queue, slightly frowning.

"Are you alright, Princess?"

"No," she admits.

"Tell me what's bothering you; is there something wrong with the food or the ceremony?"

"No, not exactly." She glances at her hands before looking in the direction of the border.

"You miss him."

"It's just... we went through so much together. I know we hated each other at the start, but then it changed. He's the first person since Leora that I feel has truly cared for me."

"I couldn't agree more."

"I wouldn't even be here right now if it wasn't for him, Zomo. None of this would be happening if it wasn't for him."

"Ciana, if I might say, I believe you and King Kieran brought the best out of each other. You brought out the good in him, the good I never thought he had, and he brought out your confidence."

"So what if we did? Our sides are just too different—Kieran and I are too different... it would never work. It's better that we don't see each other again, to prevent another war and breaking the balance again. It's for the best."

"It is not for the best. You were happy with him, Ciana. Despite everything you two went through together, I've never seen you happier than when you were with him. So what if our two sides are different? We can't keep living in the past. I know that if there was anyone that could harmonize the two sides, it would be you and him. Yes, you and Kieran are different as well, but your differences complement each other. That's why you two managed to get to where you are now, because you worked through the differences and helped one another."

"Zomo, all we did was fight with each other, we didn't—we don't get along."

"Not from what I heard. I know it started that way, but it didn't end like that."

"Zomo—"

"No, you're right. You two are so different that it hurts to say goodbye. It could never work because Kieran fixed everything for *you*. You're right. I'm just being silly. It is for the best that you two are separated for the rest of your lives, never to interact again to try to prevent another war and keep the balance in place by separation, not unity. That's the right thing to do." He bows, striding back into the palace.

Ciana watches him, considering his words. Shaking her head, she leaves the balcony, walking to the garden where Patches is playing with another cypup. He perks up, running to Ciana's feet, barking.

"Hey, puppy, how are you doing?" She carefully squats down, rubbing him behind the ears and under his chin; his foot shakes violently. "Oh, so that's your sweet spot." She giggles, standing back up.

Patches darts behind her, stopping as if he was expecting someone else. "What is it, pup?" He looks at Ciana and the empty air, tail wagging. "What is it? There's no one there." She tilts her head, trying to understand him. Patches turns around to face her, tail slowing down. "No one is there." Patches runs around in a circle, barking. "Patches, I don't know who you're looking for. Are you wondering where Kieran is?" Patches stops, his tail wagging faster at the mention of Kieran. "He's not here." His tail and ears drop, his blue eye widening. "He's not here, puppy. He's back home. We won't see him again. I'm sorry." A tear escapes Ciana's eye which she quickly wipes away. Patches lies down, whimpering. "I know, puppy. I know."

On her way back inside the palace, Ciana plucks a freshly bloomed red rose. Closing the garden door, she turns to Zomo who's patiently waiting.

"Are you ready? Everyone is seated."

"Where are the children?"

"They're in the front seats, just as you had requested."

"And the tiara?"

"Your crown is polished and waiting."

"It's Leora's, she was never queen."

Zomo smiles. "We aren't using her tiara."

"Why not?" Ciana asks, confused.

"King Kieran wanted to make sure you had your own crown for the occasion. It's not right for a queen to wear another's tiara or crown. This is *your* kingdom now."

"I can't wait to see it." Ciana smiles, tucking the rose in his suit jacket pocket.

He offers her his arm, escorting her to the closed throne room doors. Ciana closes her eyes, taking in a few deep breaths.

"Are you ready?"

"As long as everyone else is."

Zomo gently releases her hand from around his arm, quietly knocking on the doors. "The floor is all yours, Princess." The doors open, and Ciana looks at the smiling faces in the packed room; everyone stands respectfully.

Ciana smiles at Zomo, beginning her elegant march down the aisle towards her silver throne. Light piano music plays in the background. Everyone beams, bowing and curtsying as she passes, some whispering their love of her dress. Ciana spots the orphan children near the end; they whisper excitedly, waving at her. Ciana gives them a little wave as she walks past, stepping up to the officiator, who positioned himself in front of her throne.

A gentle but loud rustle comes from behind as everyone takes their seats and the music fades.

"Her Royal Highness, Princess Ciana, does take upon her the duties to rule over the Kingdom of Luxregnum, as the Queen of Light. From this day on, all that she does is for the good of her people and the kingdom. Never to rule in hatred, greed, selfishness, but in love, kindness, and hope. In her reign, may the kingdom flourish and be bright, to have no harm threaten our peace, and, if there be any threat, may she lead us proudly and be sure to protect. In all her days, may they be long, not only shall she provide for the people, but the people provide and support her in her decisions in return. May she take the crown in love and light, to be the best queen she can be for our kingdom. In the eyes of those here..." The officiator steps back and away, allowing Zomo and Ritesh to approach with the sparkling silver and floral crested crown on a royal purple pillow.

Zomo stops in front of Ciana, gently picking up the coronet and carefully placing it on Ciana's bowed head. She smiles, lifting her head up to see Zomo put a fist to his heart, bowing deeply.

"My Queen," he whispers, straightening to stand aside with Ritesh. Ciana takes her place on the throne. Everyone stands up, respectfully bowing or curtsying.

"I present Her Royal Majesty, Queen Ciana of Luxregnum," the officiator declares. Everyone cheers, clapping loudly.

Beaming, Ciana looks over them all, taking in the love.

Upbeat music fills the golden ballroom. From her spot on the small platform, Ciana watches the crowd dance and socialize, pausing to chat with people who offer her congratulations. Zomo smiles, standing guard in his armor next to her.

Abrie and the orphans run up, laughing and jumping.

"Princess! Princess!" they call.

"I'm not a princess anymore. I'm a queen," she reminds them sweetly.

"Queen Ciana!" They laugh.

"You can just call me Ciana."

"Your dress is so pretty! And you get to wear the crown now since you're queen!" The girls admire with bulging eyes.

"You're right, I do. You were listening. I love your dresses and suits. They're just as beautiful and handsome."

"Uh... Ciana?" The boy, Chris, gets pushed forward by his friends.

"Yes?"

"Can I have a dance?" His voice softens as his face turns beet red.

"Of course, I'd be delighted."

Ciana grabs his hands, leading him to the floor. She gently places his hands on her waist, resting hers on his shoulders, slowly turning in a circle. He looks around, avoiding eye contact with anyone. One of the other boys comes over, cutting in, taking his turn with Ciana. Each boy takes their turn, some attempting to go twice.

"I wanna dance with the princess," one of the little girls requests, shoving through the rest of the children.

Ciana takes her hands, dancing with her to the music, giving each girl a turn too.

"Okay children, let's leave the queen be." Abrie gathers up the children. They groan and whine, causing Abrie to quickly hurry them off. "Thank you, Your Majesty," she says before shoving off. Ciana walks back to a laughing Zomo.

"Those children adore you. It was sweet of you to dance with all of them," he says, gaining his composure.

"It's only fair, and you said they shouldn't have come."

"You're right; it was a good idea to have them here. They enjoyed it."

"Ciana?" Hamill approaches in a deep blue suit.

"Hi Hamill." She smiles.

He smiles back. "Can I give you a hug?"

"Sure," she laughs. Hamill steps onto the platform, hugging the air out of her. "I still need to breathe," she warns.

"Sorry." He lets go, stepping back down. "I'm just so happy for you. I am so sorry for everything that I did to you in the past. Please forgive me."

"I already have, Hamill. You and everyone else."

"Oh, thank you. You really do have all the makings of a great queen."

"Thank you, Hamill, I appreciate it."

"I'll let you be now. I'll see you later." Hamill bows, disappearing into the dancing crowd.

"Have you decided who you're going to dance with for your first dance as queen?" Zomo asks while watching Hamill leave.

Ciana frowns. "No, not quite. If all else fails, would you be willing to do it with me?"

"Of course, Your Majesty. I would be honored."

"Thank you."

"Although I doubt there will be any need for me to." A grin spreads across his face.

"Why do you say that?"

Zomo points to the back of the packed room, where a young man in a black tuxedo with messy brown hair is making his way through the crowd of people towards her, the light illuminating off the guests contrasting against his dull skin.

"Why is he here?" Ciana swallows, taking a few steps back.

"You invited him, didn't you?" Zomo reminds her.

A mix of feelings overcomes Ciana. Flustered that Kieran was here, but also excited. She had missed him, but they weren't supposed to interact. Struggling to catch her breath from the anxiety rising in her, she quickly picks up the front of her dress, walking out to the garden, the sun painting the sky pink and orange as it sets, tears welling up in her eyes.

"You know, I'm pretty sure it's rude to hide from your own party," Kieran's warm voice teases, walking up behind her.

"What are you doing here?" She keeps her voice steady. "You said—"

"I know what I said. It's part of the reason as to why I'm here." He moves to get in her view, but she turns away. "That and I had to see you be crowned queen." Ciana crosses her arms, not responding as she holds back her tears. "You look beautiful tonight."

"Thanks," she whispers.

"Ciana." He moves to stand before her, but she walks away to a nearby bench, carefully sitting down, and turning her back to him. "Ciana, please listen. I know what I said. I know what you said."

"You were right, though."

"No, no, I wasn't. *You* were right. Listen, Ciana, you were right that we shouldn't stay living in the past. We can't change what happened and what people grew up thinking about our sides, but we can prepare a better future, one that could lead to combining our kingdoms. We could start with the younger generation, like you said, and maybe we could devise something to slowly get our people used to interacting with one another to avoid any problems and keep the balance intact."

"We can't, Kieran, you said so yourself, it's too risky." Tears trickle down her cheeks.

"No, no, forget what I said. Here..." He grabs her hand, sitting beside her.

She looks down at his hand, which is dark compared to her emanating light.

"It's like this flower." He puts an unopened pink rose in her line of sight. "Right now we're like this unbloomed rose—tight, small, and restricted. Now, the rose can stay like this forever until it dies, but it wouldn't grow into anything. But it has the opportunity to grow and bloom into its full potential. A beautiful flower that gives to many things around it. If we don't try to combine the kingdoms, we may never grow and turn into something that could benefit everything and everyone. Who knows what we could do if our kingdoms combine, but we won't know unless we start small and take the risk. We can't stay bordered forever." He replaces the unbloomed rose with a fully bloomed pink rose.

Ciana looks into his brown eyes, smiling. He wipes away her tears.

"I know what you're trying to say, but you're just as bad at explaining things as I am," she says with a giggle.

"I try." He returns her smile, gently tucking the rose behind her ear. "What do you think? Can we please give it a shot? We can't get anywhere if we don't start somewhere."

"Yes, we can give it a shot."

"Good, we'll start small, but we'll make it work. Now I have a gift for you." He pulls out a small box, handing it to her.

Ciana withdraws a beautiful glowing silver chain necklace with a diamond 'C' in the middle. Mouth falling open, she looks between the glowing necklace and Kieran, realizing he is no longer glowing like her and her people.

"You didn't—" she gasps.

"I figured it would be best for you to keep all your power. You are tied to it after all, and this way it won't be too accessible to others, and we don't have to worry if my power would make it disappear or not. Besides, I was tired of looking like a glowstick."

"It's beautiful, Kieran. Thank you." She pulls him into an embrace, admiring the necklace.

"You're welcome. May I?"

"Of course."

She pulls her curled hair out of the way, so he can put it on as she straightens it out in the front.

"Your Majesty?" Zomo calls from behind.

"Yes?" Ciana turns to him, letting go of her hair.

"It's time."

"Thank you, I'll be right in."

"Of course." Smiling, Zomo goes back inside.

"Time for what?" Kieran asks.

"It's time for my first dance as queen."

"Oh, I see, and you're dancing with Limbo?"

"Zomo." She laughs. "And no, he was just reminding me."

"Then who has the honor of dancing with you?"

"There's only one person who I'd ask."

"Who?"

"This prince I met and went on a long journey with."

"Oh? And has this... prince shown up?" Kieran cocks an eyebrow, smiling.

"He did. Just like I hoped he would."

"May I have this dance, Your Majesty?" Kieran stands up and bows, offering his hand.

"You may." Ciana curtsies, taking his hand in return, walking back inside to the middle of the dance floor.

Resting her hand on his shoulder, she picks up her dress slightly. The music changes into a waltz and Kieran glides and twirls Ciana around the room with everyone watching.

"Kieran?"

"Yeah?"

"Tell me something,"

"Anything."

"Why were you going to leave without saying goodbye?"

"I had to." He stares into her green eyes. "I can't say goodbye to someone I'd never see again. Especially if it's someone I... I care so much about."

"That's when you're supposed to say goodbye."

"No. I couldn't. It would hurt more than if I didn't say it. It hurt when Olcan had poisoned you. It hurt when Hamill was insulting you. It hurt when *I* was hurting you. It hurt when you died. It hurt me more hearing you cry. Even though my heart was already broken, I couldn't stand the hurt that would come if I actually said goodbye." His eyes start to glaze over. "I never in a million years thought I would care so much for someone that it would physically pain me, let alone care for the most amazing, nicest, selfless person to have ever existed. You're the good thing in my life that makes me happy. Happier than I've ever been. That has brought me true happiness for the first time in my life.

"Ciana, being with you has made me a better person. The person I want to be, not who I'm supposed to be. You're the light hidden in my darkness, Ciana. I don't think I could live without it—without you. I need you in my life, Ciana. I never thought I'd be saying this, but... I love you." A tear rolls down his cheek. Ciana wipes it away, tears falling down her own.

"We all need a bit of darkness in order to see the light within. Without the darkness, without you, I never would have gained the confidence to rule as myself. Without you, I wouldn't even be here, none of us would. I don't know what I would do without you in my life."

Kieran wipes away her tears, stopping as the music slows. "Our kingdoms have a chance of working out together, do you think we have that same chance? As the Queen of Light and King of Darkness?"

"I do as long as you're always there for me."

"I will always be there for you." Kieran smiles, gently rubbing her cheek with his thumb.

Ciana smiles up at him, gazing into each his eyes, leaning in. Kieran gently presses his lips against hers, cupping the side of her face, pulling her close as she wraps her arms around his neck; the music concludes in the background.

"Wooooo!" Iris cheers from the side of the suddenly quiet room. They look over in her direction, laughing.

"It's about time! Took you two long enough." Liko joins with a sigh of relief, taking a sip of his drink.

"You go Ciana!" Hamill hollers from the back.

Kieran turns his attention back to Ciana. "So, my queen, where should we start?"

The music starts up again with a lively tune, and everyone returns to what they were originally doing as if nothing happened. Ciana smiles, interlocking her fingers with Kieran's, dragging him back towards the garden door.

"You're going to teach me how to build a fire."

"As you wish."

# Acknowledgements

Writing a book has always been a dream of mine and having one published is amazing! When I first started, little did I know how much actually went into writing and publishing a book, but I've loved the process and can't wait to do more! I am grateful for all those who have been there for me in this journey.

I'd like to first thank my heavenly parents. Without being given this god given gift, none of this would have been possible and I am so grateful to grow the talent I have been given and to share it with those around me.

To all my school teachers: Without you I wouldn't know how to write and you've taught me to enjoy the writing aspect of reading and I will forever be grateful for it.

To my parents and siblings: Thank you for your support and for helping me achieve this dream. Even though it's hard for me to let my own family read my work, I'm so glad for the feedback and suggestions you gave to help it grow and for raising me to be the person I am today.

To my friends: Thank you for your support and encouragement! Also thanks for letting me send you random scenes from the book or from other random stories I have written. It means so much knowing you have my back along, with my family.

To my editor: Jessica, I've loved working with you and you've made this whole thing easier! Your feedback and hype for my book helped my confidence so much! You've really helped my book shine and I am so grateful for you!

To my cover artist: Faith, you did such an amazing job and it's everything I could ever want! Thank you so much for helping out and for being a part of this.

To Abby: If it wasn't for us writing a book together, I wouldn't have had the motivation and determination to publish my own book. As one of the first people to read my work, you helped give me confidence in it and I will forever be grateful.

Thank you to everyone who has been with me on this journey and has made this possible! I am so grateful for you! I love you!

# About the author

Dakotah has always loved writing for as long as she could remember with her go-to genres of fantasy and romance. Born and raised in Washington State, she currently resides in Idaho. She loves the beach, flower arranging, the Temple and spending time with her friends and family. "Bordered By Darkness" is Dakotah's debut book which she published at the age of 21.

Instagram: @dakotahanne_writes